PROTECTORS OF THE VALE

Curtiss Robinson

Eloquent Books
New York, New York

Eloquent Books
An imprint of AEG Publishing Group
845 Third Avenue, 6th Floor – 6016
New York, NY 10022
http://www.eloquentbooks.com

ISBN: 978-1-60693-470-8, 1-60693-470-8

Printed in the United States of America

Book Design: Bruce Salender

Dedication

I dedicate this book to all of those who contributed no matter how great or small, but special thanks goes to the creative team who never gave up on me.

To Sean Mann (author of the Streeker Boglash series) who taught me writing is the ultimate adventure. Thanks for your mentorship.

To Lynn Galloway who helped proofread and edit the first draft as well as serving as a great sounding board in my work. Thanks for your kindness.

To Chris Capps, my gunner and friend, who read the first draft in three days and said, "Hey this is good. You got anymore?" Thanks for your vote of confidence.

To Vicki Robinson, my dear, loving wife, who endured countless hours of role-playing, helped me develop the female personas, served as a second set of eyes to get things right, and loved me through it all. Thank you for your love and patience. You are the greatest!

God bless you all.

Contents

Prologue

Breathtaking awe and paralyzing reverence best describe the first impression of Celes'tia, capital city of elves. Truly, it is more than the home to thousands of elvenkind. It is the northern stronghold for the Dae'gon Alliance, a bustling meeting place for trade, and the center of learning for the goodly races of the Western Kingdom. It is also a spectacular manifestation of Nature, magic, and civilization. In spite of all these remarkable aspects, Celes'tia is best known for its perfectly sculpted landscape, massively towering trees, and an amazing collection of wildlife, such that its sheer beauty cannot be described with mere words.

Just outside the city limits, dark leaves swirl with the wind coming off two slender elves running through the forest. Their soft leather boots and form-fitting clothes help them blend perfectly with their surroundings as they pass quietly through the forest. In fact, the scurrying animals and chirping insects of the forest make more noise than the near-silent runners. As they glide across the soft ground, their trail is barely perceptible along the thin roadway. Outsiders have been heard saying that phantoms and specters leave more evidence behind than an elf of Celes'tia. Such is the way of elves in their forest.

"Come on, Rosie, you can run faster than that," Wavren called to his sister. At nearly six feet, Wavren was tall for an elf, his body built for speed and agility with long legs and a tightly muscled torso. He wore his thick black hair in a topknot that made his angular features seem even sharper. His deep green eyes were like pools of emerald-colored water. His defining characteristic, a boyish smile that was not only charming but also a little mischievous, made him both handsome and dashing.

Rosabela was only a few steps behind her brother, huffing from the nearly two miles they had already trekked through the deep green and brown woods, but she sprinted up to her slightly larger and faster twin. She managed to pass him, never uttering a word. Wavren's broad smile showed his love and respect as she left him behind. He was always impressed by the mental determination his sister so often called on to boost her physical abilities. She seemed to have a virtually endless physical reserve when she set her mind to overcome pain or fatigue. It was a magnificent gift.

Discipline wasn't Rosabela's only asset. She was a perfectly proportioned she-elf with grace and beauty that turned many eyes from work, play, or other activities and often held the attention of both elf and human alike as she passed. Her long, coal black hair seemed to have a life of its own and her sparkling green eyes, slender nose, and full lips completed her angelic features. In spite of her feminine charms, she was no arm ornament. She was a hardworking and serious she-elf known for meticulous study and diligence. Even though she and Wavren were fraternal twins, their looks were quite different as were their personalities, but they were inseparable nonetheless.

Wavren took a deep breath, unwilling to be outdone. He pulled from his own reserves to keep up with the slender she-elf and moved up beside her. Their competitive nature had kept them close for as long as they could remember.

The twins were rushing back to Celes'tia, not wanting to be

late to a celebration in honor of many returning Protectors of the Vale. It was an event being held in honor of several warriors, mages, rogues, and priests who had recently returned from successful campaigns against the marauding orcs, tauren, trolls, and undead, known as the Bloodcrest Forces. A huge feast, music, and dancing were always on the schedule, but most important to the twins, were the epic stories that always followed. These battle tales were often the reason so many elves had joined the famous band of fighters. It was Wavren and Rosabela's dream more so than most.

The two siblings arrived just as the festivities kicked off. Several gnomes had been hired to design a huge display of fireworks, perhaps the biggest display in the history of Celes'tia, which made everyone nervous. In the years past, fireworks were often used to signal the beginning of the festivities, but this tradition had nearly ended when the reckless gnomes had an accidental misfire that set the roof of the Great Temple ablaze. As a result, the city elders decided to appoint a fire brigade to oversee the gnomes from that day forward. Coincidently, several gnomish engineers had taken up that duty as well, and more often than not, were unable to get their water-pumping devices to work in time to douse even small fires. Many of the local elves still cringe to this day when the tiny gnomes start to set up the grand display of rockets and colorful explosions, but the outsiders and small children love the show.

A large outdoor feast always followed the fireworks display. It was set up with every delicacy imaginable. There was roasted boar seasoned with herbs and spices that drew dwarves from all over the realm, steamed clams from Port Archer, the trade city to the south, and succulent lamb that was so tender even the most cultured nobleman used his fingers instead of a fork. These dishes were only to start the meal and were followed by an assortment of side items like tubers with Brie, herb-roasted bread of every possible grain, and vegetables from all over the realm. The elves of Celes'tia took great pride in celebrating their heroes.

There were scores of goodly folk dancing to the light and

jubilant music played by elven musicians. The drummers kept an upbeat rhythm on a variety of percussion instruments. There were simple gourds, which gave a shallow *thump, da-da, thump* sound as well as deep kettle-drums that radiated a strong baseline: *ba-boom, boom, boom, ba-boom, boom, boom*. To the front of the drummers, flutist's trilled high notes, trumpeters carried the melody, and a myriad of stringed instruments, including lutes, harps, and mandolins, which seemed to hum the sounds of Nature. The swirling blend of music was almost magical and seemed to entice many to grab partners or spin around solo in the clearing adjacent to the band. It was an amazing sight to behold.

The oldest standing tradition, the recounting of battle tales, was about to begin. It was more than an historical recounting of combat; it was a visceral sharing of tales that made the spectators feel as if they had been there on the battlefield. In the past, only elves were allowed to recount their battles, but as the goodly races fought more and more as elven allies, this telling of tales became an interracial event and attracted citizens from every walk of life. One unusually stout elf named Karok, who was clad in well-worn plate armor, had already gathered a crowd with his recounting of a battle in Deadmist Valley. Deadmist Valley was a battlefield in the contested lands between the Bloodcrest Force Territory and Dae'gon Alliance Territory. It was a place where the blood of both groups flowed daily as humans, elves, gnomes, and dwarves of the Dae'gon Alliance defended the lands of goodly races from the Bloodcrest Forces. This was no mere chance encounter. Karok was part of the war contingent in the last deliberate assault on the Bloodcrest Forces, and he had the scars to prove it.

The warrior announced with great hand gestures and dramatic tones, "There we were, standing on the war-torn battlements looking across the gulch. We could see the Bloodcrest stronghold in the distance with its black wrought-iron gates and dark gray stone walls. It was the antithesis of our own white marble keep. The open battlefield was strewn with twisted armor, shattered weapons, and the carrion of a hundred poor souls whose flesh was rotting in the morning sun. Some say hell itself is paradise compared to the battleground at Deadmist Valley."

Many elven heads nodded in agreement and more than a few human, dwarven, and gnomish heads bobbed up and down as well.

Karok continued, "The portcullis clanked noisily upward and out spewed the forces of evil, and our mortal enemies. I saw the motley collection of orcs and trolls raising spears and swords as they rallied their wicked brethren. Slightly to their flank was a platoon of tauren shock troops that moved forward with death in their eyes. These powerful half-men, half-bull warriors snorted and stomped their cloven hoofs in response to the orcish rally. Bringing up the rear was the last group. Rotted flesh, exposed bones, and tattered robes identified these as undead spell-wielders, mostly mages, but a few priests as well. It was a fearsome and unholy gathering of hell itself."

A few elves unconsciously gasped and stepped back, while the majority simply stared with endless awe as the warrior continued.

He pantomimed drawing his sword and spoke again: "We moved forward as a unified fighting force of elves, dwarves, gnomes, and humans. We held our lines with grim determination and weapons at the ready. Not one hesitated as the charge came on. We were honorable soldiers, disciplined, and ready for battle. I heard our wizards call for great bolts of lightning and fire, which slowed the charge just long enough for our archers to send volley after volley of arrows into the screaming villains. Many shields were raised, but elven longbows punched right through. By then, the battle was well underway as the undead cast their wicked spells of black energy that saps one's strength and steals the very warmth from his blood.

"Our close combat warriors pushed forward as the Bloodcrest infantry marched our way. I headed for the tauren shock troops with five other warriors and a paladin named Landermihl from Griffon's Peak, the human capital city. As we closed the distance, I realized that the enemies were massive, beyond my own expectation or description from tales told around the fire. Even on my *windwraith* feline mount, the tauren were huge, looking eye to eye with me."

One enraptured young elf actually stumbled forward as he unknowingly leaned toward Karok with anticipation, too immersed in the story to realize he was overbalanced.

The warrior slammed his mailed fist into his other hand for effect and said, "We hit those tauren maggots with such speed and precision that the enemy lines buckled like the knees of a coward, but they held as we drove into them.

"I found myself engaged in deadly combat with an ax-wielding beast that had only one horn. The other must have been lost in one of the other countless battles this vicious monster had fought. I smelled blood and sweat, which covered his body, no doubt from other battles that day. His armor showed the wear of numerous battles before.

"The beast came in unbelievably fast for being so large. He slammed his great two-handed ax into my shield and sent me back a step, but the 'oak bends with the wind and snaps back,' as the saying goes. I moved to his side and angled my own blade into the beast's armored midsection, but his breastplate turned my strike. His next blow sundered my shield, so I drew my off-handed dagger and moved in with both blades in unison. The sword was parried by the tauren's ax handle, but fine elven steel sank deeply into his tree-trunk-like leg when my dagger slipped through his defenses. His howl was accompanied by a rapid flurry of strikes that I dodged and blocked. Luckily, I had him hamstrung. He sought to cleave me in two with a powerful overhead swipe of his ax, but his wounded leg slowed him enough and allowed me to spin around to his rear and run my broadsword though his spine."

Several in the crowd cheered, but the elven warrior never heard it. Karok was still there on the battleground in his mind, and more than a few of the onlookers noticed his welling battle lust, which was matched by the awe of a dozen spectators.

The warrior continued, almost in a state of hallucination: "Pulling my blade from the tauren made a wet metal-on-metal scraping sound that was eerie and unsettling, yet somehow satisfying. I saw our archers focusing their volleys on the undead wizards who would fall soon enough. Our own spell casters were blasting the trolls and orcs with frost that slowed or held them in place long enough to roast them with deafening explosions of fire. We had the initiative and pressed onward, sensing victory.

"I looked around for my fellow swordsmen, but could not find the other five warriors; they had fallen in the initial charge. I turned to see the lone paladin of our company holding three of the other shock troops at bay. His great hammer rained holy justice down on his enemies while his prayers called healing down from his God. I sprinted forward and felt the blood in my veins pounding through my body. My anger and hatred boiled into overwhelming fury. The landscape seemed to be glazed in a blood-red hue and the battle sounds seemed distant, but I knew I was barely a few strides from my next target.

"Ally and enemy clashed, fought, and died without discrimination. I reached Landermihl's assailants before they could overwhelm the paladin. Using my sprinting momentum, I lashed out mightily with my sword and blasted through the first tauren's neck while my dagger sunk deeply into its now headless body. I turned to see the human holy warrior take numerous hits from the remaining two villains. His blood flowed from nearly every crevice in his radiant armor, but he held on somehow. I spun left and sliced both tauren simultaneously, hoping to draw their attacks my way. One turned on me and the other continued to attack the paladin without regard for his own life or that of his fellow shock troop. I took a solid hit from the spear my enemy held. I never felt it. I sheared off the spearhead, still embedded in my shoulder, and threw my rage at the monster who had struck me. Suddenly unarmed, the tauren dove for a sword and shield that failed to save their previous owner. The beast absorbed my first swing, but that was all it could manage as I rained more than a dozen stabbing and slashing attacks on him. My enemy was lying dead in a pool of blood before my last series of strikes landed."

It was apparent to most of the older elves that this warrior was more than a skilled fighter. On the battlefield, he was a killing machine out of control. He was an enraged berserker who lived to fight and willingly gave in to battle lust as a source of power. The younger spectators watched on in admiration and disbelief as parents guided their toddlers away in horror.

Fully consumed by the story, the warrior continued, “The paladin defeated his foe long before I came out of the rage, and it was his deep voice filled with serenity that brought me back. He told me to be at ease and accept healing from his hands. As I calmed into rationality, I noticed the spearhead that protruded from the front and exited out the back of my armor. It was a serrated tip, blacked with dirt and dried blood. I was lucky to be alive. With a nod from Landermihl, I removed it myself and the paladin purged the wound with healing magic.

“I surveyed the grim carnage. The Bloodcrest Force was in full retreat, but we had lost far too many good fighters to claim a true victory. We picked up our dead and wounded and headed to the rear, where priests and healers were bandaging us up for the next battle. We fought twice daily as either skirmishers or dedicated regulars for the entire month until we pushed the hell-spawned Bloodcrest Force back into their desolate lands. Hail to the Dae’gon Alliance and the Glory of Celes’tia!”

As the crowd cheered, Wavren stood motionless and pictured himself amid the enemy corpses, standing victoriously among the Dae’gon Alliance companies. He was certain his fate lay among the Protectors of the Vale. Rosabela was affected in much the same way but felt a sense of duty more so than the longing for glory.

The twins spent the day feasting, dancing, and rejoicing. It was the last day of their youth and the perfect precursor to an adult life spent adventuring.

Chapter 1
The Twins

Wavren awoke early the following day. It was his fiftieth birthday, the day when the vigor of his adolescence would become tempered by the maturity of adulthood—or at least, that was what the elders always said. He stretched and yawned to purge the sleepiness from his well-toned body and smiled as he considered the importance of this day. Today would be perhaps the greatest day of his life as he embarked on the rite of passage into manhood. This was more than simply being recognized as an adult. The fiftieth birthday rite of passage was the day when he would find his path among the noble careers as a Protector of the Vale. His father's ancestors had long been masters of the blade and bow and had often become dedicated warriors or skilled rogues, serving as both frontline fighters and deadly infiltrators during the many wars of the realm. He was excited about the chance to follow in their footsteps, and he intended to make his name among the great legends of Elven Lore.

Excitedly, he donned his leather trousers, matching vest, and soft-soled boots. Wavren belted on the dagger and leather pouches favored by his kin and in no time, he was ready and out the door. As he stepped onto the soft leaves and moss that covered the ground, he smiled with the knowledge that he left no trace of passage and made no sound at all. Perhaps the ways of the rogue were more his nature. He padded softly down the trail and came to a gathering of elves that were waiting to be selected as Protectors of the Vale. The line was long and he fell in place at the end, behind a female elf.

Wavren spoke aloud as he approached, "The rite of passage for housewives and famous elven cooks is on the other side of the clearing."

The female elf nodded and returned, "Then you must have taken a wrong turn dear brother, but I can give you directions if you like."

Wavren smiled and patted the female on the shoulder. How he loved Rosabela, his sister, and how alike they were. He realized that they were no longer children. They were adults today. He saw it clearly, as he gazed at his sister who stood almost as tall as he and was beautiful beyond compare. He has always admired her wit and steadfastness. She would have made the perfect wife for any elf, but as so many she-elves before her; she lived for adventure and would never resign herself to the quiet, yet noble life of motherhood and wife. She had a higher calling, just as Wavren had. They were born to be Protectors. She was in line awaiting selection and the rite of passage into womanhood just as he awaited the rite of passage into manhood. She was his mirror reflection in so many ways that he couldn't imagine himself without her. In fact, they had never been apart more than a few days throughout their entire lives.

Wavren watched those elves ahead and knew the selection process was simple. Any elf having come of age would walk up to the Grand Seer of Celes'tia and ask him to prophesize their path. He would put his ancient, virtually gnarled hand on their shoulder and whisper the answer into their ear. This had been the way for ages and none had ever denied their calling. Many elves became Protectors, but not all. Some elves became merchants or skilled craftsmen. It was the true calling of their heart, which the Seer used to set them on the path.

Wavren felt sure that he would become a warrior or rogue as his line had been since his great-great-grandfather, the Patriarch, and founder of Celes'tia itself. As for his sister, Wavren guessed that she would be either a mage or priestess as nearly every female had been since their great-great-grandmother, who married only after attaining the rank of Grand Mistress of the Arcane, the highest rank in the arcane arts and one reserved for only the most disciplined and dedicated spell-wielders. In fact, it was all but guaranteed, since he was certain that she possessed the skill and intelligence to follow that course, and after all, surely Rosie had her heart set on it.

Time somehow raced forward and before he knew it, Rosie was standing before the Seer and he was next. Rosabela stood proud and tall and called out mightily, "What shall my fate be?"

The venerable elf rested his twisted claw of a hand on her shoulder and said, "Protector of the Vale," and then he whispered the path that she was destined to follow. Rosabela was shaking with excitement as she nodded and walked past. Wavren assumed she must have been granted the path of mage by her expression.

He moved forward with confidence anew and called forth, "Prophesy my future great Seer, I am ready."

The Seer stretched out his hand and touched Wavren. "Protector of the Vale," he exclaimed. His quiet voice breathed the path into Wavren's ear. "You shall serve as brother of the forest. You shall follow the path of the hunter."

Although the appearance was nearly that of his sister, Wavren shook with emotion that was not excitement, but instead bordered on rage. He walked away fighting the turmoil in his heart and confusion in his mind.

Wavren thought to himself. What just happened? Was there some mistake? Was this a joke? I am destined to be a warrior or rogue just as my ancestors were. How could this happen? This must be a mistake! He thought of turning back and asking again, but no one ever defied the path selected by the Seer.

Rosabela ran over to her brother and hugged him, but no

embrace was returned. She looked into her brother's eyes and knew that he was distraught. She asked in her loving, sisterly voice, "Wav, what troubles you on this all important day?"

"I am not to be a great warrior or a rogue infiltrator as our fathers and their father had been. I have been selected as a hunter, a mere woodsman," he said with resignation.

"Being a hunter means you can commune with Nature. It is a fine path and a noble one at that," Rosabela said halfheartedly.

"Tell me sister, have you been selected as we guessed, to follow in our matriarch's footsteps as a wizard?"

Her eyes brightened and she threw her shoulders back and pronounced, "I have not been selected for mage-craft."

"Then surely you have been given the honor of priestess," Wavren returned.

"No brother, I have been called as a druidic shape-shifter."

Wavren stared intently at his all-too-proud sister. She had wanted to be a mage. She had her heart set on it. How could she be so happy with anything else? She simply continued to smile. Then it dawned on him. She had the best of both worlds. She would be able to heal with the magic of Nature like a priestess, and have the raw power equal to that of any wizard in offensive spells and shape-shifting forms she would command. But why was she still smiling as she stared at her brother?

"You do not realize what has happened here, do you dear brother?" she asked with the grin of one who knows an all too obvious secret. "You have been assigned as a Protector of the Vale with both the skills of the warrior and the skills of the rogue. The hunter is a blend of your heart's desire, just as the druid is the blend of my heart's desires." She explained, "You will scout and fight beyond what any rogue or warrior could accomplish individually and your connection to Nature will sustain you."

Wavren smiled sheepishly and although he was far from convinced, he did feel a little better about the path he was on as a hunter and a Protector of the Vale. "It could be worse," he thought, "at least I wasn't chosen to be a priest. I can't imagine wearing holy robes in combat. It might as well be a dress."

Rosabela laughed as she pictured her very masculine brother in a dress.

Wavren moved over to a small glade not far from where he and Rosabela were selected. There were several elves milling about, waiting for the confirmation process that was more of a modern, *welcome to the group,* than a solemn rite of passage graduation ceremony. In a copse of trees barely one hundred yards away, Wavren could see his sister waiting for her confirmation as well. In fact, there were seven different groups awaiting separate confirmations. The hunters and druids were the smallest groups followed by the mage, priest, and rogue groups. The largest was the warrior, and of course, the merchant and craftsman groups.

Wavren's heart was still in turmoil over not being in the rogue group or the warrior group, but perhaps Rosabela had been right. Perhaps the hunter was his true calling. Regardless of his second thoughts, he was on the path of the hunter now and he was duty bound to serve his kinfolk, as well as the elven nation, and serve he would, with every breath he took, even if it were his last. He thought about the stories his father had told him of the deadly battles the elves had fought over the ages. Great battles with powerful orcs, cunning trolls, fearsome tauren, and the grotesque undead had been more than fanciful bedtime stories. These tales had been woven into the very fabric of Wavren's spirit. They were as much a part of his life as the long pointy ears on his head. Yes, Wavren and his sister had been raised on the courage, valor, and honor of fighting these enemies as much as their own mother's milk. It was now his time to serve and he would do so honorably.

The time for reflection had passed and Wavren found his group being addressed by an elf of many years. The withered hunter's long double-recurved bow was now as much a walking staff as his weapon of choice. He wore his long hair in silver braids with feathers and strips of leather that made him look more like a barbarian nomad than a civilized elf, but his eyes sparkled with fire that told the real story of this elf's life.

Those eyes were wizened with experience and yet still held the look of strength found in far younger elves. His quiet resolve and powerful spirit showed through. The forest itself seemed to respond to him, empower him, and even give way to his steps. This man was not only at peace with himself, but he was one with Nature. In fact, this hunter was the embodiment of the forest.

The elven hunter brought forth his hands and began, "Welcome brothers and sisters of the forest, I am Daenek Torren, your guide on the hunter's path. You are the chosen few who will serve as the eyes and ears of the forest. You will see what the forest sees, hear what the forest hears, and even smell what the forest smells. Ultimately, you will know what the forest knows, and with that knowledge, you will find the enemy, fix his location, and unleash the power of Nature's wrath to ensure their destruction. This is your duty, your mission, and your life. Welcome, hunters."

Wavren was impressed with the simplicity of the speech and yet overwhelmed by the power of the words. Nothing more could have been said to unite the small band of initiate hunters further with purpose, direction, and motivation. He was ready to begin, and all thoughts of being a warrior or rogue had evaporated from his mind like the desert rain. His life's work lay before him. Adulthood had come and adolescence was no more.

* * *

Rosabela was intently concentrating on the moment as her group awaited their introduction to the druidic ways. No fanciful thoughts or daydreams danced in her head as in those of many of her contemporaries. No delusions of grandeur or images of epic conquest were present to distract the elf-maid. One word described Rosabela, and that word was *focused*!

The crowd was quietly chatting when a subtle change in the wind made Rosabela turn toward the tangle of massive roots that served as the speaker's stage. Something was amiss here.

She could not quite put her finger on it, but her group was no longer alone. Almost out of thin air, a great black panther appeared on the stage, and just as quickly as it appeared, there was a flash of light and where the cat once stood, an elf now appeared. It all happened so quickly, that only Rosabela actually witnessed the truth of what happened. Everyone else merely assumed the druid had magically appeared as if by teleportation, not uncommon among high-ranking mages, but unheard of among druids. It was a dramatic entrance planned to surprise and confuse the young druids to be. Rosabela knew the truth, however. Few things caught the insightful elf-maid by surprise.

The speaker began his speech with a question. "Who among you knows the heart of the forest?" he asked. None answered. A few of the initiates shuffled uncomfortably from foot to foot wondering if it was a trick question. Hackles raised and in a stern voice, he repeated the question and again none answered. Rosabela knew what was in her heart, but what the mysterious druid asked was vague. The speaker thundered loudly for the third time, "Who among you knows the heart of the forest?"

Rosabela locked gazes with him and suddenly knew the answer. It was apparent to her, not only in the depth of the speaker's voice, which was almost the growl of a great bear and at the same time, the howling of wolves, and roaring of lions. It was all too apparent in the feral stance the druid took, in his clothing, and headdress that was fashioned to make the wearer seem more beast than man.

Rosabela stepped forward and said, "The heart of the forest is steeped in change just as the life of a druidic shape-shifter. I know the heart of the forest because I embody the heart of the forest!"

The crowd murmured at the boldness of the statement and yet slowly came to realize that it was indeed truth. The speaker glared at Rosabela as if his gaze was meant to cow the young she-elf. She held her ground and waited for an eternity while the druid took in full measure of her spirit. Her mind set was rooted like the great redwoods of the forest. His gaze was steeled and fire seemed to spew from his soul, nearly consuming Rosabela. She felt his presence enter her mind and spirit. It was as if he was forcing his will into her, but her determination was as endless as the sea. He poured out his feral rage as he battled her mind, but her inner strength was no less than the speaker's. Finally, the speaker's gaze softened, his stance relaxed, and his words came forth like a proud father holding his newly born daughter for the first time.

"I have chosen my apprentice," he said, and the crowd became unmoving statues as he and Rosabela walked away to begin the path of the druid.

* * *

Daenek brought the newly commissioned hunters to a meeting hall formed in the bough of an ancient oak. He motioned for all of the neophytes to sit, and he began to speak.

"Each hunter will have a mentor responsible for his training in the ways of marksmanship, survival, and beast mastery," he said, as a line of seasoned hunters moved into the great hall. "Each of you will be tested for aptitude and paired up with the appropriate mentor based on your skills and abilities."

Wavren already knew that he would likely be the superior marksman, and his survival skills were good, but he knew nothing of beast mastery. After all, what did an elf who had planned to be a warrior or a rogue know about beast mastery? This concerned him greatly. The pressure was definitely high, and Wavren had been thrown into a career path that he had not mentally prepared for.

When the procession of hunters had ended, Wavren noticed that there were fifteen hunters in his group and only fourteen mentors. This was odd. Could it be that one hunter would simply be cut from the program? It was unthinkable that the Seer had been wrong with the selection process, but there was no other explanation for the missing mentor. It wouldn't matter anyway. Wavren intended to be at the top of the class, if not the best of them all.

Daenek Torren cleared his throat and introduced each mentor. "From Port Archer, allow me to introduce Clan Eagle, Mage-bane of the Vale. These five hunters are masters of great birds of prey who seek to cast down the wizards, priests, and other spell casters of the Bloodcrest Forces: Aris, Varamin, Kaldor, Jaereg, and Phaelen." The first group of elven hunters stepped forward and bowed. When they stood up and in unison, the hunters whistled, chirped, hooted, screeched, or cawed. Within seconds, five birds of prey flew in and perched on their master's arms.

Wavren admired the devotion of the majestic birds. He noticed that each hunter held a different raptor. He recognized two large falcons, noble and proud, two great horned owls, wise and alert, and oddly, a wretched buzzard, which was foul with the smell of carrion, but undeniably fierce in appearance. Although impressed by the display, Wavren hoped that he could avoid this group of loud, squawking bird masters.

Daenek cleared his throat again as the Clan Eagle left. He said, "From Forestedge, allow me to introduce Clan Jaguar, infiltrators of the Vale. These five hunters are masters of the great cats who seek to disrupt the Bloodcrest Forces through stealth. No assassin can match the cunning and power of these jungle cats or the skill of those who tame them: Alerac, Demetus, Narral, Samu, and Rhayne." Each elven hunter stepped forward and called to his ally. Two mighty striped tigers entered, followed by two dark panthers called *windwraiths*, and one pure white tigron—half-tiger, half-lion, and very rare. These magnificent beasts appealed to Wavren, who thought himself more apt to the rogue-like nature of these silent predators. Perhaps being a hunter would work out in his benefit after all.

Last, but not least, Daenek introduced the remaining four mentors. "From here in our home of Celes'tia, let me introduce Ursa Clan, battle-masters of the Vale. These hunter-warriors are more than scouts who relay information and use beasts to protect the Vale. These are the greatest marksmen in the realm who command nearly 1500 pounds of raging claws and teeth: Vaalic, Graemin, Saddik, and Braemish." As each elf's name was called, he stepped forward and growled or roared to call his massive friends. Two huge brown bears came in followed by two black bears. Each bear was easily 1500 pounds, and although they seemed friendly enough, the tracks they left showed that the front paws were as wide as a man's chest and the claws were wickedly hooked scythes. Few shields could withstand the crushing power of these beasts, and even finely crafted chainmail would be shredded under the ripping power of those claws. Wavren was now torn between Clan Ursa and Clan Jaguar. Perhaps fate would continue to propel him forward as it had done so far today.

As the last of the mentors departed, Daenek announced that one Ursa Clan mentor was late due to a critical mission, but his arrival would be forthcoming. Nothing more was said about the last of the mentors, but at least this meant no one would be *cut* from the hunter's program.

Wavren and his hunter brethren were marched out of the hall and into the glade where various testing stations were being set up. Several targets, both moving and stationary, were already prepared and ready for the new hunters. Dozens of tamed beasts were lined up and sitting contentedly in spite of many of them being natural enemies or predator and prey. The discipline among the beasts amazed Wavren. Last, but not least, the survival stations were being constructed. Wavren nearly trembled with excitement at the great opportunity he had before him. He felt confident that he could easily pass these tests, but he wanted to excel, and the competition would be close.

Daenek called each hunter forward, and in spite of the tough competition, the hunter who was currently participating in the test was cheered by his fellow hunters. The beast-handling test was first and was more a measure of affinity toward the various beasts and simple courage than anything else. As with the early selection process, the truth in each hunter's heart was felt by the appropriate beast. Coincidentally, there were five who seemed drawn toward the great birds of prey, five hunters who were fondly rubbed by the great cats as they chose their hunters, and five who were literally knocked down and playfully wrestled with by the massive bears.

Wavren knew the raptor birds were not for him, and it was evident by his inability to perform well with them. In fact, he almost lost a finger to one of the falcons when he offered a treat to coerce the bird onto his falconer's glove. He interacted well with the windwraiths and great tigers, but the bears seemed more to his liking. At just over 160 pounds, Wavren was no match for the great beasts that were ten times his weight, but he rolled around with them and had a great time. As the bears took turns roughing the new hunters up, Daenek and the mentors all made various observations and wrote down scores for each new hunter. Wavren scored highest with the bears, but he was not particularly high scoring among his peers with the beast handling tasks as a whole.

The tracking and survival events were next, and although Wavren managed to arm and disarm some simple traps, and work through a variety of escape and evasion tasks, he still only produced average scores. He was able to identify more than a dozen animal tracks and even make a good guess at the length of time the tracks had been around and the weight of the animals that made them, but so did many of his fellow hunter neophytes. This was somewhat depressing for the highly competitive elf, but he hoped that he would do better in the marksmanship events.

Wavren walked through the marksmanship course and observed the lay of the land and the targets he would have to engage. There were three lanes of events. The first was an accuracy lane where long-range marksmanship was measured. The objective of that lane was to score points by hitting ten successively distant targets until the hunter failed to hit a target, which would terminate the event. The second was a timed event in which the hunter must hit ten moving targets with ten arrows in ten seconds (the turn of a small hourglass). The last was a shoot-on-the-move event, where the hunter was tasked to fire off ten arrows at various targets to his left and right in twenty seconds while running at a full sprint.

Wavren knew he would perform well here. He was, after all, a master of the elven longbow as well as the more conventional composite bow, but so were many of his peers. Wavren was first in line, and he knew he would set the bar quite high. He approached the accuracy lane and took a deep breath. As he let it out, he felt the wind gently blowing to the southeast. He tested the taut pull of the bowstring and selected a finely crafted elven arrow. His first shot was a mere ten strides away. He hit dead center. The second shot was again ten strides beyond the first. He sunk the arrow deeply in the center as well. This process continued until he was using great elevation and windage to compensate for the range. Out of ten stationary targets, he hit all ten dead center, but so did three of the fourteen other hunters. It was a testament to the archery heritage in the elven community.

The moving target lane was much more difficult. On the command "fire," Wavren took his longbow and fired arrow after arrow into the moving targets that were no more than the size of an orc's head. In the blink of an eye, he had hit all ten perfectly. This time, only two of his peers matched his skill. One was a male who had excelled with the survival tasks, but had no affinity with any animals. He would have made a fine scout. The other was a female who seemed to be Wavren's equal in all events up to this point. He was keeping his eye on her to track her progress.

The final event, the shoot-on-the-move lane, was tough because it was timed. The hunter's aim was jostled by each step, and the targets moved up and down quickly. Wavren centered himself and nodded for the event to begin. Daenek Torren was watching the competition closely, and this made Wavren want to excel all the more. The course began and Wavren took off down the lane in a flash. The first target popped up on the right almost as he passed it, such was Wavren's foot speed, but he angled and fired, hitting it squarely. The second was immediately to the left, and he turned and hit it, too. There were three that came up simultaneously, and Wavren hit the first, then drew two arrows at once and hit the last two before they went down. The next one was at a bad angle behind a tree, but Wavren banked his arrow off the tree bark and hit it, too. There were two side-by-side, spinning like a top, and Wavren had to take a moment to time those two shots, which cost him a few strides, but he was almost at the end. The last two targets were barely the size of an elf's fist, and they came up and went down in less than two seconds, but they went down with two arrows embedded in them nonetheless. Wavren had mastered the entire marksmanship course and he had done it in record time. This time, only one hunter matched his perfect-hit record, the slender she-elf called Galaa, whom the crowd cheered as they called her name.

Just out of curiosity, Daenek declared a rematch of the last event between Wavren and Galaa. There was a catch, however. Daenek set the hunters on the lane at the same time to see who would get each shot off first and knock the target down, leaving no target to hit for the slower marksman. Wavren took full measure of his competition and restocked his quiver. The aged hunter gave the signal, and the two were off.

Just as before, the first target was set to pop up almost behind the runners, but Wavren poured on the speed anyway, easily taking the lead. When the first target popped up, Galaa was almost to it and Wavren was actually past it. Both fired and Galaa's shot hit the front just as Wavren fired blindly and backward, hitting it from the back, which knocked Galaa's arrow out of the target. The crowd cheered now calling his name instead of hers.

Both turned to the left and hit the second simultaneously. Wavren drew two arrows for the set of three targets that came up simultaneously and fired just as Galaa fired. Both hit the first two, but Galaa had drawn and fired three arrows, an incredible feat even for elven archers. Wavren never got his last shot off. The score was tied again.

Wavren was in a good position, well in front of Galaa, for the angled shot behind the tree, but somehow Galaa managed to hit the target before it went down with Wavren's arrow in it. The two spinning targets were going to be tough. Wavren drew and fired as Galaa fired. Both hit one target each, and both missed the follow-on shot. The last two small targets were suddenly up, and Wavren pulled back his bow to try an impossible two-arrow split. Just then, an arrow whizzed past and cut his bowstring. A smiling Galaa stood ready with her last arrow nocked and ready to fire. Wavren was furious, but he knew she had simply outsmarted him. He had arrows left, but no way to shoot them. The she-elf released her arrow and was confident she would hit the mark when a flash of silver intercepted the shot and sent her arrow off course. The crowd cheered as Wavren stood confidently with arms crossed, his fine elven dagger protruding from the small target. Both ran across the finish line with an equal number of arrow hits, with Wavren scoring an additional, unprecedented dagger hit. The day was won, and Wavren congratulated his female counterpart, who was not at all pleased with the outcome. Daenek awarded them both with praise and promised to record this event in the great History Book of Celes'tia.

The day ended with a feast and the selection of hunters by the corresponding mentors. All were chosen except Wavren. Daenek Torren announced that the greatest marksman would become the pupil of Gaedron, who had not yet arrived from his last mission. No one seemed to know this hunter named Gaedron, but Daenek assured Wavren that Gaedron was the finest marksman in the realm and a member of Clan Ursa. It was reputed that he had tamed a great white arctic bear from the northlands, which seemed odd, since elves tended to stay in warmer climates. In fact, only the traders who traveled to the dwarven city of Dragonforge spent any time at all up north.

Chapter 2
First Lessons

Rosabela walked quietly behind her master, who was leading her to a small pond surrounded by massive oaks and gnarled ash trees. The air was thick with the earthy smell of moss and leaves. The wind hummed with sounds from crickets and frogs.

Rosabela's master whispered, "This is a sacred place of druidic power. Show reverence here, and Nature will reward you. It is a mutually rewarding companionship that a druid has with Nature."

Rosabela only nodded and continued to walk softly, as if disturbing the leaves or the soft moss would somehow desecrate this lovely place. Upon their arrival, Rosabela felt a strange tingling and was almost uplifted into euphoria by the peace and tranquility in the sacred grove. This was a magically blissful place and one she was certain was hidden from non-druids.

"You can feel it, can't you?" the powerful druid said. "You can sense the magic that flows here. The power of Nature and interconnection with all life is a magnificent thing to behold," he said, as if answering his own question. "This is the nexus of Celes'tia."

Rosabela replied solemnly, "Yes, I feel the energy, and it is indeed magnificent."

The mysterious druid continued, "It is time for formal introductions. I am Da'Shar of Celes'tia, and I am a Protector of the Vale, just as you will be. I am required to find one student every century and show her the ways of the druid, that we may sustain Nature's balance and protect her from those who would see her destruction. You are that student. Your formal training with me will take some time, but your apprenticeship to Nature will last for your entire lifetime and then some."

"I understand, and I am honored to be your pupil, but what of the others?" she asked. "Will they become druids as the Seer has foreseen?"

"They will become druids under other mentors, but I have chosen you because of your innate strengths. You alone were able to commune with me as beasts do. You alone had the focus and the will to look into my eyes and connect to my soul. We are now bound, just as a brother is to his sister. With that connection, you will learn the arts of druidic balance, restoration, and even feral combat," he continued.

"I am grateful to be the student you have selected, but how can we sustain our numbers with so few being selected every century?" Rosabela asked.

"Our numbers are few because this calling consumes those who answer. All too often, those chosen few cannot endure. Once you start on the path of the druid, you may never turn from it. You must endure until death itself releases you back to the Spirit of Nature. Failing to do this, or betraying our order, will bring the fury of Nature upon you. Be forewarned that I am charged with carrying out your education as well as your destruction should you fail," he said solemnly.

"I understand, and I am ready," Rosabela answered without hesitation, "but you already know that, don't you?"

Da'Shar smiled and set his hand on the young elf-maid's shoulder. "I do," he returned. "You must now take the oath of our order and receive the Spirit Mark. Repeat these words and brace yourself:

"I am a Protector of the Vale by office, and Druid of the Grove by calling.

"I will live and die by the solemn promise that I now make.

"My mind is my own, my body is freely given in service, and my soul is bound to nature."

Rosabela repeated the words and closed her eyes. The master druid placed his hand on her bare shoulder and spoke words that were more the breath of wind and the rumbling of thunder than any language, but Rosabela heard them clearly, as if they were common tongue.

"Receive the mark which ties you to our order. It is the key to speaking nature's voice and death to those who betray it. Welcome, Rosabela, Sister of the Grove."

Suddenly, white fire poured from the druid's hand and burned deeply into Rosabela's flesh. The pain was excruciating, and the smell of charred skin was thick in the air. The master had conferred his palm print on his student and forever marked her as a member of his order and direct lineage. Rosabela was weak from the pain, and when she looked at her shoulder, she was surprised to see the mark was not merely a brand; it was a hideous, black, oozing blister. The pain and the stench of her own charred flesh almost made her vomit.

Da'Shar spoke: "The burn is made by moonfire, which is a talent you will learn. But more important, is the talent I now use to restore your skin. Be healed, young one."

With that, an eerie green light surrounded Da'Shar's hands, and as he laid them on Rosabela's shoulder. The wound healed, leaving a perfect impression of the Master's hand. Not only was the wound healed, but Rosabela actually felt invigorated. She was overwhelmed with happiness, shock, and awe, and actually fell to her knees and wept with the rite's completion.

The following days of training for Rosabela were much less painful than the initiation. She learned a few minor healing spells that she put to good use while practicing weapon sparring and unarmed combat. Rosabela found she had a gift for offensive magic and quickly picked up moonfire, the very spell that left its mark on her and now served as an everlasting reminder of her oath as a druid.

Her mentor spent countless hours expounding on the interconnection of all living things. How druids used that connection to speak with animals, find herbs for healing, and cast powerful spells for offense and defense. After several weeks, he concluded with the ever-mysterious subject of feral transformation, in which a druid could learn to shape-shift into the very beasts she communed with. As usual, these conversations strengthened the bond between student and master. Rosabela grew very close to her spirit brother, Da'Shar. She thought of her true sibling, Wavren, on several occasions, but the bond of spirit seemed very strong indeed, and the bond of blood was now somehow lessened. She did wonder how Wavren's training was coming, but was more excited about her own.

It was not long before Da'Shar felt Rosabela was ready for her first solo run. She awoke one morning to find a note from Da'Shar in fine script.

Rosabela, you have been a fine pupil and a good friend since we first met several weeks ago. It is now time for you to exercise the lessons I have taught. Travel beyond the grove to the north. You will find a small encampment of kobold squatters who have been slaughtering the wild deer and boar population with reckless abandon. They will soon deplete the northern fields of these animals and upset the balance of nature. The loss of these creatures will have a devastating effect on the local ecology. "CONVINCE" the kobolds to leave the area or use the appropriate force to evict them.

Rosabela took the note and packed a few supplies for the short trip that seemed more a grand adventure than an errand. By late morning, she was moving northward through the forest with grim determination. She knew that although kobolds were the weakest of all the *goblinkin*, they were very territorial and could be quite nasty. She also knew that the dog-like humanoids shared a pack mentality and were led by an alpha male. If she could not reason with him, she would eliminate him. The tricky part was guessing if the pack would be loyal to him if they had to fight or if they would cast him aside for a stronger pack leader. If the pack rallied behind the Alpha, she would be outnumbered and literally torn apart. If not, she would fight the Alpha in single combat and leave a vacuum of leadership that could be assumed by the next strongest member of the group.

Rosabela circled the small camp several times and took complete measure of the resources and manpower within. There were well over twenty scraggly kobolds and two larger ones that she could see. The smaller ones ran about chaotically trying to improve the camp development. There were several who were rebuilding the large open pit for cooking the deer and boar they had killed. They lined the pit with stones and then branches that served to hold the heat of the fires they built. It was an efficient oven for the uncivilized dog-men. There were others who were busy skinning the animals and preparing the hides for curing. She was sure they meant to make clothing, armor, and tools with the leather. Yet another group was taking the meat and cutting it into manageable portions for smoking into jerky and for immediate consumption.

The two large kobolds were discussing attack plans and were using the common tongue so the lesser kobolds couldn't understand them as well. This worked to Rosabela's favor. The older of the two, likely the Alpha, wanted the small tribe to "kill stupid elves" and take over Celes'tia in order to be King of the region. Rosabela thought this was laughably ambitious since there were thousands of elves in the city of Celes'tia and more than three times that in the surrounding area. The younger of the two, perhaps the son or nephew of the Alpha, was shaking his dog-like jowls, insisting there were too many for the small pack. He wanted to move back to the caves in order to increase the size of the group. This debate went on for several minutes, until the Alpha finally drew his amazingly shiny, short sword, and said that with his new pig sticker, he would kill elves and be King. The younger of the two backed away and let the Alpha have his moment of grandeur.

Rosabela lurked in the shadows for some time and observed the chaos until she had enough information to form a plan. She spent the next day waiting for the next conflict to boil between the two larger kobolds. Inevitably, it happened. The Alpha was talking to a smaller scout about the things he had seen, and he decided that he would plan his invasion. He gathered the small clan and began raving about killing all the elves. The scraggly commoners did not look convinced as the Alpha bellowed about how easy it would be to kill the stupid elves. The younger of the two taller kobolds stood back and shook his head, which infuriated the Alpha.

"You not thinks we can kills stupid elves?" the Alpha accused.

"Krek Grolkin thinks we can kills elves on road and in small groups, but no kill all elves in great town of Celes'tia, just too many. Yous can be King Grol of Celes'tia with shiny sword ifs we gets more kin from caves, but yous be King Dead Grol with empty hand ifs we attack now."

It was apparent to Rosabela that King Grol did not like what Krek had to say, but Krek was obviously better at adding up the chances of success than King Grol was. The smaller kobolds seemed to fear King Grol, but they agreed with Krek. Perhaps this was Rosabela's chance to intercede.

Grol looked like he was about to pull his sword and attack Krek when the attention of the crowd was immediately drawn to the edge of the camp, where Rosabela made her way through the crowd of kobolds who were growling and yipping at her heels.

King Grol took this opportunity to strengthen his case. "Yous see, I told yous that elves were stupid. This one must be extra stupid to come here alone. We having funs now," he taunted.

Krek looked utterly confused. He was suddenly wondering if his uncle was right about elves being stupid. Maybe they could win against such stupid elves, no matter what the odds.

Rosabela spoke in the common tongue: "I am Rosabela, Protector of the Vale and Druid of the Grove. I have come to you as a messenger from Celes'tia."

King Grol laughed. "Yous not Protector of anythings if yous dead."

Rosabela countered, "Hear my words first, and if I do not offer you information of value, then kill me."

King Grol returned, "Elves got no words of val-u for us, only tricks and lies that King Grol too smart to listen to."

Suddenly, Krek spoke up: "Speaks she-elf, yous have braveness to comes here and die, we wills hear words and kills you after."

This drew a threatening glare from Grol, but the crowd seemed to rumble in agreement with Krek, especially the part about killing. Rosabela quickly took the opportunity to speak.

"Celes'tia knows that you plan to attack the elves," she said, which drew a surprised gasp from the group of kobolds who looked suspiciously at each other. "We do not desire any battle with you."

King Grol jumped in: "Yous elves is scared of Grol and magic pig sticker is why yous want no battles with Kobolds. This shows we can wins."

Rosabela looked into Grol's bloodshot eyes and said, "I have been sent to show you that we do not want battle, but that we will destroy you if you do not go back to the caves of your kin."

Krek shouted, "Hows you show that?"

Rosabela returned on cue. "I challenge Grol in combat for rulership of the tribe."

The crowd grew deadly silent.

Grol laughed a wheezing laugh and said, "I told yous elves was stupid. First, this one comes to us alone. Then says stupid words and thinks she can be King of Kobolds. No elves can be Alphas, and no girls can be Alphas, and no dead girl elf cans be Alpha King, but okay, I kills you now and show kin what happens to stupid elves when King Grol gets mad."

Rosabela had only her staff and her magic against the

magic sword and anger of Grol, but she was sure she would be more than able to best the kobold. The druid stepped back and took up her fighting staff, which she spun overhead and down under one arm, signaling she was ready. Grol unsheathed his finely crafted magic sword and pulled a wooden buckler off his back in a fluid motion that showed he was no stranger to combat. He banged the sword on the shield a few times and howled to the crowd, who returned the howl and stomped clawed feet on the ground.

Rosabela whispered a few magic words and became slightly stronger and faster as a result. She circled to the right and felt very aware that she was outnumbered more than twenty to one if things went bad. Grol also circled and took measure of his opponent. Krek watched intently, as did the rest of the clan.

Without warning, Grol rushed in and slammed his shield into Rosabela's face, causing dizziness and a nice-sized knot under her eye. It staggered her back far enough to make Grol's follow-up slashing cuts miss by several inches. Rosabela reoriented herself and brought her staff up in front of her body in anticipation of the next attack. Grol came in with a quick overhead chop that the she-elf parried with the lead end of the staff. He made a short thrust, which Rosabela dodged with a quick hop backward. The return flurry from Rosabela was more than just wild swinging and flailing; she spun the staff in a figure eight pattern, forced Grol back a step, and then ended with a powerful two-handed overhead attack that slammed into Grol's shield. Grol smiled and came in hard and fast. His next three diagonal cuts mirrored Rosabela's figure eight move, and he ended with a spinning horizontal cut that she barely blocked with the middle of her staff.

Rosabela was faster, but Grol was stronger and better armed. It was apparent that Rosabela had to change tactics. She hopped back and circled again to buy some time. Grol circled and prepared to make his next attack. Rosabela whispered the words of the forest. To the surprise of Grol and the onlookers, roots grew up and trapped his clawed feet. He was entangled now, but also enraged.

"Yous cheats, stupid elf! When Grol cuts free, you die," the Alpha promised.

As Grol cut away at the mass of roots, Rosabela called to the sky and whispered the words that were more than a spell; they were the words that Da'Shar had spoken at her initiation. She called down moonfire. The light flashed, and Grol screamed. He flailed about, trying to put out the white flames that had engulfed his body. The smell of burning fur and flesh was revolting, and Rosabela remembered the pain all to well. As the white light faded, Grol was released from the intense agony; he then came on with fury unbridled. He swung wildly and hacked at Rosabela with reckless abandon. She dodged and parried several attacks, but when the clash was over, Rosabela had a severe gash on her right thigh, and most of her leather armor was destroyed on both shoulders where Grol's "pig sticker" had gotten through her defenses.

Grol had been burned horribly on most of his back and shield arm, but he was determined to kill the druid. He took a deep breath and rushed in again. Rosabela predicted the charge and ducked low. Her change of tactics took the kobold by surprise and Grol tumbled right over Rosabela's back. The druid wasted no time back peddling to a safe distance, where she began whispering the deadly words again. Grol had jumped to his feet and was almost on her when the moonfire hit him. He screamed and howled as the magic fire danced on his flesh. He fell to the ground and writhed in agony. Between labored gasps, Rosabela took a moment to whisper the healing words Da'Shar had taught her. She felt the healing magic mending her wounds. The bleeding stopped, and the pain eased within a few seconds. Rosabela turned her attention back to Grol.

Grol was alive, but little more than a charred and blistered mass of smoking flesh. She walked over and took his gleaming sword from the ground where he had dropped it. She placed the point at his throat.

"Do you yield to me the rights of leadership?" she demanded.

"Stupid elves and their tricks," was all he replied.

Grol died without another word. Krek walked over to say farewell. He put one hand on the burned corpse and raised a sad and eerie howl. The smaller kobolds gathered around and took their leader away to be prepared for the next life.

Krek spoke: "Yous killed Grol, but yous not Alpha. Yous give Krek shiny pig sticker and we goes back to caves. We lets you live and we no attacks elf city."

Rosabela nodded and handed over the sword. It was a long walk back to the grove, during which she contemplated the outcome over and over. The smell of burned flesh with the image of Grol writhing in pain stayed with her. She had indeed learned much on this first of many missions.

* * *

Wavren had spent the first day of his training waiting for his mentor to show up and was beginning to feel somewhat neglected. He wandered about the outskirts of Celes'tia watching several other hunters working with their trainers. The first day was more or less a meet-and-greet affair, but Wavren did see some basic tasks being taught by the more aggressive mentors, who wanted to get a jump on the training plan. Day two of Wavren's training was much like the first. It was nearly dark and Gaedron, the master marksman and well-respected hunter was nowhere to be seen. Wavren walked over to Daenek Torren, the grizzled old hunter who had given the welcome speech, and asked him about Gaedron's latest mission. All that Daenek could offer was a simple outline of the general location and mission parameters. He led Wavren to believe that Gaedron had been called to work alongside the humans to the East and that he should have returned from the pirate infested waters of Baradin Bay long ago. This was more than enough information for Wavren to secure his pack and a bow, and set off to find his wayward mentor.

Wavren told no one where he was going or what his intentions were. He just headed south toward the human-run port city of Seigeport. It was a three-day journey to Seigeport on foot, but the route was well marked and Wavren knew that he would be safe if he stayed on the road. He also knew that once he arrived in Seigeport, a ship would take him to the Wetlands, which was due east across the Great Sea in far off Stou'lanz. He was very excited about his first real adventure, but he was also apprehensive about having to look for his mentor. What kind of mentor got lost or held up for so long, when duty compelled him to be on time? First impressions were everything, after all.

Wavren took care to travel during the day and sleep well out of sight to avoid detection at night. It was an easy thing for an elf to conceal himself among tree boughs and out of sight depressions along the way. He made excellent time, even for a young elf. Perhaps his excitement drove him faster than most, or perhaps he knew that it was somehow important to make haste. Whatever the case, he hit Seigeport just after the rising of the sun on the third day, several hours ahead of schedule.

Seigeport was a paladin outpost that had become a thriving port city over the years of battle with the orcs and trolls in the nearby orc capital city of Dek'Thal. The need for supplies, black-smithed goods, and healing herbs had propelled Seigeport into rapid development, such that now it was a veritable fortress of high stone walls and towers, with a central citadel. There were also shops of all sorts, a tavern, and, of course, training halls all around, but Wavren was most concerned with the docks. He slowed from a sprint to a fast jog and managed to maneuver through the local populace with little trouble. He noticed a number of stares from the various humans who were not accustomed to seeing moon elves in the city, but he smiled and moved onward.

The dock master was a sharply dressed human who looked more like a pirate than a businessman. His tight wool breeches and puffy white shirt confirmed that he was probably more at home on a ship at sea than looking over shipping manifests in Seigeport.

"Hail, good sir, how I may help you?" he said with a confident smile.

Wavren replied, "I seek passage to Blackmarsh in the Wetlands, and I hope to make haste. What do you have leaving Seigeport immediately?"

The dock master replied, "Well, I hope you are not running from the law as the reach of local justice is long indeed, but you need a ship, and I have one due out this afternoon. Go to the end of the dock and see Marcus Brightsail. He is the first mate on the *Sea Fare*, a fine passenger ship that sails the route to Blackmarsh regularly."

Wavren bowed politely and headed to the end of the dock, where he inquired of Marcus Brightsail. After being directed to speak to several deckhands, Wavren found Marcus reviewing a map of the Great Sea with an older gentleman who wore the uniform of the Imperial Dae'gon Alliance Navy: a broad jacket with many golden buttons and long tails, much like the regalia found in royal courts. His neatly trimmed mustache and goatee marked him as a gentleman, but the wind-toughened, sun-baked skin proved that he was a lifelong sailor.

Wavren waited until the two men had concluded their discussion as was fitting and proper manners and then spoke: "I seek the first mate of the *Sea Fare*, Marcus Brightsail."

The younger man extended his hand in the common human fashion and said, "Aye, mate that be me."

Wavren noticed that the older gentleman was still standing by, apparently intrigued. Wavren felt compelled to introduce himself to alleviate the growing tension. "I am Wavren of Ce-les'tia, Protector of the Vale, and elven hunter." He extended his hand to the high-ranking naval officer.

The sharply dressed sailor snapped to attention and offered a formal handshake with an unexpected greeting. He said, "I am Commander Samuel Bailey of Blackmarsh, and I am proud to shake the hand of a Protector of the Vale. It is my deepest honor to meet you."

Wavren was a little shocked, but he smiled and shook the commander's hand solidly. "I am new to the ways of men-folk, so forgive me for being direct, but why do you show such respect to one you have just met?" he said.

The commander smiled broadly and said, "One of your fellow Protectors served with me on a naval mission to Goblin Port, one of the few contested ports south of here. He was as fine a marksman as I had ever seen, and he saved my life and that of my men when we boarded a pirate ship and found ourselves greatly outnumbered by Bloodcrest Force soldiers being transported from Goblin Port to Pirate's Cove in the Jaggedspine Valley. The battle did not go well and many of my sailors died, as would I had it not been for your brother in arms. He almost single-handedly held the enemy at bay long enough for a few of my men and me to get back to our ship and roll out the long-nines, which finally sank their warship. Well, he did have that great white bear, so perhaps it wasn't single-handed, but he won the day, nonetheless. The greatest honor for a soldier or sailor is to sacrifice one's own life that others might live. I shall never forget the sight of him cutting down orc, troll, and tauren alike while his great bear's massive claws and crushing jaws sent dozens to a watery grave."

Wavren was shocked by the realization that his mentor may have been the very hunter who had saved this man's life. "Was the marksman you described called Gaedron?"

A huge smile replaced the commander's serious and sad countenance, and he said, "Then you knew him, I see. You knew the hero of Bladerun Bay, as we now call him. Yes, his name was Gaedron."

Wavren stood aghast for a moment. His mentor was slain near Goblin Port, which was why he never made it to Celes'tia. What did this mean? Would another mentor be assigned to Wavren? It was all so surreal. Wavren looked up and spoke: "You saw Gaedron fall in battle? When did this happen? Did you recover his body?"

Samuel looked uneasy but answered, "Gaedron was on board when the Bloodcrest warship went down. As I said earlier, he fought to the last. We recovered no survivors, friend or foe, as the waters were perilous. Dear Wavren, it was his wish to die in combat, and he was given the burial of an officer in the Imperial Dae'gon Alliance Navy with full honors. I have his personal affects on my ship. I will gladly surrender them to you for internment, but he is gone, and I fear nothing can change that."

Wavren only nodded. His quest to find Gaedron had just begun, yet now it was at its end. All he had left to do was gather the equipment Gaedron left behind and go home to bear the news. He found himself trudging behind Commander Bailey and was soon in an elegant stateroom on the massive Dae'gon Alliance battleship, *Crusader*. "Welcome to the *Crusader*, scourge of the sea. I have a small pack and some clothes that Gaedron left. They are stowed in my locker. Please make yourself at home while I retrieve them."

The commander went to an ornate footlocker and pulled a golden key from his neck, which he used to open a stout lock securing the box. He opened the locker and pulled out a variety of clothes and a large field pack. Wavren didn't bother looking at the clothes, but he did open the pack. Inside he found a few days' rations, some spices, and flint with tinder. But two distinct items especially drew his attention. The first was a large pouch of finely crafted bronze spheres that looked like marbles. It was an odd item, but perhaps it was a gift for a small boy back home. The second item was a capped ram's horn. He pulled the stopper and found a fine powder inside. Wavren had heard of mages who used potions and powders as magical reagents, but this was an odd item for a hunter to have. Wavren packed the items back up and carefully placed the neatly folded clothing inside as well.

"Thank you for taking these items and delivering them to his next of kin. I am sure Gaedron would have wanted his story told and his personal affects returned to his people," the commander said solemnly.

Wavren nodded and headed back into town. He planned to leave at first light for Celes'tia. It would be a long journey back. When he awoke the next morning, his thoughts were burdened with great uncertainty as he headed for the open road. The excitement that had fueled his trip to Seigeport was now replaced with the grim determination of getting back home and finding a new mentor.

He was almost to Forestedge, a few days' run from Celes'tia, when he came upon a lone dwarf who had recently set up camp. The dwarf was stocky, even beyond the norm for his race. He had a black and gray beard that was braided with a variety of leather strips and beads. His deep-set eyes were gray-blue like a stormy sky, having a piercing, almost savage look. His chainmail armor was dusty, but appeared to be *mithril*, the exotic dwarven metal that was harder than steel and half as heavy. It was also worth its weight in gold coin. This was a most unusual dwarf, but the elf was not feeling particularly friendly, so he decided to pass by and continue his trek. The dwarf called out as he approached.

"Hey, laddie, ya don't happen to have some hot spice in yer pack, do ye? I am cooking up some jungle stew, and it just ain't the same without the kick of hot spice," the lone dwarf said.

Wavren sighed and paused as he remembered the spice in Gaedron's pack. He nodded, said nothing, and unpacked the seasoning. After handing it to the dwarf, he packed up and prepared to leave. The dwarf called to him again.

"Hey, laddie, ya seem in a great hurry, but I got plenty o' chow here fer all o' us if'n ya wanna stay fer a bite. I cook a mean stew, ya know," the dwarf offered.

Wavren thought he needed to move on, but the stew did smell delicious, even if a dwarf was cooking it. He started to walk away and said, "My thanks, good dwarf, but I have urgent business in Celes'tia."

"I be headin' to the elven city meself. Perhaps ye might stay at camp 'ere and give an ol' dwarf some company on da road t'morrow. Be a fine thing ta have some back up if'n rogues or beasts come upon either o' us along the way," the dwarf persisted.

Wavren was sure he did not need *back up*, but Protectors of the Vale were obligated by duty to help others when possible. So, reluctantly, he agreed and sat down beside the grizzled dwarf who quickly served up a bowl of jungle stew.

"I got a friend out'n the hills gatherin' food fer his dinner, so fill yer belly now, and we can chat a bit 'til he makes it back," the dwarf mentioned.

Wavren only nodded. They sat in silence, as it slowly got dark. The campfire crackled and popped with the sounds of the night, making a comforting setting for sleep. Wavren was still thinking about his failed quest, when he heard a loud rustling noise. The sound was far away, but getting closer. Wavren perked up his elven ears and noticed the smell of beast fur on the air. In one quick motion, Wavren jumped up, bow in hand, and nocked an arrow. The dwarf was sipping on his stew broth and nearly choked when Wavren sprang into action. It was apparent that the dwarf was trying to say something, but it came out garbled around a mouthful of stew. Suddenly, a massive beast appeared from the wood line and charged the camp. The beast was so large; Wavren could feel the ground shake as its paws hammered the ground. Wavren prepared to defend the dwarf with his life, but fear struck him, as the beast let out a deep roar not twenty strides away. The beast came into full view and at the last minute, stood on its hind feet, and bellowed another deep roar. It was huge, well over eight feet tall, with deadly paws ending in six-inch, gut-rending claws. It was not just any bear; it was the largest bear Wavren had ever seen, and in the firelight, it looked like some demon from the very pit of hell.

The dwarf lunged forward, perhaps in an effort to shield Wavren. But still half-choking on stew, the dwarf managed to trip on the logs in the fire and fell face first in the pot of hot jungle stew. Wavren dodged the dwarf's fall and drew on his introductory hunter's skills to try to pacify the beast, as it was far too close to shoot with his bow, and his dagger would have had no effect. The hunter looked deep into the bear's bloodshot eyes as they reflected the firelight. Wavren held his gaze and called out to the bear as he had heard the members of Ursa Clan call to their massive allies. The bear cocked his head to the side in an almost human expression of confusion. Wavren continued. The bear dropped back down on all fours and seemed to calm. Wavren willed the bear to submit. The bear walked closer and approached the sputtering dwarf who was covered in jungle stew.

Wavren had never tamed a beast before, but he was sure it had worked on this massive specimen. It suddenly occurred to Wavren that this bear was not the common brown or black bear found in the nearby forests. This was a great arctic bear of the northlands, which would be a rare ally to find and tame there. It seemed impossible that he would find and tame one here on the outskirts of Forestedge. What was truly amazing was that this bear was now licking the jungle stew off the dwarf as a domesticated cat laps up milk from a bowl.

The dwarf was still struggling to get up, the stew kettle on his head. He finally got to his feet and dislodged the kettle, in spite of the bear licking him clean from head to toe. He was half-laughing and half-cursing, as dwarves are prone to do when embarrassed.

"Of all da fool things I ever did see, ye coulda made him mad wit' that silly bow. Be thankful ye chose not to shoot him or he mighta taked yer fool head off yer fool shoulders," the muttering, sputtering dwarf said. "Ol' Blackmaw here don't take kindly to fool elves eatin' his dinner neither."

Wavren stood silent, utterly confused. He finally came up with a few words: "Who are you, and where did you find this bear, er … Ol' Blackmaw?" he asked.

"Heh, so now ye wanna be acquainted, do ye? Well, I be Gaedron of Dragonforge, Protector o' the Vale, and Master Dwarf Hunter. Ye already met me ally, Blackmaw."

Chapter 3
Training the Twins

Rosabela had returned to the grove and spoke with Da'Shar about the success of her mission with the kobolds and the despair she felt at having to kill Grol. Da'Shar congratulated Rosabela on her success and provided counsel on her feelings about Grol.

He explained that the world was bound by the laws of nature and governed by the actions of its inhabitants. Druids were responsible for maintaining the balance through selfless service, as directed by nature itself. Grol was a threat to the balance of nature, as he led his kobolds in the slaughter of countless deer and wild boar. This was a mere symptom of the disease called evil ambition. As Rosabela discovered, even worse was the pestilence of Grol's ambition to attack Celes'tia. Ambition, especially through evil means, was the single greatest threat to the delicate balance that the Druidic Protectors of the Vale sought to maintain.

Da'Shar also painted a vivid hypothetical picture for Rosabela. He said that she should imagine if Grol had attacked Celes'tia and was repelled. He would have likely returned to his kin and mustered a stronger force, only to return and be repelled again. The cycle would have raged on until all kobolds or all elves were dead. No race should be exterminated with impunity, in spite of ideological differences. To do so would upset the balance.

"By challenging Grol," continued Da'Shar, "you removed the cancer in an otherwise healthy body of kobold civilization, such as it is. You could have come back to Celes'tia and rallied warriors and mages to seek and destroy the entire camp, stamping out innocent life in the process of removing the source of the problem. Instead, you chose the noble path, the one nature intended. You have shown wisdom and have maintained your honor. You have served the office you hold with justice and prudence.

Rosabela knew Da'Shar was right, but she still heard the screams, smelled the charred flesh, and even saw Grol writhing in agony in her mind's eye. Da'Shar wrapped Rosabela in a fatherly embrace.

"This is the sacrifice of self that hurts more than moonfire and weighs like mountains on the hearts of goodly folk," he said. "I told you that this calling often consumes those who answer it. I also told you that you must endure, and you will. I have faith in your inner strength, as I know with certainty that it is limitless. I have seen your heart and measured your spirit. You will survive, of that, I am sure, but this is only the beginning, dear child. It is only the beginning."

Rosabela wept.

The next morning was beautiful. The sun peeked over the horizon and flooded the sky with brilliant orange, yellow, and red rays. The few thin clouds only enhanced this magical effect. Rosabela headed to the center of the grove to begin her daily lessons with Da'Shar, who was sitting on the branches of a large oak, watching the sunrise. Rosabela scurried up the tree and sat down by her mentor. No words were said, but each bathed in the glory of the morning warmth and the dazzling display of beauty. Da'Shar inhaled deeply and closed his eyes.

He hummed a soft melody for a few minutes and his humming turned into words that were soothing and reassuring. His light tenor voice was accompanied by the birds, beasts, and the wind in an almost magical quartet. The words were in an ancient form of elvish, but Rosabela picked up the meaning.

The sun pulls the blanket of night from our beds and we rise to the day.

Our hearts are strengthened by its warmth and our spirits soar.

Morning is a gift of renewed hope that nature gives to us.

We serve, in return, that others might live in harmony and find peace.

It was the song of morning dedication, and Rosabela realized that her life was one of service that required balance. It was a solemn song that somehow gave Rosabela perspective on life and her duties. As she suffered, so must she find joy. As she grieved for others, so must she find closure. She not only stood for balance, but she must live in balance as an example for others and as the living avatar of nature itself. It was all beginning to make sense.

Da'Shar spoke then: "Today is a special day, dear child. You will become more than a druid in training. You will become the personification of nature itself, so that through you, balance may always be achieved."

Rosabela did not fully know what her mysterious mentor was talking about, but as always, she trusted him and was prepared to follow him as he directed. Her only reply was, "I am ready."

Da'Shar jumped down from the branch of the oak and looked up at Rosabela. He looked deep into her eyes, and his spirit touched hers. Though no words were spoken, he explained the next lesson to her in detail. His mind reached out to hers and the sounds of nature exploded with utter clarity. She heard the birds, the beasts, the insects, the wind, the ground, and even the very words of her own soul. She heard Da'Shar's breathing, the beat of his heart, and even the blood flowing in his veins. She heard the sound of her mentor's soul.

Da'Shar had a look of determination on his face that drew Rosabela into his very being. He seemed to grow with magical energy as his face elongated, his shoulders broadened, and his torso expanded. His transformation was slow as she witnessed his delicate elven hands become huge paws, his mouth became a huge muzzle filled with fangs, and his body became covered with blue-black fur that gleamed in the morning sun. Da'Shar had become an unbelievably large black bear. His roar shook the trees and sent birds flying and beasts running. Rosabela was awestruck.

Da'Shar quickly turned back into his elven form and waved Rosabela down from the tree. "You will learn to shape-shift, but first, you must commune with Nature to set up terms of this pact. As you borrow from Nature, you must return to Nature a part of yourself. It is all about balance. Go into the forest and find your spirit match in *Ursa Major*; find your bear counterpart. She will teach you."

Rosabela set out immediately to seek her bear form. After a short walk, she felt drawn to a small cave in the foothills, where she was confident she would find her counterpart. The cave was quiet and dank. There were huge tracks that could only be those of a bear. There were also several carcasses littering the cave opening, including that of a wolf, a deer, and an elf. All had been torn apart by powerful claws and teeth. Rosabela felt certain that this event was required, but fear slowly moved into her mind and tried to push courage and determination out.

As she fought with her own fears of what could go wrong, she was confronted with an immediate and very real fear that stood five feet tall at the shoulder and was covered in thick, blood splattered, black fur. Rosabela steeled her will and gazed into the eyes of the bear that had not so long ago killed beast and elf alike. She sent her thoughts into it and received a blast of hot rage in return.

"I am not your enemy," Rosabela sent, more with her body than words.

"You are trespassing here," the bear returned in like manner.

"I need help and Nature has called me to you," she affirmed, with projected mental images.

"I do not trust your kind, as many have come to harm me and my cubs," the bear accused in return. "Leave now, and do not return."

"Your bond with me will ensure your future protection from invaders," the druid offered.

"I need no protection, as you can plainly see," the bear said, referring to the mauled elf at the entrance.

"You will not always be around to protect your present and future cubs. I can help with this," Rosabela stated.

The bear sniffed Rosabela and seemed to sense neither fear nor malice from her. The druid could tell that the bear was unsure what to do, but knew it somehow felt compelled to protect its cubs at all costs. Rosabela projected her willingness to help, although the bear might not be able to imagine how. She certainly looked small and weak. She had no claws or fangs to fight with and no hide or fur as protection. She had no real weapon other than a thin staff that would likely break if the bear stepped on it.

Rosabela spoke: "I see uncertainty in your eyes. I will explain. Your den is known to many in this area. I found it easily enough. What I offer is a part of my spirit that you might use as a ward against enemies. I also offer knowledge so that you might be hidden from detection. There is nothing more that I can say to explain, but you will become part of me as I become part of you. We will both serve each other for mutual gain, or we will both die. It is in our nature to survive, and this you can trust."

The bear acknowledged Rosabela's words, and Rosabela peered even deeper into the bear's eyes. She whispered the Incantations of Binding as energy passed between the elf and bear. Rosabela felt awash with a surge of power, the raw strength of the bear. The bear was calmed with the wisdom of understanding of itself and those who dwelled nearby. The exchange was mutual and yet separate. Somehow, the bear just knew how to better conceal its tracks and den, while Rosabela gained the knowledge of shape-shifting into a bear. The pact was made and sealed in spirit rather than blood, but was no less binding. Rosabela returned to the grove with excitement and a spring in her step. The trail she left was not that of a lithe she-elf. Her tracks were huge clawed impressions, not unlike those outside the cave.

* * *

Wavren walked toward Celes'tia with his mentor, Gaedron the Dwarf Hunter. He was still in shock at the turn of events. By recollection, he had been selected as a hunter by the Grand Seer, not a warrior or rogue as he had thought was his destiny. He had been assigned to the greatest marksman in the realms by Daenek's telling, but his mentor had not even showed up for the scheduled training. He had been ready to seek his mentor and had found that even among men, Gaedron was already a great hero by the account of Commander Samuel Bailey. He had resigned himself to return to Celes'tia with the news that Gaedron was killed in action on the high seas, having sacrificed himself that others might win the day, and yet he had found that his mentor was neither sacrificed nor even an elf! Now, he walked alongside the oddest possible mentor, marksman, and hero, who was also considered the greatest marksman and a hero by many, yet he still smelled of jungle stew and bear saliva. What sort of cruel joke was fate playing here? Surely, there must have been a mistake. Wavren found that he suddenly missed his dear sister. She always seemed to understand his turmoil. She knew his heart better than anyone. *Rosabela*, he thought, *how I need you to help me sort through this*. He pleaded thoughts over and over, but to no avail.

The dwarf stopped and opened the pack that Wavren had returned to him from Commander Bailey's stateroom. He pulled out some dried rations and threw them to the massive bear that seemed more of a big, loveable puppy than nearly two thousand pounds of fur-covered rage.

"Lesson number one, laddie. When ye get yerself an ally like Ol' Blackmaw here, ye gotta keep 'em happy. That means ye need ta be more'n just a good marksman. Ya gotta be a hunter worth his salt, boy-o, 'cause, guess who goes hungry when yer rations run short? Ever try to wrestle a piece o' mutton away from a hungry bear? It ain't easy, an even if'n ya win, it is always covered wit' bear slobber, and ain't no hot spice can cure that for flavor," the dwarf complained.

Wavren shuddered at the thought of eating half-chewed mutton covered in dirt and bear spit. It almost made him retch just thinking about it.

"By that pale look, I'm fer guessin' ya got yerself a good 'magination. Well, whatever ye be thinkin', it's still worse. Good news is, I'm here to train ya, laddie. So, let's see what ya got," the dwarf challenged. "See that squirrel; let's see if'n ya can get 'em with that silly bow ya got hangin' on yer back."

In one fluid motion, Wavren un-slung his bow, nocked an arrow, and fired. The squirrel was pinned to the tree from head to tail, ready to be roasted with the arrow shaft serving as a spit. Wavren yawned at the ease and expected outcome.

"So, ya thinkin' yer pretty hot wit' that arrow trick there. Well, I guessed as much. Cockiness might git ya in trouble later, but okay, so ya got yerself some skill with a bow, but what about when yer arrows run low? Can ye survive on the land and keep twenty pounds o' meat on the table fer yerself and yer ally each meal, an' not includin' snacks?" the dwarf asked.

Wavren nodded and moved about setting fish nets across a nearby stream, as well as snares and small one-way spike traps that allowed game to squeeze its head in to get bait, but not pull back to escape. Gaedron watched and made mental note. He had to admit that the boy was good, even for an elf. It reminded him of his youth, nearly five hundred years ago, when he first became a hunter. He had been a little cocky, too, but life taught hard lessons and Gaedron had the scars to prove it.

By nightfall, Wavren had trapped a brace of coney, two small deer, and a dozen river trout that were as big as

Gaedron's sizeable forearm. Ol' Blackmaw ate all the fish. Wavren and Gaedron dined on the coneys, and the deer was smoked as rations for the road and hidden in caches for weary travelers who knew where to look for emergency supplies.

Gaedron was fairly satisfied with the knowledge Wavren already had, but a Protector of the Vale had to have more at his disposal than snares and a fine bow. The lessons were going to be long and hard. And there seemed to be something holding this young hunter back. Wavren seemed distant and unfocused, which would never do. The relationship between a mentor and his pupil had to be strong. Trust and reliance were keys to a successful education, and that did not seem likely at this point. Gaedron considered the obvious differences between elves and dwarves, but perhaps there was something else. Time would surely tell.

The following morning, Wavren set about breaking camp as the dwarf was busy cooking breakfast. The smell of roasted venison with hot spice was strong in the air, and Wavren found himself wondering if his mentor ever ate anything without the powerful seasoning. Elves had a somewhat more delicate palette and sensitive digestive tract than dwarves, who, much like the bear, could eat nearly anything.

Gaedron called to Wavren, "Laddie, come join me. I have here a dish made for a king."

Wavren thought, *Perhaps a Goat King*, but said nothing.

Gaedron called again, "Truly, this be a fine morn fer roasted deer, join me that we might eat and discuss yer next lesson."

Wavren was frustrated, but not wanting to be rude, he sat down, cut a slice of meat from the spit, and took a bite. It only took a second for Wavren to register that the dwarf had over seasoned the morning meal. His mouth was on fire, and as he tried to keep calm, he realized that his water skin was missing. He tried to hold in his agony, but tears welled in his eyes from the burning that started in his mouth and was now scorching his throat and had even climbed up into his sinuses.

Gaedron held a straight face, but Wavren knew this had to

be more than an accidental overuse of hot spice. This was bordering on poison. Wavren looked around frantically for something to drink. Gaedron was busy munching venison and seemed not to notice. Wavren was holding his breath to keep from gagging, and he knew he had to do something quick. The only thing he could think of was to swallow. He did so, and the meat burned all the way down. Wavren managed to wipe his tears and take a breath, which only made matters worse. The air seemed to multiply the effects of the spice in his mouth, and the juice that was saturated with the fiery seasoning was now in his eyes.

Wavren jumped up, howled like a demon-spawned wolf, and ran for the river. The air from running enflamed the heat on his face, but pain was limited by insanity, which was the only possible description of Wavren's current state. He dove, headfirst and mouth open, into the frigid water and thrashed about like a giant fish on a fisherman's hook. His screams were now garbled as he gulped in the brackish water, but they were screams nonetheless. After what seemed like an eternity, the pain subsided into a dull, throbbing numbness from lips to stomach. Both of Wavren's eyes were bloodshot and swollen into mere slits that barely provided any sight at all. He dragged himself out of the water and onto the bank of the river. When his vision cleared enough to realize where he was, all he could see was a pair of dirty dwarven boots. He looked up and saw a smiling dwarf using a sliver of wood as a toothpick.

"I might'a used a tad more spice than usual, but it gets yer blood flowin' eh, laddie?" the dwarf mused.

Wavren felt like punching the dwarf right in the mouth, and then in both eyes to get even, but exhaustion had him beat. He just rolled over and lay down on the muddy bank to rest.

Gaedron put his hands on his hips and spoke with true dwarven ire: "Well, laddie, now dat I got yer attention, let's get a few things straight. I ain't no city lovin', genteel, well mannered, elf pretty boy like'n yerself. I be Gaedron of Dragonforge, Protector of the Vale, Dwarven Master Hunter, and proud friend of Celes'tia. You might be as good an archer as ever been born, but if'n ya wanna survive, ya gotta get tough; an' that's where I come in. So, ya got yerself two choices as I see it. First choice is ya can be accept'n that I ain't no elf like'n yer kinfolk, but I can teach ya to be a great hunter anyways. Second choice, ye can take yer fool notions that only elves can be teach'n elves and go home to learn to be a nursemaid or whatever it be that failed fool elves do."

Wavren was shocked by the astute assumptions this dwarf had made. Was he really feeling at odds because Gaedron was a dwarf and not an elf of Celes'tia? Was he really that superficial? Was he a racist? His mind made a hundred calculations in less than an instant, and the answer came vividly clear in the form of his earlier thought. Wavren stood up, and with the speed of elven fury, he belted Gaedron right in the eye, sending the dwarf backward a step.

Gaedron smiled and said, "Well there always be option three, but I did'n think ya had it in ye." He sucked in a deep breath and called his dwarven battle cry: "FER STONE AN' STEEL," and the dwarf charged forward.

Wavren dodged the initial charge, which was meant to tackle the significantly lighter elf and give the close-quarter combat edge to Gaedron. As the dwarf rumbled by, Wavren turned to reset his stance for the next charge. The dwarf had stopped and pivoted with amazing speed. When Wavren reoriented on the dwarf, he only saw the knuckles of a dwarven mailed fist coming right at him. The blow was solid, but Wavren was able to roll with it enough to spin around and circle kick the dwarf right in the face, which surprised the more experienced dwarf. The following rapid succession of punches hit the dwarf more often than not, but the only thing worse than fighting the grim determination of a dwarven adversary, was realizing that hitting them in the head was like smithing mithril: it took a heck of a lot of blows to make a dent.

Gaedron got in close and finally locked his vice-like grip on Wavren's tunic with his left hand, while his right hand went to work on the slender elf's midsection. The rapid delivery of body shots was devastating. Wavren was in trouble, but a quick knee to the short dwarf's chin gave him some respite. Wavren came in with both feet and kicked the dwarf in the chest, which sent the dwarf flying onto his back. Gaedron stood up and smiled. With his right hand in a fist, he hit his left open palm to make it clear that this fight was far from over. Wavren never saw what hit him next, but whatever it was literally hit him from behind, blasted the wind from his lungs, and was now on top of him. The weight was enough to crush ribs. It nearly broke his back, but somehow he was able to suck in just enough air to keep from suffocating.

"All right, laddie, ya had enough? Or should I set Blackmaw to chew yer fool elf head right off'n yer fool elf shoulders?" the smiling dwarf asked.

Wavren squeaked a sound that Gaedron took to mean, "I surrender." The bear lazily got off the battered elf. The resulting inhalation was painful from the beating and squashing that Wavren endured, but it was delicious clean air that Wavren savored. He was alive and that was joy itself.

Slowly, the elf got up and tried to dust off. "You cheated me, Gaedron. We were fighting one-on-one, and I was holding my own when you called in that smelly hunk of fur," Wavren stated.

"Might be yer head was waterlogged from the flailin' ye did in the river, but I told ya, I was no genteel, well-mannered, pretty-boy elf. Ya pick a fight with a dwarf, ya fight by dwarf rules, or ya get what's comin' to ya," Gaedron said, with that same dwarven smirk he had since the fight began. "Now, ya git it?"

"Lesson one: feed the bear or go hungry, and lesson two: fight like a dwarf. I got it," Wavren replied with no shortage of sarcasm. "I am ready for lesson three at your discretion, Gaedron of Dragonforge."

"Aye, laddie, that ya are," he replied as he walked over, helped him up, and shook the young elf's hand.

Chapter 4
Professions

Rosabela had taken her new bear form for quite a run. She had rumbled around the outskirts of Celes'tia looking for challenges. It was exhilarating to snap small bushes and saplings like twigs. She could smell the sweet honeysuckle and sharp pine like never before. Her ears seemed to detect birds, insects, and small animals from much greater distances than ever before. It was as if the world was newly created and she was experiencing it for the first time.

She had found that in bear form, along with her great increase in senses, strength, and raw power, she had a massive increase in appetite. Those great pangs of hunger were in equal proportion to her massive girth. Never being a bear before meant that she had to experiment a bit to figure out how bears get through the day, and eating seemed pretty important. She came up the main river that split Celes'tia and emptied out into the Great Sea. The riverbank was lush with flora and alive with small animals that made the landscape seem like paradise. She noticed movement in the water, and her instincts told her that fishing might be a quick way to satisfy the increasing hunger she felt.

She remembered that the water was frigid at this time of year, but in bear form, she hardly noticed. Rosabela moved out into the shallows and tried to snap her jaws on a nice long trout, but the refraction of the water made her miss completely. All she managed to do was gobble up a mouthful of water. She tried again, and again she came up short. She decided to take a swipe with her huge paw. She didn't hit the next fish squarely, but the force of the swipe stunned a decent sized river catfish and she quickly snapped it up in her jaws. She giggled inside with the revelation that the stunning tactic was working. She wondered how she looked as a bear swatting fish in the river and giggling with each success. *Could bears actually giggle?* She wondered. It was an odd thought. It became apparent to Rosabela that creatures of higher thought took things like giggling for granted. *We take a lot of things for granted*, she mused.

Rosabela ate a score of fish and managed to satisfy her appetite, but the effort of fishing as a bear was pretty tiring. She had the urge to curl up and take a long nap. The sun was warm on her thick black fur, and with a recently filled stomach, it just seemed right. Something in the back of her mind told her to head back toward the grove instead and talk to her mentor about these new revelations. As she headed back, she continually felt the overwhelming urge to sleep or perhaps eat again. The trip back was uneventful, and before long, she was back in the grove.

"Da'Shar, I love shape-shifting, but I found the experience made me ravenously hungry. I managed to catch a few fish, but that effort made me weary. I felt like sleeping, as a bear often does, but I thought that when I woke up, I'd need to feed again. Something told me to return to you for guidance. I want to consult your wisdom about this cycle that seems to leave little time for anything other than eating and sleeping," she said.

"As I have continually taught, dear child, this calling often consumes us. We must be cautious not to let the desire to live as a beast, the desire to serve our own instincts and other carnal needs, become the meaning of life for us. Many have fallen from the druidic ways to become more beast than elf. This is especially true of humans who choose to follow the path of the shape-shifter. Their desire for power can turn a beautiful gift from Nature into a perverted disease of evil. The disease that turns a druid into a flesh-eating monster is called *lycanthrope*, the plague of werewolves. These fallen druids become savage killers, and the darkness of their hearts becomes a sickness that passes from carrier to victim without end. Oftentimes, this results in a plague of evil on the land, a perversion that seeks to unbalance good and evil as well as law and chaos. Never allow this to happen, lest you become the target of destruction for the righteous," the master druid warned. "Ultimately, you would become my enemy."

"Master Da'Shar, your words are taken with full understanding. I will be cautious of my own desires and wary of the balance, but what of those who have fallen? Is there no redemption, no turning back?" she inquired.

Da'Shar smiled and said, "Death is the ultimate redemption. It is the final release from the decay of age, sickness, and pain. Death of a were-creature will similarly provide rest for those tormented souls and those of its unwilling victims, but be warned; just as in all beasts in the animal kingdom, the instinct of survival is strong, and no were-creature will readily give up its existence, even if death promises to ease its pain and misery. Thus, dear child, each fallen druid must be killed in order to give it release and restore the balance of Nature. Never give in to the base instincts of your animal forms, lest this be your end as well."

As she looked deeply into her master's lush green eyes, Rosabela saw the unconditional love, a father's love, but she never doubted for a moment that his warning would be fulfilled if she became a *lycan*. He would hunt her down and end her life without remorse and without compassion. It was his duty.

Da'Shar changed his serious demeanor into that of her dear friend and mentor with a smile. Then he spoke again: "The ordeal with the never-ending hunger you face while shape-shifted is one that I fought with for many years. I have a very special gift for you that will not only quench that hunger, but will also be a means for you to find peace and seek introspection in times of uncertainty. This gift must be mastered, so I encourage you to train hard and seek to practice often with it."

Rosabela beamed and promised, "Of course. I am thankful that you give your wisdom so generously. You are truly a friend and ever the dedicated mentor. Just tell me what to do." Rosabela was as eager as a small child anticipating gifts on her birthday. This made Da'Shar smile broadly.

"Meet me by the river, and I will bring the gift for you. Remember your promise: train and perfect the gift, and you will find peace and self-mastery," he said.

Rosabela's mind raced. She loved surprises and would treasure any gift from her mentor. She skipped down to the river like a little girl and waited anxiously for Da'Shar. Within a few minutes, he appeared with a long wooden tube that had a red ribbon wrapped around it. He handed it to her and left.

Rosabela examined the tube and noticed the fine craftsmanship that had gone into the carving and woodwork. It was simply beautiful with scrolling tree branches and leaves intricately carved with perfection. She opened the end of the tube and saw the butt of what appeared to be a thin staff. Her excitement grew. She delicately pulled the spindly staff out and was immediately confused. The staff got thinner at one end until it was barely the width of her little finger, and a long string was tied to the thin tip. Attached halfway down the string was a piece of carved cork that was painted half-red and half-white. At the end of the string was a very sharp metal hook. Da'Shar had given her a simple fishing pole. Her confusion turned to blushing embarrassment. She had promised to master this gift all too eagerly. A fishing pole was for fishermen, not for a Protector of the Vale. Rosabela sat down on the bank and wondered if her mentor thought he was being funny. She knew she had been duped, but a promise was a promise. She pulled a grub from under a nearby log, placed it on the hook with disgust, and plopped the line in the water. *Da'Shar is going to pay for this*, she thought with a smile and reddened cheeks. *Somehow, he is going to pay.*

After fishing for a while, Rosabela gathered up the tiny sunfish she caught and headed back to the grove. Her entire catch might feed a small housecat, even though she was supposed to have found the solution to the hunger problem with the bear. She noticed Da'Shar sorting through several herbs as she approached.

"Nice gift," Rosabela mocked, as she looked over her mentor's shoulder.

Da'Shar ignored her comment and said, "You will need supplies, armor and weapons during your adventures. How much money do you have?"

Rosabela was perplexed. "I have a few silver and a handful of copper."

"That will never do," he said. "Take these herbs to the market, and fetch a good price so you can properly outfit yourself. Always be on the lookout for herbs in your travels; they will not only be useful in healing, but others who do not understand how to find them will pay handsomely for your surplus."

Rosabela nodded and took the carefully packaged herbs. She noticed that her mentor had given her enough herbs for a small fortune. She counted a dozen *swifthistle*, ten *mageroyal*, five *briarthorn*, and a few *steelbloom*. She was confident that after visiting the markets she would be well equipped with the armor and weapons these herbs could buy.

The market was a bustling, almost chaotic meeting place. Rosabela saw dozens of elves, a few humans, a dwarf, and a gnome. The dwarf was selling all sorts of blacksmith items from Dragonforge, the dwarven stronghold in Stou'lanz. She would definitely have to stop back by to see him after she concluded the sale of her herbs. The gnome was selling a variety of cloth items made of fine silk, *mageweave,* and linen, but he had the look of a wizard. In fact, the gnome was arguing with a wicked little imp about appropriate prices for the tailored items. Apparently, the gnome was a summoner, a warlock of dark magic, and the imp was bound to him by his dark magic. Rosabela had heard of these little demons who aided their warlock masters. They were especially talented with fire magic, but not much for durability. This one was cursing at the gnome for being too generous with his customers. Apparently, the gnome had had enough of the profanity, for he banished the wretched little creature with a few words of his own.

"Care to buy a pouch, a bag, or a backpack from Granmillo of Silvershire?" the gnome asked in a high-pitched voice. "I sell cloaks, robes, and bandages, too."

Rosabela smiled. "Granmillo, I have need of such items, but I must sell my own wares first. Where would I find the apothecary or alchemy vendor?"

The gnome smiled broadly, showing perfectly chiseled teeth that matched the little fangs of the recently banished imp. "I will buy your herbs, or barter for these fine goods if you like."

Rosabela knew that she needed a cloak and some pouches for her adventures, but she was not sure if the gnome could be trusted. She preferred to sell to the elven vendor, who had posted prices that were accepted throughout Celes'tia.

"Come now, show your wares to me. I am in the market for a few rare ingredients to make potions. Do you have *stranglekelp* for water-breathing potions, or perhaps some *briarthorn* for healing potions?" the diminutive warlock asked.

"I have briarthorn, but no stranglekelp," Rosabela returned.

The gnome greedily snatched the carefully packed bag of herbs and dumped them out on his table. He sorted out what he needed with amazing speed and agility. Rosabela felt angry about his rudeness, but she couldn't help laughing when the gnome rubbed his hands together and smacked his lips like a starving dwarf at a great feast.

"I'll take all the briarthorn, mageroyal, and swiftthistle you have here for two gold. I will barter the steelbloom for store credit since you need some of my items for yourself," the gnome offered.

Suddenly, the little imp appeared again. "Fool of a gnome!"

the imp hissed. "Why not give the elf wench yer right eye and the shirt off yer back, too? I have seen murlocs with more sales savvy."

"Excuse him, miss, he is cranky, even for an imp, and I can't seem to be rid of him. Every time I banish him, he comes back somehow, I think just to torment me," the gnome explained with sad resignation.

Rosabela smiled and watched the exchange with amusement.

"She has beguiled ye, ya stupid shrimp. No one is fool enough to offer such a price for weeds and roots if they had their wits about them. You have always been lured by the round, soft flesh of women. Snap out of it, or better yet, kill her now that we might have her wares for free," the imp begged.

The poor gnome smiled sheepishly as if to say he was so very sorry for the rude little imp. Then he pulled out a magic wand and shot a glob of blue energy at the imp, which knocked the imp backward into a tangle of wizard robes. The gnome pounced on the imp and punched him in the face. The imp, being soul-bound to the gnome, could not fight back, so he screamed curses and belched brimstone to try to get the gnome to back off. The gnome grabbed the imp by its rather long, bulbous nose and then bit the little demon right on the face with those pointy teeth. The imp howled in pain and disappeared in a puff of smoke. The gnome stood up, brushed himself off, and tried to continue as professionally as he could. "My apologies, miss; I will gladly offer five additional silver pieces for your trouble if you agree to my initial offer."

Rosabela was more than happy to accept those terms and would have said yes immediately, but she was biting her lip and using all of her willpower to keep from bursting out in laughter at the bizarre scene. She managed a smile and a handshake with the now-dusty gnome, who smelled of brimstone. Granmillo quickly gathered up the herbs and stashed them in a hidden pocket of his robes. Rosabela collected the small fortune and negotiated several pouches and a fine cloak with the store credit she had. The deal was fair and probably in her favor, so she left happily.

Her next stop was for armor. She moved over to the dwarven armor merchant who had various shirts of mail and breastplates of mithril on display. She noticed several types of swords, hammers, and axes as well. They seemed bulky and far too heavy for the nimble druid. She couldn't imagine fighting with these items, much less running through the woods clanking and banging all the way. She asked the merchant, "Do you have anything made of hide or leather that might be more suitable for me?"

The gruff dwarf laughed a low, grumbling laugh that sounded like gravel bouncing down a mountain. He replied, "Lass, I be Gromin o' Dragonforge, master smith and outfitter o' warriors. I got no leather or light hide items that ye might find suitable. I got steel, mithril, and even thorium goods fer da infantry. Go down da way and try Draek the rogue, he be a bit high on prices, but he be more to yer likin' fer lighter wares."

Rosabela bowed politely, which seemed even funnier to the dwarf, and then she headed toward the leather merchant. She came upon a strong human wearing a hauberk of thick wyvern hide, with matching bracers and leggings. He smiled in a charming way and bowed low before her. "I am Draek of Griffon's Peak, and I am at your service," he said.

Rosabela liked this human immediately. He seemed refined, for a man wearing wyvern hide, and he was polite. She asked, "I need leather armor from head to toe. It needs to be stout and yet affordable. Can you help me?" she asked.

Draek looked the druid over in a very business-like fashion and went to a trunk with various items in it. He sorted through the lower end items and came back with a fine set of black *worg* armor. It was lightly oiled and smelled like a wet dog, but it seemed to be stout. "How much for the set?" she asked.

"One gold buys all eight pieces. You get a helm, pauldrons, chestpiece, bracers, gloves, belt, leggings, and boots," he offered.

"That seems high," Rosabela said, after remembering the dwarf's warning about Draek's prices. "I will look elsewhere and return later if I cannot find a better deal."

Draek's eyes narrowed, and he stared intently at Rosabela for a moment. "Very well, I will discount the sale by ten percent, but not a copper more, and if you happen to hear rumors about my prices from a certain dwarven blacksmith, I would appreciate it if you would set the record straight," the human replied.

Rosabela agreed and counted out ninety silver pieces to pay the man. She had gotten another good deal, and she was happy. She gathered her items and headed back to the grove. On the way, she smelled the sweet fragrance of *peacebloom* and then the earthy dank smell of *darkroot*. She stepped off the road and collected them both. Having seen the high demand for herbs in the merchant's district, Rosabela decided that she would never pass up an opportunity to exercise her herbalism skills. This would keep her well covered in the cost of supplies and equipment.

* * *

Gaedron and Wavren made it back to Celes'tia and met with the venerable hunter, Daenek Torren. He advised them to jump right into training, since they had been so delayed by Gaedron's last mission. Wavren wanted to discuss the obvious oversight on Daenek's part regarding the key information that his mentor was a dwarf. The opportunity never presented itself, and oddly enough, Daenek never acted as if Gaedron *wasn't* an elf. It was still odd that a dwarf was a Protector of the Vale from Celes'tia, but Wavren chalked it up to cruel irony.

Gaedron had already shown his apprentice many things regarding beast training and survivalism, but other than observing Wavren shoot a few small animals, Gaedron hadn't shown any marksmanship skills at all. Wavren had made a mental note that he didn't even have a bow or a quiver of arrows. It was very odd.

Gaedron called to his apprentice, "Laddie, come 'ere an let an ol' dwarf show ye a thing 'r two 'bout huntin.'"

"I am curious how you mean to show me anything without a bow," Wavren stated.

"Bow? I don' use no bow, laddie," the dwarf returned.

"Well, I don't see a crossbow or any throwing knives or even a sling," the elf said, his with hands on his hips.

"Boy-o, ye still don' get it, do ya? I be a dwarf from Dragonforge, an' just as elves be preferrin' a longbow, dwarves are more akin ta real firepower. I lost me last weapon when them durned fool humans tried ta drown me in da bay, but I plan ta get me a new one 'ere soon," Gaedron remarked.

"I have been meaning to ask you about that battle. I spoke with Commander Samuel Bailey who said you were dead after you sacrificed yourself that his crew might live to sink the orc warship," Wavren recounted.

"Ha, o' course that be da way them fool humans saw it. Truth is, I was blastin' them hordies left an' right wit' the help of Ol' Blackmaw here, who had himself a good deal o' fun, too. We was winnin', an' next thing I know, *BA-BOOM*, I was bein' dragged ashore by me bear an' I was empty handed. I lost me weapon and me ammunition. I woulda lost me life if me ally wasn't around. Good thing Ol' Blackmaw is as good a swimmer as he is or I'd be at the bottom of the bay. Not easy swimmin' in mithril chainmail with these short arms and legs, ya know."

Wavren was shocked that the dwarf blamed the humans. Sinking the warship probably saved dozens of lives at that moment and countless lives in the long run. He could see that the dwarf still had some deep-seated anger about the situation that he would not likely forgive or forget anytime soon. Wavren let the matter drop for the time being.

Wavren said, "Back to the original issue—if you don't use a longbow, a crossbow, or sling, then what do you use, a catapult?"

For a second, the dwarf paused and then shook his head. Wavren wasn't sure if Gaedron was confused that he had suggested such a foolish idea or if he was actually considering it as a future possibility.

“Follow me,” the crafty dwarf said.

Wavren followed his mentor to the craftsman’s section of the city. Gaedron bought a strange carved chunk of wood and several bars of mithril from the blacksmith’s shop. He purchased various pieces of mageweave cloth from the tailor and then gathered some strange powder from the apothecary. He took all of the items to a large anvil and said, “This might take a minute.” After several hours of non-stop hammering that left a dull ring in Wavren’s sensitive ears, the dwarf paused. He said, “It’s almost done, boy-o.”

Wavren couldn’t tell what was almost done. The dwarf grabbed a handful of metal screws and started piecing the crafted parts together. When he was done, Wavren saw that the carved chunk of wood was now attached to a long, hollow metal pole.

“What is it, Gaedron?” the elf asked, puzzled.

“Laddie, this be the weapon o’ the future. This be a weapon o’ dwarves. This be me *blunderbuss*,” he said with loving satisfaction.

Wavren took the item and looked closely. He grabbed the metal end with both hands and swung it like an ax. “You made a battleaxe with a wooden ax head that isn’t sharp and a metal shaft that is too smooth to grip as a handle. I don’t get it,” the apprentice said.

Gaedron’s expression showed such utter confusion that Wavren thought the dwarf might never snap back to reality. When Wavren looked back with a dumbfounded look, Gaedron snatched his finely crafted blunderbuss out of the apprentice’s hands and stormed out of the smithy and into a clearing. He took the powder and one of the *marbles* from his pack and stuffed them into a slotted chamber where the wood and the metal came together. He took a knee, propped the strange weapon against his shoulder, and peered down the metal shaft at a wooden target across the field. He said, “Shoot the target yonder wit’ that silly bow o’ yers.”

Wavren unslung his bow and fired an arrow at the impossibly far target. Using elevation and windage, his arrow hit the target dead center. No sooner had his arrow hit than Gaedron clicked a mechanism on the bizarre weapon he called a blunderbuss. The result was a terrifying explosion that nearly deafened Wavren and sent small animals scurrying about. When the smoke cleared, Gaedron was standing up, smiling. He pointed to the target that Wavren had just bulls-eyed. Wavren noticed that not only was the arrow gone, but the center of the target was gone as well. Wavren realized that this new weapon was not only powerful with excellent range; it was a weapon of fear and awe as well, which would likely send enemies running if it didn't kill them outright.

"Dwarven engineering, laddie, 'tis the way o' the future," Gaedron said.

Wavren responded with an open mouth and two simple words: "Teach me."

Chapter 5
The Bear

Learning to master the druidic ways was second nature to Rosabela. Da'Shar was amazed at how eager she was and how quickly she learned. Perhaps the most incredible characteristic was the endless energy Rosabela showed. She managed to balance her offensive spell casting, healing arts, feral combat skills, weapons training, herbalism, and even found time for fishing. Da'Shar continued to pour his knowledge out, and she soaked it up like a sponge. He was well pleased with his student, well pleased indeed.

Da'Shar felt confident that Rosabela was ready for the final lesson of her druidic training. Much had happened in the weeks since he had met her. It had all led to this moment, and he was sad that it was almost at an end. The druid had one last gift for his student, and he knew she would be excited to receive it. He wasted no time heading to Rosabela's favorite spot by the river.

"I knew I would find you here," he said.

Rosabela sighed in feigned exasperation. "I am meditating,

looking for inner strength, and seeking reflection," she said, hauling in a huge river catfish that matched three others already on the bank. Rosabela had become quite the fisher in spite of her initial doubts.

Da'Shar walked up and sat beside the young elf-maid. He opened his pack and handed Rosabela a package that was carefully wrapped in delicate silk cloth. Rosabela smiled and rolled her eyes in mock exasperation.

"Have you brought me another fishing pole, or perhaps a hammer and anvil to teach me to smith steel like the son you never had?" she taunted.

Da'Shar smiled broadly and said, "Perhaps this gift is poorly timed. Perhaps you are not ready for the next step in your training." He put the gift back in his pack and started to walk away. He had only gotten a few steps away when he heard familiar words of magic coming from behind him and suddenly his feet were well ensnared by a tangle of roots and vines. He wobbled and nearly fell at the abruptness of his entrapment.

"You won't be going far; now, hand over the present," Rosabela commanded.

Da'Shar turned and scowled at his student, although inside he was beaming with pride. He chastised her, "You must not abuse your gifts from Nature so readily. Remember patience and …" He couldn't even finish his sentence before his student was pulling on his pack to get to the present. "Rosa … bela … stop … this … child … ish display!" he ordered, as he struggled to outmuscle his persistent student. He was stronger, but he was also trapped and immobile. His pack slid off his shoulder, and the tug of war was on. Da'Shar began his own whisperings, and suddenly he was transformed into a six-hundred-pound jungle cat that Rosabela could never match for strength. She held on with grim determination and invoked her own incantation of shape-shifting. Now a huge bear that was more than double the size of Da'Shar's cat form was dragging the cat with ease across the grove, leaving long rows of claw marks behind until finally Da'Shar gave up and resumed his elven form.

"Have it your way," he said. "Perhaps one day you will learn some self-restraint." He loved the playful exchanges they shared. He had indeed wanted a son, just as his student had teased earlier, but Rosabela was more than a student or a son could ever be. She had captured his heart in a way that only a little girl could. She was beautiful, witty, good-natured, and fun to be with. He realized at that moment that she was the closest thing to a child he would ever have. She was his dear friend, and that was a rare thing among the isolated druids. Da'Shar smiled inwardly as he considered this last gift for his student and the joy giving it brought. He was getting too attached to this elf-maid, or maybe he was just getting soft.

Rosabela was oblivious to her teacher's thoughts as she transformed back into her elven form and carefully opened the pack. She pulled the silk-wrapped present out and opened it. It was a carefully bound book of hand-penned alchemy recipes. She opened the book and saw the ingredients Da'Shar had taught her to find and collect, but more importantly, she now had the exact amounts to combine in order to make a variety of potions, salves, and powders that could heal, grant strength, induce wisdom, and even explode with devastating effects. This was a wonderful gift indeed. She turned to thank her benefactor, but he was gone without a trace. He was no doubt hidden in the shadows well on his way back to the grove. Rosabela decided to gather up her things and head back as well. Once she stowed her belongings and her newest gift, perhaps she might scout round the forest for some new herbs.

* * *

The life of a hunter was a hard life. Many nights would be spent under the stars with only the campfire and the hunter's animal companion for company. As a result of being far from the amenities of home, and having a huge beast to feed, many hunters learned how to cook using wild seasonings, roots, leaves, and the meat from their hunt. They also learned to preserve the food with sea salt or smoke to make jerky for long trips where food might be scarce. This had been a hard lesson for Wavren, who thought cooking was more for the she-elf than the male.

Gaedron, however, was an excellent cook, when he was careful not to overuse hot spice. He continually showed Wavren that being self-sufficient was critical to the lonely life of a hunter. This point was well made over several weeks of training and by being nearly poisoned on more than one occasion with hot spice. It had gotten so bad that Wavren went hungry or ate plain tubers from the ground, until he finally gave cooking a shot. When he got the hang of it, he learned that he enjoyed creating a delightful meal as much as eating it. It was actually a lesson in growing up that could not be taught with a blunderbuss, trap, or beast. Now that he could cook, it was time for the last lesson Gaedron had to offer.

"Today be the day, laddie that ya go out an' find yerself an ally. Being that yer one o' Clan Ursa, I suggest ya find yerself a nice bear. Don't get me wrong, boy-o, a cat be a fine ally for cuttin' down hordies, an' a bird be fine, too, if'n ya find yerself in a scrape wit' a mage, but a bear has raw power. A bear be a pow'r to be reckoned wit' an' as such, he can keep the attention o' dem hordies, while ya hammer 'em with yer gun," Gaedron explained. "Go on now; get yerself a big 'un."

Wavren set out and hoped to make his mentor proud. He had come a long way from the foolish idealist he was before his training. He had learned to craft the dwarven blunderbuss, which was now his weapon of choice, as well as the shot and powder it required. He had also learned to engineer a few other items that Gaedron had taught him, including a long tube with a small convex crystal in the small end and a larger one at the opposing end. Gaedron called it a lookin' tube, but he had heard of rogues using items like this for long-range infiltration and calling it a *spyglass*. He had mastered tracking and survival as well. This was the final test of his training period.

The forest opened up into a beautiful glade, and Wavren picked up the tracks of a fair-sized bear almost immediately.

The bear had been catching fish along the riverbank and had moved back toward the hills, where its den was most likely located. Wavren knew enough about beasts, and bears in particular, to know that going into a bear's den was not a good idea under any circumstances. Many foolish elves had found this out the hard way when they let their desire for high-priced bear pelts outweigh good sense. Few lived to learn from this mistake.

The tracks led from the river to the hills and then to the edge of the city. This bear was lucky to have survived living so close to civilization, but Wavren dismissed those implications and continued to track the beast around the forest. When Wavren finally caught a glimpse of the beast, he was shocked by its size. This bear was perhaps the patriarch of black bears, by the looks of it. He was excited about befriending such an ally, but he remembered the words his mentor had shared just days ago. He had explained that befriending a bear was more than walking up and offering it food. Befriending a bear was about thinking like a bear and understanding what a bear wants from its companion. In many cases, the bear just wants to be left alone, and that makes befriending one a tricky matter. Most importantly, the bear can never feel in danger or at risk. Such mistakes are often fatal.

Wavren approached the bear from the southwest, so that the wind would bring his scent to the bear. The bear may have noticed Wavren's scent on the wind, but its reaction did not indicate any such detection; or perhaps the bear simply did not care that Wavren was stalking it. This made him a little more concerned. He did not want to spook the great beast, nor did he want to take for granted any patience the bear was showing. He approached very cautiously. In the corner of his eye, Wavren saw Gaedron in the distance, ever watchful of his student.

The bear turned and sniffed the air. It was now very aware of Wavren and possibly Gaedron as well. Wavren was now committed and had to move forward. He relaxed his body language and looked deep into the eyes of the beast. He held up his hands and acted like a bear on its hind legs. He lumbered around on all fours and even rolled around on his back playfully. The bear watched with interest. Wavren was sure he was somehow connecting to the bear, but he was not getting the reaction he expected. He half-expected some interaction like the bears gave during his indoctrination. He doubled his efforts by circling the bear and made a few more bear-like attempts on all fours. He even went to the river and pretended to swat at the fish as if looking for a quick meal. The bear actually sat back on its haunches and lifted one huge paw as if waving and then continued to watch.

Wavren was perplexed. He got close and began to imitate the bear exactly. He sat down and looked straight ahead at the bear. The bear appeared to lift both paws and its shoulders in a very comical shrug. Wavren imitated it exactly, thinking this must be the strangest bear in the realm. Finally, Wavren offered the beast some food, which it took gingerly and ate in one bite. Wavren thought he must have succeeded in taming the bear since he wasn't dead yet. He called to his teacher with confidence that his final test was done.

Gaedron came up slowly to make sure he didn't spook the new ally. The closer he got, the more he looked befuddled until he finally stopped, scratched his head, and looked into the beast's eyes. Gaedron's normally dour look of disdain slowly broadened into a smile. Wavren smiled too. Gaedron's smile turned into a giggle, then into a laugh, and finally Gaedron actually fell on the ground and laughed until his face was red, tears were streaming down his face, and his once-confident student was very confused.

"What?" Wavren asked.

Gaedron could not speak as he was fighting for air just to breathe.

"What is it?" he asked again

After several seconds had passed, Gaedron finally composed himself and said, "Congratulations ya fool o' an elf, ye just tamed yerself a druid." This was followed by another bout of hysterical laughter that Wavren still did not understand.

The bear looked at Wavren again, shrugged in a rather un-bear-like way, and shrank into a smaller form—that of a lovely she-elf he immediately recognized.

"Rosie?" he asked.

"Hi, Wav. Uh, what are you doing here?" she asked in return.

"Oh no, I am never going to hear the end of this," he thought out loud as he walked away, heading back to town.

Gaedron just kept laughing until he realized that Wavren and his new tamed *bear* had long since left him behind. He finally composed himself after gasping for air and smiled, saying, "Oh that was good. I been needin' a hardy bit o' humor fer a while."

Chapter 6
Reunion

Rosabela and Wavren had so much to catch up on since their separation several weeks before, when they had been selected as Protectors of the Vale. Their training had taken them to different classes within the calling of being a Protector, but now they were side by side again. It was an exciting and joyful reunion, to say the least.

Rosabela told her brother many things about life as a druidic shape-shifter. She recounted the early selection process and the "branding" ceremony where she was initiated. Wavren shared his selection process and "initiation" of becoming a hunter where he met Gaedron and later punched it out with him over the hot spice incident. Rosabela laughed so hard when she heard the story that she thought she might pass out from a lack of air. Wavren did not see the humor in the story, but he took the lightheartedness of his sister with great maturity. Wavren was a bit shocked that his sister was now tattooed, but she seemed so fulfilled in spite of the moonfire palm print that he just accepted it as part of her rite of passage.

Wavren and Rosabela spent the next day together, then finally parted company when Da'Shar and Gaedron came looking for them. They noticed that Da'Shar and Gaedron seemed to know each other well. It was an odd thing to see the ever-stoic, almost aloof Da'Shar greeting the dour and determined Gaedron with knowing nods and more-than-strained, yet casual greetings. It was as if they had been lifelong associates and yet never managed to see eye to eye. At the parting, Wavren and Rosabela embraced as siblings often do, while Da'Shar seemed to spin on his heel all too quickly, and Gaedron merely rolled his eyes and huffed away.

Rosabela asked her mentor about the exchange, and Da'Shar explained that dwarves and elves rarely see eye to eye on matters of Nature. From Da'Shar's point of view, Rosabela understood that elves were very much in tune with Nature, and elven druids even more so. He felt that hunters, especially dwarven hunters, were more interested in killing things and stomping around the forest in heavy mail boots than serving the balance. This caused Da'Shar much consternation, so much so that he had spoken to the gruff dwarven hunter about it decades ago. The conversation had not gone well, and Da'Shar was still at odds with Gaedron as a result.

Wavren had also taken a few minutes to broach the subject with his mentor, who mumbled something about elves, druids, and how next time they would be discussing it with Blackmaw and the business end of his blunderbuss. Wavren just let the matter drop, turning the subject back to the business of being a hunter and finding his own ally, just as Gaedron had Blackmaw at his side. Gaedron agreed to stay focused on hunter business and snickered at the thought of Wavren trying to tame his sister's bear form. Wavren knew he would never live that down, but at least he had distracted the dwarf from the unpleasant memories of Da'Shar.

Several days passed with Wavren and Gaedron on the hunt for an appropriate ally. The seasons were changing again, and the cool spring mornings were nearly gone, leaving the oppressive heat and powerful summer sun to slowly bake the elven realms. Wavren had been cautious about any bear that seemed too comfortable with his presence, not wanting to accidentally repeat the last mistake with Rosabela. As a result, he let many suitable bears pass him by. When asked what was wrong with the latest prospect, Wavren always said he was looking for a magnificent ally like Blackmaw, not some weak cub. Gaedron knew the truth and giggled on more than one occasion.

Wavren's obsession with finding a bigger and tougher ally led him to the Thunderidge Mountains, where he tried unsuccessfully to tame a massive brown bear with a bad disposition. The bear had turned on Wavren and would have mauled him had it not been for Gaedron and Blackmaw. The resulting swat from Gaedron's great white northern bear stunned the brown bear into reconsidering his initial attack on Wavren. This further pushed Wavren into seeking the ultimate bear ally. Gaedron liked that his pupil was determined. It reminded the older hunter of himself not so many decades ago. In fact, Wavren was becoming more and more dwarf-like the longer they worked together, which was very unusual for an elf. Gaedron smiled broadly at this revelation, but Wavren never saw the grin.

The day finally came, after many trial beasts had been tamed and released for being too small, or too gentle, or, in one case, rabid. It was a sunny summer day when Wavren came upon perhaps the perfect bear. He had traveled far across the Great Sea, north of the Wetlands and into the Raptor Highlands. This was where he had first seen the massive bear tracks and other beast signs that indicated the presence of a huge bear. No other beast in the area was interested in competing for this territory. Wavren picked up the pace and moved into grass-covered, rolling hills. He was confident this was the ally he had been seeking, as he compared the large bear tracks to the only slightly larger tracks that Gaedron's bear left. This one was definitely the right size, and there was only one way to see if it was the right temperament.

The final realization that this bear was perfect came to Wavren with the discovery of a rather large tauren lying in shredded pieces outside the bear's den. This tauren had obviously been a hunter with the Bloodcrest Forces. The tauren was also obviously unfit to tame such a magnificent ally, but Wavren never doubted his ability to befriend it.

The battle between the tauren and the bear must have been one-sided, yet of epic proportions. Wavren could see where the half-bull, half-man tauren had been standing when he made contact with the bear. The tauren must have been hit hard with a vicious bear paw that sent him reeling hard to the right. The tauren's tracks painted this picture as clearly for Wavren as if he had been there to witness it. A large splatter of blood was spilled where the brave, or perhaps foolish, hunter had regained his composure and made his second attempt to tame the bear. The bear's next attack had come as a bone-crushing bite that took the tauren's hand off at the wrist. The crippled hunter had tried to run, but his hoof prints ended where the bear had obviously risen up on its hind legs and swiped downward with both sets of claws. The resulting double-paw blow had broken the tauren's back and sheared its flesh cleanly in ten perfectly gouged rows. The tauren hunter was most likely dead before the bear's final bite to the back of his neck all but decapitated him.

The site was gruesome, but Wavren approached with confidence nonetheless. Wavren replayed the images in his mind to get a feel for what the tauren had done wrong. The ability to reconstruct events in unbelievable detail was a powerful skill of all great trackers. It was much more than simply following evidence from start to finish.

Wavren moved forward. Gaedron was far behind, well out of blunderbuss range, and Blackmaw was off scavenging for food. Wavren would either have his ally or die, as the tauren had, not so long ago. He considered the mind of this bear, trying to think as it would think and feel as it would feel. The bear was used to being a loner. It was the master of its domain. This bear was the king of the land. What would appeal to such a beast? Wavren thought of his childhood with Rosabela and his close connection with Gaedron. He considered the even closer bond Gaedron shared with Blackmaw. The answer became obvious. He would never master this beast. He would never tame it, as the foolish tauren had tried in vain. Wavren knew he must offer the great bear the one thing it could never have on its own: friendship.

Indeed, friendship was the key. Who would be beside Wavren both day and night? Who would fight, and if need be, die beside Wavren in battle? Who would be the sole guardian when sleep finally took the hunter at night? In Gaedron's case, who pulled the blasted and drowning dwarf out of the sea as the ship he fought on sank to the bottom? The answer to all of these questions was not a pet, nor was it even an ally. The answer was a friend. This was the bond a great hunter had with his ally, and so it would be with Wavren and his chosen bear.

Wavren removed his leather armor and stacked it neatly in a pile with his dwarven blunderbuss and elven dagger. He knew they would never be able to help him if the bear chose to attack. He centered himself and thought of the love he had for his sister and the friendship he had with Gaedron. He called to the bear in a guttural growl, and the response was terrifying and exhilarating at the same time. The bear's roar was a powerful bass tone that warned of certain death. Wavren called again with a bear-like roar that conveyed honor, respect, and somehow, even friendship.

The bear appeared between a short hill and a huge rock outcropping that made an excellent entryway to its den. It was massive, nearly the size of Ol' Blackmaw. Instead of being white like the bears of the North, this bear was a deep, ruddy brown with almost-red highlights and long black claws. Beast lore named this bear *Ursus Arctos Thunderidge*, or Great Bear of Thunderidge. Wavren stared in awe and determination. The bear's side-to-side swagger spoke volumes to the hunter: it said, "None are my equal," and "all who stand in my way are crushed!"

The bear sniffed the air, then swaggered forward and growled as if to say, "Last chance to leave, elf; the last hunter chose death over discretion." Wavren held his ground and fell to all fours in a very bear-like fashion. The bear watched for a moment, not sure what to make of the bear-like elf. This gave Wavren confidence. He rolled around on the ground in mock play and then growled a bit. The bear was curious, so it allowed the hunter another moment of life. Wavren took the pause as a good sign and emoted friendship and equality to the bear instead of a desire for domination over this powerful ally. The bear seemed to understand, but made no move to accept the elf as its comrade. Wavren pulled a leg quarter out of his backpack from a boar he had slaughtered earlier. He set it on the ground as a show of friendship. The bear's interest peaked. Wavren moved closer; once the bear had consumed the meat, he sniffed at the bear, again in a most bear-like fashion. The bear allowed the sniffing and even circled Wavren for inspection.

Gaedron's student was now out of his sight and sound range. Gaedron also noticed the large tracks that ran parallel to those his student left. Gaedron had great confidence in his student, but as a measure of safety, he called to Ol' Blackmaw and stepped up the pace to find Wavren. What Gaedron saw next made his heart drop into the pit of his stomach.

Wavren had stripped down to his leggings and was engaged in a most feral form of communication with the biggest bear Gaedron had ever seen, short of his own ally. Gaedron was thrilled to see that Wavren was still alive, but he could hardly believe the foolish elf was naked from the waist up and seemed to be communing with the beast. The dwarven hunter decided that his pupil was either brilliantly courageous or stupidly insane. Gaedron was still out of range to shoot the bear if things went wrong, so he watched in grim confidence, hoping he had taught his student well. If he had not, Wavren would be meeting his ancestors very soon.

Wavren and the bear circled a few more times, and then the bear stood up on its hind legs and growled. To Gaedron's amazement, Wavren stood up and growled back. The bear swatted at Wavren with a paw that could easily crush or disembowel the young hunter. The elf ducked and swatted back, hitting the bear with an open palm that seemed so tiny against the bear's massive head. The bear responded with an open maw that completely engulfed Wavren's head! Gaedron closed his eyes and waited for the loud crunch that he knew would be the end of his student. Instead, he heard another growl, somewhat muffled; when Gaedron opened his eyes, he saw that Wavren had the bear by one ear and its lower lip, and was prying the huge bear's mouth open. Every muscle stood out on the slender elf's body as the bear's paws wrapped the elf in a deadly bear hug.

Gaedron had always been a great marksman and a canny survivalist, but his experience with training new hunters was limited to the elf that had his head in the bear's maw. Gaedron was frozen with fear that his student might soon be dead. He'd never get close enough to intervene in time, and even if he could, his shot would probably hit the student he was hoping to save. The world seemed to stop, as he felt nothing but dread.

The dwarf knew the bear should have killed the elf by now, but as Wavren extricated his head from the bear's mouth, he could see why the beast had not simply bitten the small hunter's head completely off: Wavren had his own teeth locked on the bear's tongue. Although quite disgusting—even by dwarven standards—the tactic had been effective. The bear was unable to close its own jaws, being uncertain of the damage being done to its tender tongue. In fact, the bear was thrashing about quite bizarrely, trying to get the crazy elf out of its mouth. When it finally dislodged Wavren, he did the last thing Gaedron thought he would do. Instead of running, he jumped on the bear's back and bit it on the ear! The bear bucked and reared, but the elf was embedded like a tick. Finally, the bear rolled over and squashed the elf. The bear got up and shook itself, roaring in victory. Gaedron snapped out of his trance and loaded finely crafted mithril round into his blunderbuss. Even if saving the elf was no longer possible, he would avenge his student.

Ol' Blackmaw was already in a full gallop toward the brown bear, when the dwarf called his famous battle cry: "FER

STONE AN' STEEL!" Suddenly, the elf's head popped up. The dwarf rumbled on faster, thinking he might still save his poor student. Wavren jumped up and put his body between the oncoming attack and the bear. "STOP!" he yelled. Time stood still as the two hunters and the two bears looked at each other in great confusion.

"All is well," the younger hunter said. Then he added, in his best dwarven accent, "I'll not have ya killin' me new friend."

Gaedron did stop, as did Blackmaw. They stared at each other for a long moment, and finally Gaedron spoke. "Well done," he said, and then he turned and walked away, grumbling something about being too old and needing a vacation. Wavren's new ally turned and headed back to its den. Ol' Blackmaw turned and followed the dwarf. Wavren stood there, somewhat battered and bruised, but smiling. He thought, *I am alive, and now I have my ally. May our enemies tremble in fear from this day forward.*

Wavren spent the next several weeks training his new ally; he felt the massive brown bear was more a friend than a pet or beast of burden. Wavren decided to call the bear Stonetalon, for his nearly unbreakable claws that looked like blackened granite. The great bear seemed to like the name well enough, and he learned to respond not only when the hunter called him by it, but also to the mere sound of the elf's voice.

Stonetalon could distinguish various degrees of urgency as well as the general intent of the hunter by his tone, pitch, and cadence. This developed to a point where Wavren's mood often dictated the response of his ally. When the elven hunter was tired, he gave tired signals that the bear followed slowly or not at all. When Wavren was energized or serious, the bear reacted accordingly. This was particularly true when Wavren was in danger, and the bear sensed worry or fear coming from him. It was simple bear psychology. The bear looked at Wavren as a cub in need of protection, in spite of the exceedingly loud blunderbuss he carried and the skill that made that weapon quite deadly. Stonetalon was also jealous and territorial. Since he considered Wavren to be his favorite toy that was not to be played with or abused by anyone other than him, Wavren was well protected. It made for a strong bond of loyalty and mutual gain.

The relationship between the hunter and his ally had grown quickly as Stonetalon learned how reliable and devoted Wavren was. In turn, Wavren learned that Stonetalon would always give fierce protection and loyalty.

* * *

Rosabela returned to the wildly beautiful grove, where she saw a serious look on her mentor's face. She knew immediately that he had bad news, but there was also something else. He looked sad, almost despondent.

"What is it, Da'Shar?" she asked.

He smiled weakly and replied, "You know me too well, child. Your initial training is complete, and you have been assigned to the ranks of the Protectors in Forestedge."

Rosabela beamed, but she noticed the sadness again in the older druid's eyes. He was going to miss her just as she would miss him. It was like sending the fledgling from the nest for her first flight. Fear and hope mixed poorly and made a thick emotional soup between Rosabela and Da'Shar.

"I know you will miss me," she said. "I will miss you as well, but won't we see one another often?"

"The world is an uncertain place, but I believe we are destined by the will of fate and Nature to visit again soon," Da'Shar said.

Rosabela launched herself forward and hugged the stoic elf like a little girl hugging her father. Da'Shar returned the embrace, a single tear rolling down his sharp features. He smiled with pride.

Rosabela moved off to the druidic enclave where she was scheduled to meet a coordination officer who had her mission orders in hand. The enclave was built among a mass of redwood trees so that it looked like the building was actually part of the trees surrounding it. The long, winding stairs that led to the Forestedge liaison's office were also designed to look like the undulating roots and branches of the trees. It was beautiful.

Rosabela entered the liaison's office and saw a well-dressed nobleman behind a desk. She presented herself, and he handed her a rolled up parchment. The parchment gave the following directions:

> *Travel from Celes'tia to SurCeles'tia Village. Take the ferry to Port Archer and ride south to Forestedge. You will meet with Councilman Joram Panni. He will assign missions for your tenure in Port Archer. Serve well, Rosabela, Protector of the Vale.*

Rosabela nodded to the nobleman, spun on her heel, and headed out the door. She was determined to serve honorably and accomplish great things. As she made her way across Celes'tia toward the small port of SurCeles'tia Village, many commoners stepped aside to let her pass. Some waved and others bowed. She took the show of respect in stride and never let it go to her head, but it was amazing to see both strangers and elves she knew well stop their activities and acknowledge her as she passed. It was as if she was already some sort of hero—or maybe they thought she was going away, never to return. Whatever the case, she kept her pace steady until she arrived at the outskirts of Celes'tia and the path to SurCeles'tia Village.

A voice that she recognized called to her: "They let anyone become a Protector these days, don't they?" Wavren asked

She replied without ever looking back: "No, but it appears they dropped the standards just for you."

Wavren laughed heartily and spun his sister around into a huge hug that reminded Rosabela how much she had missed her twin. She smiled and hugged him back, but looked questioningly at him after a moment.

"I have orders assigning me to Port Archer now that I have

completed my initial training. I am a Druidic Protector now," she said proudly.

"I, too, have completed my initial training and have been given my assignment," he returned.

"Have you been assigned to Port Archer?" she asked.

"I was originally assigned to Dwarven Darrow. For some stupid reason, they apparently thought I was a dwarf, but I got the assignment changed when I heard you were heading to Port Archer," he answered.

"That is wonderful, Wav. I hope we get to see each other often, once we get our final duty orders," she said. "You need someone to look out for you."

"Funny you should mention that. I have someone looking out for me," he returned with a smile on his face.

Wavren whistled loudly, and from the edge of the tree line, Rosabela saw a huge reddish-brown bear heading right toward them. She looked at Wavren with awe as the massive bear rumbled up to them.

"Now, that is a good trick!" she exclaimed. "Or have you charmed another druid?"

"Trust me, this is neither druid nor some pet; this is my ally. His name is Stonetalon," Wavren said. "You might want to use caution around him, lest he swallow you whole."

"I think I know a few things about bears," she said.

Rosabela immediately walked up and scratched the bear's ears, which Stonetalon seemed to tolerate more than appreciate. Wavren was a little concerned that his bear might not allow such affections, but all seemed to be well. Wavren thought for a moment that it was foolish to take such liberties with a wild bear, but perhaps Rosabela had a way with bears since she could shape-shift into one. He smiled and put his arm around his sister as they headed for the docks at SurCeles'tia Village. There was much left to share about the time they had been apart, and Wavren wasted no time along the way.

The ship arrived moments after they passed through the portal that connected SurCeles'tia Village and Celes'tia proper. It was actually more of a large shuttle than a true ship for open waters, but it was a huge caravel nonetheless. It transported passengers from the island city of Celes'tia to the mainland at Port Archer every few hours. The sea was calm, and the smell of brine was thick in the air. With a clear sky and a favorable wind, life seemed just about perfect.

The twins walked down the long dock and up the short plank to the ship. They boarded with a large group of elves and found a broad deck filled with passengers bustling about. Wavren was given a wide berth with Stonetalon at his side, and Rosabela followed in their wake to a small cabin. They dropped off their personal belongings and were soon underway for the Elvenshore Coast and the port city of Port Archer.

Chapter 7
Port Archer

"Where are the messengers from Forestedge?" Councilman Joram Panni demanded. Joram Panni was an important man and hated to be kept waiting.

Security Captain Helio shook his head as if to say they were probably dead somewhere between Port Archer and Forestedge. He had learned that it was better to maintain silence around the councilman, who preferred the sound of his own voice to anyone else's.

"I cannot push supplies forward to the troops in Forestedge, who support the battle in Deadmist Valley, without solid intelligence on the enemies' whereabouts!" the councilman exclaimed to the captain.

The captain saluted and left the volatile councilman behind as he set off to find his personnel officer. He half-ran, half-walked in an effort to make haste and maintain his composure, but urgency always seemed essential when working with Councilman Panni. It wasn't always so hectic. Panni used to be a soldier, but he left the military to serve in politics. The transition from duty and discipline to negotiation and compromise had left Panni at his wit's end, and Helio always seemed to bear the brunt of the frustration.

Captain Helio moved purposefully into the small personnel office where his company controlled all incoming and outgoing assignments, as well as payroll and a myriad of other personnel duties. Sitting at a small desk with stacks of paper strewn about, was one of the few non-elven inhabitants of Port Archer, a tiny gnome named Asanti.

"Asanti," the captain called.

Amid tumbling stacks of paperwork and a long string of gnomish curses, the captain heard his chief of personnel reply, "Here, sir."

"Asanti, I believe the two messengers we sent to scout the road from Port Archer to Forestedge were captured or killed by the Bloodcrest Forces. I need two new recruits and I need them now," Helio insisted.

Asanti replied with disdain, "So the councilman wants us to sacrifice two more of our troops?" Asanti sighed. "Well, there is a pair of Protectors due in from Celes'tia today. Let me find their orders … one second … ah, here they are."

Helio considered the situation for a moment. Protectors of the Vale were elite troops, not regulars that he normally commanded. It would be unprecedented to send a pair of Protectors to reconnoiter a road. It was a waste of high value resources, and more importantly, what would the elves back home say if word got back that elite troops were being required to run these menial tasks instead of his own scouts? He would be the laughingstock of Port Archer, or worse, Celes'tia.

"I want regulars, not elites. Where are my replacement scouts?" he asked.

"We are low on the O.M.L., sir," Asanti said.

The captain looked at the gnome questioningly.

Asanti shifted uncomfortably in his seat and clarified, "The *Order of Merit list,* sir."

Helio continued to wait for the proper disclosure of information.

"Sir, we are low in priority for scouts from our higher command because we have the simple mission of supplying troops, who actually fight the battle, instead of being on the frontlines like those in D.M.V.," the gnome explained.

Helio looked exasperated, and the gnome continued, "D.M.V. is the official acronym for Deadmist Valley, sir."

Helio finally commented, "For the love of Nature, can you just stop with the acronyms and abbreviations? We are both from extremely long-lived races. We can afford to take the time to say the whole message and get the full meaning without the fear of dying before we finish. Leave abbreviations and acronyms to the humans who need to conserve every moment as if it were their last."

The gnome frowned, saluted, and said, "Wilco—I mean, I will comply, sir."

Captain Helio took the new arrival orders of the two Protectors to the docks and waited for them to pull into Port Archer. He rubbed his temples and thought of his younger days when life was simpler. He wished he could be the scout to run from Port Archer to Forestedge and back with nothing more than a report of enemy sightings to worry about.

The ship pulled in by midday, and the captain waited for the passengers to unload. He was confident that he would have warriors or rogues, the mainstay of the elite Protectors, but he was willing to work with anyone at this point. His surprise was profound when two very young elves, who distinctly favored each other, stepped off the boat. The taller male had a massive bear in tow and didn't even have a bow or a sword. He carried one of the newer weapons, a gun, which, in Captain Helio's opinion, was a disgraceful weapon, not like the longbow and elven blades of traditional warriors. To make matters worse, the wispy female carried a stick and wore armor, which indicated she wasn't a mage or a priest, but some sort of fighter with a staff. The captain thought, *This is preposterous!*

Wavren moved forward and greeted the captain with a firm handshake and a warm smile. He introduced himself: "Well met, sir, I am Wavren of Celes'tia, Protector of the Vale and

Hunter of Clan Ursa. This is my sister, Rosabela of Celes'tia, Protector of the Vale and Druid of the Grove. My companion here is Stonetalon. We are at your service, sir, and ready for assignment."

Helio was taken back by the formal greeting and had to pause for a moment to collect his thoughts. "I am Captain Helio of Port Archer, commander of the security forces here. I welcome you to our town. We are shorthanded in personnel, so please forgive me if I skip the formalities and get right to business. There is an immediate need for you to scout the road from Port Archer to Forestedge and secure word from the high councilman in Forestedge regarding his re-supply needs."

Wavren looked at Rosabela and then replied to the captain, "Sir, we will gladly accept this mission, but is this not an errand more fitting to your scouts?"

"This is an important mission that requires completion, and I have no one else available to send. My last two scouts are missing in action, and as I have previously stated, we are undermanned here," the captain returned.

Wavren smiled broadly, took the dispatch from Captain Helio, and nodded to Rosabela. They were off to Forestedge without even taking the time to settle their personal belongings. Captain Helio was relieved to see the eagerness of the two new recruits, but he felt guilty about sending them on this simple, yet uncertain, errand. His thoughts went back to his scouts who were missing in action. The uncertainty was troubling, but his job was to make the mission happen, and he was long overdue with his update to Councilman Panni. His personal regrets and concerns would have to wait.

Wavren padded alongside his sister and Stonetalon at an amazing pace. Rosabela seemed to have that look of determination on her face, and the bear loped along nearly oblivious to both Wavren and Rosabela.

"Well," he said, "what do you think?"

Rosabela never looked his way. "About what?"

"Don't you think this is a silly errand for us?" he asked.

"Wav, we are new, the captain is shorthanded, and this

mission is just a start. Don't make the situation more than it is," she replied.

"Sure, but I was thinking we might see some action, you know, fight some orcs or maybe a platoon of trolls," he commented. "There's not much chance of that running messages on a secure road between two Dae'gon Alliance-controlled towns."

Rosabela looked at her brother for a moment and saw the gleam in his eye. She had seen that gleam before. It usually appeared just before Wavren got them into a lot of trouble as kids, and now that they were grown, the gleam usually meant adult trouble. She just pushed ahead at nearly a sprint in order to keep his mind focused on breathing instead of talking. Wavren got the hint and picked up the now-faster pace.

Stonetalon was able to keep up for short distances, but at nearly two thousand pounds, the bear could never sustain their pace to Forestedge. After a few minutes, he slowed to a walk and then disappeared into the forest. Wavren just kept running, having full confidence that the bear would move through the forest alone at a faster rate than he could run along the winding road. If Wavren needed him, Stonetalon would be there.

Not long after the bear had departed, Wavren picked up barely distinguishable signs of orcs passing this way. The normally deep depressions made by heavily armored orcs had been nearly wiped clean from the road, but few things were missed by an elven hunter. He signaled to his twin, who immediately took up a defensive posture. The hunter moved in and out of the adjacent wood line and crossed the road back and forth several times trying to discern what the signs meant. He noticed various other tracks and signs of passage by elves and beasts, but his attention was drawn to a small trail that branched off the main road. It was little more than a rough path through the brush that was probably made by deer or other wild game.

Wavren motioned for Rosabela to follow, then whistled for Stonetalon. The bear had not gotten far and was at his side in no time. Silently, the two elves and the bear worked their way down the path for about a mile and angled around a small clearing. Wavren peeked around a huge tree and saw two elves bound with cords and gagged. They were lying face down on the ground and seemed to be unconscious.

"These could be the missing scouts," Rosabela whispered.

Wavren nodded, but his previous gleam was now replaced by a serious, almost scowling expression.

"I don't like it," he said. "Where are the guards?"

Rosabela shrugged and replied, "We have to help them."

"There are heavy humanoid tracks all over this place. I am betting we have an infestation of orcs nearby," he returned quietly. "The tracks were all but invisible at the road, having been neatly covered by a cautious rogue, no doubt, but these are obvious," he said.

Rosabela nodded and kept an eye out for the burly green savages that made up the more vicious fourth of the Bloodcrest Forces.

"Scout to the left, I'll go right. We can meet on the other side of the clearing to make sure the area is clear," Wavren said.

Rosabela moved carefully to the left, being certain that she moved silently and stayed hidden from view. She noticed that no birds were singing, no insects chirping. She knew immediately that she was not alone. Her circuitous route brought her around a few small trees and close to a poorly concealed pit. The pit would have been a reasonable trap for a beast, but Rosabela detected the unusual thatch that covered the opening. She smiled and was thankful for her awareness of the trap. She started to move around it when she noticed a very slight click under her foot. It was a pressure release mechanism that was no doubt the trigger for another trap. She looked around quickly and noticed that she had fallen into a well-planned snare. If she moved now, the trap would spring and she would be yanked off her feet and into the air, where she would be seen flailing about by the trapper. Whoever set this trap had concealed it by drawing her attention to the pit. Deception was better than camouflage in this case. She looked around, but Wavren was nowhere to be seen, and she could not alert him without alerting the enemy. She was stuck.

Wavren circled around to the other side and saw no other signs of orcs; at least none were present at the moment. He paused and listened for any sound that might indicate where the enemy was, but he heard nothing. A few moments passed, and he became very aware that Rosabela was taking too long. He peeked out at the two elves on the ground again and made his way in the direction his sister should have come from. He stepped carefully, keenly aware that his earlier assessment of the road being safe could not have been more wrong, not with all the orc-sign he saw in this camp.

Out of nowhere, a huge tusked orc came barreling toward Wavren. The orc had a wicked looking saber in one hand and a long, curved dagger in the other. He was clad in leather armor and appeared to be a long-range scout for the Bloodcrest Forces; more than likely he was an assassin.

The orc came forward and slashed at Wavren with both blades and then alternated stabs with each. Wavren dodged out of range quickly and dove forward into a roll to get some space between him and the remarkably fast orc. The orc was hoping for a quick kill and was caught by surprise when none of his initial attacks found their mark. He was even more surprised when Stonetalon blind-sided him with a massive paw that knocked him back ten feet to land hard on his rump. The bear was on him with both paws, which would have ripped the orc apart had it not been for the sturdy leather armor that suddenly seemed all too thin. Wavren completed his roll, un-slung his blunderbuss, and prepared to fire when three more orcs came out of nowhere. Each looked like the first and carried similar weapons as well. These were no mere scouts. This was the advanced party for a raid, and they were well armed and well trained.

Rosabela heard the fighting commence and felt confident that stealth was no longer her primary concern. She knew she had to act, but with no way to disarm the trap, she had only one choice. She braced herself and shifted her weight. As predicted, the pressure released the trigger, which set off the unavoidable snare, and she was whisked upward, to hang by one foot. She called on her feral might and became the great black bear. The sheer weight was more than the snare could hold, and Rosabela felt the tree give way. She fell back to the ground and shook off the pain of the fall. The rope was cut with one mighty bite, and she was crashing through the woods in a flash.

She came through the brush and saw that the fight had moved into the clearing. Wavren was dodging attacks from three orcs, and Stonetalon was shredding the armor of a fourth on the ground. Rosabela roared mightily and charged in; the three orcs turned to see her approach, enabling Wavren to get his shot off. The sound was incredibly loud, and the effect was tremendous. One orc was blown backward. He had a huge black powder burn on his chest that surrounded a now profusely bleeding hole. The other two were stunned for a moment, caught off guard by the deafening explosion. This gave Rosabela the time she needed to close the distance and make her assault.

Wavren backed away from the mass of orcs and bears, which was now the center of the battle. He was amazed by how powerful his sister's swipes were, even compared to Stonetalon's attacks. He marked the orc on the ground under his ally's paws and fired. The assassin moved no more. He drew his sights on the orc who was on the ground bleeding from Wavren's first shot and fired. Now only two remained. The odds were growing in their favor. Rosabela smashed one of the two remaining orcs with a one-two combination, and he fell to the ground with a broken neck. Stonetalon bit the last orc on the back of the leg just as he moved to stab Rosabela. The orc screamed just as Rosabela turned and lashed out with a mighty paw. The sickening crack followed by an agonizing scream told Wavren that as Rosabela struck, Stonetalon's bite snapped the orc's femur. He would likely bleed to death if they decided not to finish him off. Rosabela shifted back into her elven form and Wavren called his ally off the wounded orc. The scout was in terrible pain, but still conscious. This lucky turn of events meant information might be gathered.

The twins took a few minutes to check on the elves that were still tied up and gagged in the middle of the clearing. Both were alive, but unconscious. They had sustained various wounds that had been bandaged by their captors. They were most likely being kept alive as hostages, or possibly dinner. Rosabela cut their bonds with a small knife and rolled them onto their backs. She spoke the words of Nature and healed their wounds just as Da'Shar had taught her. She used herbal potions to restore strength in their arms and legs, which had been tightly bound for too long. When the elven prisoners finally regained consciousness, they thanked the twins and explained that their mission was urgent. They had to return to Port Archer immediately, and they wasted no time leaving. On the way back to the road, they both spat on the dead orcs and headed out. Wavren and Rosabela turned their attention to the last living orc, who was being watched by Stonetalon.

"Do you speak common, the trade language of the Western Kingdoms?" Wavren asked the dying orc.

Through gritted teeth, the enemy growled in rough common, "I do."

"Well, give us your name that we may speak civilly," Rosabela said.

"I am called Borik of Dek'Thal," he replied, grimacing in pain.

Wavren replied, "I am Wavren, and this is Rosabela. We will spare your life if you give us information."

The orc obviously doubted Wavren's offer and replied, "You cannot save me now. I will be with my ancestors soon."

Rosabela whispered the words of minor healing to show the scout that his life could be spared, though it revolted her to ask Nature to heal this wicked member of the Bloodcrest Forces. The orc's leg was still mangled, but the bleeding slowed. The look of intense pain melted away from the assassin's face, but there were no thanks in his eyes to replace it.

"As you can see, I have the power to save you, as promised. We are not required to slay you, and we have no love of senseless killing, but we also have our duty to fulfill," the druid said with calm resolve.

Borik laughed and looked away, but made no agreement.

Wavren switched to the language of elves and asked his sister, "Well, we can't just kill him. He is an unarmed prisoner, and although I bet he would prefer to see us dead, we have a code of conduct to follow."

The druid replied, "I agree. We must bring him to Forestedge for questioning. To do that, we must bandage his wounds for the trip. I am willing to sustain him, but he will be eager to kill us both if given the chance."

"Then we don't give him the chance," the hunter returned with a sly smile.

Wavren fashioned a crude, but effective, field-expedient stretcher from two stout saplings, vines, and a spare cloak. The stretcher was designed with a harness that could go around Rosabela's waist in bear form and support the injured orc's weight, but the end would have to drag along the road. Wavren lashed the orc to the stretcher with thick cords and tied the assassin's saber across its throat for insurance. If the orc struggled too much, it would cut its own throat. If it was compliant, it would live long enough to see justice in Forestedge, after much *convincing* to reveal the enemy's plans.

The rest of the journey was quiet, with Rosabela hauling the crippled orc on the stretcher and Wavren scouting ahead for trouble. Stonetalon watched the prisoner to ensure he behaved himself, which was a fair guarantee considering he was lashed to the stretcher and pinned under his own blade. The most convincing argument was still the massive brown bear trailing behind, ready to finish the job it started.

Chapter 8
Forestedge

The twins made it to Forestedge with fair speed, considering that they could not jostle the injured orc prisoner they had in tow without decapitating him. It had been very clever of Wavren to secure him in such a way that his own blade would inhibit any escape attempts along the journey. The town guard received the newcomers with caution and more than a few questions and concerns. It was not unusual to have Protectors pass through, but having two bears and an orc prisoner seemed very bizarre to even the seasoned sergeant of the guard. After routine questioning and intense scrutiny, they let the odd group enter.

Wavren and Rosabela, now in her elven form, were escorted to High Councilman Kalin while the restrained and injured orc was turned over to the local interrogators. The message from Port Archer was presented to the high councilman, who frowned at the realization that the previous two scouts had been delayed in their mission to get the supply requests back to Captain Helio.

"I assume that two Protectors of the Vale can accomplish what the last two scouts could not," the high councilman said, as he motioned for his secretary to reconstruct the last supply requests.

Rosabela replied stoically, "That mission is already underway. We rescued the two scouts from a band of orcs who were likely part of a larger force not far away. The scouts are now on their way back to Port Archer to complete their mission. Our work here is done, but we hope the prisoner we brought to you for questioning might give some indication of the enemy's plans."

The high councilman thought for a moment before speaking. Finally, he said, "I would like for you two to take word back to Councilman Panni. There will be two scrolls to deliver. The first dispatch will contain our findings from the prisoner. The second will be a list of future needs from Port Archer." The councilman sat back heavily in his finely crafted chair, which creaked in protest to his weight.

Rosabela merely nodded and she and Wavren walked away.

"Well, what do you think about our new mission?" Wavren asked.

Rosabela responded matter-of-factly, "We are heading back to Port Archer regardless of the mission. It is convenient to carry the dispatch."

Wavren added, "But don't you think we are supposed to be doing bigger and better missions? I thought we would be fighting more and running from town to town less."

Rosabela thought back to the fight with the kobold leader, Grol. His suffering at her hands made her somewhat less inclined to go out looking for battle. Even the recent battle with the orcs seemed surreal. It was obviously not so with Wavren. Her brother seemed more interested in fighting the enemy than negotiating. Maybe it was simply a male characteristic. She walked alongside her brother and thought back to Da'Shar's teachings. Could it be that druids were more in touch with Nature and all life than hunters, who, by profession, hunted and killed? The answer seemed obvious, but she would consider this more later, for now she had to prepare for the trip back to Port Archer.

Wavren split off from his sister and took Stonetalon out hunting for some food. This seemed to be an ongoing task for the hunter, who could never fully satisfy the hunger of his ally. Rosabela took this time to walk over to the large pond behind the local inn. She took out the fine fishing rod that her mentor had given to her and plopped the line in the water. She watched the bobber and the ripples that endlessly circled outward from it. She meditated on the events of the recent past and the missions that lay ahead while she hauled in several beautiful catfish from the freshwater pond.

* * *

Barely two hours had passed since the twins parted company, and High Councilman Kalin had already gotten a fair amount of information from the interrogators. Apparently, the Forestedge interrogators were very good at getting information out of the enemy. The latest information included plans for probing attacks on Forestedge and even Port Archer from the contested region of Deadmist Valley. These attacks were meant to measure the capabilities of the local forces as well as to disrupt the supply lines between the smaller towns and had been reasonably effective up to this point. The orc could not give the exact size of the enemy forces, but he did reveal that his team was one of many in the area. With this knowledge, Kalin called a meeting of his guard forces and key leaders to brief them on the situation.

"Listen carefully, folks. I have urgent news, and we need to plan and act quickly," Kalin announced.

The crowd that had gathered around the high councilman grew quiet. Kalin paced heavily back and forth across the wooden platform. His footsteps seemed unusually loud for an elf of small stature.

"Our interrogators have discovered information that will

require change to our battle posture and defensive fortifications. An orc prisoner, delivered to us by two Protectors of the Vale, has revealed a high likelihood of numerous small scouting forces infiltrating our territory. These advanced scouts have penetrated our outer perimeter-roving patrols and are now scattered throughout the land between Forestedge and Port Archer. They are well armed and well trained in combat operations and tactics. Their mission is to gather information, disrupt supply lines, and harass our forces. No doubt these scouts precede the larger invasion forces already assembled and awaiting orders to move," the high councilman explained.

An unusually tall elf warrior spoke: "So we send out more scouts to find these vermin, and when they do, we take them out."

"That would be a fine plan if we had more scouts," Kalin concurred, "but we have no more scouts, so we must restructure our defenses to enhance the forward operations. Every third warrior will be reallocated into the scouting troop along with every other mage. We must protect the outlying areas."

One mage stood up and exclaimed, "This is ridiculous! Without the mages and warriors guarding the rear area, the Bloodcrest Forces will raze Forestedge to the ground, leaving the forward operations with no support or re-supply. The scouts must not engage if the enemy is beyond their capabilities. By sending warriors and wizardly firepower, you are encouraging combat. We need information on the movement of our enemies, not a harassing force that cannot win decisively with skirmish tactics."

There was much murmuring in the crowd, and the spokesman for the scouts stood up and protested, "The warriors are too loud with all the armor and weapons they carry, and the mages are not well suited for long journeys in the wild. Our mission would be compromised with this blending of combat professions."

This brought nods from the warriors who had no intention of leaving their heavy mail and plate armor behind and who knew the mages to be of low constitution. The mages remained silent, not wanting to refute or validate the claims about having lower constitutions, but each quietly knew magic could always be used to enhance any ability.

The high councilman spoke again: "I realize that these seem like drastic changes, but the alternative is to surrender the roads to these orcs or have our current scouts spread too thin to be effective. The mages will provide fire support, and the warriors will lead the attacks. The scouts can serve as skirmishers at range or take part in the melee as they deem necessary. Imagine the advantage of surprise we gain when scouts fix the enemy location and the warrior charges in and disrupts the enemy's ranged attacks, while the mage calls fire and arcane bolts down on their heads!"

Again, there was much grumbling, but the plan was solid in theory. Two scouts, one mage, and one warrior would be able to handle similar encounters like the one Wavren and Rosabela faced not so long ago. The real question was if they could work together and learn to overcome the reduced movement speed and stealth problems. Change was always tough to accept, and after hundreds of years of traditional scouting missions where elven archers in leather armor moved quickly and quietly, this was especially difficult.

The decision had been made, and new teams were already being formed. The new blended teams did seem to be a motley collection of elves, but no one could deny the sheer power that each team had available. The high councilman signaled Rosabela and Wavren. They followed him to the town hall, where he addressed them apart from the loud group.

"You two have a special mission," Kalin began, as he returned to his office chair; again, it protested under his weight.

"Yes, we already know that you have critical dispatches that must get to Port Archer," Wavren said caustically. He imagined the pompous elf falling flat on his back with the collapse of the creaky chair.

"No," Kalin returned to Wavren's surprise, "I want you to perform a special task for me. You must de-fang the snake as the old proverb goes."

Rosabela and Wavren looked at each other in disbelief.

"I want you to seek out and remove the central leader of the advanced forces. The prisoner you captured was *convinced* to give us his name and general location as well as a brief description. I think you will find this task not only challenging, but rewarding as well," he said.

Rosabela spoke with a very noble air: "We do not require payment, we are Protect—"

Wavren elbowed his sister somewhat obviously and picked up where she left off. "We are indeed Protectors of the Vale, but we require new equipment and weapons. Please continue with your offer."

Rosabela glared at her brother.

Kalin offered, "Forestedge will pay you fifty silver pieces each for the bounty of Neggish Grimtusk, the orcish scout commander. He is located in the mountains east of where you found the prisoner."

Rosabela thought for a moment, then asked, "How is it that you were able to get this critical information from the orc in such a short time?"

Kalin responded, "Actually, the orc volunteered this information. He dared me to send anyone to face his commander. My guess is that the commander is very powerful to inspire such awe in his followers. All orcish leaders must earn this awe from great displays of power or uncanny demonstrations of sadism to be able to rule over their lawless minions. It is simply their way."

That was pretty much how Rosabela assumed the information was obtained. She also assumed the leader would be no mere scout or warrior. Wavren thought nothing of it. He was more interested in the reward and the challenge than the reputation of the orc leader.

Kalin asked, "Do we have a fair arrangement?"

Wavren replied, "We will also need supplies and equipment repairs, as I mentioned."

The high councilman agreed with a nod, and before nightfall, the twins were heading back up the road toward Port

Archer. Wavren was given a fine set of studded leather armor to wear under his loose fitting clothes. The city's armory was full of it. For armor, it was amazingly light and certainly able to protect him from edged weapons and possibly arrows. He was feeling more and more like a professional every day. Most importantly, this was finally a quest worthy of two Protectors, and Wavren was beaming with joy. Rosabela was excited, but also wary that this orc leader would be no pushover.

Night fell quickly with all the business of war preparations going on. The sounds of insect chatter started up with the frogs soon joining in. The collective sounds were musical, almost magical. Given the clear night air and the music of Nature, it was hard not to forget that the land was not secure and death could be waiting to pounce at any moment.

The twins picked a small clearing to set up camp and went about preparing the evening meal. Wavren produced a variety of smoked meat he had in his pack, while Rosabela found wild roots and herbs to throw into the pot. It did not take long for Wavren to complete his famous jungle stew, just as Gaedron had taught him. That sumptuous smell and the crackling fire brought back memories of Gaedron and Ol' Blackmaw. It hadn't been so long ago since he had his first taste of the dwarven recipe he was currently using. Of course, his version was missing one particular ingredient that Gaedron was very fond of, but Wavren now had an aversion to dwarven hot spice. He wondered how the gruff old dwarf was doing.

Wavren stirred the stew, and Rosabela hummed an old elven tune that he couldn't remember the words to anymore. Stonetalon was off on his own, no doubt looking for food, but would be back for a fair portion of the stew. Wavren had to smile at the irony of the entire situation. He was cooking and reminiscing. His sister was waiting for the meal to be served, and the bear was carousing. How different this was from his preconceived notion about the roles of men, women, and friends. After all, shouldn't Rosabela be cooking, while he was out and about? Perhaps not, but it was odd that he had been so wrong about so many things since he became a Protector of the

Vale.

"Rosie," he asked, "what is that tune you are humming? I can't seem to place it."

"It is the song of the road," she replied. "Mother often sang it to us when our father was gone."

"I thought I recognized it, but I just couldn't place the tune, and the words wouldn't come to me," the hunter remarked.

Rosabela continued to hum the song, and Wavren scooped out two bowls of jungle stew and gave one to his sister. No sooner had they sat down to eat than Stonetalon came through the brush with his nose leading the way. The bear had an excellent sense of smell and excellent timing for dinner. Wavren pulled the pot down from its place over the fire and let the bear have at it in order to prevent him from overturning it and spilling the stew into the fire. The bear eagerly gobbled up the stew and began looking for more. Wavren knew it was pointless to deny Stonetalon whatever food he wanted, so he sighed and gave the remainder of his portion to the bear. When Stonetalon was done, he headed for Rosabela's bowl, but quickly turned aside when she glared at him and growled a very bear-like message that must have promised a long and painful fight if he tried to take her bowl. Wavren sat half-amazed and half-confused with a half-full stomach. Rosabela returned to her bowl as Stonetalon headed back into the woods for more scavenging.

"She-bears and she-elves have many things in common. Never mess with our young, never take our food, and never forget who the boss of the den is," she said between mouthfuls of stew.

Wavren' jaw dropped. He realized right then that he had many things to learn about life. It was even more confusing that, somehow, these things seemed common knowledge to his sister. He also thought that if Gaedron were here, he would agree. No wonder Gaedron was a loner. Women were complex and unpredictable.

* * *

Barely two miles from Wavren and Rosabela's camp were four orc scouts moving through the forest with amazing speed and stealth. They were heading back from the outpost where they had recently found three out of four of their brethren quite dead. The scouts could not tell exactly what had happened, but two of the dead orcs had been killed mysteriously, and one had apparently been mauled by a bear. The report would be sketchy at best, but they knew their leader would want the information while it was fresh.

The four scouts made it to the base camp in record time and were immediately escorted to Neggish Grimtusk, a particularly sadistic orc with large, protruding lower tusks that gave him a never-ending scowl. They came to their commander and took a knee in unison as a show of respect.

Neggish crossed his thick gray-green arms over his leather cuirass and growled, "Report!"

The leader of the scout platoon stood and looked his master in the eye. "Our outpost has been sacked. The two elven scouts we were sent to escort to you are gone, and three of the orcs are dead."

Neggish frowned even deeper than usual but remained calm. "What of the fourth?"

"It was obvious that he was taken. We could find no trace of him, his armor, or his weapons. We did notice many beast tracks and two parallel lines that lead from the outpost toward the elven town of Forestedge," he stated with confidence.

"Were they killed by warriors with swords and axes or at range by elven longbows?" the commander inquired.

"Neither sword cuts nor arrows were found. Two had been killed by something else, and one was mauled by beasts," the scout replied.

"Explain how the other two were killed," Neggish demanded.

"There was a scorch mark surrounding a hole that pierced armor and flesh alike, but nothing burned. It was as if the elves drilled holes through their armor with a fiery auger. I cannot explain beyond that," he returned.

Neggish thought for some time and then dismissed his scouts with a wave of his hand. He was perplexed by the description. He had been prepared for the possibility that his outposts could be discovered, but not that his men would lose the initial engagement or that one of his orcs might be captured alive. He knew that elves were clever foes, but he had no idea that they could have so easily taken out his elite scouts. He was also concerned about the magic that was known to be powerful among the elves. But something was not right with the two killed by fire. They were not killed by the great bolts of fire that traditional mages preferred.

He needed to know how his orc scouts had been so easily defeated. Perhaps the beast tracks were the key. It was not unheard of for the Dae'gon Alliance troops to have beast pets. In fact, orcs also tamed various beasts for fighting. Nearly every race in the realms did. Although all of his men were scouts, he had known several beast handlers who were very cunning warriors. Clearly, he would have to investigate this matter further, but first he had to report this to his leader who would need this information to determine the next step of the invasion. After all, bad news never gets better with age and timing was critical in war.

Neggish Grimtusk had never been known for great intellect, but he was a shrewd survivor. This was often the case with orcish leaders. Those who made critical mistakes were often killed on the spot, poisoned, or slain while sleeping. Knowing full well that Gorka, his regional commander, would not be pleased, Neggish sent his report by courier, not willing to be in the wake of his commander's fury. It was certain that his courier would not be coming back once he delivered the bad news, but that was an acceptable loss in orcish society and expected in the life of a courier. The scout commander never gave it a second thought.

One day later, Neggish received word back from Gorka. The message was clear that failure would not be tolerated. The dispatch was one simple sentence that read, "*I will see you after the new moon.*" The moon would be all but gone in two weeks, and Neggish knew his life depended on having better news to report by then. The unspoken message was also clear since the words were penned in a brownish-red ink. More than likely it was the blood of the courier who had not come back with the return dispatch.

Neggish had personally assembled the four best orcs under his command as platoon leaders. Each had a warfare specialty and was given a codename based on that skill. Blackbane was an assassin who preferred the use of toxins to slow, weaken, or simply kill his enemies. Nightshade was more gifted in the art of stealth than even expert rogues who could hide in almost broad daylight. Rumor was that his skills were magically enhanced by wretched undead wizardry. Shadowblade was a weapons master. His combat tactics were flawless, and his battlefield strategies were drawn from a myriad of experiences learned while fighting the Dae'gon Alliance his entire life. Last was Doppelganger, an orc who had the ability to shape-shift. His power was rumored to be nothing more than arcane illusions, but some believed evil druids had trained him and that he could become nearly any beast or humanoid. As Neggish considered each orc and his specialty, he smiled broadly, knowing that he had done well selecting his subordinate officers.

Neggish called a meeting of his scouting platoon leaders, who assembled in the feast hall. Each orc had the same dark leather armor that had been crafted specifically for the scout who wore it. They looked fearsome, and he knew each orc took pride in conveying that fear. Still, the armor was unprecedented for two reasons. The first reason was that orcs were rarely disciplined enough to serve in an organized military force. They preferred the chaos of overwhelming numbers to win victories. Secondly, orcs rarely had the financial backing to provide finely crafted and individually tailored matching armor for soldiers. The norm was to have scavenged armor from victorious battles that was often damaged or too small for the hulking orcs. As a result, most of the patchwork armor was altered to cover vital organs but not much else, leaving many holes for enemies to take advantage of. Not his scouts. His scouts were the best and deserved the best in equipment. Ultimately, Neggish thought his scouts were more than a ragtag band of invaders. He thought they were professionals, and that was how he treated them. This was yet another unprecedented aspect of the situation.

One by one, the platoon leaders took their places and waited for their commander to speak. Each orc was anxious to get back to his assignments and uncomfortable in the presence of their volatile commander. It was better to send messengers with reports of failure than to come in person, but each orc knew better than to defy the official summons from their commander.

"I called you here to discuss the failure at outpost three," Neggish started.

Unconsciously, three of the platoon leaders slid away from the fourth, who had been in charge of overseeing outpost three and charged with leading the initial scout mission. The orc in question, Shadowblade, sat unmoving. He dared not even breathe, knowing that anything could set his commander off.

Neggish continued, "All we know for certain is that the outpost was sacked, three members of Shadowblade's group are dead, and one was captured. The two prisoners we had in custody were released or escaped, and tracks appear to point to Forestedge."

The three platoon leaders who had previously slid away from the focus of Grimtusk's anger now seemed to be leaning slightly away from the responsible orc. It was as if they had looked into the future and witnessed Neggish unleashing his fury on Shadowblade with such reckless abandon that all suffered a grisly and painful death. Still, the orc lieutenant sat motionless and now dared not blink.

The commander asked, "Shadowblade, do you have anything to contribute to the situation at hand?"

"Commander," he said, "there is no additional information available; however, I have a plan that should remedy the situation. If you will give me access to our resources and three days to execute the mission, I will personally deal with the problem."

Commander Grimtusk smiled in such a way that his oversized tusks made it look like he was snarling. He asked sardonically, "If I give you full access to our scouts, supplies, and three days to work, you can rebuild my outpost, raise three scouts from the dead, recapture the two escaped elves, free our orc brother from Forestedge, and erase the knowledge of our presence from the elves?"

Shadowblade had fallen right into a battle of wits with his commander. If he said no, then he would be torn apart by Neggish for failing to live up to his word. If he said yes, he would be torn apart for promising the impossible. He said the only thing he could think of at that moment: "If I can't convince you, then I expect death, but allow me to share my plan with you. We already have our best agents in place, and we can move forward with our conquest."

Neggish Grimtusk wanted to kill the arrogant orc so badly that he could hear his own blood pulsing through his veins, but Neggish was no fool. He had to allow his followers room for improvisation, room to maneuver. He had freethinking orcs under his command, not the uneducated fodder that could be easily replaced. In addition, he had risen to great levels of power by employing those free thinkers. The trick was maintaining the balance between severe discipline for failure and opportunities for redemption. In this case, Shadowblade's punishment for failure should be death, which had to be weighed against the glory he might achieve for Grimtusk if he managed to pull off a miracle. Shadowblade was a resourceful tactician, and with the full complement of Grimtusk's forces, he just might be able to salvage his own life and the reputation of the elite scouts under Grimtusk. This gave the scout commander an incentive to listen, even if it meant killing the platoon leader afterwards.

"Speak, but know that my patience is nearing an end and *death* constantly whispers in my ear that you would be better off in the abyss. *Death* tells me that you should be his already."

Shadowblade began without hesitation: "My plan is all about stealth. This is what I need."

Chapter 9
The Hunt

The twins had scoured the area for signs of their enemies. Two days of searching had turned up little new information about the location of Neggish Grimtusk. They had visited the outpost where their last fight with the orcs took place, but it had been cleansed. The dead bodies were gone. The outpost supplies and shelters were gone. Even the signs of battle were gone. This was amazing to Wavren, who was trained to track as a professional hunter. He had scouted the area, the outlying perimeter, and even the narrow trails made by deer and boar that were indigenous to the forest. He had found nothing.

Rosabela had followed along quietly, not sure how to contribute to the process of locating the enemy. Tracking was indeed her brother's specialty. Hours passed, and as boredom set in, she began foraging for herbs. This area was lush with briarthorn and *kingsblood*, which she needed to make healing potions. She also spent some time fishing, while Wavren and Stonetalon were methodically searching for clues. The mission seemed to be heading for failure.

"Rosie, do you think the interrogators were given false information about Grimtusk?" Wavren asked.

"According to Councilman Kalin, the information was volunteered. That makes me think it was accurate, but who knows the mind of an orc?" she returned.

"I just can't help but think that we are wasting our time here. I should have found something by now. I haven't seen a footprint, a broken twig, or even a discarded bone from orc rations. It is so empty of orc sign that I am beginning to wonder if we actually fought here or if we somehow imagined it all," the hunter mused.

"Well, I am sure we fought here," Rosabela said, as she mentally retraced her steps from Forestedge to this location.

Wavren nodded and tried to think like an orc as he paced the area. He just couldn't imagine a band of orcs being so thorough with hiding their camp or even their tracks. Orcs were bold and fearsome. As a race, they were best suited as warriors with huge muscles and limited patience. It just didn't make sense that these scouts were virtually invisible. Orcs were violent and aggressive, which should make them predictable. On top of those facts, orcs were heavy humanoids known for stomping around haphazardly, leaving deep tracks from their easily three-hundred-pound frames. Tracking them should have been easy.

Wavren thought out loud, "If I was an orc, what would I do? I would never run and hide. I would rather muster my forces and attack. I would make my enemies suffer for killing and capturing my comrades. I would want revenge. Yes, revenge is the key."

Rosabela noticed Wavren as he stopped his seemingly endless survey of the area. She noticed that he paused as if his mind were so engaged that his body could not draw on its resources. She became suddenly aware that something was wrong.

"What is it, Wav?" she asked quietly.

Wavren could not answer. He was so immersed in his thoughts that he could not afford distraction.

"Wavren," she pressed.

The veil of confusion lifted slowly from the hunter's mind. He took the one piece of information he was confident of and began to build. Revenge was the key. Wavren knew the orcs would want revenge. He remembered that the councilman had said that, according to the prisoner, the scout commander, Neggish Grimtusk, would be east of the outpost. If that were true, then the orcs would have found him and Rosabela by now. The orcs would have jumped at the chance to get revenge on any elf, but they would have been particularly eager to kill the twins if they knew that they had personally sacked the outpost.

Wavren was on to something, but he still couldn't figure out why there had been no contact with the orc scouts. Even more bizarre was the obvious lack of any past orc presence. In fact, the hunter's only clue that he was in the location where he and Rosabela had fought was the nearly obliterated twin marks made by the field-expedient stretcher that Rosabela dragged all the way to Forestedge with the heavy orc prisoner in tow.

Wavren mumbled, "Forestedge …the deep twin marks … the heavy orc prisoner … heavy …"

"What did you say?" Rosabela asked.

"Is it possible?" the hunter wondered.

Rosabela, confused, said, "Wav, what are you saying?"

Wavren looked stunned, as if someone had thrown frigid water in his face. He turned and immediately began running back toward Forestedge at top speed. He called to Stonetalon with a sharp whistle through his fingers and unslung his deadly blunderbuss. Rosabela sprinted after him.

"What is it, Wav?" the druid begged through rapidly increasing breaths.

"Pray that I am wrong, sister, but I think the high councilman is in league with the Bloodcrest Forces," he huffed. "He might be an orc!"

"How can that be?" Rosabela asked.

"Call it instinct, but our orders came from the high councilman, and the orcs are all gone without a trace," he panted.

"There is a traitor among us, and I have a feeling he is a wolf in sheep's clothing."

"What does that prove?" she asked.

"Nothing. I said it was instinct … a gut feeling … a piece of the puzzle," he gasped.

Rosabela might not understand how her brother *knew* the councilman was involved, but she fully understood his body language and the urgency of getting back to Forestedge. Now was not the time for questions. Rosabela had to focus on running, and focus she did.

Wavren was moving at a full sprint with Stonetalon lumbering along behind him. Rosabela was barely keeping the pace as her look of focus turned to grim determination. The twins pushed their limits, knowing they would never make it to Forestedge at the speed they were running. It simply wasn't possible to sprint the distance they had taken a full day to walk. Yet onward they moved at breakneck speed. The trio ran as a pack of wolves in pursuit of a herd of deer. They drew strength from each other as they flew down the road. It was a hunter skill Wavren had learned. Their determination to see the edge of town was such that a synergy of motion and breathing enhanced their bodies beyond their physical limits. This enhanced speed lasted until they saw elven corpses.

Barely ten minutes before they hit the edge of town, Wavren noticed four dead elves. Two were scouts from Forestedge. Both were dead with dozens of crossbow bolts protruding from their bodies. Both scouts had their weapons still in their sheaths.

Not far from their bodies, the hunter found an elven warrior lying in a pool of deep crimson. The various wounds he had sustained before collapsing indicated that he'd been slain by overwhelming odds. His finely crafted elven broadsword was still in his hand and lay untouched, not far from his severed arm. The warrior's shield was mutilated beyond repair, having turned dozens of deadly blows.

The last body was that of an elven mage. Although his body was mutilated and dismembered, Wavren could tell that the wizard had cast several spells before being cut down. There were at least forty small puddles where the attacking forces had been held in place by a frost spell, and there were no a leaves or bark remaining on any trees in a perfect circle around the dead spell-wieldier. Clearly, the wizard had seen his own end. He had chosen to immolate the invaders with arcane explosions as his final act of defiance. He died a hero just as the warrior had. The fact that concerned Wavren more than the dead elves was that there were no dead enemies. Not one single dead orc could be found.

Wavren and Rosabela moved forward with caution and found scores of dead elves in the same group configuration. There were always two scouts, one warrior, and a mage, just as the councilman had decreed. Wavren let out a low growl as he grew more and more convinced that the councilman was behind this. If he was, the hunter meant to make him pay.

The town of Forestedge was still standing when the twins arrived. Wavren had half-expected it to be a smoldering pile of rubble littered with elven corpses from one end to the other. Instead, the townsfolk were milling about, trying to prepare defenses for another attack. The hunter let out a sigh of relief and headed directly for the town hall where High Councilman Kalin was usually found.

"Wav, we don't have enough information to accuse the councilman," Rosabela warned.

He moved forward with no response.

"Wav, did you hear me?" she asked emphatically.

He paused outside the building in the large, open courtyard and took a deep breath. He had always been the more impulsive of the two, just as Rosabela had always been the more patient. Deep inside, he knew the councilman was involved, but he also knew that his sister was right. With a great battle raging inside, Wavren turned away from the town hall and headed for the jail, where he hoped to find some answers.

Rosabela was truly proud of the maturity her brother had developed in the last few months, but deep inside, she seethed with anger that she had probably saved the life of a traitor who might somehow be an orc. She decided, at that moment, that if she could find evidence against Kalin, she would personally proffer charges, and if he tried to escape, she would kill him herself.

The guards had abandoned the jail with the first call to arms, but the door was still locked and intact. Wavren called to his ally. Stonetalon came forward and leaned on the huge oak door, but it held. The hunter stepped back and fired two shots into each hinge. The mighty bear pushed and the door creaked, groaned, and then buckled. The trio moved inside. The corridor was dimly lit and smelled of sweat and excrement, but it hardly mattered. Rosabela came in behind her brother, and together they moved past several cells. All seemed in order until they saw the orc prisoner from their first battle. He had been quietly assassinated amid the confusion of the attack. The low growl rumbled out of Wavren's throat. Rosabela stepped aside and let her brother pass. She knew where he was going, and she knew nothing she could say would stop him.

High Councilman Kalin was meeting with his security advisors about the defenses when the large double doors to his meeting hall were thrown wide open. Wavren and Rosabela stepped through and did not look happy.

"Ah, the Protectors have returned. I assume you have Neggish Grimtusk's head and a report of the enemy's whereabouts," Kalin commented.

Wavren glowered and answered the councilman through clenched teeth: "We have a report of the enemy, but it is not Neggish Grimtusk's head we seek."

There was a moment of confusion and silence. Kalin waited impassively and seemed very much at ease, in spite of the hunter's obvious rage. He waited for another moment and then went back to reviewing the situation with his advisors as if Wavren was nothing more than an annoyance.

Wavren spoke: "The orcish outpost we hit is now gone without a trace. There is no sign of it ever existing. No tracks or even blood from the fight could be found. We searched for Neggish Grimtusk, and he was not east of the outpost. In fact, there was no sign of any orc in the area."

Kalin didn't look up as he spoke: "Perhaps the prisoner lied." He went back to discussing the defenses.

Wavren spoke again: "The prisoner is dead. He was assassinated during the attack. Your forward scout teams were also slain. I saw them just outside of town."

Kalin had a look of sadness, as if the loss of so many elves was tragic. The slender elf sat back in his chair with a thump. The predictable creaking of the chair made Wavren glare at the councilman, who asked, "Do you have anything else to report?"

Wavren noticed that the guards were gathering now, and the advisors seemed more than a little annoyed. Kalin remained calm. Rosabela nodded to Wavren, ready to fight if need be. Wavren was infuriated, but he was powerless to act without being forced to fight everyone in the room. He elected discretion and turned to leave.

Kalin didn't even notice the twins leave as he went back to discussing the recovery plan to get the town back to normal.

Rosabela smiled as her brother moved out into the courtyard. She called to him saying, "I'm proud of you, Wav. You did the only thing you could do."

"No, Rosie, I did exactly as I meant to do. I know the truth, and now Kalin knows that I do. We aren't finished here, not by a long shot, but before we're done, we will have Kalin right where we want him," the hunter replied, "and then he dies."

"I still don't fully understand what you are planning, but I trust your judgment, brother. What's our next step?" she asked.

"We need back up. I don't think Kalin is in this alone," Wavren said. "Then we need to wait for nightfall. I want to check out the councilman's office."

"We can't break into his office and rummage though his desk. That would be dishonorable, and we would probably get caught," Rosabela stated.

"I don't plan to get caught, and I don't plan to rummage. I just want to sit in his chair," the hunter replied with a smile.

"His chair?" she asked.

Wavren replied with a nod, and Rosabela started to catch on.

* * *

Gaedron had been running missions for the Dae'gon Alliance in Jaggedspine Valley when he found a message at the inn where he had been staying. Gaedron could tell that the message had come by way of messenger through the Dae'gon Alliance Mage Guild due to the recently dried ink and the smell of sulfur on the envelope. In essence, the messenger had been transported across the Great Sea by magic to expedite delivery. The envelope had been sealed with the Clan Ursa symbol, a bear on its hind legs with a bull's eye background. It was obviously from Wavren. He took the envelope up to his room in the inn and closed the door to ensure he had privacy. He opened the letter and read it by candlelight.

> *Master Hunter Gaedron of Dragonforge,*
>
> *Forestedge has been compromised. The elves there are in league with the Bloodcrest Forces, and I need your help. I cannot explain all of the details at this time, but be assured that I cannot trust anyone other than you. Make haste, old friend, the fate of the Dae'gon Alliance is at risk.*
>
> *P.S. Don't forget your Blunderbuss and Ol' Blackmaw. We will need them both.*
>
> *Wavren of Celes'tia*

"Durned fool elves done made a deal wit' da devil," Gaedron said to himself. "Seems like the minute I leave the Western Kingdom, the whole place falls apart an' I git called to go fix it, but that's what I git fer bein' friend o' them long-eared elf types. Well, I better pack some hot spice fer the road, 'cause I'm knowin' how bland food can be when ya got a silky soft stomach like them elves do. All a bunch of weak mama's boys if'n I ever did see one."

Within two days, the gruff dwarven hunter arrived at Darkshore and the port of Port Archer. He was welcomed by many local townspeople as both friend and hero, but time was short and Gaedron had to make his way south to Forestedge. Being a dwarf allowed for many things, including always being busy, in a hurry, and somewhat less than polite. This worked well for Gaedron, who appreciated the thanks for his years of service to the Dae'gon Alliance and the Protectors of the Vale, but was always uncomfortable in large crowds, especially when that crowd consisted of non-dwarves. Not that he disliked elves, humans, and gnomes, but he just felt misunderstood by them.

Gaedron was back on the road in less than a quarter hour when he heard his name being called. Gaedron looked about, but saw nothing. He called for Ol' Blackmaw and unslung his weapon. "Who's that?" he asked.

"Put your gun away," the voice said. "I am no enemy."

Gaedron sensed the voice was coming from his left among the dense thicket, but he was still unable to see anyone. He did recognize the voice, although it was altered slightly. The voice was elven, and although it had a feline, purring undertone, the dwarf was confident that it belonged to a certain, rather annoying, elven druid.

"Da'Shar, unless ye wanna be a permanent trophy on me wall in Dragonforge, I suggest ya make yerself seen," the hunter called.

Da'Shar came out of the shadows of the woods. He was in his dark windwraith form, which was perfect for moving with stealth through the jungle. He noticed that Gaedron had his blunderbuss aimed his way and that the huge white bear was ready to charge. Da'Shar knew the dwarf would never attack, but the sight of the massive bear and the grizzled old dwarf made a profound impression. He changed into his elven form to ease the tension.

"What are ye about?" the hunter asked, lowering his weapon.

"I was wondering the same of you, Gaedron of Dragonforge. Shouldn't you be back in the Eastern Kingdoms, killing all manner of wildlife?" the druid asked sarcastically.

"Nah, I came to the Western Kingdom to hunt big, black cats," the dwarf replied, equally sarcastic.

"You haven't changed a bit, have you?" the elf asked. "Still a savage killer in Dae'gon Alliance clothing?"

"Aye, but though I be a savage killer, I also have friends who be needing me, so be gone lest I let Ol' Blackmaw have his way wit ya," the dwarf threatened.

Da'Shar suddenly turned pale. "Don't tell me that you are going to Forestedge."

Gaedron didn't turn pale; he turned red and then stormed off, muttering, "Dern fool elves, this is what I git fer choosin' the life o' a Protector instead of a miner or a smithy."

In spite of their differences, Da'Shar and Gaedron traveled the road more or less together. They stopped only once for a quick snack of dried fruit and salted pork, so that by morning, they reached the outskirts of Forestedge. It hadn't changed much in the last decade except for one thing. Both Da'Shar and Gaedron got the feeling that they were not very welcome. The people seemed on edge, and even though both were lifelong Protectors of the Vale and heroes, neither seemed to be treated as such.

Rosabela and Wavren met their mentors soon after their arrival, but chose to lead them back out of town to a small encampment before sharing any information.

Chapter 10
Unearthing the Truth

Night had fallen by the time the foursome had moved out of the town limits to a small alcove cut into the hills. Wavren started a fire and set up a large pot for cooking. Rosabela rummaged through her pouches and produced wild rosemary and sea salt for flavor, as well as a bit of willow tree bark to take the aches and pains of a long journey away from the travelers. Gaedron immediately dug into his pack and produced three deep red peppers that seemed small and dry, but were unmistakably known for potency. Wavren crossed his arms and frowned deeply. The dwarf threw them into the pot in spite of the silent protest and added various tubers he had been saving for just such an occasion.

"Master Gaedron and I have come a long way to help you with no idea why we were called here. Can you tell us what the urgent need is?" Da'Shar inquired.

Rosabela smiled and said, "We believe there is treachery afoot in Forestedge such that few can be trusted. It goes beyond fighting enemy skirmishers. We had to be cautious when you arrived, and we must be cautious now, but this place should be free of prying eyes and traitorous ears. Wavren will explain everything."

"Aye, let the boy speak an' I'll tend the pot here. Who likes jungle stew? It be me own special recipe an' there be plenty enough fer us all," Gaedron announced.

Wavren winced at the thought of his mentor's cooking. He composed himself and recalled their story from the time they departed Celes'tia. After several minutes, Da'Shar began rubbing his brow in deep thought. Gaedron was unaffected, seemingly interested in nothing but his stew. Wavren remained silent upon completing the story.

"Well?" Rosabela asked after a long silence, half-expecting the two mentors to sound their battle cries or stomp about in fury.

"This is a tightly spun web of events and deception," the older druid remarked.

"I say we kill some orcs since we're here, but ya got nothin' to go on and tryin' to prove that elves be in on it won't be well received. We need proof," Gaedron returned. "Who wants a bowl o' me best stew?"

Da'Shar rolled his eyes and went back to rubbing his brow. Wavren and Rosabela exchanged looks of confusion.

"Master Da'Shar, don't you believe me?" Rosabela asked, pain in her voice.

"Dear child, of course I believe you, but as the gruff old hunter so eloquently stated, we need proof. Without substantial proof, we would be nothing more than fools who accused well-respected elves at best. At worst, we would be murderers if things got out of hand," he stated, nodding in the dwarf's direction.

"Like I said a'fore, lassie, gotta git 'em red-handed if'n ya goin' fer elves, but there always be open season on orcs! I say we kill orcs," Gaedron said while scooping out stew for the group.

Wavren smiled at his sister, who nodded back. There was proof, but getting it was not going to be easy. Thinking back to the slender elf councilman in his fine, high-backed chair, Wavren was sure he could convince Gaedron. Da'Shar might be a different story. For this reason, Rosabela would have to make a miracle happen, while he focused on his mentor.

The darkness of night had already covered Forestedge completely, but the foursome waited until just after midnight to creep back into town. Wavren and Rosabela had hoped the locals would be in bed and fast asleep when they returned. They all knew that the fewer witnesses, the better. Forestedge's late-night shift had just changed, and the elven guards were fresh and alert. The group moved toward them.

"Halt and state your business," a sturdy warrior challenged as the group approached.

Wavren called out, "We are Protectors of the Vale in the service of Forestedge. We have returned with reinforcements from abroad."

"Approach and be recognized," the warrior directed, as the druids and hunters moved into the firelight of the guard's torch.

"It is good to see you all," the warrior stated. "I know Rosabela, Wavren, and Master Da'Shar, but who is your dwarven companion?"

Wavren spoke formally: "This is Gaedron of Dragonforge, Protector of the Vale and Master Hunter of the Dae'gon Alliance."

Gaedron extended his hand in friendship, and the elf grasped it firmly.

"I know of you," the guard said humbly. "You are the hero of Bladerun Bay. It is my honor to meet you. I am called Bray'min."

Gaedron's thoughts raced back to the naval battle where he fought alongside men and elves and nearly died. He remembered the rumble of the long nines as they blasted the enemy ship he was standing on. He remembered the cold blackness of the water as he sank below the surface. He would have drowned had Ol' Blackmaw not dragged him out of the water. The moment passed.

Gaedron looked into the guard's eyes and said, "I was

there, but I be no more a hero than any who fought there beside me."

"Although we never met, I saw you go down with that hell-spawned ship as I watched from across the bow of the *Crusader*. You were thought to be lost, but not before you took a dozen or more orcs, undead, and tauren with you. Your name was called with the bell tolls of the entire Dae'gon Alliance Navy as a final honor. The death of a hero and always to be remembered," the warrior stated with sincere respect.

"Aye, that's what they always be thinkin', but n'er count Gaedron out till ye see me dead and rottin' corpse fer yerself. Just fer the sake o' knowin' me ally saved me that day, an' many since then, but that be the way o' things," the hunter returned with a wink and a cocky smile. "Ain't the first time the bells tolled fer me, and I'm guessin' it won't be the last."

"If ever you need my service, noble Gaedron, know that Bray'min of Forestedge will stand with you until death takes me or time ends," the warrior swore.

Gaedron smiled and walked past. Wavren and Rosabela followed the dwarf, and Da'Shar stood awestruck, having heard less than a handful of elves ever swear a life debt in the thousands of years he had lived. Among those who swore, he had never heard an elf swear allegiance to a dwarf. He doubted that it would ever happen again.

Wavren motioned for Gaedron to follow him and headed for the chambers of the high councilman, while Rosabela headed to the opposite edge of town with Da'Shar in tow.

"Boy-o, I hope ye know what yer doin'. Politicians don' much care fer common folk pokin' around in their business an' breakin' into the councilman's office won't get us invited to supper," the dwarf said with measured tones of concern.

Wavren moved silently from building to building until they stood at the town hall's great door. Gaedron looked around and motioned for Wavren to proceed when he was sure no one was watching. Wavren tried the door, but it was locked. Gaedron came forward and produced an odd-looking device that looked like a miniature spring-loaded letter opener. He slid the odd contraption into the lock, and after a slight whirring sound and a click, the door opened.

"Dwarven engineering, laddie," Gaedron whispered.

"I know, I know," the elf said, "'tis the way o' the future."

The two walked inside and approached the high councilman's desk. Gaedron paused and shrugged, not knowing what to do next. Wavren motioned to the exquisite high-backed chair behind the desk. The old dwarf looked dumbfounded and stood motionless.

"Sit in the chair," Wavren whispered.

"Fer what?" the dwarf whispered back.

"Just sit in the stupid chair," the elf repeated, almost too loudly.

The dwarf shook his head and walked behind the desk. He pulled the heavy chair out and plopped down.

"Get up," Wavren said with a smile.

Gaedron stood up, and Wavren plopped down on the chair with a silly, ever-broadening smile. He stood up again and sat down again.

"Are ye daft, fool boy? What are ye about?" the dwarf begged.

"I weigh about one hundred seventy pounds; what about you?" Wavren asked.

"Fer heaven's sake, what does it matter?" the dwarf spat through clenched teeth.

"The high councilman's chair groans when he sits," was the elf's reply. "How much do you weigh?"

The dwarf was perplexed but answered, "About two hunnerd."

"You're a dwarven engineer; how much weight should this chair hold?" the elf asked.

Gaedron scratched his beard and finally concluded, "More 'an any elf can weigh."

* * *

Rosabela led her mentor out of town on the opposite side

from where they had entered. Da'Shar knew Forestedge well, but he could not begin to guess where she was leading him. The only thing on this side of town was the graveyard, and he could think of no place he wanted to avoid more than the resting place of the dead. This was especially true at midnight. Restless spirits were never pleasant, and the thought of encountering one made the seasoned druid shiver as if a cold chill crept up his spine.

Rosabela took him through the graveyard and beyond it for nearly a mile. This place was not familiar to Da'Shar, but he was glad to have passed the elven graveyard. He immediately noticed a small clearing not far ahead. This patch of ground had no markers, mausoleums, or headstones, but he sensed the dreary pull of the dead on his spirit. They were standing on unhallowed ground where enemies of the Dae'gon Alliance were buried in an unceremonious manner. Although apprehensive, Da'Shar trusted in his young pupil. Rosabela walked on until she was in the middle of the clearing.

"We are here," she said.

"Very well," the elder druid stated. "Now, why have we come?"

Rosabela opened her backpack and withdrew a large, silk-shrouded book. It was the grand book of alchemy that Da'Shar had given her as his last gift before departing Celes'tia for Port Archer. She unwrapped the tome and began searching through pages.

"Here it is," she said as she pointed to one of the last pages. The writing was in an ancient dialect of the night elves that few could read and even fewer could pronounce in the manner required to invoke the potion's properties. It was old even by Da'Shar's measure.

Da'Shar planted his staff into the soft ground with little effort and whispered, "*Illumani.*" The crystal at the top of the staff glowed a faint green and produced enough light for the druid to clearly see the words Rosabela was pointing at. He held the heavy volume of alchemical recipes in one hand and traced the words with the other. Slowly his eyes widened, and his impassive expression turned downward in disapproval.

"This is a recipe for making a potion that conjures the spirits of the dead. This is necromancy," Da'Shar commented. "Dear child, you must only use this potion with approval from the Druidic Conclave, and I am certain they would never grant you permission without reviewing the reason in committee. Even then they would probably refuse to grant you the right to awaken the dead, whose eternal rest is a sacred thing."

"I understand the policy of the conclave regarding this issue. However, under exigent circumstances, two Druids of the Grove, who are also Protectors of the Vale, can create the potion and conduct the 'commune with the dead' ritual if the information is critical to survival or security of the Elven Nations," the younger druid nearly quoted from the bylaws of alchemy doctrine.

"I know the doctrine, but you do not have sufficient cause," the elder druid said, "and the risk is far too great in this ceremony."

"I know that Wavren seems more like the dwarven mentor he follows than an elf. He may not rely on wisdom and intellect as you and I do, but his instinct and intuition are powerful. He rarely understands how he knows the things that he knows, but he is convinced in this, and we are charged with proving or disproving his conclusions," she explained with more passion than impartial judgment. Her faith in her twin brother was absolute, and her determination to convince her mentor was resolute.

"And what of the risk, young one? What if the spirit is an evil one who seeks revenge for its death? Are you prepared to deal with that?" Da'Shar queried.

"There is no uncertainty here. The spirit is that of an evil being. It is the spirit of an orc who we captured and interred with the local authorities. This orc was killed during the invasion of Forestedge, and I believe he was killed because he had information about the enemy's future wide-scale invasion plans. I also believe he can confirm what Wavren suspects about the high councilman," Rosabela said without fear.

Da'Shar stared at his student. His eyes peered into her soul, not unlike their first meeting. He searched for doubt or fear or any sign of uncertainty. He saw the perfect integration of a brilliant mind and an iron will. Rosabela was a fortress of determination with no flaw or weakness, yet still he peered deeper. His consciousness left his body and pierced that of his student like an arrow shot from an elven longbow. Rosabela stood frozen as the intrusion rushed past her mental defenses, now left willingly open. She had nothing to hide and bared her soul under Da'Shar's scrutiny.

Da'Shar found the inside of Rosabela's mind to be a lush circle of massive oaks with a small, clear blue pool of water in its center. It was a reflection of the druid grove where she had been trained. He moved in closer and saw his student fishing in the glade.

"Welcome, master," her consciousness said.

"There are no secrets here, and all things are evident to me, so speak plainly," he whispered, not wanting to disrupt the peaceful reverence of Rosabela's sanctuary.

"I have no secrets, master. I have full faith and confidence that you will see as I see while you are here," she returned with a gentle smile.

"You have mastered your focus and concentration just as I have instructed you to do. You have found inner peace at a very young age, and for that, I am proud. But now I must ask you to show me what you see if we proceed with speaking with the dead. This could be painful for you, but trust in me," the druid urged in his fatherly tone.

Rosabela smiled and pulled the leather-armored pauldrons she wore over her head. She pulled her shirt to the side, revealing the white mark of her master that was now a permanent reminder of her lineage to Da'Shar and the Druids of the Grove of Celes'tia. "Can there be any doubt that dedication and trust often come at a price?" she said with a dutiful expression on her face.

The master druid now wore a dual expression of pride in his student and of sadness that he had hurt her in the past and would now hurt her again. He began to whisper words in an ancient tongue that Rosabela could not understand. The sanctuary that she had built in her mind was now gone with a rush of wind. The sky in Rosabela's mind grew dark, and a new scene formed.

To Rosabela's amazement, the new scene was that of the Elven Kingdoms, but as she had never seen them in her life. The landscape was beautiful beyond measure. There were no palisades or fortifications, which now protected the land from invaders. There were no modern buildings or structures. She saw only the ancient trees, which grew into massive communities where the elves lived thousands of years ago. The only words she had to describe the scene were joy, peace, and harmony.

Da'Shar spoke: "This is the elven past as I have seen it in my youth; it is part of the collective unconscious that all elves retain from the beginning of time. This was when the lands were pure, before the legions of the Bloodcrest Forces polluted the world. It has changed greatly in my lifetime and will continue to change throughout yours."

The lovely elven lands slowly flew away like leaves caught in the fall wind as Da'Shar whispered the ancient words again. The scene in Rosabela's mind shifted forward to the recent past. Along the way, Rosabela noticed that she felt weakened as Da'Shar apparently drew on her mental strength to invoke the spells in her mind.

Rosabela recognized the scene forming in her mind's eye as the events starting with her selection as a Protector of the Vale and ending with the arrival of Da'Shar and Gaedron to Forestedge. She saw herself move through town and then stop just past the elven graveyard where she knew her body still stood. It was all very surreal. It took an enormous amount of discipline to maintain the understanding that she was still in her subconscious mind, not in reality. These events were memories and nothing more.

The elder druid called again to the arcane powers, and again Rosabela felt drained, as if her life force was being extracted from her body with each of her mentor's incantations. She felt dizzy and even nauseous. The world was spinning while the dark sky swirled with a myriad of colors. Rosabela pinched her eyes closed tightly to avoid the madness that was causing her vertigo.

"Da'Shar," Rosabela gasped, "when will it stop?"

"Nature is tied into all things, but divination is not easily accessed," he replied. "This may take a few moments."

"What are you trying to divine?" she asked with clenched teeth.

"The future of Forestedge as you will see it if we proceed with communing with the dead," he replied.

"It feels like it is killing me," she said weakly.

"It is," Da'Shar returned, "in a manner of speaking. A druid's power comes from the flora and fauna of the forest as well as the four elements. I am seeking answers within you, Rosabela, and thus you are the source of power for these answers. Your very life essence is being drained away in order to divine the nature of your decision to commune with the dead.

"Know that this is our only recourse without the Druidic Council present to authorize us to proceed. If we must invoke necromantic powers, then we must do so righteously. Without knowing the consequences beforehand, we can be charged with treason against Nature by the Druidic Council. We would become criminals hunted like vermin and slain as such."

Rosabela winced and trembled while saying, "I do not understand. Aren't we ultimately trying to divine information from a dead orc?"

"You are the center point of time regarding this decision," he said with no emotion. "You are the critical junction where our future splits like a fork in the road. If we choose the path you have suggested, then the divination will take us to the outcome of that decision. If we choose the other option, not to commune with the spirit, then our future will continue along a different path. It is one that follows the natural order of events already past. This is the nature of divination. This is why you now suffer."

Rosabela's head felt like it might explode while her body felt like it was withering away. She could not tell if it was real pain or part of the divination in her mind, but it was tremendous. Just as she was convinced that she would not live through the ordeal, the landscape changed. The journey from present to future was complete, and as the drain on her life essence ceased, the future of Forestedge unfolded.

The vision was clear. Da'shar and Rosabela witnessed many dead bodies, one of which was the high councilman. There were scores of dead elves, but many were left standing. Conversely, of all the scores of orcs in the vision, none survived.

Mere moments later, the vision faded and Rosabela found herself lying on the soft ground with her mentor pressing a vial to her lips. The liquid within the vial was cool and sweet as it flowed down her dry throat. She felt the effects immediately as her energy returned and brought strength and vitality along with it.

"What happened?" she asked

"You fainted from the stress of the vision," Da'shar replied gently.

"No," she said, "what happened in the vision? I don't understand what happened."

"All I can say is that if we speak with this dead orc's spirit, then the high councilman will die, many elves will die, and the orcs will die. Beyond that, I cannot say. The vision did not show your suspicions that the high councilman was anything more than an elf. I can only assume that a battle is coming one way or the other," he explained.

"Then, what have we truly learned by this divination?" Rosabela asked with obvious distress.

The elder druid smiled and said, "We have learned by your sacrifice that you are worthy to make the decision on how we proceed. You know what is at stake, and you have seen a glimpse of what could be. Now, you must choose."

Chapter 11
Decisions and Consequences

Gaedron and Wavren moved through the city swiftly and silently, having completed their reconnaissance mission in the high councilman's office. The two hunters picked up the trail of Rosabela and Da'Shar, which led them out of town toward the burial grounds. Before long, they rendezvoused with the two druids who were sitting silently among numerous unmarked graves.

Wavren spoke to his sister and Da'Shar: "We believe the high councilman is in league with the Bloodcrest Forces. Gaedron and I confirmed that he must be an orc or perhaps a tauren in disguise. I can only assume that his appearance has been altered by powerful magic so that he looks like an elf, but that magic has not concealed certain other indications. What have you discovered?"

Rosabela stood up and spoke: "We have not yet confirmed anything."

"Did the prisoner's spirit reveal nothing of use?" Wavren asked.

"We haven't spoken to it," she returned calmly.

Wavren looked at his sister with confusion and then asked, "What are we waiting for? Isn't this a necessary step?"

Da'Shar crossed his arms and scowled. "Druids do not take such things lightly. There are sacrifices and consequences that you can never comprehend."

Gaedron's face grew red, and he came forward with fists clenched. "Sacrifice, ye say? What can a hunter know 'bout sacrifice? I tell ye this: I done lived more'n a few centuries on da edge of civilization where protectin' those who choose ta live in cities means takin' out scouts an' lead elements of enemy invaders a'fore they can git close enough ta threaten ye and yer kinfolk. It means makin' a family of a bear and the only comforts of home are a warm fire and what e'er I can carry on me back. It means bein' ready to die for what ye believe in an' never gettin' so much as a thanks from those whose lives yer protectin'"

Wavren physically restrained his mentor and tried to calm him. Da'Shar turned his back and stepped away. Rosabela was left staring into the night sky. She reflected on the words of her mentor and on the vision that she had endured. Doing the right thing meant making tough decisions, and her mentor had dropped the responsibility squarely on her shoulders. She felt confident that the spirit of the orc prisoner had information that would be useful, but her mentor was unconvinced. Her decision to move forward with communing with the dead could have serious repercussions, but those consequences were unknown. It was the fear of the unknown that made Rosabela hesitate.

Da'Shar moved over to his student and placed his hand on her shoulder. He said, "This is your decision, and as I have said, you are worthy to make it. I want you to know that I support you regardless of the decision you make, so be at ease, and make your choice without fear of reprisal from me."

"I have decided," she said. "We must know what the orc knew and why he was killed during the invasion."

"Very well, my child; let us proceed," Da'Shar returned.

Rosabela nodded and retrieved her book of alchemy. The potion called for a mixture of kingsblood, purple lotus, and grave moss suspended in a solution of pure water drawn from greater water elementals. None of these reagents could be found easily, and each item was from a completely different part of the world. In spite of their rarity and the difficulty of acquisition, the young druid had all of these items on hand except the pure water that Da'Shar contributed. Da'Shar looked somewhat uneasy as Rosabela prepared the concoction. It was as if he knew some terrible secret that no one else could fathom. The potion did not boil or bubble; in fact, it looked rather innocuous.

Da'Shar confirmed, "It is ready. Gather the hunters; we may need them."

Wavren and Gaedron were called over. The foursome gathered around the spot that seemed to be the most recent burial. Rosabela held the potion and nodded to her mentor, who would bind the spirit to speak truthfully, once she summoned it. She looked to her brother and the dwarf who stood ready with their massive bear allies at their sides as back up if anything went wrong.

Unlike the summoning of demons that warlocks were known for, the summoning of a spirit was tricky business. The druid or priest needed to be certain to bind the spirit to the material world long enough to get the answers they sought, yet release them back to the spirit world before they are able to take control of the summoner by possession, or worse, call forth the undead to attack the world of the living.

Ever focused on the required steps to complete the summoning, the younger druid poured the potion over the burial plot and spoke loudly: "I call to the spirit of Borik of Dek'Thal, slain prisoner of Forestedge. *RESTORIAUM ESPIRITOS*!"

The ground darkened where the potion had been poured. The wind blew, and a dank, moldy smell of death permeated the air. The soft whistling of the breeze turned into a bone-chilling howl that announced the arrival of the spirit.

Da'Shar moved forward and whispered arcane words as

green energy engulfed his hands. He bound the spirit to speak truthfully and serve the group against its will. The orc spirit growled and hissed at him in response as it tested the limits of its bonds. It came at the group even though visibly restrained by unseen chains that pulled at its limbs and neck, not unlike a prisoner chained to the wall of its jail cell.

Rosabela called out in a high-pitched, yet powerful voice, "Spirit of Borik, you have been summoned and bound to answer our questions. Speak truthfully, and we will release you back to your eternal sleep. If you choose to deceive us, your torment will be far beyond anything you have experienced in this life or in the afterlife."

The spirit said nothing. Although tormented by the memory of life and the knowledge that it was now bound into service, the spirit of Borik seemed to resign itself to compliance. Rosabela knew that the spirit would only answer simple and direct questions. She also knew that if she did not phrase her questions carefully, the spirit would be able to answer either literally or figuratively. This latitude could be confusing or misleading.

Again Rosabela spoke: "Give me the name of the master you served in life."

In a distant, almost watery voice, the spirit replied, "Neggish Grimtusk."

Rosabela had been given that name by High Councilman Kalin. Neggish was the local leader of the orcs near Forestedge. She had expected it.

"How many orcs does Neggish Grimtusk command?" she asked.

"Three score," the orc said.

Sixty orcs was not an army, but Rosabela had already assumed the local band of orcs was an advanced party of scouts.

"How many orcs, tauren, undead, and trolls are in the next higher command that threaten Forestedge?" Rosabela asked.

"Many hundreds," the spirit answered vaguely; Rosabela wondered if it even knew the exact number of minions threatening Forestedge.

Rosabela had at least confirmed what she needed to know about the imminent attack. It was time to ask the real questions. It was critical that she use exact wording to discover the truth about the high councilman of Forestedge.

"Has High Councilman Kalin of Forestedge been replaced by an imposter?" Rosabela asked.

The spirit twisted in its arcane bonds and pulled against them with unholy strength. It howled and hissed like an animal while the foursome watched with weapons ready. Da'Shar called the orc's name, the one word that held the creature bound, and then he called a pillar of bright energy down on the spirit. The spell was called *starfire*, a more powerful version of moonfire that pulsed with brilliant, arcane energy. The spirit screamed and begged as the spell engulfed him. When the spell ended, Borik was cowering in a huddled position with his face buried in the crook of his arm.

Borik spoke one word in whispered tones: "Yes."

"Then the imposter Kalin must have orchestrated your death to serve our enemy's purposes," she stated.

"He controls the city, the defenses, and even the fools on the council with him. He is the high councilman," Borik offered, still trembling from Da'Shar's spell.

Rosabela actually felt pity on the soul of the orc, but she had more to ask. This had been a tough decision to make, and even now, she wondered if the information would be worth the price. The vision of divination had shown many dead elves in spite of all of these efforts. She wondered what the outcome would have been if this information had not been gathered. Steeling her will, Rosabela refocused on the task at hand.

"Tell me when the attack is coming," she demanded.

The orc looked up from his cowering and huddled posture. He managed a weak smile and said, "The Bloodcrest Forces attack at dawn, but you will die long before."

The spirit vanished, having served until the spell expired, but the ground where it had been summoned suddenly cracked open. Black sulfurous fumes spewed forth, and the moaning of undead announced the coming battle. From the unmarked graves came shambling corpses of the enemies of Forestedge. Leading the desiccated zombies was Borik, but he was no longer an orc, nor was he a spirit. He was a hideous ghoul with blackened fangs, flesh-rending claws, and red eyes filled with hatred.

"And now, you die," Borik announced, as he waved his shambling troop forward.

Rosabela was already casting her moonfire when the thunderous charges of the two bears passed her. Da'Shar dropped to all fours and sprang forward as a six-hundred-pound black cat. He tore into the zombies with speed and grace only matched by his awesome fury.

"Git ye some space, boy-o," the dwarf called out. "We gotta give them bears our best, or they'll fall, and then we die."

Wavren shuffled back a dozen steps, leveled his blunderbuss, and fired a finely crafted bullet through the chest of one zombie. It never slowed. He took a breath, reloaded, and fired again. The second shot took the walking corpse in the head, which exploded in black oozing gore. The now headless zombie stumbled forward, blindly groping for anything to attack. Rosabela called to the elements, and a white pillar of energy engulfed the unholy being. Now, the headless wandering zombie was ablaze and still searching for a target. It seemed drawn toward Wavren.

"I said git back, ya durned fool elf," Gaedron called, lobbing a small, reddish-brown stick at the flaming zombie, which exploded on contact.

Wavren was thrown backward from the blast, but came up smiling.

"It's called dynamite, lad, an' afore ye ask, the answer be yes. I'll teach ya how ta make it," he said with a wink and a huge smile.

Wavren moved back another ten yards and took up a good firing position where he could best support his ally, Stonetalon. He began firing his weapon again and again.

"Ye gotta keep hittin' 'em till they fall," Gaedron called out to the twins as he fired nearly a dozen shots into a skeletal warrior, blowing several ribs and both arms off it. He continued to fire until he had literally dismantled the skeleton's entire body.

Ol' Blackmaw and Stonetalon lumbered forward shoulder to shoulder, each taking huge chunks out of the slow, but determined, zombies. The bears seemed well equipped to deal with this enemy. Their thick fur coats turned the ragged zombie claws, and powerful jaws crushed anything that got past their great swipes.

Da'Shar leaped from zombie to zombie, causing a great amount of chaos for the uncoordinated enemy attack. His paws did not have near the power that the bears' had, but his claws were razor sharp, and his attacks came nearly twice as fast. He moved through the enemy ranks like a flash of black lightning and finally came to Borik. The orc-turned-ghoul had watched the battle up to this point, but now he gnashed his teeth and howled like a beast of the night.

Borik had been a massive orc in life and was no less imposing in undeath. His large orc tusks were blackened with the foul poison that made ghouls so terrifying. It was that very poison that paralyzed the ghoul's victim so it could be eaten *alive*. The ghoul held no weapon; instead, he now had long, jagged claws that would rend flesh like fine elven daggers. To complete the package, ghouls were known for unlimited stamina and a true lack of fear. After all, what could a ghoul fear? It lived in perpetual undeath.

Borik met the druid head on. Da'Shar slashed Borik, leaving several deep lines in the ghoul's face before springing away, just evading the monstrous claws and dripping maw. The cat circled and roared as the evil being hissed in fury. This was not going to be a quick fight. It was too evenly matched.

Da'Shar pounced, hitting Borik with both forepaws and sinking his own fangs deep into the creature's shoulder. The ghoul howled and fell back with the massive cat's momentum. He managed to get his feet up and planted them in the large cat's midsection. As his momentum carried him backward, he kicked up and sent Da'Shar flying. The cat spun in the air and landed on his feet. Borik was up and running for the druid, intent on closing the distance while he had the initiative. The two clashed with claws raking and jaws snapping.

The wound on Borik's shoulder was oozing a putrid *ichor*, but the ghoul didn't seem to notice. He raked deep red lines down the cat's sides and almost ended the fight with his paralyzing bite, but Da'Shar's speed and size enabled him to swat the ghoul's gaping maw to the side at the last second.

Da'Shar transformed back into his elven form and called out to Nature for healing. His wounds glowed with an eerie green light and mended right before Borik's eyes. The ghoul was enraged.

Borik charged again, thinking he had the slender elf at a disadvantage in his elven form, but Da'Shar was no fool. He called to Nature again, and long vines ensnared the ghoul, holding it rooted in place. He called to the elements, and this time starfire blasted the ghoul with arcane light. The scream was blood curdling as the arcane blaze engulfed Borik entirely. Da'Shar left nothing to chance; he called for starfire again and again until the ghoul was nothing more than a charred mass of blackened bones and ash.

Da'Shar was spent. He went down to one knee and breathed deeply. The wounds given by the wretched creature were nearly mended, but he felt terribly hot, as if his blood were boiling. It was obvious that further healing would be required, but dizziness and an overwhelming need to vomit prevented him from any casting. His vision blurred and growing darkness was the last thing he saw.

Rosabela was alternating between casting healing spells on the two bears and blasting zombies with moonfire. At least ten zombies and skeletons were down, but nearly a score were still coming, and the two bears had taken dozens of hits already. Weariness was taking its toll on the young druid, but her work was far from done. She was nearly tapped out of magical reserves when she noticed her mentor was no longer in sight. She quickly scanned the battlefield and could not find the huge black cat that had been dashing about the enemy ranks earlier. She stopped long enough to visually search through the carnage, and a smoking corpse caught her attention. She guessed it was Borik, but from this distance, she couldn't be sure. It was then that she saw the elven form lying prostrate far behind the enemy lines.

Fear for her mentor turned to frustration. She knew she would never pass through twenty undead. The frustration turned to anger and that anger turned into rage. She had to get to Da'Shar, and she had to hurry. Tears rolled down her cheeks as she screamed. Her high-pitched wail became a deep roar.

Gaedron and Wavren had fired hundreds of rounds into the mass of zombies as their allies fought valiantly not twenty meters away. The bears took turns swatting zombies that seemed to press forward in spite of being mauled by the great beasts. It was a stalemate in the classic sense. The zombies were the proverbial irresistible force being held back by two hunters and their bears, the proverbial immoveable object. Something had to give. Suddenly, a high-pitched voice cut through the air, drawing the attention of friend and foe alike.

The hunters looked in Rosabela's direction, where the sound was originating, and saw the beautiful elf maiden change into her massive black bear form. Thick black fur, powerful paws ending in deadly claws, and a muzzle filled with large fangs replaced the elf's delicate form. Rosabela stood up on her hind legs and roared with a deep, powerful voice. The zombies immediately converged on her.

"Durned fool elf bought us some time lad, but she ain't gonna last long," Gaedron said as he looked to his pupil.

Wavren was already training his blunderbuss in his sister's direction, unable to speak as the realization of her imminent death hit him. A shudder ran through his body, and a single tear fell as he pulled the trigger. One zombie fell and then another. He heard his mentor call out, "FER STONE AN' STEEL!"

Gaedron shoulder-slung his weapon and moved forward with a red stick of dynamite in each hand. He heard the report of Wavren's blunderbuss over and over. The bullets whizzed past his head not more than a few inches away. He saw zombie after zombie pitch forward as the bullets cut through their flesh. It almost seemed pointless, but the dwarf cast his explosives and hit the ground. The dynamite exploded into a massive fireball followed by a shockwave that obliterated four zombies and leveled several more. Gaedron jumped up and started firing.

Rosabela had five of the undead on her at once. She hit one zombie hard enough that the momentum of her blow knocked a second one down. The remaining three pummeled her with clubs and rusted swords. She felt none of it as she ravaged the enemies on the ground. She tore the arms and head off the first one as the second one fought from its back, kicking and punching at her futilely. She stomped down, crushing it with her massive weight, and shredded it with fangs and claws.

Wavren fired and fired again, but the three remaining zombies were swarming his twin. He knew any stray shot would hit Rosabela, so he decided to cast his fine weapon aside and drew his elven dagger instead. He sprinted forward and dove headfirst into a roll beside a fallen ax-wielding skeleton. When he came up, he held its reverse curved ax in his other hand to accompany his dagger. The three zombies never saw him coming.

Gaedron now had to pick his shots carefully as Wavren shot forward into the fray. The dwarven hunter fired one round through the head of the zombie on Wavren's right. Desiccated brain matter splattered across the twins, but the zombie kept swinging wildly.

Wavren thrust his dagger through the now headless zombie's back as he repeatedly hacked it with his ax. It fell to the ground, lifeless and unmoving. The second zombie hacked deeply into Rosabela's shoulder with its rusty broadsword. The reflexive snap of the druid's jaws severed the zombie's arm. Wavren removed its other arm and both legs with an upward swing followed by a spinning backhand slice. His dagger sank in deeply, embedded in the vile creature's chest all the way to the hilt.

Gaedron fired his weapon just as the last zombie turned on Wavren. The shot staggered it and gave Rosabela enough time to latch her powerful jaws on its torso. Wavren brought his two weapons about and hacked at the thing until it moved no more.

Rosabela dashed over to the fallen druid, returning to her elven form along the way. She was bleeding profusely from the shoulder wound and various minor wounds as well, but her concern was directed toward Da'Shar. Her mentor was unconscious, but alive. Although he seemed uninjured, Rosabela could not wake him. She noticed his skin had become clammy and his muscles were rigid. She realized he was suffering from some sort of poison or infection within. Calling on her healing talents, she laid her hands on his forehead and tried to strengthen his body's defenses. His condition did not seem to change. She drew her great tome of alchemy from the silk wrappings and began searching.

"Lass, yer bleedin' pretty good there," the dwarf whispered with concern.

She ignored him.

Wavren put his hand gently on her back and asked pleadingly, "Rosie, your death will not help save Da'Shar."

"I can save him," she snapped.

"Aye, lass, we know ya can, but we canna save you," the dwarf murmured.

She paused, drank a healing potion, and allowed Wavren enough time to dress her wound. It was only then that she realized how much blood she had lost. Dizziness started to cloud her mind, but she willed it away. She looked at the arcane symbols in her book and steeled her will to find an herb or potion to purge her mentor's body. Although the words seemed to run together, she finally found a possible solution. The potion called for wild steelbloom, *liferoot*, and *silverleaf*, which she had, but Da'Shar would never be able to swallow it in his unconscious state. She needed another way to administer the antitoxin, but the book was geared toward potions, not salves or poultices. She began searching frantically through the pages.

"Rosie, what can we do?" Wavren asked.

"He can't drink a potion," she said. "I need a different medium to administer the herbal concoction."

Gaedron thought for a moment and then began digging in his bag.

"What are you doing?" Wavren asked.

"Got me an idea," he replied.

Gaedron retrieved a handful of dark red peppers and said, "Mix yer potion and soak it up wit' these."

Wavren quickly made a wave-off motion and shook his head while mouthing, "No," over and over.

Gaedron pushed him aside and handed the deep red peppers to Rosabela, saying, "Ever notice how hot spice spreads through yer mouth an' down in yer gullet wit' just a tiny taste? Well, have ye?"

Rosabela had never eaten hot spice, but it seemed reasonable.

"It be a fine catalyst fer pushin' dat there potion through his system an' the heat might just wake ol' boy up. Ye mix yer potion an' crush these up in it. Next, ye put 'em under his tongue. It be pow'rful, I tell ye, pow'rful indeed," the dwarf said confidently.

Wavren was still pantomiming a definite no to the idea.

Rosabela was unsure, but with no other option, she did as she was instructed. The peppers were dry and soaked up the antitoxin quickly. The resulting smell was awful, and the fumes burned her eyes. Tears welled up and ran freely down her face. She looked at Wavren, who had a look of utter disbelief on his face. He was amazed that she would even consider going though with this ridiculous plan. Rosabela looked over to Gaedron, who was smiling eagerly and nodding emphatically. Without another course of action, she opened her dear mentor's mouth and placed the odd poultice under his tongue.

At first, nothing happened, and Gaedron frowned. Then, tiny beads of sweat appeared on the druid's face. His gray pallor began to fade returning to normal then a ruddy red color. Finally, his cheek twitched, and then his entire face began to move in a contorted spasm.

Rosabela was worried, and Wavren was, too, but Gaedron just smiled and nodded more and more.

Gaedron mumbled, then spoke, and then yelled, "It's working. It's working! IT'S WORKING!"

Da'Shar suddenly sat straight up, then went to all fours and vomited. His eyes were open far beyond their normal range, and the pupils were dilated wide open. A long line of saliva drooled out and slung back and forth as he shook his head from side to side. He said nothing, merely stared forward with a look of sincere pain and horror. And then it happened: he drew in a long, deep breath and screamed like nothing the three onlookers had ever heard. The sound raised the hairs on the backs of their necks and sent waves of pity through their souls.

Rosabela was elated that he was alive, but thought it might have been more merciful to let her mentor die than to see him suffer in such agony. Wavren thought death would have been better by far, having tasted the hot spice firsthand. Gaedron smiled and only felt sorry that he was now out of his favorite seasoning. Da'Shar suffered for several more minutes, but after the hot spice antitoxin deadened his sense of taste and numbed all sensation of pain, he was able to compose himself.

Da'Shar tried unsuccessfully to wipe the long line of thick saliva from his lips. Trying to regain some measure of dignity, he stood and brushed the dirt from his clothing. Finally, in a somewhat slurred and pathetic voice, he half-whispered, half-croaked his suspicions to Gaedron: "You … you … are behind this … aren't you?"

Gaedron smiled and said, "Welcome back, 'ol boy, we got work ta do."

Rosabela hugged her mentor, and the two hunters smiled as they looked across the carrion-covered battlefield.

Gaedron patted Ol' Blackmaw and said, "A fine battle, me friend, fine indeed."

Wavren remarked, "Truly. Any battle you can walk away from is a good one." The foursome headed back into town to prepare for the battle yet to come.

Chapter 12
Orcs and Elves

Forestedge seemed unusually quiet and peaceful when the four heroes approached the pair of guards. These two grim-faced elves wore matching armor and weapons, making them the epitome of professionalism and deadliness. Both were alert to the approaching Protectors, but oblivious to the attack they would likely face at dawn. Neither guard presented their weapons as the foursome approached. Instead, they called to them as friends and welcomed them in.

"Hail, Protectors of the Vale!" the closest elf sentry called.

Gaedron stepped forward and said, "Wake yer captain of the guard, an' be quick about it."

The sentry asked, somewhat awkwardly, "Is there a problem, master dwarf?"

"Aye, there be a problem. If'n ye don' go get him, ye'll have me boot up yer—," he started, but was interrupted by Wavren's calm hand and clearing of his voice.

The sentry scowled and exchanged looks with each of the four Protectors.

Wavren spoke: "We must speak with the captain of the guard. It is urgent, and it concerns the security of Forestedge and the lives of the good elves within."

The sentry spoke with an official tone: "I am Sarim, sentry of the south gate. If you have information regarding security, give it to me at once, and I will determine if it warrants waking the captain."

Da'Shar quickly stepped forward and spoke in the ancient elven tongue, saying, "I am Da'Shar of Celes'tia, Druid of the Grove and Protector of the Vale. I represent the Druidic Council and the Dae'gon Alliance in the Western Kingdom. You will rouse the captain of the guard, or I will kill you on the spot for dereliction of duty and risking the security of the entire city, after which your companion will be forced to rouse the captain to report your untimely death. Either way, I will see the captain now."

Sarim turned, nodded to his companion, and then sprinted to the Guard Headquarters. The remaining sentry held his composure.

Wavren and Rosabela stood awestruck, having fully comprehended the entire tirade. They had never heard Da'Shar speak so harshly to anyone. Gaedron stood with arms crossed and mailed foot tapping as if the entire fiasco was simply a waste of time. Da'Shar acted as if nothing unusual had happened.

Several minutes passed before Sarim returned. Following closely behind was the captain of the guard and no less than twenty warriors from the city guard's quick reaction force. Each warrior was outfitted as the two sentries were with matching armor and weapons. The only exception was a distinctive cloak each wore that was embroidered with a fierce windwraith, the great, black, panther indigenous to Forestedge. These were elite warriors assigned as the first line of defense for the city.

The captain walked up to Da'Shar and spoke in a formal baritone: "I am Captain Jael'Kutter of the Forestedge Security Forces. What is the emergency?"

Before the heroes could answer, two of the windwraith warriors fell to the ground with crossbow bolts deeply embedded in their throats. A gurgle of blood followed by a spray of crimson was more than any explanation could offer. Captain Jael'Kutter was in motion.

"Windwraiths form upon me, archers in range!" the captain ordered.

Instantly, the warriors dropped in place with shields interlocked to form an impenetrable wall against the ranged weapons. Gaedron and Wavren moved to the outer edges of the defensive wall and scanned the wood line for enemies. They saw no one. Rosabela and Da'Shar went to work on the two fallen warriors with herbs and healing magic, but the damage was severe and would likely be fatal.

The captain of the guard grabbed Sarim by his tunic, pulled him close, and commanded, "Sound the alarm, get the perimeter defense prepared for invasion, and send word to the high councilman to advise Port Archer of our situation in case we need to evacuate."

Sarim saluted and sprinted for cover behind the closest tree. He was nearly there when a crossbow bolt pierced his thigh. He collapsed, but found cover behind the tree. The next gap was slightly farther than his first ten-second rush, but with an injured leg, he would never make it before the deadly archers cut him down.

He looked back and saw his commanding officer coordinating the movement of the formation forward to flush out the archers. Injured or not, he had a mission, and failure was not an acceptable alternative. He broke the shaft off and tied the wound with a strip of cloth.

Sarim looked at his next position and saw a low spot halfway between. It might be low enough to provide cover from the deadly archers. There was a tree, as well as a long gully just past it that he could use to crawl safely once he got there. He took a deep breath and stood up. The leg had some strength left in it, but it throbbed with agony. He hobbled for a dozen steps and dove into the small dip that provided nearly enough cover from the archers. Several crossbow bolts flew past, but none found their mark.

Captain Jael'Kutter pressed his men forward in small, shuffling steps. The cadence he called seemed very dwarf-like to Gaedron, as did the entire shield phalanx maneuver. Wavren fired his blunderbuss again and again, but the enemy was well hidden. The return fire was obviously coming from the direction they were moving in as the steady sound of crossbow bolts on steel shields rang out rhythmically.

Sarim scurried face down until he was able to gain cover behind the last tree along his path to the great horn, which would alert the entire city. He smiled for a moment as he watched his fellow guards push forward in their armored formation. With one last glance across the landscape, he searched for any sign of the enemy, but none were in view. Sarim checked his wound; it was bleeding profusely. He tightened the bandage and summoned his courage with a few deep breaths. He focused on the great horn barely fifty yards away and took off. The pain in his leg was bearable with the adrenaline he was pumping. The distance closed in slow motion. Each step seemed an eternity, but the goal was getting closer.

Rosabela and Da'Shar stopped the bleeding on the two fallen Windwraith Guards, but they would likely be at death's door after this battle was concluded, if they survived at all. The two druids looked at each other and knew that they had done all they could do for these two. They looked about and saw the progress of the small elven force as well as the lone guard trying desperately to get to the great horn to alert the city.

Da'Shar leaped forward, transformed into the sleek, black panther, and quickly faded into the shadows. Rosabela dashed forward and ducked behind the wall of elven shields. She kept her eyes on the lone guard who was limping his way along with limited cover and concealment. She silently prayed that he would make it. Just as he reached the great horn, his body jerked twice and he went down to one knee. Rosabela knew he would not live long, as she saw the black fletching of two crossbow bolts protruding from his chest. The guard summoned his remaining strength and stood once more. He inhaled and pressed his lips to the mouthpiece as several orcish bolts pierced his body. The guard blew into the great horn and sounded one long, deep, bass note before he collapsed. Rosabela felt great pity for him, and yet a surge of elven pride accompanied her grief. He had fallen while courageously doing his duty.

Da'Shar heard the alarm sound and knew reinforcements would assemble soon. Nearly invisible, he crept silently through the brush. His course was along a circuitous route, toward the crossbowmen's location. Although he still had no visual confirmation of their attack position, he could now hear muffled voices and movement up ahead. He heard a quiet murmuring and realized that it was chanting, probably spell casting. The sound put the caster a few yards away and although the caster was obviously invisible, Da'Shar could tell the mage was facing in the opposite direction. The druid in panther form crouched, calculated his next move, and suddenly pounced.

The invisible wizard fell forward with six hundred pounds of teeth and claws already shredding his mystic robes. Had the robes been made of natural fabric instead of enchanted mageweave, he would be torn limb from limb by now. Instead, the now fully visible undead mage had a second to react before the feral druid destroyed him.

"*Incantus protectori*," the undead mage called, followed by, "*Novas Arcti*."

The first spell surrounded the caster with a magic shield of protection, and the second blasted Da'Shar with frost, immobilizing him temporarily. The mage rolled away from the druid and hopped back several steps before beginning to cast his next spell.

Da'Shar felt his muscles lock up from the icy blast and saw the mage move into a better position to cast. He rotated his hands in circles and summoned a ball of fire, which grew bigger with each rotation until it was the size of a pumpkin. The druid braced himself for the flaming missile, knowing full well that he would never dodge it in time. He felt the blood flowing warmly in his body and knew the frost spell would fade soon, hopefully before the next attacks. The mage cast his fireball and sent Da'Shar flying backward. The blast singed his fur and stole his breath, but the druid was alive. The wizard was not the only one with enchanted possessions.

The rotting corpse of a mage called forth more fire and cast it just as Da'Shar regained his bearing. The panther-druid dodged with amazing agility, yet still suffered more damage from the intense heat. But now he was on the attack. Da'Shar pounced forward and hit the enemy with his full weight and both front claws. The mage could not get his offensive spells off with the rapid pounding from the mighty cat, so he vanished and reappeared some twenty feet behind and called for the frost spell again. This time the spell failed to hold, and a look of fear washed over the mage as Da'Shar pounced. His full weight and both forepaws came down on the mage. Once Da'Shar's claws dug into the corpse-mage's shoulders, the great cat bit down on the enemy's head and began to rend his abdomen with both back legs. The undead mage simply came apart under the assault.

Da'Shar transformed into his elven form, took a few moments to inspect the damage, and healed his wounds with Nature's magic. He needed rest, but many enemies were still alive, and that meant there was work to do. The shape shifter couldn't help but retch as he considered the foul aftertaste of the mage's putrid flesh. He put it out of his mind and returned to his feline form, prowling unseen through the thick vegetation, on the hunt for more enemies.

* * *

Wavren and Gaedron had been lying down covering fire, hoping to wound or scare off the unseen enemy. Suddenly an entire war party of orcs appeared out of nowhere. The orcs were out in the open, having relied on magic to remain unseen. They had to assume Da'Shar's work behind the front line had been the break the two hunters needed. With visible targets, the hunters might be able to turn the tide of battle back in their favor.

The closest target was an orc in black leather armor with a shaved head. He was reloading his crossbow when he realized that he was suddenly visible. Gaedron and Wavren fired simultaneously, and the orc went down with a surprised look on his face and two smoldering holes in his chest.

The orcish war party threw down their crossbows, drew blades, and charged just as Blackmaw and Stonetalon entered the enemy lines. Stampeding shoulder to shoulder, the two bears plowed through the orcs and disrupted any chance they had of forming up on their commander. A grand melee of fighting erupted as the small band of elven warriors broke ranks and charged. Swords and shields clanged loudly amid the growls of bears and reports of gunfire.

Rosabela scanned the field of battle and counted nearly two score orcs and less than half that number of elves. Gaedron and Wavren were firing from the cover of a huge oak, and the two bears were nearly swamped with enemy troops. She knew immediately that the battle would be won or lost based on the timing of reinforcements. The brave guard, Sarim, had given his life sounding the massive horn, but so far no one had responded.

The druid turned away from the battle and dashed toward the great horn. As she sprinted for cover, she saw two elven warriors climb weakly to their feet, supported by grim determination and duty to their countrymen. These were the two guards who had been mortally wounded and then brought back from the brink of death with her druidic magic. They must surely feel indebted to Da'Shar and Rosabela for saving them, but Rosabela knew immediately that they would not survive their wounds if they entered the battle. They stood up and drew swords anyway.

Rosabela moved past them and came to the great horn where Sarim's pierced body lay. She couldn't get to the horn without stepping over the fallen hero. Gently she took the body, now soaked with blood, slid him out of the way, and placed him slightly in front of the great horn. Swallowing hard to keep from sobbing, she rested his head gently on the soft grass and stood up to finish her task. As she pressed her lips to the mouthpiece and drew in a deep breath, she saw a lone orc leveling his crossbow at her. Her instincts told her to dodge or seek cover, but her heart overpowered her sensibilities, and a long, deep blast came from the horn instead. The orc fired and a black, orcish arrow raced toward her heart in slow motion. Death was upon her when suddenly an elven shield appeared just in time to deflect the shot. Rosabela looked down and saw Sarim's arm hanging limply between the shield straps. He looked at her, grimaced in pain, and closed his eyes.

The orc cursed and set to reloading his crossbow. Rosabela blew the horn again. The orc raised his crossbow to fire just as two blood-covered warriors charged into him. The three went down in a jumble of flailing weapons, blood, and grime. Rosabela blew one final time. The orc drew his twin blades and quickly dispatched the two wounded elves that Rosabela and Da'Shar had saved earlier. Looking past the mouthpiece, Rosabela witnessed their sacrifices for her, and her heart felt heavy with their loss.

Enraged that the alarm had been sounded, and that he had been unable to kill the she-elf with his crossbow, the orc came forward with murder in his eyes and blades spinning, red with fresh blood. Rosabela didn't flinch. She didn't look for cover; she just waited. She wanted this fight. Fear and sadness were now gone, drowned in righteous fury. The hate-filled red eyes of the orc were evenly matched with her own intense, deep green gaze. The orc was twice her size, armed, armored, and ready to kill. Rosabela balanced lightly on the balls of her feet in anticipation of the coming attack.

The orc picked up a trot, growled, and came on with both blades thrusting. The lithe druid dropped down to her back and kicked up with both feet just as her attacker overbalanced forward. The unorthodox maneuver caught the orc mostly in the groin and sent him flying head over heels onto his back. He hit the ground and scrambled to his feet. The pain in his groin was painted across his face, but hate and anger were enough to keep him in the fight.

Rosabela called to the forest for entangling vines, which held the orc in place. His taut leg muscles strained against the creeping entanglement, but could not budge. The highly trained orc kept his eyes on the elf while he sawed at the vines around his feet. The druid called to the elements and blasted the orc with moonfire. To her amazement, the orc's armor absorbed the blast, leaving him unharmed. She saw that he would be free from the entangling spell soon, and with his resistance to her elemental magic, the druid knew the battle would be fought at close range. She growled a deep, throaty warning and transformed into the massive black bear that was best suited for melee. The orc did not look surprised, but as he finished cutting through the vines, he elected to circle the druid, who was now in bear form, instead of coming in directly.

Rosabela moved in with long strides. This time, the orc waited on the balls of his feet to dodge at the last minute. As Rosabela rumbled forward, the orc deftly rolled right and came up just behind her. His blades came down heavily on her back, but only drew small lines of red after being mostly absorbed by the thick fur and dense muscle. The quick turn and swat from Rosabela caught the orc off guard and sent him flying backward several feet.

The orc rolled backward and came back to a standing position with swords at the ready. His battle stance was strong, but Rosabela stood eight feet tall on her hind legs. The orc thrust one blade in at her soft midsection, but the bear-druid saw it coming and parried the thrust with a lightning quick paw that caught the orc on the forearm. The distinctive pop followed by a howl indicated that she had dislocated his arm at the shoulder. The orc backpedaled as his right arm swung limply at his side.

Rosabela remembered the look of Sarim as he departed this life. She envisioned the two wounded guards who had sacrificed themselves for her to sound the alarm. She felt a surge of rage and came forward with both paws raking downward. The claws scraped across the orc's scalp, face, and chest, leaving ten deep, bloody gouges. The orc screamed and tried to scramble away. Rosabela brought both paws down on his chest with most of her considerable weight. Ribs gave way with a crunching, grating sound and he moved no more. Rosabela tore out his throat for good measure.

The main battle was going poorly. Although several of the orcs were dead, the elven warriors were all but decimated. Two warriors fought beside Stonetalon and Blackmaw as Gaedron and Wavren fired relentlessly. Captain Jael'Kutter, was barking commands to hold the line while he pulled wounded elves out of the fray. Rosabela transformed back into her elven form and moved to treat the wounded. As she surveyed the carnage, she suddenly realized that no reinforcements had come.

The warriors had been well trained and battle hardened, but fell as if they were new recruits. As Rosabela called to Nature for healing, she noticed that the wounds would not close. The enemy had poisoned their weapons. She had to purge the wounds before they could be healed. This would be a simple matter with time and the appropriate salves, but she had neither.

"The enemy has poisoned their blades," Rosabela called out to the captain. "I need herbs to treat them."

"Do what you can," Jael'Kutter spat, turning toward the battle with vengeance in his eyes.

The enemy surged forward, and in spite of the tremendous damage the two hunters were doing, the two bears and two warriors could not hold them back. Orcs swarmed past and came into close combat range, where they met Captain Jael'Kutter now holding his finely crafted double-bladed polearm. The captain spun the polearm overhead and stepped aside as the first orc came in range. The blade on one end knocked the orc's curved sword to the side, and the other bladed end came around with a flash, lopping the villain's head off cleanly. This happened so swiftly and efficiently that the other orcs paused and gave a wide birth for Jael'Kutter. He charged into them with reckless abandon and inspired renewed vigor in those few left around him.

Gaedron dropped his blunderbuss and drew twin axes. The enchanted mithril of the weapons trailed a glimmering blue radiance that seemed to make the weapons move impossibly fast as he leapt forward and called his battle cry: "FER STONE AN' STEEL!" One of the orcs, avoiding the elven captain, walked right into Gaedron's hacking frenzy. The orc's fine leather armor lasted less than a split second under the fine edge of the dwarven-crafted mithril axes. The orc never saw what hit him, but he managed to howl under the dwarven assault before he died.

Wavren drew his dagger and pulled the reverse curved ax he found in the cemetery and followed his mentor into battle, but the odds were nearly three to one with both bears, both warriors, and both hunters fully engaged.

Rosabela hated to abandon the dying elves, but she shifted into bear form to spend her last moments alive fighting beside her brother. She charged into the throng of blood and carnage with determined focus. In mere moments, her thick black coat was covered in gore and foul orc blood, as well as a mixture of her own and some of her peers'. Through the fighting, she wondered where the reinforcements were. The long blast of the great horn should have alerted the city. Arrows and mage fire should be raining down on the invaders right now, yet they fought alone.

The orcs continued to apply pressure to the small band of defenders. These orcs were well trained. They knew better than to let their battle lust overcome their tactical advantage of numbers. This battle could be won or lost depending on even a single tactical mistake, and the orcs seemed to be following their plan to the letter.

A swift black streak entered the fray from the edge of the forest. Claws and fangs tore into the orcs with deadly precision and caused great chaos among the reserve ranks of orcs. Da'Shar, in his windwraith form, had arrived just in time to see his comrades nearly swamped with orcs. He quickly entered the fight to help balance the odds. He knew the battle was nearly lost, but a little confusion might allow his allies the respite needed to regroup.

Jael'Kutter saw the windwraith move in and attack. He saw how effectively chaos worked against the disciplined orcs. This was ridiculously contrary to any historical battle between the Bloodcrest Forces and the Dae'gon Alliance. Normally, the Dae'gon Alliance would hold ranks and use tactics to defeat the chaotic, barbaric assaults the Bloodcrest Forces were famous for. He decided that a change in tactics might throw the orcs off balance just enough to make a difference. There were no reinforcements on the way, and they would all likely die anyway, so there was nothing to lose by trying.

Jael'Kutter inhaled deeply and howled his final order to his allies: "Break ranks! Kill these beasts!"

The two warriors and Jael'Kutter, who had been fighting side by side in a triangle, dove apart in different directions. Jael'Kutter rolled backward as the two warriors on either side rolled outward. The pressure of the disciplined orc assault quickly gave way with the sudden release, and the orcs came forward right into Wavren and Gaedron's slashing blades. Their surprise was complete when the two hunters split outward after landing several cuts, and the orcs found themselves facing a now-standing Jael'Kutter with his deadly polearm already spinning. Both fell dead in moments.

The former wedge-shaped fighting force of elves had now become a V-shaped envelopment, and the odds were now somewhat better. The two hunters moved in and out of orc melee range while the two warriors charged back into the weakened sides of the enemy formation. Two more orcs fell, and the score was nine heroes to fourteen villains.

Rosabela and the two other bears held the mass of enemies at bay with powerful swipes and crushing jaws, but all were bleeding from multiple wounds. Rosabela knew it was a matter of time until the loss of blood slowed their attacks and the wretched orcs overwhelmed them. She roared and swiped mightily, dropping one orc; two more came in to replace him.

Stonetalon and Ol' Blackmaw took numerous hits, but they rushed in, and each grabbed an orc in its powerful jaws, allowing Rosabela room to retreat a step. It was at that moment that Rosabela saw her mentor pouncing from orc to orc with fury and unbelievable speed. She stood up on her hind legs and came in again with renewed hope. The unfortunate orcs trapped in the mouths of the two bears never noticed Rosabela's downward strikes. Each massive paw raked through armor and flesh, leaving two more dead enemies. The count was now twelve to nine.

The battered enemy invasion force suddenly realized that its tactical advantage was gone, and with the loss of so many troops, the call to retreat was made. In an instant, the orcs broke ranks and sprinted for cover in the forest.

A cheer went up, but no one followed the fleeing enemy. Battered and exhausted, the heroes regrouped in preparation for a second wave of attacks. Jael'Kutter immediately took charge setting up defenses while Da'Shar and Rosabela tried to heal the wounded.

"Gather the wounded and form up around them. The orcs might return any moment," the captain of the guard ordered.

"There are so many wounded," Rosabela whispered as she viewed the carnage.

"Save whom you can, child; the others will meet us in the afterlife," Da'Shar replied stoically, as he healed his student first and then himself. "It is Nature's way to choose who stays and who returns to dust in death."

Rosabela moved from warrior to warrior, calling to Nature to heal them. She was amazed by how many wounds these elves had sustained. Da'Shar supplied the needed herbs to counter the wicked orcish poison, but her job seemed hopeless. Bones were broken and flesh was torn, yet these hardy souls had endured. She noticed that Wavren and Gaedron were not among those she healed. Concern nearly turned to panic as she moved from elf to elf and could not find her brother. Finally, she saw two lone figures still on the battlefield. Her brother and his mentor were lying face down over the two great bears they had fought beside.

Rosabela jumped up and sprinted toward them. She noticed that both the dwarf and her brother were moving. She thanked Nature that they yet lived, but as she drew closer, she noticed that their prostrate state was not due to injury, but mourning. Stonetalon and Ol' Blackmaw had not survived.

Wavren's face was covered in blood and grime, creased by two well-defined trails of tears. His sorrow overcame Rosabela, who collapsed to her knees. Wavren hugged his sister and placed one hand on the blood-soaked, ruddy-brown fur of his companion. Gaedron hugged the neck of his now-red-covered great white bear. The grizzled old dwarf said nothing, but a single tear fell and rolled down his cheek, disappearing into his beard.

Da'Shar appeared behind the trio and spoke in a quiet tone: "Is it too late, master dwarf?"

Rosabela replied in a weepy voice, "They gave their lives that I might live."

Gaedron remained silent.

Da'Shar asked again, "Is it too late?"

Wavren stood up looked into the older elf's eyes and said, "They are gone."

"Gaedron," Da'Shar murmured, as he patted the dwarven hunter on the shoulder, "you must decide. Is it too late?"

Gaedron stood up. Head bowed and with his back to Da'Shar, he replied, "Nay, not yet."

Da'Shar placed his other hand on the old dwarf's shoulder and said, "Let us revive them, that they might mete out justice against our enemies."

The old dwarf looked over his shoulder at the elf and nodded. He turned to Wavren and said, "There be one lesson I ain't teached ya yet."

Wavren's heart skipped a beat as he hoped that somehow he would have his companion back.

Gaedron explained with an unusually somber voice, "Hunters an' druids got one thing in common an' that be a connection ta Nature. Sometimes a druid can jump-start a fallen comrade, but when it comes to beasts, they canna do it. Has somethin' ta do wit' where a soul goes after death. Humanoid souls linger, animal souls don't. If'n ya wan' yer ally back, ye gotta go git it. When all be said an' done, a part of yerself will be giv'n ta yer ally ta bring him back. Sometimes nothin' can bring 'em back."

Wavren immediately nodded.

Gaedron continued, "Don't be so quick, lad. If'n ya can't find yer ally's soul, you die in the effort. Not ta mention the fact dat even if'n it works, it still hurts like hell! Be sure ya know what yer gettin' yerself inta."

Wavren nodded again

Gaedron sighed, mumbled something about fool elves, and then nodded to Da'Shar to begin.

The elder druid began chanting the ancient words of magic and Nature. Gaedron drew his dwarven dagger and cut open both palms. He moved over to Ol' Blackmaw and knelt down by the massive bear's head. He made two cuts along the bear's broad face and placed his palms over each incision. He pried its eyes open with his thumbs and forefingers and looked deeply into the deep dark eyes of his companion. Da'Shar called out again to the elements, and a bolt of white energy shot out from his hands and blasted right into the dwarf. The master hunter shook with agony. The energy drew on his life force and channeled into the bear through the blood connection. The bear twitched and then convulsed, but the dwarf held on. Da'shar fired another bolt of energy into the dwarf, and finally, Ol' Blackmaw's great chest heaved. The dwarf fell unconscious, but the miracle was done. Ol' Blackmaw began breathing on his own. Gaedron had the look of death, with dark, recessed eyes and a gray pallor instead of the normally suntanned skin of a hunter.

Da'Shar looked a little weak from the ordeal, but he managed to remain standing and even smiled a bit with the satisfaction of helping the hunter return his ally from death. He moved over to Rosabela and put his shaky hand on her arm.

"You must now aid your twin and his bear, as I have aided

the dwarf," he said.

Rosabela was unsure how to proceed. She had never attempted this sort of magical feat, and although she fully understood the words her mentor spoke, she had no idea what might go wrong.

Da'Shar sensed her apprehension and said, "Just ask Nature to lend you strength; the spell will do the rest."

She nodded and then walked with Wavren over to his ally. Wavren looked somewhat unsure of his role, but he trusted in the words his mentor had spoken. He had to find Stonetalon's soul and bring it back to his body. He drew his fine elven dagger and repeated the steps Gaedron had taken. As his blood mingled with that of his ally, Wavren felt suddenly very aware of his surroundings. He pried the bear's eyes open, looked into them, and saw emptiness. He heard his sister calling to Nature for strength and then she called to the elements. He immediately felt very hot, as if he was on fire.

He noticed that his perspective had changed. He was floating above the scene as a disembodied spirit. He saw himself, Stonetalon, and Rosabela. The view expanded to include the others and even the entire battlefield. He saw more than the living beings and the corpses of the dead. He saw the spirits of the fallen still clinging to the bodies that had housed them recently.

The spirits of the orcs turned and looked his way. They snarled and drew ghostly weapons and meant to engage him! He was unarmed and defenseless. The spirits came forward with malice in their undead eyes. Wavren tried to run, but where could he go? He noticed the spirits of the fallen heroes clinging to their bodies. They were oblivious to him in their sorrow. Wavren ran to them.

"Brothers," he called, "we fought together in life, aid me now in death!"

One by one, the fallen elves looked his way and recognized him. They noticed the charging orc spirits as well. Each drew their ghostly weapons and gathered to meet the enemy again.

"We will stand with you, brother," they said in unison. "Your time has not yet come to join us in the afterlife."

"I must find the great bear, Stonetalon, and then I will depart. Can you delay these enemies long enough?" Wavren asked.

"None shall pass," they said in unison, and the battle erupted in an eerie spiritual melee.

Wavren moved down where his ally had fallen and inspected the area. To his amazement, ghostly tracks led eastward. He picked up the trail and moved with amazing speed, easily ten times that of any horse; no object, tree, or building barred his way. He followed the tracks for several miles and finally came to the easternmost edge of the Western Kingdom where the Great Sea opened up and met the sky. The tracks vanished into the sea.

Wavren could only assume that Stonetalon had continued across the water toward Stou'lanz. He pushed forward across the water as if it were land. Water-walking—or water-running in this case—was possible for ghosts and spirits since their mass was almost nothing, and the water could support it easily.

In mere moments, he saw land again. Upon making landfall, he picked up the trail, and what's more, he knew where Stonetalon was going. He was heading home to the Raptor Highlands where they first met. Wavren pushed on faster than before. He made the trip in moments that would normally take days on land and by ship.

As predicted, Wavren found his ally in the cave where they had first met. The bear was walking around confusedly when he entered the den. At first, the bear roared a deep, ghostly roar, but then recognition set in. Wavren called to his ally, who came forward sadly.

The bear emoted, *I am sorry to have failed you.*

Wavren spoke: "You have not failed. Because of you, I have not tasted death."

But you are here.

"I am here to return your soul to your body. Our work is not yet finished."

The bear seemed unsure. *I am weary.*

Wavren spoke: "I need you, old friend. If you choose not to

return, I must remain here with you forever."

Stonetalon perked up, sensing the urgency in his friend's voice.

Wavren asked, "Will you come back with me, that we might have retribution against our enemies?"

Stonetalon came to his side. When they touched, the world around them flashed, and Wavren found himself back on the battlefield. He saw Stonetalon's body come to life. He also saw the spiritual battle between the fallen elves and the fallen orcs still raging. He gave a silent prayer that they would soon find rest and then moved back to his own body.

The shock of returning from astral travel was great indeed. Wavren saw his sister and Da'Shar smiling, and then blackness overcame him.

Jael'Kutter was lingering beside the fallen guard by the great horn. Rosabela put her hand on his shoulder and said, "He died with honor and did his duty. He even saved my life with his dying breath. His name will always be remembered."

Jael'Kutter was nearly boiling with rage. When he looked up to the druid, he had tears on his face and such hatred in his eyes that she felt certain he would draw his weapon and attack her or anyone close by. Instead, he stood up and turned away from her, saying, "We will have vengeance. On my honor, we will have vengeance!"

Chapter 13
Infighting

The first rays of sunshine crept through the dense mass of trees as dawn approached from the east. The battlefield remained cloaked in darkness as dawn approached. It was littered with orcish and elven bodies from the evening's battle along with more than a few carrion-eating vermin. The stench of death permeated the air and the wind carried it in all directions. By midday the sun would amplify the smell, leaving no doubt that many lives had been lost the night before. The old proverb said good news traveled fast, but in this case, bad news knew no bounds.

Midway between the battlefield and the city proper, a dozen wounded heroes staggered warily to warn Forestedge of the imminent raid.

"Quickly now, the attack starts at dawn," Rosabela urged the tattered band of survivors as the less injured elves and Gaedron half-walked, half-dragged the more seriously injured companions into the city.

"Aye, lass," Gaedron returned, "but them orcs are knowin'

they lost the advantage of surprise. They won't be in a hurry ta hit a well-prepared city o' elves. I'd bet me last mug o' ale on it."

Rosabela could not help wondering where the city's reinforcements were. Sarim had blown the great horn, and it had ultimately cost him his life. The reinforcements did not come then or even when she sounded it soon after. Rosabela watched Sarim fall, impaled by crossbow bolts, repeatedly in her mind. Each time, her rage grew. His last breath was spent saving her life. It was all more than the normally calm she-elf could bear, and she meant to find some answers.

Anger was not an emotion Rosabela normally indulged. But she was haunted by the image of the young guard giving his life to alert the city and by his last act of defiance of the invaders when he deflected the crossbow bolt meant to end her life as she sounded the alarm. She knew there were reinforcements barely minutes away, yet none had come.

* * *

Neggish Grimtusk knew full well what had transpired during the night before his scouts returned from their mission. He had heard the great horn just as every living being within several miles of Forestedge had. He assumed that every friend of the elves for miles around was now alerted to the failed attack. He knew he would have to alter his plans in order to continue forward. He also knew that his own life was now at risk if there were additional failures. Most importantly, he had to return to step one of leadership, and that was the need for discipline.

The commander sent a runner to summon Shadowblade, the platoon leader who had promised so much more than he could ever deliver. Neggish Grimtusk already had his plan in place for discipline when the failed platoon leader arrived.

"Commander," Shadowblade began.

Neggish held up his massive hand and shook his head, quietly dismissing the platoon leader's attempts to explain the situation. He nodded his head to the other platoon leaders who surrounded Shadowblade on three sides, leaving the only escape route through the massive commander. They were prepared to tear Shadowblade apart if he made any attempt to resist or run.

Shadowblade was perhaps the finest fighter in the group, but he knew there would be no way for him to kill his peers and the mighty Grimtusk in order to escape. It was obvious that his life would end today. He stood straight and proud as his brothers in arms closed in. He had failed, and he knew the price for failure. If he was lucky, they would give him a clean death.

Commander Grimtusk spoke: "You have failed me and your brethren. Due to your incompetence, we have lost many warriors and the region is now at risk. Your initial failure to protect the outpost and now the failure to regain your honor by raiding Forestedge proves that you are a liability to this command."

Shadowblade stood perfectly still and said nothing.

Neggish spoke again: "You are hereby reduced in rank from platoon leader to thrall. Your name shall never be mentioned in my presence, and any evidence of your existence will be erased by fire. You will be publicly executed as an example for all to learn. Do you have anything to say on your behalf?"

Shadowblade had never feared any living being and had never even feared death. He had always known that his life would be short, most likely concluded in battle. But now, his mind raced with the anticipation that he would die as a lowly peon without so much as a sword in his hand when the end came. He said the only thing he could think of at that moment: "Send me to die at Deadmist. At least there, I will die with some measure of honor." Shadowblade requested.

The other platoon leaders were astounded. Deadmist Valley was the battleground of contested lands where the Dae'gon Alliance and the Bloodcrest Forces had lost countless soldiers in daily combat. It was a desolate wasteland of blood and gore from which few ever returned. It was suicide to volunteer, but the glory was equally inevitable. Each platoon leader took in full measure of the request and nodded with a newfound respect for their comrade. Perhaps this would win some favor with the ruthless commander as well.

Grimtusk paused for a moment to consider this last request. He knew that discipline must be enforced and that justice demanded a severe punishment. He thought for a moment and made his decision with the characteristic twisted smile that was his namesake. The smile on his face nearly took in his ears and prominently showed the yellow tusks of his orc heritage.

"You will die in combat if that is your wish, but you will not die the honorable death at Deadmist. I have a better idea," the commander replied. He then commanded, "Strip him of his armor and weapons. Bring his remaining platoon members, our healers, and every shaman in the area to the edge of Forestedge. We will have justice and a bit of revenge as well."

* * *

Forestedge was already fully engaged preparing for war. Soldiers lined up with weapons ready and faces grim with the knowledge of the coming battle. The city itself was in a valley, which provided a natural barrier of mountains on the northern and southern edges. To the east, a narrow road wound through the hills leading to Port Archer. To the west, a narrow road ended at a bridge that spanned the small moat leading to enemy territory and beyond. This bottleneck had been the site for hundreds of battles and would likely be the main avenue of approach for the invaders. This was barely the distance of an arrow shot from an elven longbow from the east gate where the battle had been fought earlier.

As the warriors fortified the city and the citizens prepared to evacuate west to Port Archer, the city leaders were gathering to discuss recent events. Rosabela, Wavren, Gaedron, and Da'Shar were in attendance, along with Jael'Kutter and the few surviving troops of the quick reaction force.

High Councilman Kalin began the meeting with measured calmness. He called on Jael'Kutter to recount the early morning battle and advise the council on the enemy situation.

"Captain Jael'Kutter, would you please give the council your report?" Kalin said coolly.

"High Councilman, I was summoned by Sarim, a guard on the eastern patrol, early this morning. He said there were several Protectors of the Vale demanding that the city be alerted to a possible raid," Jael'Kutter began.

"And where is Sarim, that we might have his perspective and the whole story?" Kalin interrupted.

"Sarim was one of many who fell in the battle that began soon after I arrived with my contingent of soldiers," he replied with a barely detectable quiver in his voice.

There was a moment of silence as the council stared at the captain of the guard. Rosabela noticed the small, almost imperceptible change in Jael'Kutter's demeanor. His normally perfect posture and military presence diminished somewhat, as if a massive weight was dropped on the sturdy elf. She also made note of the numerous looks of sorrow on the faces of the council of elders of Forestedge.

"I see," the councilman said, somewhat unsympathetically. "I am sorry for the loss of every elf. I am sure Sarim was a fine guard and loyal citizen."

The high councilman's aide quickly leaned over and whispered something into Kalin's ear. The high councilman nodded and tried unsuccessfully not to look embarrassed, but he was obviously distressed by the whispered words.

Kalin cleared his throat. "Forgive my oversight, Captain, but I just realized that Sarim was your son. I am truly sorry that you have not only lost one of your men, but also a dear family member."

The shock on Jael'Kutter's face became the center of attention. He spoke softly to himself in a low voice that could be heard only by Rosabela. Over and over he kept murmuring, "Sarim was known by all as 'the son of Jael'Kutter.'" He was struggling with more than the loss of his son. Why had his son had died sounding the great horn while no reinforcements came? And now, there was an inappropriate, almost frigid regard from the high councilman who had known Jael'Kutter and his son for many years.

Rosabela could barely contain herself. She had witnessed the death of Sarim and so many others. She had fought two battles back to back and had nearly lost her dear friends. She had evidence from the spirit of Borik that the high councilman was an imposter, and now she saw the turmoil in the noble elf captain as Jael'Kutter battled to understand why his son had died in vain.

She whispered into the captain's ear, "I do not believe this is the high councilman. The person before us is an imposter in service of the Bloodcrest Forces. He is a traitor, and he is responsible for the loss of numerous patrols as well as Sarim's death."

Frigid water thrown into the captain of the guard's face could not have had a more dramatic impact. Jael'Kutter knew that Rosabela spoke the truth. He was not sure how, but instinctively, it all made sense. He didn't even know if it was rational to believe Rosabela, but being overwhelmed by anger and determined to make someone pay, became paramount. He drew his mighty polearm, narrowed his eyes into slits of vengeance, and stood ready.

In this single motion, Jael'Kutter had shown Rosabela that he was with her. She drew strength and confidence with the knowledge that her allies were close. It was time to bring the truth out into the open.

Wavren couldn't hear what had been said, but he saw the mighty elf warrior draw his weapon, and as he looked over at his sister, the world seemed to move in slow motion. He saw Rosabela raise her arm and point her finger at the high councilman as she called in a commanding voice, "Traitor!"

Da'Shar was immediately in motion. He sprang into the air and transformed into the dark windwraith form. The shapeshifting druid landed perfectly on top of the high councilman. They fell backward in the high councilman's chair, and Da'Shar sank his claws into the slender elf's shoulders. High Councilman Kalin howled in pain as he lay bleeding with the six-hundred-pound cat on top of him.

"Guards! Guards!" the high councilman screamed.

Several loyal guards came forward, but the menacing look Jael'Kutter gave, along with the now-twirling polearm, stopped them in their tracks. The surrounding council members spread out, giving ample room for the captain of the guard.

"As captain of the guard and chief of security for forest-edge, I place you under arrest for treason," Jael'Kutter announced in a voice that was meant to express a promise of death should the councilman resist. It was apparent to everyone in the room that he wanted nothing more than to execute the accused imposter on the spot. He was hoping that somehow, the villain would try to escape.

"I am no traitor," Kalin returned. "I have committed no crime, and you have no proof of treason."

The high councilman's aide, a young and willowy elf, stepped forward and spoke: "Do you have proof that we might proceed in accordance with the laws of Forestedge, or shall we simply conduct a lynching here in the council chambers?"

This simple statement seemed to shock the crowd back into reality. Almost on cue, the remaining council members quickly closed in from their more distant positions and tried to resume control of the city meeting. Each member took his or her seat and tried to look dignified. The centermost elf on the council pointed to the guards in the room and directed them to secure Kalin. Da'Shar transformed back into his elf form and rejoined his friends in the common seats. Jael'Kutter had murder in his eyes, but Rosabela's reassuring hand on his broad shoulder seemed to calm him somewhat.

The senior councilman spoke: "I am Councilman Xaeris, and as the senior member of this council, I motion that we investigate and judge the accused to determine if Kalin is to be held for any alleged crime. As this situation has exigent circumstances with the real possibility of war looming, I also motion that we will convene immediately as an ad hoc tribunal."

From the council, a withered female elf stood up and said, "I second the motion."

Councilman Xaeris proceeded, "The motion is carried.

Who speaks on behalf of the accusers?"

Rosabela moved forward and said, "I do."

Xaeris nodded and asked, "Who speaks on behalf of the accused?"

The high councilman's aide stood up and said, "I will."

Xaeris announced, "Let the records show that Rosabela of Celes'tia acts on behalf of the accusers and represents the prosecution, while Jade'ena of Forestedge acts on behalf of the accused and represents the defense. We will proceed using a simple preponderance of evidence to determine if Kalin should be formally tried for treason. This is a fact-finding hearing only, and by the Laws of Forestedge, we must bring the truth to light."

The council nodded in agreement, and having dispensed with the formalities, was prepared to hear the facts.

Xaeris motioned for Rosabela to come forward. He said, "You should know that we only want the facts, and that any information that cannot be proven as fact will be eliminated from the judgment."

Rosabela nodded and started with the obvious facts. "The high councilman stands accused of treason in that he failed to ensure the safety of the city by choosing not to send reinforcements when the great horn was sounded no less than four times. It was sounded once by the noble son of Jael'Kutter and three times by me. It is standard procedure to send reinforcements at the sounding of the great horn to preclude the spread of open fighting in the city limits."

Xaeris spoke: "Let the record show that the city alarm was sounded four times last night, and High Councilman Kalin is responsible for dispatching troops in defense of Forestedge."

Jade'ena stepped forward and spoke with a melodious voice: "High Councilman Kalin has served honorably for years and knows well his responsibilities. Kalin was informed by a messenger soon after Jael'Kutter and his quick reaction force set out to investigate the eastern gate raid warning. I was present when Kalin and this very council decided to utilize every soldier, mage, and citizen to fortify the city in preparation of the coming raid. When the first alarm was sounded for reinforcements to aide the eastern gate, Kalin made a tactical decision not to send reinforcements that would be essential in the protection of the inner city. Being a leader means making tough decisions, and our beloved high councilman chose to protect his city even if the eastern gate fell. He did his duty."

Xaeris spoke: "Let the records show that Kalin was prepared to send reinforcements and elected not to in support of the inner city's defenses."

Rosabela spoke again: "The high councilman knew the situation was dire when the horn was sounded the first time, but when it sounded the second, third, and fourth times, did he consider that even a small contingent of soldiers might make the difference?"

Jade'ena quickly returned, "Kalin assessed the situation with assistance from the city's Mage Guild. He saw the battle firsthand and knew that Captain Jael'Kutter had the situation well in hand."

Quickly growing tired of the pointless debate, Rosabela raised her voice, saying, "We lost more than a dozen elves, not to mention all those remaining were seriously wounded!"

Xaeris announced, "Let the record show that numerous individuals were killed or wounded in the raid on the eastern gate."

The high councilor's aide rationally said, "Your presence and the defeat of the war party prove that Kalin made the best decision. The city stands unmolested, and you lived to tell the tale."

Xaeris announced, "Let the record show that Kalin's defense plan was sufficient to keep the city safe."

Rosabela was certain that her argument was not going well. She knew that a preponderance of evidence was merely weighing the facts of guilt against the facts of innocence. Whichever proved the most substantial would determine if the accusation would go to an actual trial. Doubt was creeping in, and time was running out. Rosabela looked to her mentor and considered telling the council about the information extracted from Borik, but proving that a spirit had been bound to reveal facts about the coming raid was not an easy thing, and Jade'ena was very cagey for an aide. She mentally reviewed her knowledge of the recent events and decided to bring up Borik's death and the information his spirit gave.

"Council members," she said, "my brother and I captured Borik, an orcish spy, several days ago and brought him here for questioning. He was slain in his prison cell. High Councilor Kalin was overall responsible for the loss of this prisoner and the vital information that he had regarding the raid. This is another failure on his part that indicates he is a traitor and failed to serve the interests of the city."

Jade'ena laughed at the preposterous stretch of the truth. , then replied, "Jael'Kutter is the chief of security. He is to blame for the death of the prisoner."

As expected, the senior councilman noted the statement: "Let the record show that Captain Jael'Kutter was at fault for the death of the orc prisoner Borik and High Councilman Kalin shares in that responsibility to a small degree."

Rosabela dared to venture into the gray area where fact and fiction met. "I have spoken with the spirit of Borik, and I present testimony that can be validated by my mentor Da'Shar of Celes'tia."

The council murmured for a moment and called on Da'Shar to speak. "Tell us of this spirit that Rosabela claims to have communed with."

Da'Shar was not happy with having to relate the tale. Druids were very private about their abilities, and this spirit summoning was an unprecedented event that had nearly killed the four Protectors. It would likely be discussed later in a Druidic Council not so different from this tribunal, where his career and Rosabela's would be at risk for the violation of druidic ways.

"Rosabela did summon the spirit of Borik with my supervision for the purpose of interrogation. The spirit informed us of the coming raid. The spirit said Kalin had allowed the living form of Borik to be slain in prison. I swear this to be truth as a

Druid of the Grove and Protector of the Vale," Da'Shar said.

Xaeris took a deep breath and was about to enter the new testimony into evidence when Jade'ena said, "The spirit must have lied. A spirit of an orc is innately an evil spirit and one who has been bound by magic would surely lie if given the chance."

Xaeris held his comments and waited for Da'Shar to refute the claim. Da'Shar did not disagree. He sat motionless, unwilling to confirm or deny the statement. The next step would take Rosabela down a precarious path that would likely lead to disaster.

Rosabela looked to Wavren who had been waiting quietly beside Gaedron. He smiled and nodded for her to continue. "Master Da'Shar, please tell us what else the spirit revealed," she pressed.

Da'Shar looked directly at Kalin and said, "Borik said that High Councilman Kalin was not only a traitor, but that he was an imposter who served the Bloodcrest Forces!"

The council murmured, and even Jael'Kutter looked doubtful. Jade'ena smiled and calmly said, "Council members, the prosecution surely has proof beyond doubt that somehow the elf in front of us all is not High Councilman Kalin."

Rosabela spoke: "Jael'Kutter can testify that the true high councilman knew him and his son well. We all witnessed earlier that the elf on trial did not know Sarim, nor did he know he was the slain son of Jael'Kutter until his aide informed him of those details. This is intimate personal knowledge that an imposter would not know."

Again, Xaeris paused before adding the information as a fact to the records.

Jade'ena spoke quickly: "The high councilman interacts with hundreds of Forestedge's citizens. He cannot be expected to remember the relationship of every man, woman, and child."

Rosabela was running out of options. She looked again to Wavren, who was smiling now. It wasn't a grand smile of happiness; it was a small, sly smile that seemed to say, "We have one more card to play."

Although unsure how to proceed, the druid knew Wavren was considering something she had missed. She called out to the council, "My Brother, Wavren of Celes'tia, also has testimony. Let him speak."

Xaeris nodded and Wavren stood up. He looked to his mentor, the mail-clad dwarf who had been leaning back precariously in his chair. The dwarf began rocking back and forth on the two rear legs of the chair. The motion made a slight squeaking. The hunter chose his words carefully and proceeded:

"Councilman Xaeris, I noticed that you have assumed the position where High Councilman Kalin normally sits. The senior councilman always gets the centermost chair as a symbol of authority. It is really more of a throne than a simple chair. In fact, that chair looks a lot like the chair in Kalin's private office, which is perhaps the finest chair in Forestedge. I was wondering if you would allow me to sit there for a moment."

The senior councilman was unsure of what to say. No one ever sat in the high councilman's chair, except Kalin and now Xaeris, the ad hoc high councilman. Just as he was about to say no, Gaedron sat up and spoke: "Let me boy sit in yer pompous, overstuffed chair fer goodness sake. He done earned it fer killin' the very orcs that would prolly be hav'n their way wit yer daughters and wives had we not been here."

Somewhat stunned by the dwarf's directness, Xaeris got up, and Wavren sat down. Wavren got up again and sat down again. He smiled to Gaedron and said, "I bet this is one of the softest chairs in Forestedge, not to mention its sturdiness. Gaedron, you have got to try this chair."

Before anyone could object, the stout dwarf ran up the aisle and plopped into the high councilman's chair. Everyone looked utterly confused. Finally, Jade'ena spoke up: "Well, now that a dwarf and a common elf have made a mockery of the council and this tribunal, I move to end this foolishness and dismiss the charges against Kalin based on a lack of substantial proof."

Wavren looked to Rosabela, and she smiled.

Wavren spoke up: "I was called to testify, and I have yet to do so."

Xaeris looked somewhat confused and appeared to be growing impatient, but he nodded.

Wavren began, "I noticed a while back that High Councilman Kalin seemed to know a lot about the local commander of the Bloodcrest Forces and even offered to pay my sister and me to go after him. He said the prisoner dared us to try to get the orc leader named Neggish Grimtusk. We went looking and came up empty handed. I thought it was odd that Kalin also restructured the defense forces so that most of the experienced warriors and mages were on patrol instead of in the city limits where they had traditionally been assigned. Now, many of them are dead or remain abroad on their scouting missions just as a raid comes to Forestedge. The connection here is that with the two local Protectors of the Vale gone on a wild goose chase, and the most powerful warriors and mages on patrol, few are left to protect the city."

Jade'ena objected, "This is all circumstantial coincidence and proves nothing."

Wavren smiled and said, "I do have proof."

All eyes turned back to him as he smiled that sly, knowing smile. He played his final card.

"Senior Councilman Xaeris," Wavren began, "I believe that the elf you see over there is a changeling. He is a cunning wolf in sheep's clothes, to quote an old saying. He is an orc from the Bloodcrest Forces, and to prove it, all you need to do is make him sit in your chair. You see, an elf like yourself, or even one outfitted in armor like me, weighs significantly less than an orc. Even the stout dwarf in chainmail to my right weighs less. An orc who can change his appearance with magic might look different, but an illusion does not change the mass of the caster. He is still a massive brute under the façade of the illusion."

Xaeris looked unsure for a moment. Then he stood up and began to call for the guards to escort the entire group of accusers out of the city limits when Gaedron jumped up. In one smooth motion, he drew his blunderbuss and pointed it at Kalin.

Gaedron commanded, "Kalin, ye foul traitor, I got me money on the boy's theory. I'm so sure'n dat he be right, dat if'n ye don't git yer arse up and try out yer ol' chair, then I'm just gonna have ta kill ya. Ya see, I'm believin' dat once yer dead, ye'll be revertin' back to an orc. Either way, we're gonna know da truth."

Dwarves were never known for subtlety, and Gaedron of Dragonforge was very convincing with his blunderbuss in hand. The high councilman stood up and tried to look dignified. He walked over to the chair and gently sat down. When the chair creaked with his weight, the entire council gasped.

Jade'ena spoke again: "I can't believe the council is even entertaining this insane notion, and for anyone to threaten a council member with deadly force is a crime against the city. The dwarf should be arrested along with his fellow conspirators who only want to see the downfall of a good elf."

Gaedron lowered his weapon and smiled. The council backed away from Kalin and Jael'Kutter moved forward with his mighty polearm held in battle-worn hands that were white knuckled from the grip he had on the weapon. The captain's jaw was set and his fury was mounting. Kalin knew the tribunal was over and the judgment was made. The verdict was death. Kalin dashed through the back door and into the courtyard behind the council chambers. There was no way to escape, but he needed room to maneuver.

Kalin was quickly surrounded on all sides with soldiers, archers, and mages, quickly gathering en mass. Jael'Kutter and his few remaining troops came forward with Wavren, Rosabela, Da'Shar, and Gaedron trailing behind.

Kalin held up his hands and spoke a few arcane words. His thin elven form dissipated with an acrid puff of smoke, and a massive orc clad in heavy chainmail armor stood where the form of Kalin had once been.

The orc spoke in perfect elven tongue, saying, "I am Ballock of Dek'Thal, soldier of the Bloodcrest Forces under the command of Doppleganger and Commander Neggish Grimtusk of the Northern Front. By the code of combat, I request my fate be decided in single battle with your city's champion. You must honor this request in accordance with your own laws of warfare."

Jael'Kutter stepped forward, and with one mighty swing of his blade, the head of Ballock fell to the ground. Through gritted teeth, he hissed, "Request denied."

The captain of the guard shook the blood from his polearm and spit on the body of the dead orc. He looked up and saw acceptance in every elf's eyes, but one expression stood out. Gaedron, the normally grim-faced dwarven hunter, was smiling broadly.

Chapter 14
Preparing for Battle

Forestedge was a swarm of hustling townsfolk. Evacuation of non-combatants, mostly the very young and the very old, was underway. Craftsmen were honing blades, producing arrows, and hammering armor. Engineers were digging in fortifications, setting obstacles, and laying traps. The leaders were already present in the council chambers with the city council, which had called an emergency meeting to discuss the coming invasion. No one knew exactly how many enemy soldiers the Bloodcrest Forces would send against the city or when they would come, having had their advanced war party repulsed, but everyone seemed determined to be ready at all costs.

A gnome with a long, twisting mustache came forward and spoke: "High Councilman, the Mage Guild has dispatched seers and divination specialists to scour the city for other orcs in elven disguise. So far, none have been found. It appears as though we only had the one infiltrator."

"Very good," he replied dismissively, as he nodded to the captain of the guard to come forward.

"High Councilman Xaeris," Jael'Kutter began, "the remaining soldiers are prepared for combat, but our numbers are few. We have barely two companies of warriors, supported by one company of spell-wielders, half of which belong to the Mage Guild and half of which are healers."

"Send a runner to Celes'tia requesting reinforcements, and make great haste," Xaeris instructed.

The captain of the guard spoke again: "High Councilman, reinforcements cannot be assembled and marched from Port Archer, much less Celes'tia, in time. We have roughly three hundred elves, which means we can hold out indefinitely as long as the enemy attacks with less than five hundred orcs, but we will be hard pressed to hold back numbers beyond that without reinforcements."

Xaeris considered the implications of the situation. "We must know how many are coming. Send the hunters out to reconnoiter the enemy numbers, and send the druids with the dispatch for reinforcements. They can make the trip faster, with Nature's help, than our fastest rider."

Captain Jael'Kutter turned on his heel and dashed out of the room. The council was murmuring about the impending doom and the much-needed preparations that remained undone. The high councilman managed to initiate a plan for every concern that came up, but underneath his calm, quiet demeanor, he was fighting back the urge to join in the building panic.

* * *

Rosabela and Da'Shar were already prepared to make the run to Port Archer when Jael'Kutter offered them the dispatch. He spent a brief moment staring at the young and beautiful elf maid. She was intoxicating, a perfect balance of Nature, and although battle hardened, she was still innocent somehow. He noticed his unconscious, lingering gaze when Rosabela smiled and quickly took the dispatch. In that moment, the captain of the guard forgot the evil in the world. For a moment, all was right and perfect. Then he came back to reality.

He spoke quickly to dispel the silence: "Fare well, my friends. Our fate may be decided before you return, but do not stop until you reach Port Archer. The road is likely crawling with orcs, so run hard, and be prepared for a fight if it comes."

Da'Shar had witnessed the small but powerful exchange of feelings between the two, but he remained focused on the mission at hand. He intervened by saying, "We will not fall prey to the orcs; neither will we rest until we have made Port Archer." As he spoke the words, he was already transforming into his windwraith form, and the words trailed off into a low growl.

The two druids sped quickly out of sight, and Jael'Kutter spun on his heel, heading back to his troops where he would plan for the toughest battle of his life. Barely a mile away from the city, Da'Shar stopped and transformed back into his elven form. Rosabela followed suit and stood alongside her master.

"It is time for another lesson, dear child," he said in his fatherly tone. "You cannot keep the pace as a bear and must now learn to travel as the wind. Just as you have bonded with the bear for combat, you will now bond with Nature itself to become speed incarnate. No other beast will match your foot speed, no hunter will find your trail, and only those keen of sight and sound will ever sense your passing."

Rosabela was thrilled with the idea of learning how to summon her travel form and watched closely as Da'Shar walked through the incantation. He closed his eyes and made a variety of hand gestures that were followed by words in the ancient tongue of druids. The wind picked up from a gentle breeze to a fair gust that whipped Da'Shar's hair back and forth. His body stretched forth into a feline form, but it was not the windwraith she was used to seeing.

The travel form was longer and much lighter with a tawny, spotted coat that somehow blended with the surroundings immediately, not unlike a chameleon. The paws were broad, though not for combat as the windwraith's paws. These paws distributed weight broadly in order to leave an imperceptible trail. To call the travel form cheetah-like would be a fair assessment, but in truth, the travel form was less substantial, almost ethereal in nature. It was not a beast of this world. It was some sort of mystical creature from another plane of existence.

Da'Shar returned to his elven form and approached Rosabela. He leaned in close and whispered the true name and incantation of the creature that she would bond with. Immediately, the words became a part of her being, not unlike the bond she had with the bear. Her mind raced with anticipation, but discipline had always been her watchword, and measured steps were always required when dealing with magic.

Rosabela calmed her mind and then reviewed the three parts of the spell: the incantation, the somatic gestures, and then the reagent expenditure. Only after she was fully prepared did she begin the transformation, and the result was breathtaking. Her body did not contort into the new form as it did with the bear. Instead, she simply faded away and where her elven body had once been, now there was a feline, astral form.

She sprang forward toward Port Archer like a flash of tawny light. The feeling of running through the forest in her travel form was unbelievable. She felt like a low flying bird, slicing through the air more than running. Suddenly, an unsettling feeling came over her. She felt the irresistible temptation to remain in this form where she was little more than a gust of wind and a blur of movement to any passersby. Abandoning her body and even her duties seemed inconsequential compared to her current state of euphoria. She paused for a moment, and Da'Shar was there, knowing full well the struggle she was facing. His presence comforted her, and with a hollow roar, like the echo of a distant lion, he reminded her that time was short, and they had to continue quickly. She refocused and dashed onward, but the subconscious desire was still there. It would always be there.

Barely an hour had passed when Port Archer came into view. Da'Shar never slowed down to change into his elven form; he merely appeared in the doorway of Port Archer's high councilman. Asanti, the gnomish personnel clerk, jumped and squeaked at the sudden appearance. Papers flew everywhere.

"Master Da'Shar, what brings you to Port Archer?" the

gnome asked.

"I bear a dispatch from Forestedge. We have reason to believe an attack is imminent. Where are the high councilman and your security commander?" Da'Shar inquired.

In an all-too-gnomish panic, Asanti replied, "The high councilman is in his chambers and does not wish to be disturbed, but this is obviously an emergency, so I will get him. Captain Helio is in the security headquarters building. I will send a messenger."

"I cannot wait; I must be off to Celes'tia. My companion, Rosabela, will deliver the dispatch and brief your leaders," Da'Shar explained hastily, then departed.

Asanti immediately dove into his numerous files, dug out a battle roster of available troops to assemble for battle, and sped off to pass the word. On his way out, he grabbed Rosabela by the hand and led her along to see the high councilman speaking in such frenzied words that Rosabela could only catch a few pieces. She heard him say something about rousing the troops, full alert, and this action being what he was born for.

Dashing up the stairs of the councilman's chambers with amazing agility, Asanti managed to half-pull, half-drag Rosabela into Councilman Panni's presence. He presented her to Panni and was out the door heading for the security headquarters in mere moments. When Panni and Rosabela took their eyes off of the high-strung gnome, they realized that both had been staring open-mouthed at the spectacle.

Panni cleared his throat and said, "Rosabela, it is good to see you. Considering the exuberance of my personnel clerk, I assume you have urgent business here."

"High Councilman Panni," she began, "I request immediate dispatch of every available soldier to aid in the coming battle at Forestedge. Time is of the essence, and unless we move quickly, the Bloodcrest Forces will likely overrun our defenses."

Being an elven high councilman meant making tough decisions, and Councilman Panni was rarely shaken even given dire news. He calmly spoke: "What is the threat Forestedge faces? I need reconnaissance reports, invasion force numbers, and siege equipment they employ."

Rosabela spoke confidently, saying, "I do not know how many or what siege equipment they might bring, but a host of orcs, well trained, disciplined, and armed with enchanted armor, are mobilized to assault the city. I personally faced an advanced party so powerful that it nearly destroyed Forestedge's entire quick reaction force in a single battle. We have assembled the remaining warriors, mages, and healers, but Councilman Xaeris requires your assistance."

"Councilman Xaeris?" Panni repeated. "Xaeris is not the high councilman; he is merely the speaker of elders."

"I do not have the time to explain everything, but Kalin was a spy. We discovered that he was an orc, disguised as Kalin, who had infiltrated the city. Xaeris is now the ad hoc high councilman," she replied, her voice beginning to show frustration at High Councilman Panni's delay.

The high councilman smiled and gently placed his hand on Rosabela's shoulder. He said, "Easy, child, I will not fail in my duty to send reinforcements, but I must have the details in order to respond appropriately. Asanti is no doubt mustering the troops. By now, Captain Helio is making preparations for rapid deployment. We have a few moments to speak at length, so please tell me everything."

* * *

Da'Shar had expended most of his considerable endurance running from Forestedge to Port Archer. Even in his travel form, he had limits, and those limits were rapidly approaching as he neared the docks. Da'Shar hoped that a ship would be in port to carry him from Port Archer to Celes'tia, but he was mentally prepared to swim if need be.

Da'Shar transformed back into his elven form right behind the dock master. "I must get to Celes'tia immediately," he said. "Is there anything available leaving the port that might carry me and make great haste?"

The dock master was quite surprised to have Da'Shar suddenly appear right behind him, but upon recognizing him as a Protector of the Vale, he snapped to attention. "No, sir, I do not think anything is outbound for Celes'tia within the hour."

"Nothing whatsoever?" the druid pressed.

"No ship, sir, but there is something that might carry you quite speedily," the dock master returned.

"Anything will work; I am willing to take a rowboat if it comes with two powerful oarsmen," he said.

The dock master squinted to the east while shading his eyes. He finally pointed to the top of the hill on the edge of a cliff facing the sea and said, "Go see the griffon master. He claims to have trained beasts able to carry a man, or in this case, an elf, to Celes'tia faster than a caravel under strong winds. He says it is the way of future transportation."

Da'Shar was off in a flash for the hill-top. He knew a great deal about most beasts, but griffons were not a natural breed found in the forest. Griffons were the magical combination of a lion and a giant eagle. Legend said they were originally guardians created to protect the great gates of Griffon's Peak, the human capitol city. Using the eagle's wings, they were rumored capable of flying to the highest parapet. From there, they would tirelessly watch for enemies at great distances with their piercing, avian eyes. They could then drop down at great speeds to attack evildoers using the powerful body and forelegs of the lion. The druid was concerned that these beasts might not be easily controlled since they were not of Nature, but his options were now limited to swimming or the griffon master.

"Hail and well met, stranger," the griffon master called as Da'Shar moved up the hill in his elven form.

"What must I do to get to Celes'tia by griffon?" Da'Shar inquired, laboring for breath. He was much more tired than he realized, but he put thoughts of his fatigue out of his mind.

"Well, friend, for a single silver coin, I will saddle up this beauty, and she will do the rest," he said confidently. "All of my griffons are trained to go from one griffon aerie— which is essentially a griffon nest—to the next griffon aerie and back. I simply whisper the destination, and off they go."

"That sounds easy, but do I require training in order to ride?" the druid inquired.

"No, sir, these mystical wonders are trained from birth to fly with even the most untrained rider to a destination of my choosing. The only way to fall out of the saddle, which comes with an idiot-proof harness, is to completely unbuckle and jump off, at which time the griffon has been trained to scoop you up, before you splatter on the ground, and carry you in its claws to the destination. Yep, it is fool-proof."

"Very well; I would like to purchase a ride to Celes'tia," Da'Shar said, handing the griffon master a silver coin.

"Would you be interested in a skin of wine, or perhaps some dried fruit for the trip? I can sell it to you at a reduced price since you are a first time flier," the griffon master haggled.

Da'Shar managed a smile and said, "I am in a terrible hurry. Please prepare the saddle so that I might depart immediately. I need nothing more than the mount for this journey."

"Very well, sir, one griffon coming up."

The griffon master was not only a fine salesman, but he appeared to be an excellent beast keeper. Da'Shar walked with him to the aerie and noticed several griffons sitting majestically in their nests. The heads of these amazing creatures were no different than those of great eagles. Their eyes were piercing and all-seeing. Their feathers were white or red, depending on the breed, and the beaks were vice-like and undoubtedly razor sharp. Da'Shar made note that a griffon could easily bite the head off an elf and swallow it whole.

The griffon master bridled a white-feathered beast and led it toward Da'Shar. As he placed the saddle and harness on its leonine back, the griffon held perfectly still. Not a muscle in its massive, tawny-colored body so much as twitched. He noticed that unlike the lions of the Western Kingdom, this beast was easily a thousand pounds of flesh tearing destruction, closer to the size of a warhorse than a lion.

"There you go, friend. Just jump up there and run these

leather straps over your legs. This belt goes around your waist to secure you into the saddle. Even a child can do it," he said with a proud smile.

Da'Shar felt a little uncomfortable at first, but the griffon showed no distress as he climbed up. Once Da'Shar was secured in the harness, the griffon master checked all the straps and buckles and gave a thumbs up. When Da'Shar returned the gesture, the griffon master whispered a few words to the griffon in a strange language that could have been magical, but may have been nothing more than chirps and whistles common to birds. The only word the druid recognized was Celes'tia, his destination. Upon completion, the griffon master blew a tiny whistle, and the beast stretched its mighty wings and dove off the cliff. The vertical plummet to the ocean was several hundred feet, and the griffon waited for more than half of that to begin leveling off.

Da'Shar had always been conservative in using Nature's gifts, but he was well versed in spectacular feats, being a shape-shifter. He was knowledgeable in numerous magical wonders; he had run as an ethereal cat, fought evil as a savage windwraith, and crushed enemies as a powerful bear, but never had he experienced the exhilaration of flying. This was absolute euphoria! He felt his blood pumping through his body as his heart beat powerfully with adrenaline. The hurricane-force wind pulled mightily on his clothes and hair and made his eyes water, but he barely blinked, not wanting to miss a moment of the ride. His arms and legs ached from holding on so tightly, but none of that mattered. Even his fatigue seemed to be washed away by the experience. He was astounded.

Da'Shar's mount landed gently a short while later. Having arrived on the outskirts of Celes'tia after the strain of flying, the druid found that he was once again exhausted. He retrieved the long staff from its resting place strapped on his back and began walking into town. He simply could not summon the strength to transform into his travel form. Luckily, his objective was not far. In fact, he was already being approached by an elven guard patrol riding massive windwraiths. They would carry him to the Great Temple where he would deliver his message to request reinforcements.

* * *

"Our forces are ready to march on Forestedge," Nightshade reported.

"And what of Shadowblade and the shaman; are they prepared as well?" Commander Grimtusk asked.

"Yes, Commander, they are ready to march as well," he replied.

"Good. I think his failures will finally bring some good fortune to our battle plans, not to mention fine entertainment," Grimtusk snarled. "Sound the war horns; we march for Forestedge and the destruction of our elven enemies."

"Yes, Commander," the platoon leader replied before departing with much haste.

The great orcish war horns sounded moments later, just as Commander Grimtusk had ordered. He thought that it was good to finally be on the road heading for battle. Orcs had never been known for patience and were often willing to fight amongst each other if no other enemy was readily available. It was a precarious balance leading such violent troops, but it was a balance that had its rewards. Great honor and glory awaited them, and that was exactly what orcs lived for. That was what Neggish Grimtusk was born for.

Unlike earlier forays into elven territory, this march brought a full-scale invasion force. The orcish infantry marched in four ranks online with fifty troops per line. They were clad in heavy armor and carried every manner of weapon imaginable. Many carried a single sword and shield, but several preferred two-headed axes and great swords that were easily as long as a human was tall.

The elite orcish troops made up two flanking platoons of fifty soldiers each and carried dual weapons of every size and design, including twin swords, sword and dagger, twin hand axes, and even blade and mace combinations. They were tasked with quickly enveloping the enemy lines while the more heavily armored infantry made the frontal assault.

The trolls made up four platoons of light cavalry riding in columns slightly behind the elite orcs. These forty mounted troops were astride great bipedal lizards called *desert raptors,* which were known for their vicious rear talons that could rend chainmail and shred flesh like dwarf-forged blades. Their ability to spring high into the air, often over the frontlines, and land amid the archers in the rear, made them extremely effective and terrifying to unprotected rear troops. They carried a myriad of ranged weapons from throwing axes to crossbows. They were deadly at medium range, but after a few volleys of missile fire, they could draw melee weapons and charge into the fray, causing great havoc and much destruction with their wickedly curved scimitars.

The undead contingent was small, but no less fearsome than the other groups. It comprised the spell-wielders, mostly wizards with a few dark priests. These were reserved to protect the command cell and served as Neggish Grimtusk's personal advisors. Their ability to call death-magic, fire, and ice made them nearly unstoppable at long range, but their lack of armor made them vulnerable at close range.

Last, but not least, were the shock troops. A powerful company of tauren warriors marched in a diamond formation behind the leading infantry ranks. It was obvious that their unparalleled strength would be used to punch a hole through the battle lines with the sole purpose of hitting the enemy commander.

In the deep rear of the enemy formation rode Commander Neggish Grimtusk and his platoon leaders. They all rode great worgs, the most vicious of all mounts. These battle-hardened creatures were fourteen hands tall at the shoulder and could easily snap the neck of a warhorse in their great lupine jaws. They were feared most of all for their pack mentality. Not unlike massive wolves, these beasts fought well independently, but they were unrivaled when two or more of them fought together.

The platoon leaders all wore matching black armor and carried matching weapons. Their only true differences were in their specialties. Blackbane was the poison specialist, Nightshade was the master of stealth, Doppelganger was a shapeshifter, and Shadowblade was the weapons and tactics expert. Each leader normally commanded ten orcs trained in their specialty, but that number had been decimated during the last night raid. Still, the remaining four platoon leaders were the finest orcs ever trained by Grimtusk and would quickly kill anyone or anything long before their commander was in danger.

Neggish Grimtusk wore layered plate armor over chainmail. The blackened chainmail was enchanted such that no arrow, stone, or crossbow bolt would penetrate into his flesh. The outer plates that covered his shoulders, chest, back, thighs, knees, forearms, and shins were studded with enchanted ivory spikes that would impale anyone foolish enough to engage him in close combat. The spikes coincidently matched his namesake, *Grimtusk.* He carried the great ax of his ancestral tribe. The blade was pure obsidian and the handle was adamantine, both of which were enchanted by the great shaman, Draken'skgar, who was rumored to have been half-orc and half-dragon. Legend had it that the ax of Grimtusk was forged eons ago, during the age of fire, when dragons ruled the realms. It was supposed to provide its bearer with protection from the elements, particularly dragon's fire. It was also a vorpal weapon, able to sever arms, legs, necks, and even armored torsos in one massive swipe. Nothing could stop the dark magic in the blade once called upon, not even dragonscale.

Neggish smiled as he assembled his massive force toward Forestedge. He knew there would be no way for the pitiful elves to stop his troops. His battalion of warriors and war beasts numbered nearly six hundred strong. From earlier reports, the forty-orc raid nearly ransacked the city by itself. This would be a slaughter, especially given the nasty surprise he had in mind with his failed platoon leader, Shadowblade.

Neggish signaled one of the undead wizards to cast a spell

to increase the range of his voice for all to hear.

Commander Grimtusk inhaled a massive breath and called to his warriors: "Brothers of Bloodcrest, today we march for Forestedge and the ruin of all elvenkind!"

The group replied in unison, "Death to the elves!"

He continued, "With our great strength, we will crush their defenses effortlessly!"

Again, they replied in unison, "Crush them!"

He called again, "Today we will show all of Western Kingdom that any who stand before us will be slain without pity and with no remorse. Today, we are the storm. We are their destruction!"

"Destroy them!" they called in unison.

"For the glory of Dek'Thal!" he called out.

"For the Honor of Bloodcrest!" was the response of his soldiers.

The march began.

Chapter 15
War in Forestedge

Wavren was carefully scouting the outskirts of Forestedge, checking the fortifications and assessing the defensive perimeter. So far everything was coming together according to the overall plan that High Councilman Xaeris and Jael'Kutter provided. Luckily, there were only two possible avenues of approach for the Bloodcrest Forces. The northern corridor was unlikely since the enemy had to move out of the east in a northwestern direction, through dense woodlands before pushing south to Forestedge. This was the long route, but offered the element of surprise. Just north of that corridor was the city of Port Archer, where allies were being mustered and would be on the move soon. If the enemy chose that route, they would likely have elven reinforcements at their back before the battle was over. The other option was to drive out of the south, then westward through enemy-controlled territory to attack along the main battle lines that had been used over and over throughout history. This was the most likely option, and the council agreed that the bulk of the forces should be positioned to receive the enemy from that direction. Wavren was certain that the enemy commander would want surprise on his side, but not at the cost of getting hit in the rear by reinforcements. The one thing that bothered him was the possibility that Port Archer had also been infiltrated by a shape-shifting spy. If this was the case, no reinforcements would come, and Forestedge would be sacked from the north for sure. Chances were that reinforcements would never arrive in time anyway, but he hoped his sister would find a way.

As Wavren moved outside of the fortifications to view the defensive perimeter from the perspective of his enemy, he had to smile. In spite of the short amount of time to prepare, the city had been able to establish a fine perimeter. The southern route had been barricaded with an *abatis,* a series of fallen, interwoven trees, cut down to slow the progress of massive troops in formation. He thought, *Thank goodness the druids were not around to witness that destruction of Nature, or the enemy wouldn't be the only force fighting Forestedge today.*

Once the Bloodcrest Forces hit that obstacle, they would be in range of the deadliest weapon in the elven arsenal: the legendary elven longbow. The abatis would also slow any siege equipment or cavalry and should isolate the forward ranks of infantry. The second wave of fighting would be the gnomish and human wizards. Although few in number, they would be able to ignite the abatis with spells of fire and cause the forward ranks to break. This would allow the warriors to move forward and hit the broken lines of troops with skirmishing tactics. Elves were by far superior in fighting skills to the orcs, but the orcs had greater numbers. It was critical for the Dae'gon Alliance to prevent the enemy from massing its forces. That was the decisive point in the upcoming battle.

Wavren moved back into the city proper and noticed that his mentor was nowhere to be found. He moved quickly from the council chambers to the marketplace and finally to the smithy's shop. It was there that he found Gaedron. The dwarf was steadily working at the bench when Wavren walked up behind him.

"I knew ye'd be about soon," the dwarf said.

"I have been out checking the perimeter defenses," Wavren said.

"And what've ye found? Did them long-eared kin o' yers drop dem trees like'n I told 'em too?" he asked.

"The abatis was your idea? Da'Shar is going to have a fit when he sees it," the elf replied.

"Aye, an' I'm hopin' he sees it soon, meanin' he done brought more long-ears from Celes'tia. If'n he fails to rally more fighters, I'll be dead 'n gone long afore he sees what we did to his trees," the dwarf returned with a very serious tone.

Wanting to change the subject, Wavren picked up one of several red sticks that Gaedron was working on and said, "Are these the same sticks you used to destroy Borik's minions at the graveyard?"

"Aye, lad, an' I recall sayin' I'd teach ye how ta make 'em," he replied with a somber, but somewhat less serious, tone, "but first ye gotta un'erstand dat this ain't like the powder ye use in yer gun, boy-o. Dis be dynamite, an' it'll kill ye faster 'n any sword or ax if'n ye get careless. Ain't no sec'nd chance 'ere."

With that disclaimer, Wavren gingerly put the red stick back on the counter and said, "Teach me."

Gaedron smiled broadly and went into a long explanation about how to combine the ingredients, package the explosive, and add the fuse. He spoke at length about testing the fuse for *burn rate* every time a new batch was created in order to avoid problems with five-second fuses setting off the dynamite in less than two seconds. "Sometimes, the darned fuse jus' fizzles and goes out, but dat ain't near as bad as when it burns too fast and catches ye in mid-throw. Had me an uncle who used ta blow holes in da mount'in side lookin' fer ore. He fergot ta check his fuse one time, an' KABOOM! We ne'er found all o' his body, but da big pieces got a nice burial," Gaedron said more to himself than to his pupil.

Wavren made a mental note to always check the fuse.

Gaedron smiled again and patted the elf on the back. He

said, "Ye'd make a fine dwarf if'n it weren't fer dem pointy ears."

Wavren felt certain that Gaedron had just given him the highest compliment a dwarf could give an elf. He swelled with pride for a moment and quietly thanked the Gods for having such a fine mentor.

Just as the last of the dynamite was stashed in padded backpacks for safekeeping, the great horn sounded. The Bloodcrest Forces had arrived on the outskirts of Forestedge. All able-bodied warriors and spell casters moved into position. The very young and the very old who chose to stay behind shuttled extra arrows, water, and bandages from stockpiles to the outer defenses. No one was left to cower in fear.

"C'mon, boy-o, let's go see what da baddies brought us ta play wit' dis time," the dwarven hunter called with no shortage of ire. He whistled once, and Blackmaw appeared out of the brush behind the smithy. Wavren followed suit, and Stonetalon appeared soon after.

From the wall that formed the outer ring of the city, scores of elven archers waited patiently. Councilman Xaeris was among them, with his fine longbow in hand. Wavren was greatly impressed that he was willing to participate in the fight given his station, but in truth, the time for policy and politics was over. The city was in the hands of Jael'Kutter now, and the citizens of Forestedge were going to follow his leadership to the end, regardless of position or wealth. The assailants would not discriminate in their desire to kill, which relegated everyone to the role of combatant or combat support provider.

As Gaedron approached the battlements, he could barely see over the wall, but after pushing his way through several archers and climbing on top of his bear, he got a clear picture of the massive army.

"By Moradin," he whispered, "dat looks like a full battalion to me; at least five hunnerd. Durned ghoul said forty was comin'. I'm guessin' we done killed that group an' this 'un is da real war party."

Councilman Xaeris asked, "Can we hold these vermin off,

master dwarf?"

"Sure can," he said confidently. "Jes' pray ye don' miss wit' yer bow or run outta arrows afore reinforcements arrive. If'n ye do, ye better be faster'n me, 'cause runnin' to Port Archer is da only other option we have."

Councilman Xaeris nodded and nocked his first arrow. "Prepare to fire on my mark!" he ordered.

Wavren and Gaedron leveled their unusual weapons as well and waited for the command.

Far below, just outside of the gate, Jael'Kutter and his small contingent of warriors stood ready to hold the onslaught back. If the Bloodcrest Forces managed to pass the abatis, under heavy bow fire, they would be in for the fight of their lives. He looked from left to right and made note that not one warrior trembled. Not one cringed. Each elf was stone-faced, jaws clenched and weapons at the ready. He knew that if the city fell, it would be only after he and all of his troops were dead. He said a silent prayer that Rosabela and Da'Shar would make it back in time. They were soon to be desperately needed.

* * *

The Bloodcrest Forces had made amazing progress through the southern route, and Commander Grimtusk was eager for blood. One of his scouts ran through the ranks to the rear of the formation and informed him that several trees were down in the roadway.

Neggish laughed and mocked the elves, saying, "The mighty elves of Forestedge have cut down their own trees to slow us. How futile! They must be desperate to buy time for their brothers from Port Archer and Celes'tia to arrive. I applaud them for their innovation, but I have a surprise that they will find most interesting. Nothing will delay my forces. Bring Shadowblade and his platoon forth. His time for penitence has come."

Shadowblade and his remaining four platoon members approached the frontlines followed by nearly a dozen venerable shamans. The platoon members and their leader had been stripped of armor and weapons. The shaman tied the platoon members together in a tight circle around a large tree stump. Each platoon member was tended by three of the holy men. Shadowblade had been recently covered from head to foot in a myriad of tattoos and magic sigils. The shaman started chanting, and the tattoos began to glow. The sigils came to life and danced across Shadowblade's body. He grunted in pain and began to gasp for breath. He screamed and writhed as if tortured and then began to grow. His body elongated and widened at first to the size of an ogre, then a giant, finally swelling to the size of a titan. The pain had been maddening, and Shadowblade howled. Even the frontline troops of the Bloodcrest Forces cringed for a moment, and then Shadowblade lurched forward toward the now-tiny abatis. Effortlessly, he kicked the once-formidable obstacle apart and moved into range of the elven archers.

From nearly a thousand paces away, Shadowblade heard a tiny voice say, "Fire!" The sky went dark for a moment as one hundred arrows arced in from above. Two tiny explosions and puffs of smoke preceded the impact of the hunters' gunfire on Shadowblade's chest. The effect was minimal. Shadowblade roared and swatted at the needle-like tiny barbs, breaking off most of the shafts and lunging forward just in time to receive the second and then the third volley.

Meanwhile, the four platoon members tied to the stump screamed in agony and erupted with dozens of arrow shaped wounds. The twelve shaman healers quickly laid hands on them and restored their health. Each volley sent waves of searing pain into the platoon members as they shared the damage of their platoon leader. Neggish Grimtusk smiled at their torment, knowing that no other soldier under his command would defy him or fail him for fear of sharing that wicked fate. None would betray him or turn and flee. The punishment was beyond cruel, but at least Shadowblade would be remembered as a hero who led the charge on Forestedge, and this lesson would be remembered even longer than Shadowblade's fame. Grimtusk would be infamous for the deed for all time.

* * *

Councilman Xaeris fired again and again alongside his countrymen with little lasting effect. Wavren and Gaedron were not doing any better. The monstrous orc just kept coming forward. He had more than a dozen volleys of arrows protruding from his hide and twice that in bullet holes from the hunters.

The time had come for more powerful attacks. The spellcasters stepped forward. No one had to call for them to fire in unison; they simply started blasting away. Each mage cast fireball after fireball. The warlocks and priests called on dark bolts of energy and pillars of fire. It was a magical display unlike anything ever seen in Forestedge.

The acrid smoke and the smell of burning flesh was thick in the air, but each mage continued issuing blast after blast until the entire landscape before the elven warriors was burning and smoke covered the field of vision. The spell-wielders stopped for a moment, and the battle grew quiet. There was a deep groan, and then the ground shook as the mighty orc-titan crashed to the ground.

The elves cheered, but Gaedron, who knew what was yet to come, held his blunderbuss at the ready. It had just begun and was going to get worse in a minute. Wavren was first to see the movement along the flanks. He called to his kinsmen, "Troll cavalry … mounted archers on the move!" His blunderbuss went up just as Gaedron fired his first round. A troll fell from his *raptor* clutching his side, but two score of other troll riders fired into Jael'Kutter's men.

"Shields to the front!" the mighty captain called. "Hold the line!"

Several elven warriors took hits, but none fell. In a matter of moments, the warriors had the shield wall in place, and the trolls regrouped and dashed back behind the cover of the black smoke. Jael'Kutter quickly assessed his troops and their injuries. No one was seriously wounded, thanks to fine elven mail and a lot of luck. He called for a healer and had the few minor injuries tended to. He knew the next attack would not be as subtle. He called to his men again, "Hold the line, and let none break through!"

Councilman Xaeris called for more arrows; a dozen young boys hauled quiver after quiver up to the archers, but there was only enough ammunition for a dozen more volleys. After that, the archers would have to draw swords and back up the front-line warriors. He realized that the cunning orc general had anticipated the huge expenditure of arrows and magical firepower. They had played right into his hands.

Gaedron and Wavren had plenty of ammunition, but they would be of little use alone in the parapets. Time was running out, and much of the firepower had already been expended on the giant orc. If reinforcements didn't arrive soon, there would be a rout, followed by the greatest slaughter of elves in the Western Kingdom's history.

* * *

Neggish Grimtusk had barely committed any of his considerable forces to the battle, and yet he had already drawn the foolish elves into expending a mass of firepower. These pathetic fools were no match for his cunning. He took the time to move forward among his warriors and examine the four platoon members tied to the great tree stump.

The twelve shamans were feverishly working to revive and restore the mutilated bodies that had magically shared the damage given to Shadowblade. The first of the four was facing east. He had taken the brunt of several fireball spells and was little more than a charred corpse, yet somehow he was still breathing. Neggish chalked it up to orcish constitution and dozens of restoration spells. He nodded for the healers to simply let him expire.

The second orc, who was facing south, was only burned on the left side of his body, but he had suffered countless arrow wounds as indicated by the deep crimson pool that filled the ruts in the ground where he had kicked and thrashed trying to free himself of his bonds. He was not breathing, and his three dedicated healers were working to resurrect his lifeless body. Neggish waved them off from their task.

The third, facing west, was not burned at all, but was no longer recognizable as humanoid. The trauma he sustained had overwhelmed the healing powers of his three shamans, and the result was some sort of magical backlash that seemed to have disintegrated his skeletal structure and most of his organs. He was little more than an empty shell of loose skin. Grimtusk was always amazed at how magic could bring about such powerful results. He was also amazed at the toll it took to do so.

The last orc, who faced north, was not only alive, but was spitting and cursing those around him. Neggish noticed that his burns were healing of their own accord and that his right arm, where the burns were the most severe, was turning from black, to red, to pink right before his eyes. The holes in his chest from the arrow wounds were closed up, and only a minimal amount of blood was present. Grimtusk was intrigued.

"Soldier," Grimtusk called, "how is it that you have suffered less than your doomed brethren?"

The soldier smiled with many broken and crooked teeth. "I'm a fast healer."

"I can see that, fool!" he replied angrily. "Tell me how it is that you are able to sustain yourself."

"If I tell you, will you grant me peace?" the soldier asked. "I have suffered and paid for Shadowblade's failures a hundred times over."

"Your work is not yet finished here. I will not grant you peace, but I will make you suffer one hundred more deaths if you do not speak quickly," the commander returned with a hiss.

The soldier knew of Grimtusk's cruelty and although he did not fear death, he did fear the suffering that he had just experienced. He truly wanted it all to end and decided that his ability to heal was now more of a curse than simply to let go and die.

There was one way to find eternal rest. He began with the truth.

"I am Hath'or, bastard son of Neggish Grimtusk," the soldier began. "My mother was Jin'ada, the enchantress. I can see, by the look in your eyes, that you remember her."

Grimtusk merely shrugged. He had numerous bastard children. Such was the way with powerful orc males. Their seed was coveted by ambitious females seeking to improve their standing in the orc community by producing favored offspring.

"My mother knew you were cruel and heartless. She also knew you were a great warrior and leader. She raised me to survive, to fight, and to learn by watching you. She understood that you would likely be the death of me, so she took ... precautions in order for me to live long enough to move up in the ranks as I have done. Now I am an elite warrior, second in command of Shadowblade's death platoon, and likely his successor. I am not the favored son of Grimtusk, but now that you know me, you should know that I would have followed you to the underworld and back. I see now that I have gone where you have never been. I have died a dozen deaths today. You are no longer my better. You are merely the orc in command," Hath'or said with great contempt.

"So, the witch enchanted an item to heal you. I admire her foresight, but in the end, it matters little. Since you think yourself my equal, then we shall have to test your resolve. Cut his bonds. Arm and armor him that we might test his mother's enchantments and my bastard son's skills. Perhaps today is the day for a new leader after all," Neggish announced. "I will wager my command, my armor, and the ax of my ancestors against your healing charm. We will find out who is the best orc to lead this army." Neggish knew he had been manipulated into combat with Hath'or, but such were the ways of orcs. There would always be a challenger.

Hath'or nodded as the shaman buckled on his enchanted black armor. The other soldiers backed away and formed a ring around the two combatants. Neggish stepped down from his mount and hefted the mighty obsidian ax with ease. Hath'or was given his two long, curved blades that were, no doubt, also enchanted by his mother. The two orcs faced off and began circling like two mighty lions fighting for leadership of the pride.

* * *

Gaedron and Wavren were certain the onslaught would begin any moment. They could see nothing beyond the thick black smoke of the burning abatis, but they knew something terrible was coming.

Jael'Kutter waited with his mighty double-bladed polearm at the ready. His warriors were holding their defensive posture, peeking through the overlapping shields, but unable to see the enemy.

The only elves scurrying around were the healers and the supply runners. Time was always against the healers, but this short respite had given them the break they needed to bandage and heal most of the minor wounds incurred thus far. They took the opportunity to cast some protective spells and call for blessings on the fighters. The runners were moving back and forth, drawing water into every available skin to ensure the armored troops were well hydrated. Other younglings carried more arrows to the archers or cross-leveled the ammunition, so each archer had an equally distributed load of arrows. Many of the old men brought spears and javelins to the walls as well. When the ability to fight at range came to an end, the orcs would gain a disastrous advantage.

Every elf, dwarf, gnome, and human in Forestedge had the same thought through all the fighting and preparation: *would the reinforcements ever arrive in time*?

* * *

Neggish Grimtusk was a veteran of a hundred battles, and he knew through experience that gaining surprise was the key to quickly vanquishing any foe. He had given that element of combat up by allowing Hath'or to arm and armor himself. But surprise was not the only factor. There was strength and endurance, as well as timing and skill. All of these elements of combat would come into play.

Hath'or had studied combat for his entire life. His mother had personally instructed him in the ways of war and survival, and he had spent the last ten years of his life climbing through the ranks and learning from the best warriors his clan had to offer. He had one advantage over the mighty commander: he knew his enemy. He had studied his father and learned how he fought. The same could not be said for Neggish Grimtusk. He had no knowledge of Hath'or. Before today, he didn't even know Hath'or existed or that he was related to him.

The orcs surrounding the two fighters cheered and made bets among themselves. Most felt sure Neggish would win, but a few secretly hoped Hath'or would prevail. Such was the way of orc society.

It began all at once. Instinctively, both orcs turned inward and charged. The massive ax of obsidian came down hard just as Hath'or came across with his double blades. The resulting clash rang out with grating reverberations. The two combatants broke contact and circled again. Neggish made note of the younger orc's strength and skill. Hath'or shrugged off the numbness from the initial shock of locking blades with the beast that was his father.

Again, both orcs turned and came inward. Grimtusk feinted with his ax and spun around, leveling a sidelong swipe. Hath'or saw the feint for what it was and stepped back just in time to avoid being disemboweled by the attack. His counter attack should have caught his opponent off guard, but as he sliced left and right with his enchanted blades, Grimtusk's ax blocked them both. The initiative fell back to the older orc, who came in with a left to right diagonal cut that Hath'or parried, which was followed by a savage kick that lifted the younger orc up off the ground and sent him reeling back into the crowd of onlookers.

The crowd cheered and pushed Hath'or back into the ring. His ribs were aching, but the magic *dweomer* of his healing charm restored him easily. A guttural rumbling came from

Grimtusk's throat as he began to realize that this impertinent fool might be a worthy challenge. Caution was not a value given much credence in orc society, but experience had taught the great orc leader that it was worth the effort to take one's time in single combat, especially when a quick kill was unlikely.

Neggish came in again. He blitzed forward with an overhead circular attack followed by another spin that leveled his ax at Hath'or's midsection. Hath'or dodged the first attack and ducked low on the second attack. He countered with a thrust that should have gutted his enemy, but the armor plate turned the stabbing attack away. Grimtusk knew that his armor had saved him. His fury grew at the notion that this young challenger had managed to score a hit. He drove forward with his shoulder plate and impaled the younger orc on its spike. Hath'or was unable to skip back fast enough. The shoulder spike pierced his fine armor and dug deeply into his chest. Blood flowed for a moment, then slowly stopped. Grimtusk growled angrily and pressed in close. More money passed between the orcs in the crowd as the odds wavered back and forth.

At close range, the ax was much less effective than the smaller blades Hath'or employed, but Neggish had spikes on nearly every joint of his body. He was a living weapon. He lifted his knee and sank a long spike into his opponent's abdomen. He thrust forward with the handle of his ax and caught Hath'or in the face. His nose bled for a moment and then stooped, just as the hole in the younger orc's belly closed. Neggish realized that he was not going to win by taking him apart one piece at a time.

Hath'or had suffered the pain of grievous wounds dozens of times today, and these were not nearly as bad. He took a deep breath and centered himself. He leveled his twin blades and came forward with the right blade across, the left blade swung under and then backhanded. The right returned, also backhand, cutting as he drove into and past his father. Four strikes hit, but none penetrated the armor or defenses of Grimtusk. He was beginning to think that given his ability to heal, and his father's inability to be hurt, this would be a stalemate. He turned, and Grimtusk was smiling with that wicked orcish grin he was famous for.

"It is *stoneskin*, boy," Grimtusk yelled. "You can hit all day and never make a dent. I guess all of your mother's lessons never taught you about such things."

"Perhaps you are right," Hath'or said though he knew stoneskin had a limited duration, "but you can't kill me either. As long as I have breath, I will fight."

More money changed hands. Grimtusk took a step forward, then another, and slowly closed the distance between the two. He took a deep breath and swung the massive ax in a tight circle in front of him. Hath'or braced for the incoming attack. Grimtusk called on the power of his ancestors and leapt forward. The sheer power of the attack knocked Hath'or to the side, opening up a vulnerable angle of attack. Neggish called his war cry and heaved the mystic ax in another overhead circle, bringing it across the off-balanced orc's torso. When it hit, it moved effortlessly through armor, flesh, bone, and out the other side. This was the true nature of a vorpal weapon. It was enchanted to sever when its power was called upon.

Hath'or's body fell in two distinct pieces. His waist and legs were twitching off to one side while his upper torso was already healing itself. The wound should have been mortal, but the enchanted charm was already closing the gaping hole, preserving the life of the younger orc. Neggish glared at him. Hath'or knew he was defeated, although still alive. He laughed and said, "Come on, Father, finish it." Neggish took his mighty ax and dismembered his son's body. The arms and head were removed from the upper torso so that there could be no doubt that this fight was over. When he was finished, he grabbed the enchanted charm from the necklace around his son's neck. As he stared at it in his hand, a picture of the enchantress appeared. It was a message.

"This is the healing charm of Hath'or, my son. Whosoever dons this enchanted charm will be given the power of healing, but be warned: this charm carries a curse for the one responsible for Hath'or's death. The blood of my son will be avenged through an eternity of suffering," the image warned, and then faded from sight.

Neggish Grimtusk knew all too well that Hath'or's mother was ever the conniving witch and that such a curse was well within her power. It was a shame to have such a powerful charm and be unable to use it. It was a cursed item for him and likely an item that would sooner or later fall into the hands of another ambitious orc. This item could still lead to his downfall. He had been undone, and now there was only one choice. He threw the item on the ground and raised his ax to destroy it. As it came down, the ax shattered the charm into two pieces. Grimtusk walked away without another thought. There was a war to fight, and time was moving against him.

"Infantry, prepare to move. Cavalry will follow in the second wave. The spell casters will follow them. The shock troops and elite platoons will wait in reserve," the massive orc commander yelled to his subordinates.

The infantry began to move forward, banging their weapons together or against their shields. The cavalry formed up on the outside edges, riding their raptors, and the undead wizards and priests held their magical reagents at the ready, to call forth their unholy blasts of energy and fire. Neggish was fully immersed in the savage tumult of the coming battle. His adrenaline was racing, and his ax was screaming for action. He called for the attack to begin: "Advance and slay the elves!"

The attack did not come swiftly, as most orc-led battles were famous for doing. Grimtusk was a seasoned warrior, and he knew that his followers would break ranks soon enough. For now, he had them advance steadily as a single fighting unit. Discipline had its uses against archers, even if not so much in melee.

* * *

"Here they come!" Wavren called, as the first rank stepped

out of the thick black smoke.

Xaeris called for his archers. “Archers, draw, ready … re-lease!”

The two hunters began scanning for elite troops or leaders to shoot. The elven archers would be able to keep the main force busy with their volley fire. The second rank of infantry came through the smoke just as the rain of arrows hit. The longbows were renowned for piercing armor and shields, and their reputation was well earned. Several of the orcs screamed in pain as the hail of arrows penetrated shields, armor, and flesh. Many of the injured were able to press forward. Those who fell were quickly left behind for the healers to care for. At this point, none were killed outright, a testament of orcish durability and excellent armor. The second volley was already in the air as the third and fourth rank of orcs appeared. The first orcs broke ranks and charged the elven defense forces. More fell, but there were far too many to make any difference.

As the orc infantry hit the elven frontlines, the trolls came in fast on their raptors. They quickly closed the distance between the cover provided by the thick smoke and the area too close for volley fire. Two marksmen were already tracking them in their sights. Wavren called the first kill of the day, hitting the lead cavalryman in the eye at well over four hundred paces. It was a lucky shot to critically hit at that range, but one less troll was always a good thing. Gaedron wounded his target, hitting the troll center mass, knocking him off of his mount. Unless a healer rendered aid quickly, that troll would be visiting the abyss in a matter of moments. They both continued to fire, trying to stem the tide of invaders, but neither was able to make much difference. They fired furiously as the invaders closed from long range into melee combat.

Down below the parapets, Jael’Kutter was directing the close-quarter battle. His troops were battle hardened and easily the match for any single orc, but the numbers were overwhelming. The first rank had been weakened by the hail of arrows, enabling his men to cut many of them down quickly, but the second and third rank pushed in too fast to hold them off. He called for a fighting retreat almost immediately after the clash began. This was going to be a short battle without a miracle.

"Pull back into the city; canalize the vermin at the gate! Fight them along the corridor!" he screamed above the ringing of steel on steel.

The infantry moved in as the elves gave ground. The troll cavalry picked off a few of the outside elves, but they were unable to get many clear shots without hitting their comrades. It was too congested to go into close combat range, so the cavalry broke off and tried to skirt around the outer wall. It was a decision made with the desire to score kills more so than with sound tactical reasoning, but that was often the way with troll troops.

The archers were about to drop down to street level when the next wave came in range. More than one hundred elite orcs wielding dual weapons sprinted forward, hoping to cross the open area before the deadly archers could fire. Councilman Xaeris called for bow fire just in time. Unlike the hardened infantry, the elite soldiers were not well armored, and none carried shields. These were the swift skirmishers that used speed and skill in melee over armored strength and endurance. These were the hit and run specialists who lived to create chaos in otherwise disciplined warfare. As the first volley came in, the elite orcs fell in great number. Many were seriously wounded and some were killed instantly. The second volley ended what the first had begun. Less than twenty of the elite force survived to engage the elven fighters. It was the first sign of luck so far.

"Gaedron," Wavren called, "should we move down into the lower levels to engage the enemy with Stonetalon and Blackmaw? It seems a pity to leave them out of the fight."

"I be jus' as eager ta have my ally squish a few orcs, but me gut's tellin' me dat there be a few left ta shoot from here yet. In fact, that be me next target comin' now," the dwarf replied.

An undead priest moved across the battlefield to raise a fallen comrade when Gaedron's bullet took the top of his head off. The zombie-like priest fell to the ground and thrashed for a moment until Gaedron's second shot ended the villain's suffering. Wavren saw a glimmering reflection at the edge of the battlefield. His instincts told him it must be a tricky mage trying to get across with an invisibility spell or a magic cloak. He couldn't be sure, so he lined up the nearly imperceptible target and fired using dead reckoning. A mage appeared on the ground where the hunter had just fired, and with the spell broken, an entire company of tauren followed by numerous robed casters also appeared.

Gaedron called to Xaeris, "Git yer skinny elven arses back up 'ere, we got new targets tryin' ta sneak 'cross the field!"

The archers rushed back up the parapets and managed to fire off a single volley before the bulk of the final wave made it into the city walls. Several of the half-bull, half-men were hit, but none fell to the ground. Gaedron and Wavren had managed to pick off several priests and wizards, but there were just too many. The flood of enemies was quickly washing over the elven forces.

"Now, we let da bears play a bit, but first I'm thinkin' a bit o' the fireworks be in order," Gaedron announced, as he pulled the pack of dynamite off his back and ran to the opposite side of the wall. Wavren smiled and join his mentor with a torch and some flint for striking.

The two hunters waited until the tauren had made it through the corridor, just before they hit the courtyard; then they started lobbing the sizzling red sticks below. After the first few exploded, sending tauren bodies flying, all attention turned to Gaedron and Wavren. They had bought some time for the warriors to regroup and for the remaining archers to fire over the backside of the parapet into the courtyard below. The few remaining elite fighters and many of the tauren pushed up the twin spiraling staircases to exact revenge on the two hunters.

"It looks like you made them mad," Wavren laughed.

"They ain't seen mad 'til they meet Ol' Blackmaw," he returned.

"Archers, fire at will! I have the northern stairwell, and Gaedron will take the southern. Don't hit the bears unless you want to be their next meal," Wavren said with a serious tone.

The archers split and began firing over the two hunters. The two Protectors held their fire until the last moment, until either a head shot or an opening in the armor presented itself. At first, the tauren tried to rush up the stairs, taking two or three at a time; but when the lead troops encountered either of the fifteen-hundred-pound bears and were swatted back down the stairs with no less than a dozen arrows and a bullet hole for their trouble, they changed tactics.

As a distraction, the elite orcs were literally thrown up the wall by two massive tauren. Several died on the way up, but one got through and landed among the archers. Before the hunters or elves could react, the lone orc had skewered several elven archers. Gaedron couldn't get through the elves to his rear, and Wavren couldn't get around either. It was a massacre. One orc had started a chain reaction, allowing several more to land on the upper level. As the archers drew swords and fought off the elite orcs, Wavren and Gaedron kept the tauren at bay. After a few moments, all of the orcs were dead, but not before they had crippled the entire group of archers in a matter of moments. Wavren looked over the side and saw the last elite orc preparing to be thrown by the two massive tauren. "Orc on the way!" he called.

Both hunters dropped their long-range weapons and drew melee weapons in their place. Gaedron's twin glimmering blue axes twinkled in the sunlight. Wavren's fine elven dagger and the reverse curved ax felt warm in his hands. The lone orc landed, smiled, and spun his wickedly curved short swords, inviting the two hunters over for some action. The dwarf turned and saw the carnage of over a hundred dead elves before him. It was more than he could bear. He was ready for some revenge, but the hatred in Wavren's eyes from across the parapet was unnerving.

"FER STONE AN' STEEL!" Gaedron called, as he barreled in.

Wavren charged as well, jaw clenched and a look of deadly focus on his face. The orc was fast for a three-hundred-pound beast. His swords batted away Gaedron's initial strikes, and he turned in time to duck Wavren's ax and dodge the thrust of his blade. The orc kicked out sideways and caught the elven hunter in the midsection, sending him back several steps in order to buy time to focus on the dwarf. The following left, right, left attack that he made bounced off of the tough dwarven chainmail and only seemed to enrage Gaedron, who returned with his own right, left, right swings. The first two were blocked by the enemy's swords, but the third cut into his armor and traced a line of red across his chest.

The orc paused and said something threatening in orcish, but Gaedron's reply in common was, "I don' speak pig language, so me axes'll do all me talkin'!"

Wavren came in again, and as he swung hard with his ax, the orc ducked right into the elf's raising knee strike. As his head flew back, Wavren spun around and circle kicked him in the side of the head. The orc's head snapped to the side, and his body spun just in time to receive two more hits from the dwarf's glimmering blue axes. The orc leaned in on the dwarf, using his size and short swords in a downward press to impale the grizzled hunter. Gaedron held his axes in an X across his chest and dropped his supporting leg back under the strain. The twin blades dug into his neck, drawing two small points of blood. Gaedron sucked in a deep breath, his massive forearms bulged, and he threw the beast off.

Wavren was positioned perfectly to drive his elven dagger into the orc's back and through its lung as it fell backward. The blade slid in to the hilt. Gaedron was already swinging his axes as the orc's knees buckled. His strikes bit into the soft flesh on the right and left side of the enemy's neck, nearly decapitating him. Wavren smiled, and Gaedron gave him a nod of approval. They turned to see that the two bears had held off the tauren quite well without them.

"See, boy-o, havin' da high ground an' a bit o' a bottleneck makes all da dif'rence in da world," Gaedron remarked.

Wavren remained silent, sheathed his ax, sheathed his dagger, grabbed his blunderbuss, and went back to work killing anything that came up the stairs. Gaedron took up his position on the other stairwell and wondered if his young friend would ever be the same. When the tauren stopped coming, they called their allies back into the safety of the parapet and waited.

* * *

Jael'Kutter was still in the fighting retreat, and his men were greatly outnumbered. They had moved from outside the wall, back through the narrow corridor, out into the courtyard, and were now fighting along the main road through the city. At this rate, he and his men would be dead or in Port Archer before the blasted reinforcements arrived. He was thankful that the archers had wounded so many of the elite dual-wielding orcs and at least a few of the infantry. But there was no winning with these odds, and the archers had stopped shooting.

"Pull back into the great hall," he yelled over the calamity of the battle. "We make our final stand there!"

The last of Forestedge's defense force was already inside the great hall when they arrived. All of the healers and mages were fast at work bandaging the wounded. Too many of the injured, dead, and dying were the young boys and old men who stayed to supply the fighting forces. They had simply been cut down by the invaders with little or no way of defending themselves. As the last of the captain's men came through the great hall's double doors, a crafty human wizard pushed the enemy back with a wall-of-force spell. It bought them a much-needed respite.

"I need healers quickly," Jael'Kutter said, surveying the elves in his small band. "Barricade the door! Every able-bodied warrior, prepare to hold this position. There will be no prisoners, so we fight to the last."

The small band of warriors assembled, the healers cast their restorative magic, and the non-combatants huddled in the small alcoves. It wasn't long before the soldiers of the Bloodcrest Forces began hammering away at the massive double doors. The wizard came forward and conjured a wall of ice to brace the doors. He shuffled back behind the main force.

"That will only hold them for a short while," the mage said.

"We are in your debt, mage. Tell us your name, so we might remember your contributions when this is ended," Jael'Kutter requested.

"I am Corin de Valle of Griffon's Peak, advisor to the King of Griffon's Peak, here by chance to discuss matters of trade and diplomacy," he returned.

"Well, my friend, your timing is poor, but your skills are greatly appreciated. I fear that there will be little to trade once the enemy forces have finished with Forestedge, but as you can see, we are always in need of allies, so perhaps a discussion of diplomacy would be in order should we survive," the captain said. "By the way, I am Jael'Kutter, captain of the city guard and defense forces."

The banging on the door grew louder. By the even spacing between each hit, it was obvious that the orcs had fashioned a battering ram. The doors buckled after several hits, and the wall of ice began to crack. The warriors looked around nervously, but held their position and set their minds to the final task ahead.

* * *

Far away in Celes'tia, the Speaker of the Stars gazed into his scrying censure. The image was one of great destruction. The Bloodcrest Forces had taken Forestedge far too easily and were busy killing small pockets of defenders who were bravely holding out for reinforcements. Da'Shar was among the high-ranking officials around the censure. Beside him was Daenek Torren, the venerable hunter and representatives from the Mage and Rogue Guilds.

The Speaker held up his withered hand and said, "Forestedge is lost. We must now make plans to save Port Archer at all costs. It is the last Dae'gon Alliance port to the Western Kingdom and the last foothold to the northern region."

Da'Shar bowed his head in utter frustration. In truth, the

lack of action had cost the Dae'gon Alliance the city of Forestedge and countless lives. He felt responsible for the destruction, in spite of his efforts to raise the alarm and gather reinforcements. He began to doubt everything in his sorrow.

Daenek Torren held up his hand, signifying he would now speak. "We have lost many warriors today, but there is hope. We can retake Forestedge if we act quickly. The Speaker of the Stars is correct in that we must hold Port Archer, but I say the best way to do so is to attack the Bloodcrest Forces before they can muster more forces.

Sarai'an, a tiny gnomish mage and representative of the Mage's Guild, stepped forward and held up her hand in the customary way to speak. "I agree with the great hunter. Daenek has long been the protector of the outreaches of the Western Kingdom, and his voice should be considered strongly. We must attack."

Lorin, the elven representative from the Rogue's Guild, moved forward, and as his hand went up; all turned their attention to him. He said, "If we attack blindly, we will lose. We must infiltrate first and gather information on our enemy. We must learn of their numbers, weapons, and weaknesses. Only then can we be sure to strike the crippling blow and send those filthy beasts back to Dek'Thal."

"There is another way," Sarai'an said. "We have agents in Forestedge who already know these things which the master rogue requires. We must evacuate the last of the defenders, analyze their firsthand knowledge of the situation, and launch a counter offensive."

"What do you have in mind?" Da'Shar asked.

"We can open a portal to Port Archer for a limited time to transport the heroes to Celes'tia," she replied.

Lorin spoke out: "But how will we get the remaining resistance fighters to the portal?"

"I will lead them," Da'Shar said intently.

Lorin spoke again: "That is suicide. You will be taken and slain for your trouble."

"Unless there is another who will go in his place, I support

Da'Shar in this mission," the Speaker concluded.

No one dared speak against those words. The Speaker of the Stars was in actuality the King of Elves and the ruler of Celes'tia. His word was law.

Chapter 16
Escape

Night was falling, and the scrying censure showed three remaining pockets of defenders. Captain Jael'Kutter and less than fifteen soldiers and casters were trapped in the great hall to the west of the city. More than fifty orcish infantry awaited the breach of the massive doors to finish them off. A handful of healers and mages had hidden themselves among the trees to the north with an illusion spell, but were trapped by roving patrols of mounted trolls and a few elite orcs. To the east in the tallest parapet were the two hunters and their beastly allies. All around them were the bodies of dead elven archers and an equal number of tauren and orcs. They were barricaded directly over the largest and most fearsome orc warrior any of the elders had ever seen. Bodyguards, undead mages, shamans, and priests surrounded him. The situation looked impossible. The Speaker waved his hand over the scrying bowl, and the image faded away.

"Da'Shar," the Speaker began, "are you certain that you can lead these souls to the portal in time? I fear for your life, old friend, and my heart tells me that you will be unlikely to return."

"I am prepared to die as Nature intends, but this is not my time. I will not be alone in this rescue, so fear not," he said resolutely.

"Who will accompany you, then?" the Speaker asked.

"I will take the finest Protector Celes'tia has ever seen; one who has the ability to move silently and the will to fight no matter the odds. I will take Rosabela, my apprentice," he replied with perfect confidence. "It is her brother and her brother's mentor in the western parapet. She will not let me fail."

Da'Shar moved swiftly to the griffon master on the outskirts of Celes'tia and paid for his flight to Port Archer. The great magical beast sprang into the air and was high above the clouds with a few powerful beats from its wings. Da'Shar was so anxious about the rescue mission that he barely realized that the trip was over until his griffon landed in Port Archer. He moved quickly to the council chamber and found a very angry and frustrated elf waiting for him.

"What in the world is wrong with these people? Their army has been assembled and prepared to march for Forestedge for hours, but the order to march will not be given," Rosabela complained.

"Forestedge has fallen," was all the older druid could say.

Rosabela was struck speechless for a moment. Great tears welled in her green eyes. She bit her lip and whispered, "Wav, Jael'Kutter, Gaedron?"

"Your brother and that grizzled old dwarf he fights with are alive, as are several other elves, including the captain of the guard. Sadly, many have fallen to the destruction of the enemy. You and I will lead them out," he said, laying a hand on her wispy shoulder.

Her jaw set and her will steeled, she nodded and said, "By Nature, I swear we will succeed."

The two swiftly moved back to the griffon master to purchase quick transportation.

"Do your griffons fly to Forestedge?" Da'Shar asked.

"Forestedge?" the griffon master asked quizzically. "The Bloodcrest Forces hit Forestedge earlier today. We have been seeing refugees fleeing from the south all day, and the army of Port Archer has been marshaled to fight if they come here."

Da'shar was a patient elf, but he was in no mood to discuss the matter. "Send us to Forestedge; I'll pay double for both of us."

The griffon master sighed and rigged up the bridals and harnesses for the two elves. Rosabela had never ridden a griffon before, but she was so focused on her mission that she never even asked what to expect. She simply mounted as if she was riding a horse, and the griffon master tied her in. Da'Shar leaned over and handed her a small vial.

"Drink this as soon as you see the outskirts of the city. It will make you invisible for a short time—long enough for us to move undetected into the outer city limits," he said.

Rosabela nodded and tucked the vial into her belt. The griffon took off, and like a bird, she was flying above the trees. Her heart pounded with adrenaline, and her grip tightened around the bridle, but she only reacted subconsciously. All other thoughts were focused on getting in and out of the city with her friends being held by the Bloodcrest Forces.

The time sped by as they passed mile after mile of forest. Da'Shar saw the outer edge of the city and signaled to his apprentice to drink from the vial. She complied and faded from sight. Da'Shar also drank and became transparent. They circled the aerie where the Forestedge griffon master should have been, but with no one there to command them, the griffons would not land. Da'Shar and Rosabela unbuckled their harnesses and jumped from a reasonable height. Invisibility prevented the highly trained griffons from preventing the druids from jumping to the ground. The griffons had no choice but turn back toward Port Archer.

"Follow my voice," Da'Shar called to Rosabela.

"I am here," she replied, as she moved up and bumped into him.

"We will travel faster and more silently in astral form once the potion wears off. We must be cautious, but our plan is to distract the enemy army so that our brethren can move to the portal. Only when all have been freed will the Speaker of the Stars know to signal Sarai'an and the Mage Guild to open the way. Timing is critical," he stated.

Rosabela nodded.

"I will be the bait. You must get through to the trapped citizens and direct them to move on my signal. When I attack the commander, all must move as one," he said solemnly.

"Do not get yourself killed, or I will be forced to stay and fight the entire army," Rosabela said, with no smile and no sign of jest.

Da'Shar nodded.

* * *

Neggish Grimtusk was well pleased by the successful conquest of Forestedge. He had lost many warriors, but never in the history of Dek'Thal had Forestedge been taken. He was certain that the supreme commander would be pleased. His name would be recorded among the greatest warriors of all time. More importantly, with Forestedge now taken, Deadmist Valley would never see supplies or troops that had been caravanned from there over the last ten years. The never-ending battle that had consumed this region would finally be won by his troops. As his mind raced, Grimtusk considered setting up his own command here in Forestedge in order to take Port Archer next. If he could do that, Celes'tia would be isolated, and all of the Western Kingdom would belong to the Bloodcrest Forces. What a glorious conquest that would be! He could be a baron or duke over these lands, maybe even one day! Surely that was his destiny.

Nightshade, the second in command under Commander Grimtusk—now that Shadowblade had been sacrificed—approached and brought word. He said, "Commander, we have taken the city with the exception of the great hall where we believe a small group of elves are barricaded. There are also reports of savage beasts in the top of the parapet above our command post, but they are trapped. The doors have been shut and locked to prevent them from causing any harm."

Neggish leaned down from his saddle and gave one simple command: "Burn them out."

The subordinate leader nodded and swiftly moved to carry out the orders. The parapet was made of shining white marble and granite. It would be difficult to do more than burn the contents of the stairwells, mostly bodies and supplies, but the great hall was made of the most beautiful wood from all around Forestedge. The doors were four inches of oak. The roof was crafted from the darkest mahogany, and the walls were cypress on the outside and oak on the inside supports. It caught fire easily and slowly spread from wall to wall. The orcs waited eagerly to hear the screams of the elves being roasted alive inside.

Rosabela and Da'Shar had transformed into their travel forms. They sprinted silently and almost invisibly to the edge of Forestedge on the northwest corner. Da'Shar motioned to the platoon of trolls patrolling the northern edge, where the mages and priests were said to be hiding. Their help would be needed to free the elves in the great hall, which was now noticeably ablaze.

Da'Shar transformed into his windwraith form and pounced on the troll farthest from the group. The troll never saw the attack coming, and within moments, he was lying on the ground with his belly torn out. He gurgled a scream for help, but Da'Shar dashed away. The other cavalry trolls pursued the windwraith, easily keeping pace with their raptors. Da'Shar dashed in and out of thickets and shrubs trying to slow his pursuers, but the raptors were amazingly agile and often leapt over the shorter bushes. He had to keep a safe lead or risk being ripped to shreds by the vicious raptors.

Rosabela took on her elven form and called to the mages. Many of the trees that made up the forest around her shimmered and suddenly became spell-wielders. Rosabela was caught by surprise, having never seen a mass illusion spell, but she quickly recovered and explained the plan. It was all about confusion and diversions. She explained that the rescue could only be complete if they kept the enemy running in circles long enough to get the elves out of the great hall and the hunters out of the parapet. The wizards and priests shrugged, having no better plan and willing to do their part.

Rosabela moved to the back of the great hall, which was almost completely engulfed in flames. She tore open her back-pack and thumbed through her book of alchemy. She took *gravemoss*, *willowsbane*, and blackroot and mixed it in a small glass tube filled with *mummy's dust*. Careful not to get any of the concoction on her, she poured the mixture on the back wall. The fine wood darkened and thinned. The potion had a rapid-rotting effect, weakening the wall's integrity just enough to break through. She shape-shifted into her bear form and began clawing through the wall. After several massive swipes, the wall ripped apart and Rosabela crashed through.

Jael'Kutter and his men were kneeling or crawling about on all fours trying to stay below the layer of thick smoke when he saw the bear come through the back wall. The bear turned into the most beautiful sight he had ever seen, and before he knew it, she was hugging him. He returned the embrace and began directing everyone to escape through the hole Rosabela had made. Had the situation been different, he would have had much to say to his rescuer, but Rosabela grabbed him by the hand and pulled him out just as the roof collapsed.

The druid spoke quickly: "When all hell breaks loose in the courtyard, run for the edge of the lake to the northwest. You will see a portal; it will take you to Port Archer. It will only be open for a few minutes, so make haste or be left behind."

All nodded except the captain. He crossed his burly arms over his thick chest and said, "I will fight until all have es-caped."

All eyes moved to Jael'Kutter. Many mouths opened, but no words were spoken. Time was too short for arguing. The few warriors, wizards, and remaining citizens moved to the outskirts of the city to lay low for the portal to materialize. Rosabela and Jael'Kutter circled around to the south and east. The bulk of the enemy force was watching the great hall burn. The central figure sat astride the ugliest beast of a worg ever seen. That must surely be their leader. Rosabela had no way to get up the stairs leading to the parapet without being seen. Even in her travel form, the orcs and tauren were too close—not to mention the sizable contingent of undead wizards who had heightened perceptions to otherworldly magical beings and creatures.

Suddenly, a streak of light flashed through courtyard and transformed into a windwraith mid-jump toward the massive orc leader. Da'Shar was right on time. He hit the orc commander with front paws extended, and as they toppled over in the saddle, Da'Shar's rear paws dug in and he sprang away, transforming again into his travel form.

Neggish Grimtusk stood up uninjured and drew his great ax. He called to his troops, "Find the changeling who dared attack me. I want him alive!"

The bulk of the infantry circled around the southern end of the city while the tauren shock troops dashed after the windwraith at a sprint. The troll cavalry arrived to report the chase they had taken up earlier, but Neggish sent them in pursuit of the windwraith again.

Only the commander, his spell casters, and his personal bodyguard remained, and they were greatly distracted by Da'Shar's recent attack. Rosabela and Jael'Kutter slipped past, opened the door, and bounded up the stairs. They climbed several dozen stairs over numerous tauren and orc bodies to find a massive white bear at the top and the business end of a dwarven blunderbuss.

Gaedron let out a deep breath in relief. Then he asked, "What in da nine hells 'r ye doin' 'ere, lass?"

"I am rescuing you two. Now come on, and be quick about it," she said.

Wavren and the dwarf looked at each other, shrugged and quietly followed the she-elf. As they carefully stepped over the dead bodies, Gaedron counted on his fingers and made a gesture indicating that he and Ol' Blackmaw had killed about ten of the invaders. Wavren flashed five, five, and two, indicating that he and Stonetalon had killed twelve. Gaedron mumbled something under his breath about beginner's luck and quickly followed the elves out of the parapet.

At the edge of the stairwell, the three Protectors and the captain carefully peered around the corner and saw that the orc commander and his entourage were still somewhat distracted. They moved quickly around the corner and headed back past the western side of the burning great hall. The smoke was quite thick and provided plenty of cover for their movement. It seemed likely that they would make it to the portal area without being detected.

Da'Shar was dashing through the forest in his travel form with no less than ten troll riders behind him. He had long since lost the infantry, who were on foot and far too slow to catch him. He began to veer back around toward the portal in a circuitous route, hoping that the last of Forestedge's warriors were already moving to the escape point. If luck was with him, he would arrive just in time to dash through the closing portal. If not, he had a long run back to Port Archer with the trolls hot on his trail.

The mages and priests were already in position along with the bulk of the warriors from the great hall when Rosabela's team arrived. The wind swirled, and a flash of light opened up into a shining circular doorway with Celes'tia at the other end. The portal was now ready for use, but Da'Shar was still out of sight. Gaedron took charge and started shoving elves through the opening. All of the very old and very young went first, followed by the mages and priests. Jael'Kutter's men were unwilling to go without their leader, but Gaedron was able to convince the first of the warriors by shoulder charging into him. He flew backward several steps and fell through the portal. Jael'Kutter looked on disapprovingly, but dismissed his men with a simple gesture. They moved grudgingly through the gateway.

"A'right, don' make me tackle ye hard-heads through the portal. I'm knowin' ye all have loyalty ta that fool druid, Da'Shar, but he be a crafty 'un. Now c'mon, let's go afore the durned thing closes up," the surely dwarf ordered.

Wavren, Rosabela, and Jael'Kutter moved in unison, grabbed the dwarf—who was kicking and cursing—and heaved him through the portal, kicking and cursing the whole time. Wavren nodded to his sister, knowing she would never leave Da'Shar, and then he followed his mentor, leaving Rosabela and Jael'Kutter alone.

"I can't leave without him," Rosabela said, still hoping to see Da'Shar appear before the portal closed.

"I won't leave without you," he replied with more emotion than he meant to reveal. His connection to the lovely she-elf was making things complicated, but he couldn't deny their attraction.

Rosabela smiled. She couldn't remember when the captain had become more than just another soldier to her. But somehow, among the chaos of war, she found his presence comforting, protective, and reassuring. She felt foolish; after all, she was a Protector of the Vale and a Druid of the Grove. She was perfectly capable of protecting herself, but this was something beyond her experience.

A flash of light indicated that the portal was closing, and Da'Shar was nowhere to be seen. The two elves looked at each other. Neither was willing to abandon the other while waiting for Da'Shar. The portal was almost closed when the master druid finally appeared. He was dashing madly through the city with nearly a dozen trolls driving their raptors faster and faster behind him. Rosabela knew there was no way he could make it in time. Instinctively, Jael'Kutter reached for Rosabela. His strength was more than enough to pick her up. She cried for him to stop and flailed wildly, but the warrior already had her airborne and heading into the portal.

"We will meet you in Celes'tia," he said grimly, as he turned to face the oncoming cavalry. The captain pulled his fine helm onto his head and drew the massive polearm from his back. He whispered to himself, "The druid saved my townsfolk. The Bloodcrest Forces destroyed the town. Now, I will repay both."

* * *

The group arrived in Celes'tia with a great cheer from the onlookers. Gaedron was still fuming about being tossed like a sack of grain when everyone noticed Rosabela crying. Wavren put his hand on her shoulder and said, "They will survive this. I know it."

Rosabela stood up, wiped the tears from her eyes and walked up to the Speaker of the Stars. The Speaker was considerably taller than the she-elf and truly imposing with his nearly god-like power and authority, but the fire in Rosabela's green eyes overwhelmed him. As she approached, he took a single step back, unsure if she meant him harm or not.

The young druid spoke a single command: "Prepare the elves for war."

The Speaker nodded politely, taking Rosabela by the hand. He led her to the magic censure and spoke a few arcane words that even Rosabela could not fathom. Then, she saw Forestedge and the two remaining elves. Da'Shar was running right for Jael'Kutter, who was standing at the ready as the trolls approached. Rosabela couldn't look away.

* * *

The first troll came in hard with his long spear lowered to skewer the warrior elf. He was quite certain the elf would die impaled on his weapon without even having to break off the chase for the shape shifting druid.

As Da'Shar flew past, the captain yelled, "Do not stop. You must make Port Archer!" As Da'Shar continued to run, he knew there was no way to save the courageous warrior. He looked back long enough to see Jael'Kutter sidestep the lance aimed at his heart, swing his powerful weapon, and sever the leg of the troll's reptilian mount. The troll went down in a heap and lay very still. His head was at an unusual angle, indicating a broken neck. The raptor kicked and screeched, but would soon bleed to death. Da'Shar was amazed by the warrior's skill, but nothing could save him from the mass of villains heading his way.

The second troll came in with his raptor as the means of attack. The beast jumped high into the air and was angled to come down with its razor-sharp claws in the lead. Jael'Kutter held his position, braced his polearm on the ground, and eviscerated the creature. The resulting death throes broke the warrior's grip on his fine weapon, tearing it away from him. The troll rolled away and came up with a sword and shield in its hands. The captain drew two long daggers from his boots just in time for the other trolls to close in and surround him.

Two platoons of mounted cavalry and one dismounted troll were odds no warrior could face. He took measure of the situation, sheathed his blades, and drew a tiny potion from his belt. The trolls could have taken him at any time, but something made them hesitate. He looked around and saw what caused their delay. Da'Shar had come back. It was a distraction that gave him all the time he needed. Jael'Kutter pulled cork in the potion and swallowed it in one deep draught. The world went red as the liquid burned all the way down. He felt his muscles bulge and his heart race with adrenaline as the potion took effect. His head pounded, and hate filled every fiber of his being. He grabbed his blood-soaked polearm from the dead raptor and unleashed his fury, the fury fueled by the death of so many elves and the death of Sarim in particular. Rage boiled in the captain's heart. He unleashed it all on his enemies.

Da'Shar was uncertain how he might save the captain from the trolls, but he simply could not leave him to die alone. His sense of duty as a Protector would never allow it. As he approached the battle already in progress, he saw that two raptors were out of the fight and one troll lay dead close by. Da'Shar prepared to join the fight, when he saw his comrade sheath his weapons and pull something from his belt. The warrior turned for a moment and looked into the druid's eyes and then drank something, a potion perhaps. What happened next was amazing and horrifying at the same time. The warrior seemed to gag for a second on the liquid, and then his body convulsed and appeared to thicken and bulge within the confines of his armor. He took a few steps toward one of the slain raptors and dislodged his polearm. Howling a battle cry in a feral voice, he leapt toward the nearest enemy with a double-handed slash. The blade cut through the troll's armor, leaving a deep gash across his chest. He fell backward out of the saddle and recovered just in time to receive the finishing blow through his chest.

The other trolls howled in rage and came in all at once. The sheer volume of attacks should have cut the elf down, but he never slowed. Jael'Kutter was in a frenzy of hacking and slashing attacks. He was hit several times, but for every hit he took, he turned and slashed the troll giving it. Da'Shar couldn't get close enough to the berserker to help fight, so he did the only thing he could. He called on healing magic to sustain him.

Jael'Kutter sliced upward and opened up the chest of another raptor. As it went down, he dodged left and stabbed backward into its rider. Another troll hit him hard with a huge spiked ball at the end of a long chain. The air left his lungs, but it did not stop him from impaling his attacker on the long blade of his weapon. He felt a sword slice into his side, but as he turned with the blow, his own weapon went up high overhead and spun outward, taking the orc in the throat. It fell back gurgling on its own blood.

A throwing ax flew past, drawing his attention. He threw his polearm like a massive spear, hitting the owner of the ax in the belly. It crumbled to its knees in agony. The remaining enemies backed away from the raging elf to hit him from a safer distance. Two arrows hit Jael'Kutter in the chest as he launched himself toward the troll dying at the end of his polearm. He never slowed and managed to rip his polearm free.

A crossbow bolt buried itself in his back. He tore it out and charged the troll who fired it. The troll tried in vain to re-cock the weapon and fire another bolt, but the captain cleaved his skull in two. Time suddenly slowed for Da'Shar as he called a warning to his friend. A desert raptor was in the air behind him before he could react. All of its weight came down behind its massive claws, shredding the fine chainmail and ripping four deep wounds down his back. The warrior went to his knees and dropped face first to the ground. It was over.

Da'Shar couldn't believe it. Even with his considerable healing skills, he was unable to cast spells fast enough to do more than prolong the fight. He ran forward to meet death beside his noble ally just as the commander and his entourage arrived. The undead mages called forth numbing cold, and the druid found himself frozen in place. He transformed into the windwraith to break free just as the priest blasted him with paralyzing magic. He reverted back into his elf-form, unable to move or even speak. The last thing he saw was a huge platemail boot covered in white spikes coming down on his head. Then, utter darkness enveloped him.

* * *

Rosabela, Wavren, Gaedron, and the Speaker of the Stars had watched the battle unfold. They had witnessed the great warrior dance with death far longer than any mortal should have. Da'Shar cast dozens of healing spells in vain only to fall beside Jael'Kutter. The death and destruction was nearly unbearable, but now it was personal. The group was silent. All but the Speaker turned and resolutely walked away. Tears flowed from many eyes that day, but none so much as from Rosabela.

The Speaker watched as the riders left with Da'Shar in tow. Jael'Kutter had been left as carrion. The infantry, cavalry, tauren, and undead had regrouped in town with their commander and were setting up their base of operations. Forestedge was truly lost.

The Speaker was about to dismiss the image when an old crone dressed in rags appeared out of the woods. Leading a small mule, she hobbled up to the ravaged body of Jael'Kutter, bent down beside him, and rolled him onto his back. The Speaker was perplexed. It wasn't clear what she was doing, but after just a few moments, she stood up, tied a rope to his leg, and had the mule drag him off to the side of the burning hall. She untied the rope and gently rolled him into the fire, throwing a small bag into the fire as well. The hag dusted off her hands on her grimy shirt and moved back to the battle site, where she gently wrapped the mighty polearm in a long cloth and strapped it onto her mule. She hobbled back into the forest and disappeared. The Speaker let the image fade away.

Chapter 17
Mustering Forces

The call for allies went out that very night. Corin de Valle, the mage-diplomat from Griffon's Peak, personally traveled to his home far across the Great Sea to summon his countrymen to the Western Kingdom. His service to the King and his personal involvement in the battle of Forestedge enabled him to convince the royal court to send aid. Griffon's Peak's contribution was a full company of the King's Royal Knights, who were by far the finest heavy cavalry in the realm. The greatest hero of Deadmist Valley, the Paladin Landermihl, would lead them. The humans would serve well in the coming fight if Landermihl could be contacted. He was likely fighting the Bloodcrest Forces at Deadmist as he did day in and day out. It was a self-imposed curse to stay on the frontlines, but one he seemed to embrace with honor and courage.

A human rogue-turned-scout named Draek was immediately dispatched to retrieve the famous paladin. The scout was given his dispatch and a magnificent palomino for the journey. He rode out of Griffon's Peak through Bladeshire and straight on to Blackmarsh, the port city at Bladerun Bay where he caught a transport ship to Seigeport, the paladin proving grounds.

The paladin training camp and human port to the Western Kingdom was a great starting place to search for Landermihl. Draek moved through the town with great haste. He asked the innkeeper if Landermihl had been a guest or if anyone knew his whereabouts. He searched the tavern, where information was often found in abundance, but with no luck. His next stop was the holy fortress at Seigeport. The scout moved swiftly through the massive double doors to the great keep. As he moved from room to room, he inquired about the great hero. All answers were the same. Landermihl was likely fighting at Deadmist.

The determined human mounted his sturdy palomino and headed for the savage battleground as a last resort. Deadmist Valley was not simply the contested land between the Dae'gon Alliance and the Bloodcrest Forces. As a location of restless spirits and corpses, it was second only to Dwarfrun. There was no doubt that it was a cursed and horrifying place. It seemed the last place for a holy warrior to be found, yet, ironically, it was the one place in all of Dae'gon where Landermihl's skills as a warrior and a healer could be fully utilized until now. He was greatly needed in the upcoming battle for Forestedge.

Draek arrived at the Dae'gon Alliance keep on the friendly side of Deadmist. He dismounted and headed inside. To his dismay, he saw row after row of wounded and dying warriors being treated by priests, druids, and paladins. It seemed a waste of life to continue this endless assault, but Draek did not come to pass judgment on those who were paying the ultimate price. He paused only for a moment as he came to the chamber of the fallen, a room dedicated to the countless fighters who gave everything serving the Dae'gon Alliance.

There were statues of humans, dwarves, elves, and gnomes who had achieved the rank and status of hero. Many had died soon after reaching the great honor. All of these were carried by rearing mounts. The humans rode great warhorses from

Griffon's Peak, the elves had their powerful Celes'tia wind-wraiths, dwarves were carried by the great fighting rams of the mountains at Dragonforge, and the gnomes were astride mechanical contraptions called striders, which resembled large, flightless birds, which only had two legs and could not rear, but had their wings in an extended upward position. The heroes who had been gravely wounded, but still lived, rode similar mounts, but only one of the forelimbs was raised off of the ground; the striders had their wings in the downward position. There was only one statue in honor of a warrior who had achieved the rank and status of hero, but had never been gravely wounded: that was the statue was of Landermihl, the paladin, who sat proudly on his elite, holy charger, a magnificent warhorse of legendary speed. This statue had all hooves planted firmly on the white marble base from which it was carved. Draek could only imagine the power and skill of such a warrior.

Snapping out of his awe, the scout moved down the long corridor to the edge of the massive keep, where a dwarf-crafted portcullis was fully retracted, signifying the warriors of the Dae'gon Alliance were already engaged in combat, and the battle was likely in full swing. He moved his fine palomino forward to seek out Landermihl. What he saw at the end of the corridor and through the portcullis was staggering.

The battlefield was at least a mile of open, rolling hills confined by two massive cliffs. It was as if the Gods themselves had constructed this place to pit the forces of good against the forces of evil for their amusement. The terrain required the force on the offense to cover a great distance under a hail of volley-fired arrows and mage-cast magical blasts in order to assault the fortress on the opposing side. Even then, the attacking force would have to fight uphill through infantry, cavalry, and skirmishing troops to achieve the goal of capturing the enemy fortress. Clearly, tactics would enable a cunning leader to make great progress, but this would always be a war of attrition, requiring hundreds of soldiers to die to close the gap. As Draek looked across the war-torn, bloody chasm of bodies, it was obvious that both sides had committed scores of warriors in this most recent battle alone.

With keen eyes and relentless determination, Draek scoured the combatants for any sign of the holy warrior. As he scanned from left to right, he saw a flanking element of lightly armored enemy troops get cut down by the charge of a windwraith-riding cavalry troop. Their screams were joined by those of a group of human infantrymen being overrun by marauding tauren who punched through their frontlines like a craftsman's awl through leather. Draek continued his visual search. He saw a motley collection of knights skirting the main battle. Among the group were dwarven ram-riders who trampled a fair share of orcs and undead as well as several human horsemen and gnomish raiders on their mechanical striders. It was an effective assault into the enemy rear. Several evil crossbowmen fell immediately along with a dozen spell-wielders. Leading the charge was a hammer-wielding knight in magnificent armor. He rode a magnificent warhorse, so powerful and majestic that it had to be the legendary elite charger of a master paladin. It had to be Landermihl.

The scout watched in amazement as the knights cut through the scantily clad mages and archers. It allowed the Dae'gon Alliance skirmishers to attack the tauren shock troopers and relieve the human infantry before they were slaughtered, but the fight was far from over. Just as the knights passed the enemy keep, the portcullis spewed forth a company of raptor-riding trolls. The Dae'gon Alliance riders were still moving at top speed, plowing over dismounted enemy soldiers, which enabled them to avoid being hit from behind. As the trolls came upon the trailing knights at the end of the wedge-shaped formation, Landermihl cut his charger back around in a wide circle, actually leading the trolls back over the injured and dying enemy forces that remained. It was a brilliant move that created great disarray in the enemy lines. The human infantry came forward in a surge and pushed back the remaining tauren.

The devastation and the chaos of the enemy's broken lines left them no choice but to retreat back to the keep. As the orcs, undead, trolls, and tauren broke ranks and fled for the safety of the portcullis, the Dae'gon Alliance quickly took advantage of the rout. Before most of the remaining enemy forces could escape, the portcullis slammed down and left the remaining troops to be cut down easily. Today, the battle was won by the Dae'gon Alliance, but there was always tomorrow.

The Dae'gon Alliance forces cheered and moved back to the safety of the Dae'gon Alliance camp. Healers and aid teams moved out to retrieve the bodies on both sides. It was the only sign of respect between the opposing sides, but one honored daily. Landermihl was among the victorious knights who had saved the day, and every warrior able to raise his hand and voice in honor of the radiant paladin hailed him.

Draek pushed his way through the masses and handed Landermihl the written orders summoning him to Port Archer. The knight read the parchment and nodded. Without a word, he wheeled his mount about and headed for the elven city. He understood the urgency of the King's summons. Draek breathed a sigh of relief and headed back to Griffon's Peak, having completed his mission.

* * *

Gaedron traveled to Dragonforge in Stou'lanz to raise an army of dwarves and then north to Silvershire to rally the gnomes. The dwarves had no real love for the elves as a nation, but when the chance to bust a few orcish heads presented itself, the dwarves found much in common with the pointy-eared westerners. Gaedron set sail immediately with a full company of King Magni's heavy infantry called the Blade-Breakers, who were known for two things: dwarven tactics and dwarven mithril armor, which, incidentally, was known for breaking weapons before being pierced. This made them the obvious choice to penetrate the enemy army's defenses. The High Sheriff of Silvershire agreed to send a small contingent of very powerful mages and warlocks to help. These diminutive casters were particularly adept at summoning denizens of the abyss and casting fire spells which would serve the war effort well. Gaedron himself agreed to lead the stout people of Stou'lanz.

Rosabela was already working to raise elven forces from Port Archer to Celes'tia. The entire Port Archer defense forces were on high alert given the fall of their sister city, Forestedge. Celes'tia was willing to send two companies of their finest elven long-bowmen, but Rosabela was persistent and very convincing among the Speaker and the elders of the elven city. She managed to haggle for a company of Forest Runners, who were perhaps the greatest skirmishers in the land. These lightly armored warriors could move like the wind and leave even less sign of passing. Captain Helio of Port Archer, who was the senior commander in the area and a brilliant strategist, would lead them.

The call for support against the Bloodcrest Forces spread throughout the lands like a great wind. Every town and shire surrounding the major cities held a meeting to call for volunteers. All of the volunteers came together under the leadership of a fairly well known human warrior by the name Vlaad. He was a most unusual looking human, having a cleanly shaved head and a dark black goatee with piercing brown eyes. His armor was a dwarven-design, custom blend of dragonscale and *thorium*, both of which were known for their resilience and resistance to elemental attacks. In addition to his unique armor he carried the *Aegis Shield of Griffon's Peak,* identifying him as the King's Champion. Lastly, he carried an elven-crafted curved blade, called a *shamshir,* rumored to be over a thousand years old. His motley group had gnomish rogues, dwarven warriors, elven archers, and even a few human priests. These would be the reserve forces, as they had great diversity and made up nearly two full companies.

The flood of soldiers heading to Port Archer required the Imperial Dae'gon Alliance Navy to mobilize. Under the command of now-Commodore Samuel Bailey, every available ship pulled into Blackmarsh harbor to transport troops, weapons, and supplies to Port Archer. It was an amazing sight to see, as the fall of Forestedge had barely a ten-day ago. These were trying times, but the men and women of the Dae'gon Alliance understood the gravity of the situation and had responded with all haste.

* * *

Neggish Grimtusk had been barking orders for two days to get his warriors and newly arrived craftsmen on schedule rebuilding the defenses in Forestedge. He was certain the elves would counter attack to retake their beloved city, but more importantly, he was concerned about the approaching new moon, which would bring his regional commander to his doorstep. Neggish had no fear of dying or of the pitiful elves mustering their forces. His only concern was that the big boss would come and find him lacking as the senior commander on the ground. His entire life had been about gaining honor and moving up the chain of command. A setback of any kind could end his desire to become ruler of these lands one day.

In retrospect, he had made excellent progress fortifying his position. He admired the newly erected palisade that ringed the outside of the city around the northern front where the elves would make their attack. Within the palisade, he had also ordered small catapults and ballistae to be built and positioned to defeat the rank and file columns of troops that the Dae'gon Alliance tacticians were so well known for. Things were shaping up well.

The second in command of the orcish forces, Nightshade approached Neggish, saying, "Commander, I have an important update for you."

Neggish nodded.

"One full company of infantry remains after our consolidation effort. We have lost the entire elite orc force. The troll cavalry numbers twenty-five, and your tauren shock troops were reduced to fifty. You still have most of your undead priests, mages, shamans, and, of course, your personal bodyguard," the orc informed him.

"What have the priests and shamans been able to accomplish with resurrection?" Grimtusk asked, a sharp edge in his tone.

"My lord," the orc replied, "they have been unable to resurrect any of the fallen. This land has been warded against those spells somehow. Our spell wielders cannot explain it, but apparently, there is a spirit guardian still watching over this place. They can work their other spells, but full resurrection is impossible."

Neggish's temper was bordering on rage. He knew time was against him, and he couldn't fight with less than half of his forces. "Send the undead priests to me," the commander growled.

A few moments passed, and then several undead priests shambled up to their leader.

"What are your ordersss?" they said in unison, with an unnatural echo.

He replied, "What can you do to strengthen our numbers?"

"Necromancy," they replied

"How many can you raise to fight with us, and how long will they remain animated?" he asked.

"We can raisssse them all … even the elvesssss, but they will only remain under our power for a few daysss," they returned hollowly.

"And then what will become of them?" he asked.

"They will wander the landssss until they find peace," they moaned.

"Very well, assemble the corpses beyond the palisade. Be prepared to animate them on my command," he ordered.

Zombies and skeletons were little more than fodder. They were nothing like a resurrected orc who retained his humanity, but like any tool, they were a means to an end. Grimtusk was concerned that when the Dae'gon Alliance came, they would quickly cut down the animated undead, and he would be unable to hold the elves off indefinitely. He was particularly uncomfortable with any troops that he could not command. Any soldier that felt no pain and felt no fear was certainly beyond his power to control. Mindless zombies and skeletons had no need for fortune or fame, either. He simply had to find more troops. He wondered if this was what the elves were feeling as his army approached. No, surely they were swamped in their fear. Neggish was merely concerned, as any good commander would be.

Grimtusk was a cunning and innovative leader. He had numerous resources to call on, but time was against him, especially with the regional commander due to inspect his progress any day now. He called to his platoon leaders for a meeting.

"Send runners to the Crossroads. It is the nearest outpost that might have additional forces to join us in the coming fight. Promise them scavenger rights for any Dae'gon Alliance soldier they kill. Give five gold coins to any who volunteer as a show of good faith, and make sure they can be here before dusk tomorrow," the cunning leader explained.

"Yes, Lord," they said as one.

"Bring me a seer. I must know how we lost so many soldiers to the elves. We cannot afford to make mistakes in the upcoming fight. The stakes are too high, and our army is weakened," he said, as much to himself as to his platoon leaders.

The seer was a shaman with special powers focused on divination. Neggish had hoped to look into the past to learn from his enemies how to best engage them, but when the seer arrived and was perhaps the most hideous beast Grimtusk had ever seen, he was taken aback by the sight. The seer was hunched over and had an unnatural growth on his face that might have been part of a conjoined twin, but could only be described as an extra bloodshot eye that moved independently and a fang-filled mouth that constantly opened and closed as if chomping down on some unseen food.

Neggish composed himself and directed the seer to recall the past by saying, "I must look into the past to discern our enemy's strengths and weaknesses. Call forth the battle of Forestedge from the point just before my elite orcs entered the fight and were decimated."

The seer said nothing in return. He opened a mageweave bag tied at his hip and drew a knife made of chipped flint from his belt. With his free hand, he walked about until he came to the southern stairwell leading into the parapet. The seer squatted down and scooped up a handful of dust. With the flint knife poised over his wrist holding the dust, he mumbled a few arcane words, cut into his flesh, and dropped the dust into the bag. After several moments of dripping his own blood into the bag, he danced about in a small circle. He paused and spit a sticky black substance into the bag. He moved about and shook the bag fervently. All at once, the wind picked up and blew in a small circle until a tiny cyclone formed. The seer opened the bag and released its contents into the newly formed vortex and called for the vision.

The seer said in a cracking voice, "Follow the vision, and it will take you to that which you seek."

Neggish was suddenly flooded with images of the last battle. He walked up to the stairwell and climbed the stairs until he was in the parapet. The vision was so real, he felt himself reaching for the massive ax on his back to fight the elves that filled the upper level of the southern wall.

He peered over the edge and saw that his infantry had taken few casualties and had successfully engaged the elven ground force. He watched as they pushed the elves back into the corridor and out into the courtyard. He saw the archers turn to fire on the heavily armored infantry, just as he knew they would. It was then that he had signaled the advance of his elite orc warriors. They started the charge across the open field when a lone elf called for bow fire on his unarmored troops. The archers, numbering close to one hundred, turned back and laid waste to his fine swordsmen. Less than twenty appeared to have survived. He remembered that loss and cursed himself for not waiting a little longer.

The elven archers turned and began to engage the infantry again. Among the archers were a single dwarf and an elf, both with a most unusual weapon. They both remained focused on the ground outside the city walls. A priest moved out to resurrect some of the fallen orcs when the dwarf fired at the priest. The strange weapon quickly dropped the priest. Grimtusk remembered the next part. He had called for a mage to conceal his tauren shock troops with a mass invisibility spell. Once hidden from sight, they moved across the field, but somehow the elf on the far end detected the caster and ended his life. The result was the reappearance of the tauren company midway across the open ground and a call for more bow-fire from the archers.

Neggish smiled as he noted that not one tauren fell from the volley fire. They plowed into the corridor safely. Just as he expected them to appear on the other side, he saw the dwarf and the elf light several red sticks and drop them among the emerging shock troops. The resulting explosion had the effect of several fireball spells. Many of his tauren warriors died in the blast wave. This was something Neggish could not have prevented. Somehow, the dwarf and his elven companion had weapons and magic he had never seen before. Just as he was about to end the vision, he saw tauren dashing up the stairs to kill the perpetrators above. Each one was greeted by an enormous bear, more shots from the dwarf and elf, and numerous arrows from the archers.

Neggish fumed and stomped around until he saw an elite orc sail over the wall and land among the archers. Then another and another appeared. Several of his remaining elite sword wielders had been tossed up to the parapet by his tauren shock troops below. Somehow, fate had shown his troops a little favor. The swordsmen utterly annihilated the elven archer company before anyone could react. In the end, the orcs died, having been overwhelmed by sheer numbers, but the victory was worth their deaths of honor. Once again, several tauren raced up the stairs only to be slain by the powerful claws of the two bears and the fire-rods the dwarf and last elf fought with.

The vision ended, and Commander Grimtusk made a mental note to never forget the two responsible for the death of so many of his troops. He would have them pay dearly, but first, he needed some information from his prisoner.

* * *

Day three after the fall of Forestedge came with a port full of sailing vessels. Port Archer was quickly filling up with warriors for the coming battle. Among the chaos was a frantic gnome running about organizing the new arrivals into companies and battle formations. Asanti dashed from commander to commander getting names, ranks, and specialties to best organize the troops. With endless energy and the help of his gnomish rocket boots—which he had fashioned himself—Asanti was quite the efficient adjutant. As he drew up the last battle roster from the ragtag volunteers, Captain Helio stepped forward and touched him on the shoulder, which of course made him jump and squeak like a field mouse.

"Be at ease, Asanti, we are making remarkable progress," Helio said soothingly.

"Sir, we have the following soldiers on standby for the C-J-T-F-C-O-O-S," he said, almost too fast to be understood while handing his boss the manifest.

Helio closed his eyes for a moment and patiently asked, "What was that you just said?"

Asanti paused as if his train of thought had clearly been derailed. *How could the captain of the guard and leader of the elven defense forces not know what the C-J-T-F-C-O-O-S was*? he thought. "Sir, the C-J-T-F-C-O-O-S is the approved acronym for the Combined Joint Task Force Counter Offensive Operational Strike. It is an operational term that you approved yesterday to keep the enemy from knowing what we are working on. I have the memo right here," he said indignantly.

"Let me see that," Captain Helio said. He looked over the memorandum, and sure enough, the acronym was among a dozen other cryptic code words that were supposed to be used to keep the enemy spies confused. He was certain it would work since *he* was confused by the entire list, and he was in command here. As he carefully scrutinized the signature, he noticed that it was, in fact, his signature and a spot-on match, but he had never signed nor personally approved any such memo. Finally, he said, "Asanti, this might look like my handwriting, but I am sure I never signed this document."

Asanti smiled broadly and said with no lack of pride, "I know, sir. I even made sure to add the long sweeping tail that you like on the *H* in *Helio.* It is as genuine as if you had signed it yourself!"

Captain Helio stood slack-jawed and at a loss for words, wondering how many other orders and formal documents the gnome had signed without his knowledge. For all he knew, Asanti could have appointed himself King and Regent of all of the Western Kingdom, and he would never know until the official documents made it to his desk through the gnomish channels. He finally just walked off to find his sword and shield. At least he was still in charge of swinging the blade that would actually win this war, even if the actual operation was being planned and efficiently run by a gnome with delusions of grandeur.

Asanti went back to his work, shaking his head and mumbling something about elven incompetence and a lack of trust; after all, only a gnome with his talents could ever organize this chaotic bunch into an effective campaign. He moved up to one of his kinsmen who had just stepped off the boat and started asking questions to properly place the fine gnome in the ranks where he would be most effective.

"Name, please?" Asanti asked.

"I am Granmillo the Great!" the other gnome returned, his smile showing perfectly filed teeth that looked like wicked little fangs.

"Granmillo, ah yes, I have you on the manifest. It says here you are a warlock specializing in summoning," Asanti read carefully.

"That is true, but I also sell fine goods and trade for herbs in my spare time," the other gnome said quaintly.

There was a puff of acrid smoke, and a feisty imp appeared, saying, "You mean you sell cheap wares to fools who know no better."

Granmillo smiled with flushed cheeks and said, "Pay him no mind; he is a foul-tempered beast and one that I wish I could be rid of, but I am afraid that we are spirit-joined, and I am doomed to hear his rantings until the day I die."

"Which can't come soon enough, you shrimp. I thought I was being summoned by an all-powerful warlock who would allow me to wreak a bit of havoc, but no, I get summoned by a balding freak with a soft spot for she-elves and an obsession with roots and leaves that barely bring in enough money to keep a roof over our heads!" the imp returned, tiny flames leaping off his back as he insulted his master.

Asanti looked over his tiny round glasses and watched the exchange curiously. Granmillo pursed his lips in anger and drew a tiny wand from his pouch and blasted the imp several times. The imp screamed and cursed the gnome before disappearing in a cloud of brimstone and smoke. Granmillo huffed and tucked his wand away. With a sigh of resignation, he turned to board the ship to go back home.

"Where are you going, mister?" Asanti asked, his arms crossed over his tiny chest and resting on his round belly.

"I will go home; there is no use for me here. I will end up fighting that blasted imp more than any of the Bloodcrest Forces, and what good will that be?" he replied sadly.

"Nonsense!" Asanti said confidently. "You and that imp are going to the frontlines. I know right where to put you two, and who knows? Maybe this battle is exactly what the imp needs to learn some respect for you."

Granmillo snapped to attention and said, "I am yours to command, sir."

Asanti nodded and moved on to finish his work. Time was growing short, and the army was set to march in two days. He saw a single warrior riding at an amazing speed toward the encampment. He looked over his battle roster and said, "Ah, there we are … I believe Landermihl of Griffon's Peak has arrived in time to lead the Kings's knights into battle. We are right on schedule."

* * *

Da'Shar had been unconscious for a long time, and now

that he was awake, his body ached all over. His head throbbed with the beat of his heart as if he had tried to out-drink a dwarven warrior the night before. Slowly, he came to his senses and found himself securely bound and gagged on the cold floor in the Forestedge stockade. Although his thinking was still fuzzy, he was able to remember the last battle. He recalled grimly Jael'Kutter's final stand, and then, his noble death. It was a sad moment of reflection, but heavy boots clomping down the hallway snapped him out of the past and quickly into the present. There were two people heading his way. One was likely fully armored, as the rattling of plate over chainmail made a distinctive sound. The other was lightly armored and moved more quietly. Da'Shar pretended to be unconscious as the jailer turned the metal keys in the lock and opened the steel gate. A boot came in fast, landing in his ribs. He gasped for air, staring wide-eyed at the leader of the attack on Forestedge.

"Well met," he said in the formal greeting of adventurers. "I am Neggish Grimtusk, commander of the Bloodcrest Forces here, and soon to be your executioner. The soldier beside me is Blackbane, one of my most trusted advisors. We are here to ask you a few questions."

Da'Shar noticed that the armored orc's common was extremely fluent. He took full measure of him. He was well over three hundred pounds of hulking, gray-green muscle. His eyes were sharp with intellect, and his words indicated higher learning. This was a most unusual orc. Oh, how Da'Shar hated him now more than ever.

"I am going to remove your gag that we might speak. If you so much as mumble a single word of magic, or twitch as if shape-shifting, I will cleave you in two. Do you understand?"

Da'Shar nodded.

"Good," he replied as he came forward and untied the dirty cloth that had been far too tight, nearly unhinging the druid's jaw. "First, you will tell me your name as is customary in a civilized introduction."

"I am Da'Shar of Celes'tia." His voice was dull, for he had a dry mouth and sore jaw muscles from days of harsh treatment.

"Well met, Da'Shar of Celes'tia. Tell me about the dwarf who fought beside you two days ago. What is his name?" the orc said calmly.

"By the code of conduct as a Protector of the Vale, I am only required to tell you my name. As your prisoner, I must relinquish nothing more," Da'Shar said defiantly, knowing full well that the orc would either torture him or kill him on the spot. He preferred the latter of course, knowing the brutality of the orcs.

"Ah yes, the code of Protectors; it is a fine tradition, to be sure, but you should know that compliance will get you further than the code. I brought Blackbane with me, assuming you would resist my questions. He is trained and quite talented in mixing toxins. His favorite is made of swiftthistle and firebloom. Properly mixed and applied to any open wound, this concoction races a fiery pain throughout your body. It is rarely fatal, but quite agonizing," the orc said, a wicked grin on his face.

Da'Shar spoke serenely and confidently, saying, "I am dead already. No matter how you torture me, I will be executed soon or later. I choose to die with my honor intact. I will become one with Nature, and my body will simply be no more. You have no true hold over me, only empty threats."

"Perhaps," the commander said calmly. "Bring the other one here!" he called down the hall.

Da'Shar waited stoically. A few minutes later, a hellish sight was dragged into the cell. Barely recognizable but somehow alive, Jael'Kutter was thrown beside Da'Shar. It seemed impossible, but he was breathing. He had been stripped bare, severely beaten, and healed repeatedly. The older wounds from the raptor had already scarred over and new ones lay over them from brutal lashings. In some spots, the white of his ribs showed through the flesh and considerable blood. Da'Shar struggled for a moment, but his bonds were too tight. He cursed and spit at the commander, but to no avail.

Neggish Grimtusk was not a patient orc, and his dark eyes

flashed angrily as he spoke: "You will tell me what I want to know, or I will heal this friend of yours throughout the day and shred his flesh by night until even my most powerful shaman are unable to save him. Do you need a demonstration?"

Blackbane smiled evilly and moved forward with his viciously curved and serrated dagger covered in poison. He ran the blade lightly over the open wounds on the warrior-elf's back. In spite of the exhaustion and agony he had previously suffered, the elf thrashed about, kicking and squirming as if molten steel had been poured down his spine. Da'Shar felt sick being unable to help his friend. This was one form of torture the well-disciplined elf could not bear.

"Enough!" he said with utter revulsion, "I will speak, but you must heal the warrior and release him. He has suffered enough."

"We will play a game, Da'Shar. For every question you answer, I will allow my healers to restore your friend a little. For every question you fail to answer, I will add to his torment. For every lie you tell, I will cut off one of his fingers, and then one of his toes until we get the truth. Do we have an agreement?" he asked.

"We do," the druid replied weakly.

"Who is the dwarf, and what is that weapon he uses?" Neggish asked.

Da'Shar assumed that any lie he spoke would be detected magically, but the entire truth need not be revealed unless asked specifically. This was now a mental game of chess, and Grimtusk had moved a pawn forward to start the game. "His name is Gaedron, and the weapon is called a blunderbuss."

Grimtusk nodded and continued, "Who is the elf that fought beside him and also uses the blunderbuss in combat?"

Da'Shar knew he must be asking about Wavren, but he was unsure what the interest was in the two hunters. He moved his own pawn forward and said, "His name is Wavren."

The game continued. "What do you know about their weapons? Tell me how the blunderbuss works and the explosive red sticks they use."

Da'Shar honestly did not know for certain and simply said, "I know not, but I do know that their effects are far greater than that of a wizard's spells." Da'Shar had hoped to distract the orc by turning his own fear of the unknown into a weapon. By the momentary look of shock, he had done exactly that. It was an aggressive move on the mental chessboard.

The orc commander changed tactics. "How many elves will return to Forestedge for the counter attack?"

Da'Shar leaned in closely and said, "If I were in charge, I would march every able-bodied elf, dwarf, human, and gnome from Port Archer, through Forestedge, and down into the Badlands until we pushed your kind back into Dek'Thal where they belong."

The orc did not get the answer he had hoped for, but if the leaders of Celes'tia and Port Archer were as committed as this elf, it was going to be a vast and powerful army indeed. The orc had one final question: "How would you defeat the army of the Dae'gon Alliance if you were me?"

The elf was shocked. The cagey orc had thrown an operational question his way. Of course, Da'Shar knew how to best defeat the Dae'gon Alliance forces, since he fully understood their strengths and weaknesses, but he could never divulge that information. If he lied, the commander would surely fulfill his promise and remove one digit at a time from Jael'Kutter's body, until the truth came out. After thinking for a few moments, he finally said, "I would have to see your forces and battle preparations to give you an accurate strategy, but you would never be willing to disclose that to an enemy."

Da'Shar had outwitted the orc, and had, in essence, placed the orc's king in check on the mental chessboard, but Grimtusk was no fool. He still had the upper hand, given his control over the prisoner. He leaned in closely and said, "Very well, elf; today you will learn how orcs wage war." The orc cut the rope around his ankles and pulled him up to his feet. His hands were still tied behind his back, but at least he was mobile. It was the druid's turn to look shocked. He wondered if he had just set himself up for checkmate.

Jael'Kutter was given excellent treatment. He was nearly restored to full health just as the orcish boss had agreed. Da'Shar was amazed that he had kept his word. He never expected an orc to show any mercy to an elf under any circumstance. He began to consider every possibility. First, he considered that the enemy was not so unlike his allies. Although their political views and upbringing were quite different, there was some commonality in honor and even mercy. He had seen hundreds of orc, troll, and tauren minions tortured and killed for information by the Dae'gon Alliance. He had also seen compliant prisoners well treated and even released for political gain. It all went back to Nature and survival. It always did for druids. As he considered the implications of his enemy's action, he took note of the endless work his enemies were engaged in. It was no different than the work the elves had done just a few days before.

"Our warriors have built a palisade to hold off the elven siege equipment. As you can see, we have built batteries of catapults and ballistae to cut down the rank and file troops that the Dae'gon Alliance prefers. My infantry is small in number, but their armor is strong, and their will to fight is even stronger. The cavalry is also small, but the desert raptors are fighters as well, unlike the warhorses your human allies prefer. This doubles our offensive capabilities. The tauren are savage powerhouses who will break through the Dae'gon Alliance frontline and penetrate into the deep rear where the less-armored targets will be firing their deadly longbows or casting spells. My priests and shaman will heal the injured just as your healers do, but the undead priests have a nasty surprise that your timid healers would never consider: necromancy. Finally, unlike the weak leaders of the Dae'gon Alliance, I will fight alongside my troops with my own elite bodyguards. We will inspire our soldiers as we cut through the ranks of your kinsmen. Now that you know our battle plans, tell me truthfully: what else can be done to guarantee our victory?" the commander asked with deadly serious intent.

Da'Shar knew that he was as good as dead. The orc would

never let him live, given his firsthand knowledge of the enemy battle plans. He also knew that regardless of what he said, many lives would be lost in the coming battle to re-take Forestedge. He said the only true answer that came to mind, speaking in terms of life and Nature: "Commander Grimtusk, you have kept you word by providing healing. I have kept my word and answered all of your questions truthfully. I owe you one last answer, and it must be true for the good of all. You must abandon Forestedge and return to your home in the South. You say that you want a guaranteed victory. You must do the last thing the Dae'gon Alliance will expect. You must leave. If you heed my words, you and your warriors will live. The Dae'gon Alliance will be unable to defeat you on your own ground in Dek'Thal. You know this to be true. Lastly, consider the great achievements you have already won. You have infiltrated an elven city, replaced their high councilor with a shape-shifter, destroyed the city's quick-reaction force, and sacked Forestedge; you also have slain countless elves and their allies. You have done more than any other orc in the history of the Western Kingdom. What say you?"

Commander Grimtusk smiled a wide grin, showing his ample tusks and yellowed teeth. He laughed a deep and powerful laugh. He put one massively armored hand on the comparatively small shoulder of the elf and said, "You are ever the idealist! You speak many truths, but you can never understand what it means to be an orc or a commander of the Bloodcrest Forces. You say leave. That is guaranteed suicide. Even if my regional commander failed to slay me, my men would mutiny and kill me for sure. You say we are safe within our borders from the Dae'gon Alliance. I tell you that safety is a time-relative term dependant on the growing greed for ore the dwarves can never satisfy or the greed humans have for more and more land. The elves may not be so imperialistic, but they, too, covet that which others have. Even the pathetic gnomes can never satisfy their lust for technology, which requires more natural resources than they can ever find on their own land. No, Da'Shar, you have failed to answer my question, but not out of trickery or dishonesty. You failed to answer out of ignorance, and that is considerable, given your long-lived race."

Da'Shar looked at his enemy with renewed hatred and spoke frankly: "You speak of ignorance on my part, but little do you know of elves and the goodly races on Dae'gon. We have established trade in Goblin Port, Jaggedspine Valley, Winter's Vale, and several other outposts where the Bloodcrest Forces and Dae'gon Alliance come together for mutual gain, but you prefer to focus on the contested lands where none can profit or live in peace—places like Deadmist Valley. I know you, Neggish Grimtusk. You are a feral beast, a plague on civilization. You would kill every man, woman, and child in the Dae'gon Alliance only to find that once dead, your desire for conquest would turn you against your own allies. Can you deny that the tauren, or perhaps the undead, would fall to your blade if there were no others to fight? What then? Would you turn on your cousins, the trolls, and then on your own race? When none are left standing, only then can you be the ruler of the world. All of Dae'gon can be yours."

"Only now do you fully understand me, elf. Now you and your friend must die," Grimtusk said solemnly.

"My friend," Da'Shar said, feigning confusion, "surely, you don't think your shape-shifting lieutenant could fool me. I am Da'Shar, Protector of the Vale and Master Druid of the Grove. Even if I hadn't seen the real Jael'Kutter fall in combat, I would never believe an animal like you would be willing to show mercy to an elf. You have over-estimated my patient and forgiving nature, just as you have over-estimated your pathetic chances of survival. When the Dae'gon Alliance comes, Grimtusk will fall."

Neggish drew his giant obsidian ax. Da'Shar held perfectly still. The ax went up high, as its wielder prepared to cleave the elf in two. Da'Shar smiled and waited. The massive blade began its decent. The druid sprang forward, smashing his head under the orc's chin and inside the arc of the ax. Surprised and off balance, the orc staggered back a step. The elf hopped up and over his hands. He called for moonfire and the rope disintegrated around his wrists. Neggish recovered quickly and swung his ax at Da'Shar, meaning to take his head from his shoulders. The druid ducked and called to Nature, entangling the commander's feet with vines and roots. Several of Neggish's minions stopped working on the defenses and took up their weapons. Da'Shar quickly shifted into his travel form and dashed through the palisade gate. The troll riders took up chase, but in the open, none could catch the ethereal cat-like beast. After a mile, the trolls turned around and returned to their commander.

"He got away," the lead cavalryman admitted.

"Just as we planned," was his response. "Lieutenant Nightshade will handle things from here. Get back to work; we must complete the fortifications soon."

Neggish Grimtusk smiled to himself as he walked away. The pretense of having knowledge could be a dangerous thing. The cagey orc was already engaging the enemy in warfare of sorts; it was all about sending the enemy misinformation and recovering their battle plans. The elf was very good at chess, but Grimtusk was still one move ahead.

Chapter 18
Honor and Greed

The ground shook with the cadence of the Dae'gon Alliance Army's march. Never in the history of the Western Kingdom had such a massive force been assembled to march against the Bloodcrest Forces. Forestedge had never fallen before, either.

The goodly forces made an impressive display as they closed the distance from Port Archer to Forestedge with the spectacular royal knights from Griffon's Peak leading the procession. The massive warhorses were fully covered in barding, their custom-made plate armor, and each was draped with the King's emblem, the golden griffon. The knights were no less spectacular, riding in their matching golden Armor of Valor that was earned by completing a series of trials, including trips into Ironore Mountain and the Ironore Cavern where only the bravest and most powerful adventurers dared to go.

The only rider not in matching armor was the commander. Landermihl was a paladin, not a true knight. He was a holy crusader who rode a magnificent charger as his warhorse and was covered in the sacred armor of his order. A golden sun fashioned from pure *thorium,* the symbol of his God, was fastened to his breastplate for all to see and for evil to fear. He actually seemed to radiate light—or perhaps his shining armor simply reflected it intensely from the sun. Whatever the case, he was an inspirational leader, and one his men followed unwaveringly.

The dwarves of Dragonforge, the Blade-Breakers, followed the human knights in the procession. Each dwarf was clad in the lightweight, but nearly impenetrable, mithril plate armor and walked precisely one arm's length to the left and rear of the *right guide*. They had the war ax and the mining pick, King Magni's crest, emblazoned on their shields. They drummed a marching cadence on those shields as they walked, hitting it every time their left foot struck the ground. On the fifth hit of the cadence, the dwarves sounded off in unison with a loud and thunderous, "*ZHA*!", which was an ancient dwarven word that meant war. The gnomish wizards and warlocks sent by the High Sheriff of Silvershire had no armor or matching uniforms. They simply plodded along behind their dwarven cousins. Gaedron felt somewhat out of place in his mithril chainmail and green cloak. He was actually better suited to lead the Forest Runners, but King Magni had insisted that he lead the dwarves as a matter of principle.

Not far behind the dwarves were the two full companies of elven archers. They were the finest long-bowmen in the realm and wore the tunic of Celes'tia. It was dark blue like the night sky with several small stars surrounding one bright star. It signified the authority of the Speaker of the Stars and the support of its people, the nation of elves. Unlike the dwarves and humans, the elves wore a forest-green cloak and matching boots, which enhanced their stealth skills in the woods. The Forest Runners were moving parallel, swiftly, and silently among the trees and bushes off road to the left and right of the massive procession. Few ever knew they were there, and other than an occasional glimpse of a watchful eye, they were invisible. Captain Helio was among them, having been a Forest Runner before taking responsibility for Port Archer's security. They were the eyes and ears of the group.

The volunteers marched in formation to the rear. They were ever the motley group. Most were loners and adventurers. Some were members of tribes or guilds, but none were polished and disciplined in the way the human and dwarven military forces were. They brought a different gift to the battle: independent thinking. Although led by Vlaad, a natural leader and fine adventurer, they subscribed to the belief that as long as they stayed alive and killed the enemy, they were contributing to the overall victory. It was a simple but effective strategy.

Vlaad walked quietly and somberly among his troops. Most knew him only as an adventurer, but a few had seen him in action. He was a most unique warrior called a *defender*. His skill with swords, axes, and maces was a fine spectacle to behold, but his true talents revolved around his shield. Legend had it that a true defender could hold off enemies ten to one almost indefinitely and that he lived to absorb damage, but Vlaad had surpassed those ambitions long ago. He simply drew attacks from hitting his allies almost magically. Few attacks ever landed cleanly, and those that did seemed to have no lasting effects.

Two elves ran separately from the mass of soldiers. Together, they moved due east through the dense jungle, and then south over the ridgeline that made up Forestedge's natural defenses to circumvent the obvious avenue of approach. They had to be careful, as they were just skirting the enemy forces by less than a mile. If there were any orc scouts about, their mission to infiltrate the city would fail.

Wavren whispered to his sister, "This is just like old times."

Rosabela did not smile as she ran beside her brother, but she managed a nod. She was still distraught about having watched her mentor and Jael'Kutter fall in battle.

Wavren could sense her pain and decided to keep quiet, but he knew other ways to help Rosabela get her mind clear. He drew on his hunter's skills and became immersed in the surrounding forest. By drawing on the *endurance of the pack* skill, his speed doubled and he never mis-stepped. No vine or branch slowed him, and Rosabela was quickly left behind.

Rosabela watched as her brother raced ahead at an impossible speed. Apparently, his skills as a hunter had grown considerably, but she also had talents that set her apart from common elves. Summoning her travel form, the lithe she-elf dove headlong into a sprint. She saw Wavren a short distance ahead and soon caught up to him. He was unaware of her presence until she was right beside him. It would have been easy to simply blast by the hunter, but discipline was the druid's watchword. Besides, she was already moving alongside Wavren at a pace few horses could keep, and she was unsure how long he would be able to sustain his sprint. Over an hour later, she found that he was able to run at that speed indefinitely, and her respect for his prowess doubled. They stopped on the outskirts of the graveyard not far from where they had battled Borik and his undead minions. A chill ran down the druid's spine as she recalled the fight. Da'Shar had nearly died protecting the group. She had come to realize that his selfless service was his greatest contribution to the Protectors of the Vale. She would honor that lesson always.

"Are you all right, Rosie?" the hunter said between gasps for breath.

"I was remembering the last time we were here. My desire to speak with the dead was a reckless move that nearly got Da'Shar killed. It nearly got us all killed," she said, more to herself than her brother. It was a not a mistake she took lightly.

Wavren replied quickly, "But it revealed information that we used to depose the imposter and warn the people of Forestedge. Rosie, you saved the lives of hundreds of townsfolk who would have died if they had not been evacuated. That is a fine contribution and well worth the risk you took."

She smiled for the first time since the battle and said, "Wav, you always know just what to say. I am thankful for your kind words and consideration. I am ready to get to work now if you are."

He smiled back at her, nodded, and opened his mind to the surrounding area. Their mission was to gather information on the enemy and infiltrate the city before the next battle began in order to pass the critical intelligence on to the Dae'gon Alliance. Tracking the enemy was an easy task for the seasoned hunter; getting through the city was going to be considerably more difficult.

* * *

Forestedge had changed considerably over the last few days. The once austere city of natural beauty was now nothing more than a hideous orc fortress. Most of the massive trees had been cut down to build the palisade and weapons of war. The fire from the first battle had left blackened ground and dark scorch marks on the beautiful stone walls to the south. Even the inner city was quickly becoming a dismal and dreary collection of buildings and alleyways. It was as if the city was rotting, festering … dying. The enemies reveled in the city's new look. They seemed to rally in the darkness of their remodeling, and as more orcs, trolls, and tauren arrived from the Crossroads to the south, the city became more cold and twisted.

The newcomers were immediately thrown into ad hoc war parties. Having no unit cohesion or formal training as a combat force, the newcomers would be used as skirmishers following the traditions of the orc clans. They would fight using barbarian tactics—namely, the frontal assault. A few of the orcs had come to gain honor in battle and would earn a place among the professional soldiers if they survived, but most came for the gold and scavenger rights following the battle. In mass combat such as this, any who survived would be well rewarded with plunder alone. Some might be fortunate enough to find an enchanted weapon or valuable armor. It was well worth the risk given the alternative of being a bandit or simply a highwayman. For a few, this was a quick ticket out of squalor and into a better life.

Neggish Grimtusk assessed the situation with the new additions to his army. He saw many orcs wearing hide or piecemeal armor. Many carried clubs or rusted swords. He was somewhat disappointed; but he decided that when he scraped the bottom of the barrel, he should have expected to get sludge. He summoned his two remaining subordinate leaders, Blackbane and Doppleganger.

"I want every soldier outfitted in the armor of our fallen brethren from the elite forces. Arm them with their weapons as well, and when you run out of our items, use elven equipment. No soldier will fight for my army looking like a goat herder from the Badlands," he commanded.

The two platoon leaders nodded and prepared to issue the valuable cache of equipment somewhat grudgingly.

Their leader called out one more time in a reassuring voice, "Fear not, you will have your booty when they are dead. Consider this a very temporary loan. Only the strong will survive the coming battle."

The platoon leaders understood perfectly and went about their business as ordered. It wasn't long after they gathered the new recruits together and briefed them on the plan to issue out better gear that things started moving along. The neophytes eagerly stood in line for the fine armor and weapons of the fallen warriors. They greedily grabbed up their new equipment and ran off like wild animals to avoid being robbed of their new possessions. Little did they know that their leader's generosity was superficial at best and a source of false hope at worst. The army they would soon be facing could kill them easily, no matter what equipment they brought to the fight. It was all a show for psychological reasons regarding the enemy and political reasons regarding the regional commander. Neggish Grimtusk was no fool. He worked every angle to his advantage.

Night fell, and the Bloodcrest Forces had nearly finished with the upgrades to the city's defenses. A runner approached Neggish Grimtusk to announce that the regional commander was en route. The resulting expression on the commander's face was clearly one of concern, but with all he had accomplished, the commander was certain his superior would be pleased.

The scene was not one of exorbitance; the entourage was merely a dozen worg-riders and half a dozen advisors who were all likely spell-wielders. The regional commander was unlike any orc Neggish had ever seen. He was small for an orc, a runt. He wore no armor and carried no visible weapons. At first glance, he thought the feeble orc was one of the advisors, but Neggish quickly dismissed that thought as the worg-riders quickly dismounted, and formed a triangle around the smaller orc's mount. The advisors also dismounted and took up positions on the flat sides of the triangle in pairs. The resulting formation was a security force of casters and swordsmen that allowed none of the onlookers to get within ten feet of the central figure.

Neggish suddenly felt compelled to draw his mighty ax and simply slay the lot of them. Who was this weakling to come into his compound and inspect his work and his progress? Neggish had lived a long time and had achieved greatness using his wits when he felt such compunctions. He had to mentally resist his initial instincts to attack, but it was an easy feat compared to his next action. He stepped forward and took a knee before the entourage. His entire force gasped in unison and quickly followed suit. They had never seen their leader bow before anyone or anything. Whoever this regional commander was, if the mighty Neggish Grimtusk offered him such respect, he was obviously an orc of amazing power.

"Commander Grimtusk," the regional commander said, calmly dismounting, "I am Gorka Darkstorm, regional commander of the Western Kingdom, and chosen son of Dek'Thal. It is good to finally meet you. Please rise and let us meet in private, that all of your questions about me and all of my questions about your operation can be satisfied."

Neggish rose and towered over the tiny orc, motioning for his superior to walk ahead of him to the council chambers where he had set up his command and control cell. Protocol called for such courtesies, and it galled the massive orc to offer them instead of a swipe to the back of the boss's head with his ax. He maintained the façade required to appease the orc before him.

The two arrived inside and were finally alone. The smaller orc took a seat, and the larger remained standing until given permission to sit. It was granted almost immediately.

"I am overwhelmed by your discipline and sheer will-power," Gorka said to the great warrior before him. "I can see that you recognize my station, but I have in no way inspired your respect. Your body language tells me these things. It says so much more than your outward actions and courtesies relay."

Neggish could not disagree. He merely remained silent and stared at the orc before him to see how things would develop.

"I can tell that you would prefer to slay me here and now," he said offhandedly. "Your eyes tell me much more than your words would ever reveal, so let's get to the most pressing issue. You are a great warrior and a fine leader. I appear to be a small and harmless politician, but nothing could be further from the truth. I have risen to this position by merit and deed alone, but words are boring. I am sure you prefer a demonstration; after all, experience is the best teacher."

Grimtusk stepped back, overturning his chair, and drew his great ax in one swift movement. Gorka merely stepped forward and confidently held his arms out to show he was unarmed.

"Slay me here and now. It is the way of the warrior to rise by surpassing in deed or killing those above us," he said serenely.

Neggish was certain he could cut the fool down in one stroke, but he hesitated. It was all the smaller orc needed to close the distance between the two. He drew a blue, glowing blade from his sleeve and sliced through the leather straps that secured Grimtusk's armor to his left leg. The enchanted armor clanged to the floor. The smaller orc danced away, well out of range of the massive black blade of Neggish's ancestral ax. He looked down and saw a tiny red line crossing his femoral artery. The flesh had barely been broken at all, but the point of the attack was clear. He could be bleeding to death had Gorka chosen to strike deeper.

The powerful warrior's eyes flashed pure hatred as he charged the dagger-wielding fiend. His attack came in diagonally from left to right. Gorka dodged left as anticipated, and the follow-on spin and horizontal cut should have removed the smaller orc's head, but the ax met no resistance. Gorka had danced away again and Grimtusk's right arm-piece and shoulder pauldron fell free with both straps cut cleanly. Neggish felt a slight burning and noticed another red line across his brachial artery, just below his right bicep. Again, the point was clearly made that had Gorka Darkstorm wanted to end Neggish's life, he could have severed the artery and within a short time, the larger orc would bleed to death.

"Are we finished, Great One?" Gorka asked, almost nonchalantly. "I know a fine armorer who can easily repair the damage I have done, but I am afraid I do not know anyone who can teach you your place. All you have to do is accept that I am your better, and we can move on with more interesting questions."

Neggish Grimtusk had been decisively beaten, and there was no dishonor in that. It galled him that he had been toyed with and thus disgraced, but what else could he have done? He had to know how the small orc had risen to such a prominent position and was his superior. Now he knew. Considering that he could be dead now, he realized one important aspect of the entire exchange: Gorka Darkstorm needed him. If he hadn't needed him, he would be dead. Grimtusk returned his massive ax to its resting place on his back and took a knee before the regional commander. "You have my respect and my loyalty. What are your orders?" he asked humbly.

Gorka smiled and said, "Rise, Commander Neggish Grimtusk. I will have you as my most trusted advisor and top commander here in the North, but you must not fail me. I cannot tolerate failure. If you need more soldiers, I will send them. If you need more gold to conduct operations, I will supply it. All I ask is that you command your soldiers wisely to bring blood and glory to the Bloodcrest Forces without mercy. It is what you were born and bred for. It is our function in this life, and when you can no longer fulfill your duties, you will turn you command over to me, and I will replace you with someone more capable, or I will return to finish our first engagement. Do we have an understanding?"

Neggish was beginning to like his leader very much. He nodded and replied without hesitation, "We do."

"Now, tell me everything, and do not fear the truth. I must know the good and the bad in order to provide you the support you need to keep your promise to me," the superior orc said, genuine expectation in his voice.

"Commander," Neggish began, "our forces lost many warriors in the initial engagement. I have rebuilt our army with numbers, but not well-trained soldiers. I have bolstered our weaknesses with a plan to animate a contingent of undead when the Dae'gon Alliance arrives. We have built a palisade and armed the perimeter with catapults and ballistae to crush the returning elves. Our supply trains have prepared us to hold off a siege for many months. My subordinate leaders are excellent tacticians, and I have many casters at my disposal as well."

"Tell me, Grimtusk," Gorka said thoughtfully, "how many elves and their allies will it take to break down your palisade, cut through the animated forces, and slay your new recruits?"

"If they bring three hundred well-trained soldiers, siege engines, and battle-mages, then our initial forces will fall, leaving the seasoned veterans who number nearly two hundred," he replied somewhat uneasily.

"Your honesty is refreshing. I know trust is not a common value among our race, but let me demonstrate why we must cultivate it. I believe you cannot win the next battle. You simply do not have the troops necessary. I predict that the Dae'gon Alliance will send no less than five hundred well-trained soldiers and a fair number of volunteers, but as I promised, you will have the soldiers required to repulse the counter attack. They will arrive shortly, having been dispatched several days ago. You must employ them well and bring us victory," Gorka insisted.

Never had any commander had the depth of foresight that Gorka was showing. He seemed to have great resources and an understanding of warfare that once again impressed Neggish. "Lord," he began in response, "how many will come?"

"One company of elite and one company of infantry," Gorka commented candidly. "Will that suffice?"

"Yes, sire, that is nearly the sum of our total losses from the first battle," he answered with no lack of surprise.

"I know," was Gorka's response. "Do you need anything else? Are there any other questions for me?"

Grimtusk was unsure how to ask his next question, but his superior had been forthcoming up to this point, and he was curious about the orc's … background. He simply shook his head and looked down, saying, "There is nothing else."

Gorka was surprised by the body language and quickly reminded the larger orc that honesty was part of their agreement: "I can sense your uneasiness. You have more to ask, but it is not military in nature, or you would be to the point about it. I have to assume you are wondering who I am and how I came to be the orc you see before yourself."

Neggish looked up, somewhat slack-jawed, and began to wonder if Gorka could read his mind. Gorka laughed as the obvious thought passed through Neggish's mind and displayed itself like a sign on his large sloping brow. He said, "I will tell you two things about myself, but only because you are my senior commander and should have no problems keeping my business … personal. First of all, I am half-orc. I assume my mother was a human ravaged by my father.

"I was cast away at birth and would have died if not for a kind passerby who heard my wailing and took me in for the night. He had traveled through the Badlands on various occasions and knew an orc tribe that might take me in. They did take me in, but they never accepted me, as I was a half-breed.

"I became the servant boy for the chief of the tribe. He noticed that I had some capacity for trade language as I grew older, so he sent me to learn common and dwarven at a monastery near Dragonforge, hoping that I might serve as a translator during the trade season. I learned to speak common and dwarven, but I also learned the fighting arts of the monks who lived there. I returned to my home, such as it was, and learned to conduct business in trade and the mathematics of currency. The chief was pleased with me, but I was too small to be taken seriously by the warriors of the clan or even the humans and dwarves who we traded with. I was disgraced.

"The chief sent me away to Highmount, the home of the tauren, to establish diplomacy with the nomadic people there. I was too small to be any threat, so they accepted me more as a mascot or entertainer than a true diplomat. I fell under the responsibility of the tribe's herbalist and alchemist, who taught me to mix healing elixirs and salves, but more importantly, I learned the darker arts while passing messages and agreements between the orcs and tauren. I learned the art of poison production and implementation.

"Once again, the chief felt that I was too small to carry any respect among the massive tauren, so I was replaced by one of my larger clansmen. The story goes on and on, until I finally left the orcs who raised me to live in the streets of Dek'Thal as a cutthroat. I was too small to be considered a threat to anyone, which allowed me to move in the city almost invisibly. My work became problematic for the local officials who put a bounty on my head. They had no idea who I was or what to look for, so they simply called me the *Shade*. My reputation grew until I was finally sought out by the Assassin's Guild in Griffon's Peak, the human city.

"I decided to meet with the guild master and was quickly indoctrinated and hired. I took on several small jobs and made enough money to travel for a while and take a short break from the business. I went back to the monastery and trained for several more years until I had polished my fighting skills. When I returned to Griffon's Peak, I resigned my commission with the guild and went back to work as a freelance assassin.

"The guild still called on me from time to time, but I was drawn to conquest, so I returned to Dek'Thal as a mercenary for hire. The city set up several small jobs with local patrols that required an orc of my talents. I found that my ability to learn and employ military tactics was where I needed to focus. The city guard hired me on, and then I moved into the orcish army where I ascended rapidly in rank and position. The rest is boring history."

Commander Grimtusk was compelled to believe the fantastic story, having actually heard of the killer known as the Shade, but it sounded like the tallest tale he had ever heard. He nodded, stood up, and saluted his regional commander.

The half-orc stood up and said, "By the way, the second thing I need to tell you about myself is that I don't like my authority questioned behind my back. See to it that we are unified in our positions now, before we proceed."

The massive orc said the only thing he could: "We are."

Gorka left the council chamber, mounted his worg, gathered his entourage, and departed. The battle was now left to Commander Grimtusk.

* * *

Da'Shar's injuries had been significant, but he did not want to stop even long enough to heal himself. His friends had to receive the information he had gathered from his internment in time to make the necessary adjustments. He pushed on toward Port Archer and was surprised to find what had to be the army of the Dae'gon Alliance heading his way less than thirty minutes later. Da'Shar quickly shifted back into his elven form and waited.

A platoon of Forest Runners came out of the woods and immediately recognized the druid. "Da'Shar, it is good to see you. We heard that you had been captured and killed by the Bloodcrest Forces. How is it that you escaped?" one of the runners asked.

"I cannot be sure if I truly escaped or if I was allowed to escape, but I must see the commander in charge. I have vital information regarding the defensive fortifications and enemy composition of Forestedge," he said with great urgency.

A few Forest Runners escorted the druid to the forward edge of troops where they were safe from prying eyes and ears that might have followed. Captain Helio stepped forward from among the Forest Runners and said, "I am the overall commander of troops, but each group has its own commander. The others have been called and should arrive momentarily."

The procession was long, and the last to arrive was Vlaad and a small gnome no one knew, but everyone assumed was present to represent the interest of the casters. Preceding him were Landermihl and Gaedron. All were surprised to see the druid alive, but none so surprised as the dwarf, who actually pulled the elf into a powerful—albeit short—hug. He spoke with slight wetness in his gray eyes: "Good ta see yer pointy ears again, elf. Da boy and his sis'll be sure glad ta know ye made it."

Da'Shar was shocked to receive the hardy welcome from Gaedron, but he smiled and simply replied, "It is good to be back among friends. Where is my apprentice and her brother, now that you mention them?"

The hunter said, "They be out havin' all da fun scoutin' and infiltratin' while I git stuck playin' leader o' the dwarven infantry."

He nodded and greeted the other unit commanders.

Landermihl stepped forward and spoke: "I will be leading the cavalry, Gaedron has the infantry, and Helio has the skirmishers and archers. The volunteers will be under the command of Vlaad, here. What news do you bring us at this late hour?"

Da'Shar took a knee and began drawing a simple layout of the city. He said, "The northern wall has been built up considerably by the orcish and troll engineers. They have erected a massive palisade that will make a siege inevitable. Along the top of the palisade there are catapults here, here, and here, with ballistae here and here in between. I cannot say what other fortification they have to the south, as I was bound and gagged most of the time I was with the enemy."

Gaedron spoke up: "Aye, it's lookin' like we'll be needin'

our own siege ’quipment. Given a bit o’ time, me an me boys can make a trebuchet ’r two, but we be short on time as I’m seein’ it.”

Vlaad interjected quickly: “Tell us about their manpower.”

Da’Shar looked back at his rough outline on the ground and said, “The commander is here at the command post. He is a massive brute of an orc if ever there was one. He is heavily armed and armored, but his greatest asset is his mind. He is not a barbarian, mind you. He is educated in tactics, operations, and even logistics as you can see by his fortifications. You will identify him by his spiked armor and massive obsidian ax. He will be surrounded at all times by his bodyguards and advisors. The bodyguards are elite orcs with enchanted weapons. They are undoubtedly experts in close combat. The advisors are orcish shaman, troll wizards, and undead priest and warlocks. You can bet that they will be prepared to send all manner of spells our way as well as bolster the line soldiers with blessings, invisibility, and healing.”

Captain Helio interrupted, “It sounds like he is well protected, but what of the regulars we will face on the frontlines?”

Da’Shar hesitated for a moment. “The Forestedge forces crippled his infantry, shock troopers, and cavalry during the initial defense of the city and killed his elite swordsmen down to the last orc, but I saw well over two hundred remaining. I am not sure if he has been reinforced yet, but he said his priests had a special surprise awaiting us in the form of necromancy.”

Landermihl took a deep breath and said, “I will face the reanimated corpses and grant them peace, but we must use caution. Undead are fearless and unfeeling beings that will never stop until they have been destroyed. They will serve the Bloodcrest Forces as fodder and allow the catapults and ballistae time to fire many volleys long before the first orc or troll appears on the battlefield.”

The commanders all turned to face Helio, who had operational control until the battle began. They awaited his orders.

Helio thought for a moment and then asked, “Should we stall the attack to build siege equipment, or change course and go around the valley and attack from the southern side? All in favor of laying siege to the northern wall, say aye."

Gaedron voted to siege with his, "Aye."

Helio presented the other option: "All in favor of circumventing the city and attacking into the southern wall, say aye."

Vlaad and Helio voted together with their corresponding, "Aye."

Only Landermihl abstained.

Helio turned to the paladin and asked, "You have not voted for either choice. Why not?"

He spoke in his deep baritone voice: "Da'Shar said he was unsure if he escaped or if he was allowed to escape. I believe if he escaped on his own, then we should go around and attack from the south, but if he was allowed to escape and the orc leader is as cunning as you say, then he will expect us to avoid his defensive fortifications and he will be well prepared to receive us on the southern wall. Whatever course we choose, caution must be taken to avoid walking into a trap."

The other commanders nodded and spoke freely amongst themselves for a moment.

Helio said, "The Forest Runners can make the circle easily, but the knights and infantry will be slowed greatly."

Landermihl nodded in agreement.

Gaedron said, "If we git all our hands dirty, I bettin' we can build dem siege engines in two days flat."

Then a tiny hand went up and a small voice squeaked, "Can we do both?"

All eyes looked downward and Captain Helio said, "What do you mean, both? Do you suggest that we spilt our forces and attack from both ends? That would be folly."

"No," the tiny gnome said. "I think we should attack from the south with illusionary forces to guarantee all the enemy troops are focused in that direction while the real forces simply scale the wall and open the gate on the north side. We double cross their double cross; if they really weren't double crossing anyone and Da'Shar escaped by accident, then we still surprise them!"

Gaedron started laughing and slapped the gnome on the back. He said, "Leave it ta a durned gnome ta come up wit a plan so bizarre dat it actually works. I love it!"

Vlaad and Helio smiled and nodded, but the paladin was unconvinced. He said, "It won't take long to figure out that the troops aren't real. The trick with any feint is getting the enemy to believe it is the real attack."

The little gnome smiled, showing his perfectly filed teeth, and said, "Asanti promised me that I would be fighting on the frontlines, and with a little help from a friend of mine, I think we can make the enemy think he is being attacked for real. I might need a few scrolls with illusionary magic to pull it off, but that shouldn't be too tough with this group"

"When the enemy comes, little one, you will be killed for certain," Da'Shar said gently.

Gaedron spoke up before the druid could scare the gnome out of his moment of brilliance: "I say we go wit' da lad's plan, and when da front door opens, we come in so fast dat da foul beasts never knows what hit 'em an' da lit'le 'un gets away in da confusion. By da way, boy-o, wha'cha be callin' yerself, so we can know who ta cheer fer when da day be done?"

The little gnome liked the sound of Gaedron's confidence and squeaked proudly, "I'm Granmillo the Great, and I am at your service."

Chapter 19
Bait and Switch

Wavren and Rosabela had been busy for several hours watching the roving patrols and making note of the forces on the perimeter of the city. So far, it didn't look good for the Dae'gon Alliance. Scores of orcs, trolls, and tauren had wandered in from the South, and just after sunrise, two full companies of professional soldiers marched into the city. Reinforcements had indeed arrived in plenty of time to make a difference.

"We need a closer look," Rosabela said.

"I can see fine from here," Wavren returned.

Wavren was able to magically enhance his vision to see at great distances as a hunter. It was a talent called *eyes of the eagle* and was particularly helpful when spying on enemies or trying to identify friend or foe just before a company of archers fired at maximum range.

"Well, what do you see, Wav? How many platoons are there? Do you need to take off your boots to count that high?" she taunted.

Wavren took it all in stride, knowing that his sister needed a bit of lightheartedness after the disaster with Jael'Kutter and her mentor. He certainly hoped that she was resilient enough to bounce back after that ordeal. He said, "I count eight platoons of infantry with the addition of that last group. There are four platoons of elite orcs. I can see two platoons of tauren, and it looks like three platoons of cavalry. There are also a variety of trolls, orcs, tauren, and undead who are not grouped up. I have to assume they are fillers for the regular forces or maybe a reserve force of some kind. I also see the big one. He is definitely the boss!"

Rosabela scribed it all out on a parchment and stored it in a hollow bone case for transport. She looked around and noticed the close proximity of the graveyard to the south wall. "Wav, you don't think the unholy priests can raise the entire graveyard, do you?"

Wavren remembered vividly the fight with Borik and the other undead. It had been a nightmare battle that he was lucky to have lived through. He looked into his sister's eyes for a moment, then watched her remove the scroll and add her concerns about the graveyard. She quickly drew a rough map of the area and estimated the travel time for the undead to rise and move into the city. It would happen quickly if they chose to raise all of the corpses in the cemetery. This development could be pivotal, and the twins simply had to get back to the main army to warn them. They eased back from their covered observation post and began to backtrack to the northwest.

As the two sped through the dense woodlands with great haste, they caught a high-pitched voice on the winds. The elves dropped out of sight and set up a quick ambush. Rosabela readied her arsenal of spells, and Wavren called to Stonetalon and leveled his blunderbuss in the direction of the voices. They waited for several minutes until they saw a tiny gnome approaching. Still unsure if the gnome was aligned with the Bloodcrest Forces or not, they waited until the last minute and attacked. Rosabela called on the power of Nature to entangle the gnome's feet and Wavren sent his giant bear forward. The gnome was immediately trapped among the vines and roots. He pulled out his wand and aimed it at the charging bear.

Wavren called to the trapped gnome, "That would be a bad idea, mister. You might really make Stonetalon angry if you blast him with your magic, not to mention that I would be forced to put a hole through your chest for good measure."

The gnome called out, "I am Granmillo the Great. Release me before I summon the wrath of Hades to deal with you and your bear."

Suddenly a tiny imp appeared in a black cloud of smoke and ash. "Ha ha!" it laughed. "You have finally got yourself in over your head this time!"

Rosabela recognized the gnome's name and called to him: "Granmillo? Are you the same Granmillo from the market who bought my herbs?"

Granmillo craned his neck and wiggled within the confines of his root-and-vine prison as if he could suddenly grow the required two feet in order to see the beautiful elf-maid beyond the massive growling bear. "Rosie, it that you, my dear?"

The elves came forward, and Stonetalon went back to foraging in the woods. Rosabela cancelled the entanglement spell, and the gnome put his wand away, which only enraged the feisty imp. "Fool, it is a trick! The wench means to rob you, kill you, she … she … aw, what's the use? Infernal she-elves will be your downfall. Mark my words, old one," it said before disappearing in another cloud of smoke and brimstone.

Granmillo blushed at the sight of the she-elf and felt terribly embarrassed by the imp, as usual. "I am so sorry, my dear; that blasted imp really needs a lesson in manners."

"It is fine," she said. "But what are you doing out here? We are dangerously close to the Bloodcrest Forces, and if they find you, they will likely torture you to death."

Puffing his tiny chest out proudly, Granmillo said, "I do not fear the Bloodcrest Forces. In fact, I am on my way to attack them. It is all part of the secret plan …" The tiny gnome paused and retrieved a magical stone from one of his many pockets that glowed pure, royal blue. He passed it over the two elves, then walked over to the bear and got as close as possible without angering Stonetalon. The stone was slightly less blue, but he relaxed for a moment and said, "Okay, you are all good."

Wavren and Rosabela looked at each other with utter confusion and said, "What?" in unison.

Granmillo said, "I have this stone that can detect good and evil. When I tested you two, it showed very blue, which means good. Of course, I am not so sure about the bear." He lowered his voice to a whisper: "It might be one of the bad guys in disguise, but I couldn't get close enough to tell."

The two elves tried not to laugh. Even if they had been evil, poor Granmillo would have found out too late to do anything but die. It was common among gnomes to get so wrapped up in gadgets that their functions could be more dangerous than beneficial.

Granmillo came in close and said, "As I was saying, I am part of the secret plan to attack the Bloodcrest Forces. When I get their attention and kill a few, the Dae'gon Alliance Army will come in the back door and win the battle. Well, actually, I am sort of attacking from the back door, so they are sort of coming in the front door, but anyways, Gaedron said it would work!"

The two elves looked doubtful. Granmillo, not understanding their doubt, finally said, "Oh, I get it. You must be wondering if you can trust me. We are in orc-held lands now." He leaned in close and whispered, "I can let you borrow my magic stone if you want to see if I am really an orc in disguise." He quietly slipped the stone into Rosabela's hand and took a few steps back and turned around as if to let them secretly scan his aura for good and evil. Rosabela was at a complete loss. Wavren smiled so broadly that his grin nearly took in his considerably long ears!

Wavren whispered, "Pssst. Go ahead. Check him. You never know."

Granmillo acted as if nothing was going on. He even took the time to preen a few loose strands of thread from his shirttail.

Rosabela sighed and walked up behind the gnome and began scanning when the imp reappeared. Of course, the stone immediately went red and Rosabela had a sincere look of surprise on her face.

"What … oh wait, no, that isn't … it's the evil imp … I mean … it's not me," the gnome stammered. "See there, you vile imp. Now they think I am an orc or worse. This is all your fault!" the gnome said to the imp with mounting anger.

Granmillo pounced on the imp like a desert raptor with both feet first, his tiny hands following. They rolled around in the grass back and forth, both trying to get a dominant position. Granmillo punched the little demon; the imp burped brimstone and farted tiny flames as he tried to escape. The little gnome had one hand on the imp's considerably long snout and the other around its skinny neck. The imp kicked and pushed away in vain, yelling, "Get 'im off … get 'im off!" The gnome growled, leaned forward, and sank his pointy teeth into the imp's ear, yanking back and forth like a dog with a piece of rawhide. The imp screamed in pain and finally disappeared. Granmillo slowly stood up, somewhat disheveled, wiped his mouth with his sleeve, brushed himself off, and said with some remaining dignity, "I am no orc. I am a civilized gnome with a wickedly evil imp. Please try the stone again and you will see."

Rosabela quickly walked up and scanned the gnome's aura. The stone shined a perfectly beautiful blue. She smiled, handed the stone back to its owner, and said, "You are no orc, Granmillo."

He said, "Thank you, my dear. Now, I must be on my way. I have a war to win; by the way, you can keep the stone. I have more at home."

Wavren nodded to Rosabela, indicating that she should continue on with their mission. He would watch over the tiny gnome. She smiled, pocketed the stone, and headed for the Dae'gon Alliance Army in her travel form. Wavren couldn't stop giggling as he kept pace with his new friend. He just couldn't get the scene out of his mind.

* * *

Captain Helio and his Forest Runners had been very thorough in their reconnaissance of the area just north of Forestedge's city limits. As far as patrols and traps were concerned, there were none to be found. The open field, which lay before the northwestern wall of the city, stretched out for a quarter of a mile. It was the perfect place for the enemy to see the Dae'gon Alliance's return. It allowed for maximum range of both catapults and ballistae. It was the perfect kill zone. The commanders stopped short, well before the field in order to make final preparations.

The plan was simple. Instead of taking the time to build siege engines to blast through the palisade, Gaedron collected up several grappling hooks and all the available rope they could find. He handed them off to Captain Helio and the Forest Runners, since they could move silently. With any luck, Granmillo would make a convincing distraction, the Bloodcrest Forces would mass their forces on the southern wall, and the Forest Runners would be able to get over the wall undetected. If all of that happened successfully, Captain Helio would open the gate, and the Dae'gon Alliance would enter to retake the city with greater numbers and superior firepower. They would attack just before dawn, depending on Rosabela and Wavren's return with the latest intelligence. All was in order at this point, but few battle plans ever survived first contact.

As a matter of precaution, Helio's elves rotated the roving guard patrol shifts. They had the best night vision, after all. The dwarves rotated perimeter security watch, having heat-sensing sight, and the volunteers passed out bread and dried fruit to the soldiers. There would be no campfires tonight, nor even a simple torch. Any sign of light or excessive noise would alert the enemy of their presence and surprise would be lost.

Time passed quickly for the edgy troops, and as the moon began to wane, Rosabela appeared almost magically. She rushed up to one of the Forest Runners and handed him the scroll case with her message. She turned quickly to head back, but the soldier stopped her.

"Lady Rosabela," he formally called, "where are you running off to, and what should I tell your mentor when he finds out you dropped this off and left again?"

Rosabela was stunned, as if she had been shield-bashed. "What did you say?"

He said, "What should I tell your mentor? He is here."

Rosabela could barely speak. "He … he is alive?" she whispered, as if even asking the question would shatter her hope.

"Yes, and he is little worse for the wear. Apparently, he escaped and brought detailed information regarding the enemy," the elf said.

Rosabela had seen Da'Shar fall. She knew the Bloodcrest Forces would never allow him to live, much less escape. It had to be a trick. It was certainly another enemy imposter. "You must bring me to him at once," she demanded.

The two worked their way around the encampment, looking in the dark for Da'Shar. Rosabela's excellent night vision enabled her to pick him out of the crowd almost immediately. "There he is," she said. Before anyone could react, she drew energy from the surrounding area and summoned her spell of entanglement. Vines and roots stretched forth from the ground and wrapped around the druid's feet and legs.

Da'Shar reacted by instinct and shape-shifted into his windwraith form, easily tearing away from the minor spell. Rosabela came in fast, becoming the ferocious bear she had bonded with. Da'Shar was caught by surprise as the first mighty paw sent him flying back. He twisted in mid-air and landed on all four paws. Rosabela came in quickly with her jaws snapping and paws swinging, but found a shining shield had absorbed her furious attacks. Vlaad was able to deflect two sledgehammer-like blows and the bite that would have torn the older druid's throat out. Da'Shar sprang up a tree to recover. He recognized his apprentice, immediately changed into his elven form, and weakly yelled, "It is me, Rosabela. Da'Shar." She never heard a thing.

By now, the entire dwarven force had drawn weapons and was prepared to defend Da'Shar to the death against what they thought was a wild bear. The other volunteers were scrambling for their weapons and shields as well. The Forest Runner, who had escorted Rosabela to the encampment, ran up and said, "It is Lady Rosabela. Bring her no harm."

One dwarf said, "She is bewitched."

Another said, "She attacked Da'Shar, she be wit' da enemy now."

One dwarf was completely confused and said, "Orcs bewitched Da'Shar. Git him!"

It was a powder keg set to blow until one gruff voice called out, "STAND DOWN BOYS! Nobody kill nothin' 'til I says ye can."

Recognizing the voice of Gaedron, Rosabela shape-shifted back to her elven form, shaking with fury. She pointed her finger accusingly and said, "I saw Da'Shar fall. He is dead, and this one must be an imposter like the other who took Kalin's place in Forestedge!" Tears rolled down her cheeks, and energy crackled around her as she prepared to cast the starfire spell.

Da'Shar was holding his side, painfully gasping for breath. Rosabela had probably broken at least of few of his ribs, and he felt certain she meant to finish him off. Even if he wasn't virtually defenseless, he would never counter attack his beloved student. As Rosabela's hands began to glow with the white light of her magic, a firm but kind voice said, "Ye been through hell an' back, lass, but if'n yer wrong an' that be yer good frien' an' teacher up der, ye might not be able ta fergive yerself fer killin' him when it's done."

Rosabela paused; the magic dissipated from her hands, and then she simply crumbled to the ground as if a mountain had been dropped on her. She lay there, very still. The dwarves surrounded the tree, unsure if Da'Shar was an enemy or not, and the Forest Runners quickly surrounded Rosabela, not knowing if she was in danger or if she was the danger. Gaedron walked over to the tree and said, "Well, ol' friend, it looks like ye trained da lass a lil' too good. Now, let's git ye down and have a heal'r fix ye right up."

Da'Shar closed his eyes for a moment and murmured a few words in the ancient tongue of druids. He placed his glowing palms to his injured ribs and felt immediate relief. The druid finally replied, "I need no healers, and be assured, I am the true Da'Shar of Celes'tia."

The dwarven hunter said, "Yeah, I know it, but nex' time yer told ta be on time fer a portal home, ye might not wanna be late. We could'a 'voided da whole mess if'n ye were quicker. B'sides, da lass seems ta take yer heroics harder den da rest o' us."

"I will work on my timeliness, and I shall try to be less heroic in the future," he said, as he moved over to check on Rosabela. He laid his hand on her forehead and said, "Rest, child, we have much to do in the morning."

With all of the chaos about, the runner had nearly forgotten to deliver the scroll case to Captain Helio. He quickly handed it to his leader and moved back out to his patrol. Helio uncapped the case and withdrew the parchment. On one side he saw a detailed drawing of the southern defenses. On the other side he saw a message in beautiful elven writing. The message read:

> *Commanders of the Dae'gon Alliance Forces,*
>
> *Wavren and I have seen the southern defenses, and they are formidable. The Bloodcrest Forces have well over five hundred soldiers prepared to defend the city. At least two companies are professional reinforcements and most are fresh from the Southern region. The city has not been heavily fortified at this end, but we believe this to be a trap. We suspect the enemy will call on the undead to fight from the Forestedge graveyard, which would likely be hundreds, if not thousands, of zombies. Having fought these minions recently, we recommend*

making the undead priests your highest priority targets. They must not be allowed to summon their unholy minions.

Rosabela and Wavren of Celes'tia
Protector of the Vale

Captain Helio gathered the other commanders and briefed them on the news. The battle plan was already in motion. Just before dawn, Granmillo would create the illusionary force and start the attack. There was no way to stop him or even warn him at this point. He would likely die by the hands of a thousand zombies. It was a horrible way to die, but the commanders had to look beyond the individual casualties and find a way to win the war. With the numbers Rosabela reported, there would be no way to secure victory without the element of surprise and a miracle.

"I say we move in early, before the gnome starts the attack, scale the walls, kill the sentries, and open the gate. The rest will unfold as we go," a rogue under Vlaad's command suggested.

"If we fail to silence them all, we lose the element of surprise and fight force on force. Our enemy is still in a defensible position and outnumbers our forces. We would fight valiantly, but die with Forestedge still in enemy hands," Captain Helio replied.

"Can we draw 'em out o' da city somehow an' fight 'em 'ere in de open?" a dwarf under Gaedron's command asked.

"Aye, we could, but if'n we did, we still lose da el'ment o' surprise and fight head ta head. We might win, but I dunno," Gaedron responded.

Landermihl spoke: "We must stick to the original plan, but instead of hitting the rear as we had hoped, we must push through to the priests, just as the scouts have noted. It is the only way."

The commanders nodded, all except for one. Vlaad, the commander of the volunteers said, "And what of the brave gnome we sent to face certain death to secure our breach? Do we let him die as a mere casualty of war?"

"What else can we do?" Captain Helio said.

"If the armored horsemen can drive through the main force in their initial charge, I will follow in their wake and make my stand with the gnome," the defender replied. "The cavalry will have to return to do what it does best, but I will safeguard the little one."

A female voice said, "You will not stand alone. My brother is with Granmillo, and I will be there, too."

All eyes turned to Rosabela. Da'Shar smiled and moved in close to hug her, but she met him with an uncertain look. He stopped at arm's length, cautiously remembering his last encounter with her. Slowly, the she-elf raised her hand. In her tiny palm was a blue stone glowing quite brightly. She looked at it and then at him. She smiled, hugged him, and wept. It was a tearful reunion for them both.

* * *

Not far away from the forest's edge, among the boughs of a fallen oak, was a lone dark figure. He was well hidden from sight and magically hidden from detection spells as he listened to every word spoken. He had witnessed the return of Da'Shar just as his master had instructed as well as the return of Rosabela with what sounded like the entire layout of the enemy defenses. Commander Grimtusk had been wise indeed to send Nightshade ahead with instructions to infiltrate, gather intelligence, and return before the battle began. He was certain that his time to depart was now.

Nightshade took well over twenty minutes extracting himself from his shadowy hiding place, moving slower than a snail in the winter. Once on the ground, he belly-crawled for well over a quarter mile around the edge of Forestedge before taking the chance to move into a crouched shuffle. He stuck to the shadows of the trees to avoid casting his own shadow in the limited starlight. After moving for another quarter mile on foot, the orc doubled back and waited for another twenty minutes to see if he had been followed. He was quite certain that he had not, but being a master of his craft meant taking no chances.

Nightshade slipped in through the southern side of the city undetected by his brethren. It was always a challenge to circumvent the enemy, but being able to circumvent your own forces gave a deep understanding of any weaknesses within your own forces. It was no less dangerous than infiltrating the Dae'gon Alliance. Had he been detected, he would have been fired upon by crossbowmen or run through by the sword of a patrolling orc. No one would weep for his loss, since his discovery would mean he was incompetent, anyway. It was the way of things in the world of orcs.

He appeared in the command cell across the room from his commander. Neggish Grimtusk had a knowing smile on his face as the platoon leader moved up and took a knee before him.

"You were successful, I assume?" the larger orc asked.

"I am here alive, aren't I?" he returned smugly.

"Very well, then, report," Neggish commanded.

"The Dae'gon Alliance forces are not well prepared. They have too few warriors, and even their elite units and heroes cannot begin to compensate for the soldiers you command, my lord," Nightshade reported arrogantly.

"Did they take the bait we spoon-fed Da'Shar?" Grimtusk asked. "Will they attack from the south?"

The spy responded, "My lord, they were prepared to lay siege to the city until Da'Shar gave them the report we had hoped he would. They altered their plan to attack the southern wall, but became suspicious and came up with a most unusual plan. They sent a gnomish wizard to create a diversion with magic in the south instead. They had hoped to pull our forces away from the battlements toward the diversion in order to scale the palisade unseen and open the northern gate from the inside."

Neggish Grimtusk sat quietly for some time before speaking. He considered his own forces and the report Nightshade had given. If the battle developed in the way he now pictured it, then it was very likely that the gnome's feint would be an attack made in vain and his own troops would merely wait for the elves to come over the wall. But what then? If he simply cut down the few who climbed the walls, the gate would never open, and the main force would remain well out of range, having never been given the all-clear signal. The battle would end with the deaths of a few elves and a gnome. More troops would be called in, and sooner or later, the city would fall under siege, which was not how Neggish wanted to spend the next several weeks or months. His plans to conquer the land north to Port Archer would fall apart. He reminded himself that glory always came with risk, and victory could be attained through sheer audacity. That was the way of orc warriors.

"We will proceed as planned," he said resolutely. "Tell no one of the feint, and let the battle unfold as if you had never secured any of this information. We are the mighty Bloodcrest Forces, and we will crush the fools in spite of their tricks and tactics! I will be the tip of the spear to personally command the battle, and many will die by my blade."

Nightshade nodded obediently and left the command cell, flashing back momentarily to the fate of Shadowblade. He mentally saw the relentless damage the failed platoon leader was forced to endure. He saw the results in the bodies of Shadowblade's followers. He was certain that death from the soldiers of the Dae'gon Alliance would never be as grim as punishment from his leader. It was terrifying and yet exhilarating to be led by such a tyrant. Nightshade also reminded himself that the rewards for his services included great wealth, power, and of course, glory. Limitless glory!

Chapter 20
For Blood and Glory

Wavren had slept little in anticipation of the coming attack on the enemy fortress at Forestedge. He thought over and over about the crazy gnome who was going to single-handedly start the entire battle that would decide the fate of countless elves, humans, dwarves, and gnomes. The hunter reminded himself that countless orcs, trolls, tauren, and undead would also share the ultimate fate. No matter who won, hundreds would surely perish. It was a sad fact of life in the never-ending war between good and evil. Wavren sighed as he watched over the sleeping gnome who was snoring like an ogre with a head cold. He had to smile.

The last hour before daybreak began, so Wavren gently shook Granmillo to consciousness.

"Huh … what is it?" he said. "Oh, it must be time. Well, let's get to it, then."

Wavren asked, "How will the illusions work exactly? Will they be convincing?"

Granmillo answered offhandedly, "I'm not really sure, exactly. I am not much of an illusionist, you know. I specialize in summoning the denizens of the abyss for the most part."

Wavren felt uncomfortable with the gnome's lack of certainty, but what could he do? The entire battle relied on the spell-craft of an insane gnome who wasn't even an illusionist. He just went about watching over the gnome as they collected their personal gear and weapons. If they were lucky, they might escape with their lives. If not, then they would take more than a few of the enemy vermin with them.

The distance to the southern wall was not far from the graveyard, which had served as their makeshift camp for the last few hours. Ironically, Wavren realized it was his *final place of rest* prior to the battle and could be his *final resting place* afterward. His mind went back to the matters at hand, and he noticed that the gnome was almost skipping cheerfully toward the city.

"Granmillo," Wavren began, "what is it about this mission that has you so happy? Are you looking for a glorious death?"

"Death?" he asked, as if the thought had never crossed his mind. "We aren't going to die. Our job is to set up a diversion. You know, distract the Bloodcrest Forces? The army of the Dae'gon Alliance will do all the real fighting; at least, close up they will. We should be perfectly safe."

Wavren thought the foolish gnome was probably better off in his fantasy world. He decided to let the crazy warlock think whatever he wanted to think instead of breaking it down for him in terms that might scare him out of his wits—such as they were.

"We are here, my friend," Granmillo said. "It looks like the time is just about right. I believe the sun will crest the eastern border of the Western Kingdom in less than thirty minutes. I will protect you from the Bloodcrest Forces as long as I can, but be ready to retreat if things get out of hand."

Wavren smiled and said, "I will be ready in a few minutes. I just want to set a few traps and call a friend over. He will back us up if things 'get out of hand,' as you put it."

"Well, hurry up, I am on a tight schedule, and the whole

thing is waiting on me, and now, I am waiting on you," the diminutive spell-wielder said, his hands on his hips.

Wavren was as skilled a marksman as had ever lived, but being a hunter meant being able to use the terrain in every possible way to gain the advantage. He set a firetrap that would blast several of the enemy troops well before they got within melee range. He backed up and set an ice trap, which was much more difficult to manipulate, but was able to lock one enemy in a block of ice for several minutes. The components for these traps were expensive, but well worth the price if it kept the hunter and his ally alive. Last but not least, Wavren unrolled several sticks of dynamite from his padded pack. He set them in strategic locations as he imagined the rush of orcs heading his way. When he was ready, he made a mental note to shoot any undead caster first to avoid having a multitude of reanimated corpses chasing after him and the little gnome.

"I am ready," the hunter said. He whistled loudly, and Stonetalon came lumbering up.

Granmillo smiled and said, "WHOA! That's one big dog you got there. Hope he likes Saresh, my imp. We don't want them fighting each other when the battle starts." At the mention of the imp, a cloud of smoke and brimstone erupted and out came the tiny demon. It looked at the gnome, then at Wavren, and finally at the bear. As if it sensed the coming battle, the imp rubbed its fiery hands together.

"Granmillo," the imp said devilishly, "are we going to create a little destruction today?"

The gnome smiled broadly and shook his head from side to side. "No, my little friend, today we will create massive destruction!" The gnome appeared quite malevolent as he encouraged the tiny demon.

Saresh jumped up and down in excitement and tiny flames came off of his spiny back. The gnome opened a small sack with a dozen scrolls inside and pulled the first out and began casting. Wavren took a few steps back and prepared to defend the odd warlock.

The first spell created an illusion of an archer company.

They were human, but hopefully no one would notice. The second spell brought forth a company of infantrymen. They were dwarven, which seemed more accurate. The third scroll created several catapults and their corresponding crews.

"Saresh, your job is to cast a fireball every time the catapult crews fire their flaming pitch. You need to use the big ones, so don't hold back," Granmillo said. "I will join you as soon as I build the rest of our army."

Saresh smiled wickedly. His long fangs seemed far too large for his head as he did so, but he nodded eagerly and skipped from catapult to catapult, giving the illusionary crews tips on siege warfare, even though they were unresponsive.

The fourth scroll summoned several elven warriors riding windwraiths. This was a particularly interesting spell that included defensive movement and swinging swords added in for realism. The fifth and sixth scrolls produced mages who were already casting various spells, fireball in particular. At this point, Granmillo said, "OPEN FIRE!" and actually giggled as he and his imp started casting real fireball spells and a variety of other spectacular evocations.

As anticipated, the alarm sounded, which came in the form of metal loudly banging against metal. Of course, that alarm was followed by the battle cries of hundreds of orcs, trolls, tauren, and undead who were rushing to defend the southern wall. Wavren used his hunter talents to see their approach long before the gnome or imp could. He began calling the distances and directions of the enemies to his companions, which only added to their casting frenzy. Flames shot left and right, igniting virtually everything on or near the southern wall. It didn't take long for the first responding orc infantrymen to form up and advance on the windwraith-riding elven illusions. That was the key point when Wavren hoped the Dae'gon Alliance was moving up the northern wall. If not, this was going to be a very short battle.

* * *

On the northern side of the city, Captain Helio's Forest Runners were already scaling the white stone wall with great haste. They knew time was against the courageous gnome, who had started the battle with a massive barrage of fire magic, and would die very soon without help. The elves were also at great risk. If even one sentry remained behind to report their assault into Forestedge, the diversion would be for naught, so a company of elven archers covered their ascent.

Captain Helio was the first to reach the top. He peered over the edge and saw nothing. As quiet as death itself, he signaled for the others to quickly move over the edge and down the parapets to the ground level. So far everything was going smoothly. The Forest Runners assembled at the gate and lifted the massive bar and brace that secured the way inside.

The plan had worked and the way was clear. Helio moved to the outside edge of the gate and lit a torch to signal the way was clear. He turned back and quickly dispatched his elven company into the shadows of the city to keep the area secure. Just as he was preparing to meld into the darkness himself, a voice called out in poor, but understandable, common: "Welcome to For'stedge, ci-ty of the orcs," the voice called loudly,. You have walk-ed right in-to our trap."

Captain Helio froze and scanned the area with his fine night vision. He saw no one, which was inexplicable given the nature of elven sight. He knew he was exposed, but his men were not. They would cover him at all costs, so he dared to call out to the orc. "You say we have walked into your trap, but I see no warriors. I think you are foolishly all alone, but I admire your courage. Come out and settle this in the open; settle this according to the code of honor the orcs claim to live by."

Captain Helio was scanning the streets carefully and still saw no one. He knew the entire Dae'gon Alliance Army was soon to arrive. He held his position, wondering if the orc would in fact show himself. He decided to move out of sight just in case. As he silently became one with the shadows, he carefully drew his wickedly curved polearm from its strap on his back. He crept forward a few steps and felt a tiny, almost imperceptible, breeze across the back of his neck. He knew he was no longer alone, but before he could react, a massive arm came in from behind, and searing pain shot through his back. As he looked down, he could see the tip of his attacker's sword push through his fine armor.

A voice whispered in poor common, "The war-ri-or code of hon-or is not my way. I am Night-shade, mas-ter of sha-dows."

Captain Helio could neither fight, nor call for help. The assassin had punctured his diaphragm and left him to die a quiet and honorless death. The orc eased him down to the ground gently and slowly pulled the sword from the gaping hole in his back. Warm fluid rushed out and across the orc's palms. Darkness took Helio mercifully.

The Dae'gon Alliance Army had finally arrived through the passageway into the city. The cavalry was in the lead with the infantry and volunteers close behind. The archers filtered in last with the casters intermingled as well. There was no way the entire army could move quietly, but they proceeded cautiously. The entire force halted just inside the city walls, and the commanders gathered for final checks before the assault—all the commanders, except one. Da'Shar had stayed among the commanders, feeling more akin to the leaders than the followers when he noticed Captain Helio was unaccounted for.

"We are missing a commander," the druid said with concern.

"Where is Captain Helio?" Landermihl called from his great, white charger. "He knew to meet us inside the gate."

"Aye, we all knew da plan. Hold fer a minute," the dwarf said cautiously.

Gaedron quickly scanned the area for traces of heat using his dwarven infra-vision. He spotted the other Forest Runners scattered about, but could not identify the elven commander. As he moved forward, using his hunter skills, he immediately noticed the elven footprints, which were imperceptible to everyone else.

The dwarven hunter began reconstruction of the entry. "Da lads made it o'er da wall an' came down 'ere. They opened da gates an' pushed out to da shadows fer cov'r. One remained fer a short time, most likely da Cap'n. His weight settled fer a second, well balanced on both feet. He was set ta fight … he thought he was seen, but then he moved off ta da left 'ere …"

Gaedron moved into the shadows and bent down beside Helio's corpse. He knew the smell of death before he ran his fingers through the pool of blood. It set his instincts on full alert, and he drew his blunderbuss quickly. "It be a trap! Helio's dead! Sound da charge an' push through ta da gnome! Go … go … go!" he yelled. With a grim look, Gaedron called to Da'Shar, "Ye be in charge o' da For'st Run'rs now. Take yer boys and find da killer."

The knights of Griffon's Peak looked to their leader, who was already in motion. His charger reared up high as he pulled on the reins. "Knights form up on me, wedge formation … charge!" The paladin was the epitome of leadership and courage giving him god-like referent power and, enabling his men to respond without hesitation or fear. The knights lined up behind their leader with Vlaad and Rosabela in tow. They tore through the city streets and drove into the main courtyard, where they met hundreds of waiting enemy soldiers led by a massive, worg-riding orc with cruelly spiked armor. Their charge was not going to be into the rear of an unsuspecting army as they had hoped. They somehow knew the Dae'gon Alliance was coming, and they were ready.

Landermihl called to his God for strength and pulled his golden shield in tight to ward off the incoming blows. He swung his massive hammer in a reverse circle, making the uppercut blow lift the first target off of his feet and send him flying backward into the second and third ranks of the enemy soldiers. The other horsemen followed suit, leaving dozens of dead and wounded on either side of the horsemen. The wedge formation cleanly split the first rank like the prow of a boat through water, but the second and third ranks slowed the charge, effectively stalling the knights. There was no way they could push through to the gnome and his lone protector. The ensuing melee became a chaotic battle of overwhelming odds.

The mighty paladin felt the blades and points of a dozen weapons as his mount slowed. He dug in his heels and urged the massive charger forward as he rained blow after blow down on the orcish infantry. It was unclear how many of the beasts he had slain, but he knew there were far too many remaining to have even made a dent. He hammered away relentlessly at the enemy and called to his deity for healing and strength as the wedge formation collapsed into a line and then broke apart into small segments.

Rosabela and Vlaad had seen the impending doom coming as the knights blasted into the enemy forces. They were not riding heavily armored mounts like Landermihl's men, so they broke off at the last minute and attempted to angle around the mass of orcs. As they cut around the backside of the burned-out great hall, Rosabela felt oddly drawn toward the mound of ashes and charred support beams that remained. The feeling subsided as they passed the still-smoldering building, but the druid was certain something had reached out to her, something not of this world.

The two rode on for a moment, trying to find a way back into the city, but they came to a dead end. They were surely cut off from the other forces by now and had no easy way to get to Granmillo. Rosabela jumped off her chestnut mare and moved up to the juncture where the southern wall met with the eastern wall. There was a series of buildings that tied into the wall, which constituted a dead end, but with a little luck, the druid thought she might find a way in and through the building. Not far from where she had dismounted, there was a locked cellar door, but no back door or window.

Motioning Vlaad over, she said, "Let's give this a try."

He nodded and walked forward to examine the lock. It was a simple iron lock and hasp, but both were quite sturdy. The doors were several inches of hardwood, probably oak, and he was unsure if he could bash through without alerting the enemy to their presence. Rosabela realized his concern and went into her backpack for a solution.

"Try this," she said. "It is a fairly strong concentration of acid and should weaken the lock."

Vlaad took the innocuous vial and carefully pulled the stopper. He poured a few drops and watched the resulting reaction of bubbling and sizzling metal. "Where did you get this?" he asked with a smile and genuine interest.

"I am a bit of an alchemist, you know, a potion specialist? I pick up most of my key ingredients from the land or at the marketplace. That is actually acid from a black dragon's breath attack. It was quite expensive, but as you can see, it does a fine job on metal," she replied.

The defender thought there was much about this she-elf that was unusual, but never had he heard of anyone buying acid from a black dragon. He wondered how many adventurers died in its acquisition. He surmised that it was indeed expensive and probably worth a king's ransom, but she had given it up without a second thought. Either Rosabela was quite wealthy or amazingly gifted in haggling. He noticed his eyes wandering over her lithe form. Every curve was perfect, and her face was lovely for certain. She had no flaw in her overall comeliness, which must have contributed to her ability to charm a merchant out of his goods. He looked away quickly when she cocked her head to one side and put her hands on her hips as if saying, "What are you staring at?" He went back to looking at the lock and said, "It is nearly dissolved. Are we ready to try it?"

She laughed lightly and replied, "I am ready."

With a quick downward stroke of his shield, the lock fell in several pieces. The acid was incredibly potent. It made Vlaad think back to the poor adventurers who had collected it. That was one death he hoped he would never face. He moved down the staircase beyond the door and looked around. There was a torch on the wall that he quickly lit with some flint and steel, illuminating the way ahead.

"It is a corridor of some sort," Vlaad announced.

Rosabela was right behind him when she replied, "It appears to go in the direction we need to travel. Let's make haste; our allies will need us soon."

Vlaad nodded and began to move forward. He couldn't

help noticing that the sweet smell of honeysuckle and spice radiated from the she-elf. It was light and barely noticeable, but its impact was powerful. After taking a moment to collect his wits and focus on the mission at hand, he managed to square his broad shoulders and move forward. The corridor was quite long and filled with common staples such as rice, beans, and wheat. It was a dry storage cellar of some sort, which made Vlaad think it would come up in the center of town, most likely under a general goods shop. He saw the end of the tunnel ahead and a short ladder to a trapdoor. He began moving up the rungs and felt a hand on his ankle. He looked down to see the druid signaling him to proceed quietly and with caution. He nodded and doused the torch in a water barrel at the base of the ladder before proceeding.

* * *

Granmillo and Saresh were steadily blasting away at the evil forces while Wavren held steady in his defilade position. Stonetalon was waiting patiently beside him for the opportunity to tear into the enemy. The battle had been raging for a considerably long time already, but none of the troops had actually broken through the line of fire and destruction the gnome and his imp were creating. Wavren was growing suspicious, having assumed they would be overrun by now. It was almost as if the Bloodcrest Forces were afraid to come out beyond the wall. As he considered that thought for a few moments, it occurred to him that they were not afraid; they were unwilling or perhaps unable. The hunter was not particularly curious by nature, but his instincts were rarely wrong. Without another thought, Wavren stood up and moved over to the gnome to get a better view.

The smoke and fire obscured most of his field of vision, but being an elf and a hunter had its advantages. He noticed that there was a huge mass of orcs and trolls trying to move through the illusionary forces that Granmillo had created, but they were being blasted by the fire spells before they could do so. But something was wrong here. The orc forces should have cut though the illusions like walking through fog or mist. They were insubstantial reflections of light for the most part. It just didn't add up until Wavren noticed that there were no bodies and no blood. They were fighting illusions. They had been fighting illusions at the south wall since daybreak!

Wavren called to Granmillo, "It is a trick! We have been tricked, stop shooting!"

The gnome looked annoyed, but stopped long enough to listen.

"They are illusions," the elf said.

"Of course they are illusions! I made them before we started, remember?" the gnome replied.

"No," Wavren said, "the forces we are fighting are illusions. We have been tricked."

Granmillo looked confused for a moment and asked, "Did we win?"

The elf was puzzled for a moment, not knowing what to say, but replied with the only thing that might get the crazy gnome thinking on the right track. He said, "Yes, Granmillo, you did it. You and Saresh chased the real enemy forces away and they left these illusions behind to cover their escape. Now we have to go in and help the others."

The gnome had a sudden brightness in his eyes, accompanied by a wicked grin filled with pointed teeth. He called to Saresh, saying, "We did it! We beat the orcs. Now we have to go in and finish them off!"

Saresh hopped up to the warlock, took a knee in front of him, and said, "Never have a warlock and his minion created such havoc and destruction. We are the greatest spell-binders in the history of demon-kind!"

Wavren noticed something foul smelling just as he heard the shambling steps of several creatures not far behind. The sounds and smell were coming from the graveyard over the hill. Wavren grit his teeth and hissed, "No, no, no, no, NO!" With great haste, he dashed up the hill and saw an undead priest raising the army of the dead. The entire battle with the illusions had all been an elaborate diversion to get a single priest past the hunter, and it had worked. Somehow, the Bloodcrest Forces had known what to do all along and had manipulated their own diversion into cover for the real attack. Now the re-animates were coming. They were coming by the scores.

Wavren took a knee, leveled his fine weapon, and fired past the zombies and into the undead priest, the source of the summoning. The foul caster spun about, taking the shot mostly in his shoulder blade. Wavren reloaded and fired again, this time hitting the wretched villain in the chest. The priest called on his unholy power and healed the damage with ease. Wavren reloaded and fired again, this time hitting the vile being in the face. His shot went through the priest's vacant nasal cavity and out the back of his head, severing the spine and brain stem. The undead priest collapsed in a heap of rotting flesh and bones. Granmillo moved up beside him and saw the incoming mass of zombies. Wavren looked down at him and saw the gnome rubbing his tiny hands together. The imp was to his right doing the same.

"You want us to handle this fight like the last one?" Granmillo asked seriously.

"This will be easy," the imp added.

Wavren wanted to laugh at the ridiculous pair, but the situation was dire. He made a quick calculation and realized that even if the gnome and imp could kill a hundred of the enemies, he would still have to single-handedly kill another score or more on his own. This was suicide. "We need to break off and link up with the main force," Wavren said, looking around for the best possible egress.

"What?" the imp said. "You want to run?"

Granmillo nodded. "An excellent idea, you can run and help the others. Saresh and I have this group."

Wavren looked to the sky and silently mouthed, "Why me?" He was convinced that the gnome was out of his mind, and the tiny demon was too; or maybe it was trying to get the diminutive warlock killed. Whatever the case, Wavren felt compelled to stay with the gnome. He just couldn't bring himself to abandon him after the courage he had shown from their first meeting.

"Very well," the hunter said. "I can't let you have all the fun. I will stay and fight with you." He took a knee and raised his fine blunderbuss to show he was serious.

The gnome smiled and said, "Fine, fine, fine, just don't get in our way. Magic is not an exact science, after all. It is more of an art form, like a painter with a huge brush, and it would be a shame to accidentally kill you in the middle of our masterpiece!"

As if on cue, the imp and the warlock went to work while Wavren scanned the area for targets of opportunity. The first fireball was a massive conflagration of explosive magic. It took the gnome several seconds of casting to build the fiery sphere before he projected it forward. The result was spectacular. It hit right in front of the first wave of zombies and sent a blast wave of heat and force in all directions. None of the zombies went down for long, but most of them were knocked back, which bought the foursome a little time.

The imp was next. He was not able to cast magic on a grand scale like the warlock, but he was very fast at sending grapefruit-sized fiery projectiles at the enemy. He hit one zombie three times in less than as many seconds. The zombie fell and did not rise again, having had its entire torso blown apart.

Wavren was worried that the slow but steady advance of the undead would overwhelm them. He noticed that a few were already back on their feet since the initial blast. He fired his weapon and blew an arm off of one. It never slowed. He fired again and hit the thing in the chest, but the bullet went right through, leaving a large, putrid hole that seeped black ichor. He fired again and again, making two more holes in its abdomen, but it seemed determined. Finally, he shot the thing through the eye, blowing out the back of its head. It wobbled for a second and collapsed.

Granmillo said, "Not bad for an amateur, but watch how a professional does it." He drank a red potion, shivered for a moment, and ran as fast as his tiny legs could carry him into the host of undead.

Wavren knew there was nothing anyone could do to save the poor fellow, and he was too surprised to react.

The imp smiled with evil glee, chanting, "Kill 'em, kill 'em, kill 'em."

Wavren couldn't be sure if he meant kill *him,* referring to the gnome, or kill *them,* referring to the enemies. What he saw next was incredible. The gnome was completely surrounded by zombies, and just before their horrid claws could tear him to shreds; he waved his hands and said something that sounded like, "*Evoca Immolatis*." Then he started radiating pulses of fire. Each pulse had a small concussive effect that knocked the living dead back a step, and the unthinking wretches just kept trying to get closer. They stayed perfectly in range as each wave of fire got hotter and hotter. The zombies' rusted armor and clothing immediately caught fire, and soon all the flesh was consumed, leaving blackened bones. The gnome pulsed dozens of times until nearly a score of the zombies were nothing more than ash. When he had expended the limits of his magical energy, he staggered back over to the imp and said, "Top that!" He fell to the ground.

The imp shrugged, looked at Wavren, and said in a shrill voice, "I've got one better, but since he decided to take a nap, you're going to have to be my witness."

Wavren sighed in utter exasperation and replied, "Just don't get yourself killed."

Saresh hopped forward and lit his tiny claws on fire. He bounced from zombie to zombie with great agility, slashing each one and moving to the next. Each hit left a flaming claw mark that oozed the putrid ichor and did not seem to do much damage, but succeeded in getting about two dozen enemies focused on him. He called back to Wavren, saying, "Watch this. I call it the fire spin." He started spinning in a tight circle, and the tiny flames on his back got bigger and bigger. He spun faster and faster, speaking a demonic tongue until grapefruit-sized balls of fire blasted in all directions. Each claw mark was like a flaming beacon drawing the tiny fireballs toward the zombies. Not one missed its mark. After several seconds of his spinning, dozens of zombies were peppered with the imp's attack. The whirling demon continued until every zombie he had marked was destroyed. The imp stopped spinning and wobbled dizzily to the left, and then the right, until he fell flat on his face. In a somewhat muffled voice, he asked, "Wasn't mine better?"

Wavren did not respond. He was greatly impressed that the warlock had slain twenty zombies and the imp had taken out several more than that, but there were close to a hundred still coming. His first instinct was to run and leave the foolish gnome and his imp to die—it would serve them right. But he knew his sense of duty and honor would never allow it. He simply whispered to his ally, "Now we show them what we are made of." The bear roared loudly and rumbled into melee range where his claws and fangs were most effective. Wavren took up a solid firing position to back up his dear friend. He smiled and thought, "If this is the end, then so be it, but I won't be outdone by a crazy gnome and his pet demon!"

* * *

The infantry, casters, archers, and volunteers had a long jog through the winding city streets to catch up to the cavalry. They had half-expected to find the horsemen on the far side of the enemy with a mass of horse-trampled or lance-impaled orcs between them. Instead, they found an entire company of Griffon's Peak's finest knights slain and a lone paladin surrounded by hundreds of orcs and tauren.

The holy warrior was covered in blood and gore, such that his shining armor and helm were colored no differently than the red pool he stood in. At his feet were more than a dozen elite orcs and several heavily armored orc infantry. He had rained holy wrath on the Bloodcrest Forces, but the cost was great. Every man under his command and their fine steeds were dead. His own beautiful white charger was mortally wounded and was trying to get up to fight beside its master. Landermihl was gravely wounded as well, but still standing somehow. The burning of numerous open wounds at every joint in his armor testified to the sheer number of attacks he had taken not to mention the blunt force trauma from every manner of weapon imaginable that had not pierced his armor. He saw the approach of the Dae'gon Alliance Army and raised his hand to the sky, calling for his last blessing of protection: "*Divino a Priori!*" An intense golden light engulfed the great warrior as he took a knee, unable to move or fight.

The enemy moved in mercilessly and hacked at the kneeling paladin. They hammered blow after blow on him, but could not further harm the shielded servant of good. He was encased in the light of his deity and was impervious to harm for the duration of the spell though he was immobilized as well.

Gaedron was at the front of the army. Vlaad was gone, and Helio was dead, leaving him as the only other commander available. He took charge and organized the final attack.

"Dwarven Blade-Breakers to me front. Form da block o' stone," he ordered. The dwarven infantry spread out across the street in columns of twenty across and five deep. He called for the elves next. "Archers, ready yer bows, volley fire on me order!" The elves took up staggered positions well behind the dwarves and raised their fine longbows at the shallow angle required to miss the friendly ranks, but cut down the enemy. His last command was for the Forest Runners and the volunteers. He said, "Skirmishers, circle about an' hit 'em on da flank." The elves and humans backtracked and disappeared down the side streets, leaving only the gnomish casters and a few of the human spell-wielders without orders. Gaedron called to them loudly: "Rain bloody hell on 'em, boys. Give 'em da works!" The mages fired bolts of lightning, shards of ice, and multicolored rays of energy at their enemies. Gaedron called to his long-bowmen, "Archers … fire!" Last, but certainly not least, he yelled to his dwarven infantry, "Press de attack. Grind 'em to dust! FER STONE AN STEEL!" The dwarves stepped forward in unison chanting, "*ZHA*," every other step.

The effect was amazing. Several orcs fell from the combined spell and arrow fire. Those who didn't fall were engaged by the Blade-Breakers, perhaps the sturdiest close-range, combat force in the realm. The orcish infantry was pushed back, having lost the initiative after decimating the human cavalry. They were simply unprepared to receive the disciplined power of the dwarves as well as the deadly accuracy of the elven archers. Just when the orcs seemed sure to break ranks and flee, the troll cavalry appeared from the side streets right between the dwarves and the orcs. Their desert raptors jumped across the five ranks of Blade-Breakers and landed among the archers.

Gaedron called to his casters, "Freeze 'em in ice! Don' let 'em man-oo-ver!" The elven archers dove aside, rolling to the outer edges of the street, and the human wizards threw dozens of frost spells all at once. The blue cones of heart-stopping cold and white frost novas limited the trolls to less than a dozen kills. The grim-faced gnomes already had their tiny hands in motion to finish them off with searing flame spells. Several of the tiny warlocks summoned denizens of the abyss to aid in the fight. Among the demons were fire-casting imps, whip-cracking succubi, and even a giant elemental demon that charged into the frontlines and crushed more than half a dozen raptor-riding trolls on the way. Gaedron's quick thinking and shrewd battle commands had saved the archers and destroyed nearly two platoons of the raptor riders. Those remaining were killed indiscriminately by short-ranged bow fire as the archers recovered.

The dwarves pushed hard and stepped carefully over slain knights as well as half as many enemy soldiers. They dug their heels in and swung every manner of weapon imaginable. They cut down more orcs than they lost in dwarves, but the Bloodcrest Forces were far from being combat ineffective. The tauren shock troops formed up in the shape of a diamond and plowed in through their own thinning forces and slammed into the dwarven block of stone formation. At first, the lines buckled under the massive power of the half-bull, half-human troops, but as the first line bent inward, the second rank of dwarves took their place, and the first rank broke off and circled to the rear. With fresh infantry fighting, the battle quickly pitched back in favor of the Dae'gon Alliance.

The orcs regrouped quickly as their leader moved into the fray. Neggish Grimtusk had been viewing the progress from his worg mount when the human riders had been destroyed. His soldiers had performed well in spite of being a mixture of regulars and volunteers from the Crossroads. He knew the Dae'gon Alliance would cut the less experienced troops down quickly and had waited until now to lead his veterans to victory. He dropped down from his beastly mount and casually removed the giant ax from its resting place on his back. His armor was nearly as intimidating as the weapon he carried, and his warriors stepped aside to let him pass. The Dae'gon Alliance force paused at his approach as if they, too, were stunned by his mere presence. The massive orc raised his ancestral blade over his head and bellowed, "FOR THE HONOR OF BLOODCREST!" as he charged into the dwarven lines.

* * *

Vlaad and Rosabela came through a trapdoor in the floor of the General Goods Supply Depot. There was no one around to see them come up through the floor, and as they peeked out the window, they could see the entire battle unfolding. Rosabela noticed the back and forth sway of the battle lines as each army gained and then lost ground depending on the forces joining the fight. In particular, she spotted the unbelievably huge orc commander as he dove into the battle. She felt driven to join the fight among the other elves, but she had a mission that required her elsewhere.

The defender opened the door and slipped outside and down the walkway to the edge of the southern gate. Curiously, the wall and surrounding land had been scorched and blasted by countless magical attacks, but no bodies were present. The human glanced back to his elven partner. She shrugged and motioned for him to move forward. They carefully crept toward the hill where they heard the report of what had to be Wavren's mighty blunderbuss. With increased urgency, they picked up the pace, closing the distance to the hill. As they crested the top, they saw an unconscious gnome and an imp shaking his head back and forth as if stunned. Their eyes moved forward to see an elf and a bear holding off what appeared to be one hundred zombies.

The elf was firing his gun with amazing speed and accuracy while the bear slammed into the undead with its deadly claws. For a moment, neither Rosabela nor Vlaad could do anything but stare. The elf was in a battle frenzy. He lined up a target, shot, reloaded and fired again in less than second. Each time the weapon sent its projectile into his target's head, the vile corpse would fall. When it hit elsewhere, the creature would stagger for a moment, only to be hit again and again until it fell. The bear stood up on its hind legs and raked eight deep rows in the rotting flesh of one zombie, while the hunter fired a shot into two more that were angling in to hit his ally. The only time the hunter paused his fire was to draw a short red stick out of his pack to throw among a group of shambling undead. Vlaad was unsure what the stick might do against the group that was massing in front of the bear, but then the hunter threw it and its effects became evident. The resulting explosion was perfectly spaced to cut down the farthest attackers, stun the closer ones, and allow the bear time to reposition for another bite or claw attack. They were an excellent team of ranged and melee combat.

In spite of the spectacular success Wavren was having, more than fifty undead were remaining, and all were getting closer and closer to the desperate hunter. Rosabela dashed forward and called on her healing magic to restore his bear. Its numerous wounds had been minor, but would have taken a toll sooner or later. Having been fully healed, Stonetalon fought with renewed vigor and ferocity. His mighty swipes tore zombies' arms and legs off, and his jaws snapped through tattered armor, flesh, and bone alike. Vlaad set his enchanted shield over his left arm and drew his elven blade with his right. In no time, he was positioned beside the bear, where his skills were most effective. He dashed forward and shield bashed the first zombie. His sword came around and decapitated the vile thing. He absorbed two hits from the second zombie and turned just in time to deflect another spear thrust that would have impaled Wavren's bear from a third one. He leveled his shield horizontally and caught the spear-wielding corpse in the ribs, giving the bear just enough room to bite through its leading leg. The creature fell to the ground and was torn to shreds by Stonetalon's forepaws.

Rosabela drew in the mystic energy of the elements and summoned starfire to stop an ax-carrying monster from circling around the defender's flank. The sheer white light was as bright as the sun, and the crackling corpse smoldered and popped like wet firewood before it disintegrated. The druid called on her healing magic again as Stonetalon took a few hits from the surrounding zombies. None were critical strikes, but she knew that no chances could be taken against these massive odds.

Wavren was glad to find some relief, but his part in the fight was far from over. A zombie came at him with two rusted broad swords, and he was unable to get his weapon in line to fire, so he parried the strikes with his blunderbuss and butt-stroked his enemy with the solid oak stock. The creature's head went back at a weird angle, but it was far from disabled. Wavren stepped in and kicked the wretched thing in the ribs, which shattered immediately, but it was still coming. Finally, in anger and desperation, he dropped his gun, drew his dagger and reverse-edged ax, and went to work. He dove forward and hit the zombie with the backswing of his ax; his cut hamstrung the corpse. He spun about and cut upward with the dagger, leaving a serious gash from kidney to shoulder blade. The corpse tried to turn to face the hunter, but he angled around and hacked off both of its arms and then its head. Wiping the gore from his face, Wavren moved forward and led his attacks with a dagger thrust followed by an ax swing that removed an arm, leg, or head each time.

The fight was savage. Rosabela was disintegrating one zombie for every two that Stonetalon was dismembering, and one for every three that Wavren was decapitating. Vlaad was killing only a few here and there, but somehow, he was intercepting nearly all of the blows. As if by magic, he somehow managed to keep the enemy attacking his faithful shield. His ability to predict the angle and speed of numerous attacks all at once and absorb them all made him seem like a blur of motion. Even his flashing elven sword seemed to move in slow motion compared to the magnificent shield.

The number of undead quickly dropped from fifty to forty and then thirty. As a team, the four were so well balanced that the slow-moving undead could never gain the advantage. As they massed on the defender who was nearly invulnerable behind his shield and fine armor, Wavren would blast them apart with dynamite. As they regrouped in pairs and sets of three, Rosabela would cook one with starfire, and Stonetalon would rip the other one or two to shreds. The few that attacked alone were cut down by Vlaad's blade or Wavren's ax. Before long, the battle was over, and the heroes took a much-needed break.

Vlaad came forward, shook the gore from his blade, sheathed it, and said in his Eastern dialect, "I am most impressed by your explosive rod and fire sticks. I am a blacksmith and sword craftsman by trade, but I need another skill. Perhaps you would be willing to teach me to make weapons such as yours."

The elf nodded, wiped the gore from his cheek and replied, "After your help here in the graveyard, I owe you that and probably my life. I am Wavren, Protector of the Vale and Hunter of the Ursa Clan. What is your name, warrior?"

The defender bowed low in a formal fashion among human noblemen and said, "I am Vlaad of the Mountain Steppes, defender of Griffon's Peak and professional adventurer. It is an honor to meet you."

The two shook hands and spoke briefly about the events leading up to the recent fight with the zombies. Wavren told them that the gnome and imp, who were still too weak to move, had taken a considerable number of the undead down before leaving him to fight the remaining enemies. He also mentioned that somehow, the villains seemed to know their initial attacks would be nothing more than a diversion. He speculated that the Dae'gon Alliance was unlikely to have gained any surprise at all and were likely in the fight of their life right now.

Rosabela said, "I agree. We saw the battle unfold," while she was vigorously scratching Stonetalon's massive jowls, which made his lips give off a wet slapping sound as they shook back and forth. Wavren could never understand how she was able to take such liberties with his ally, but he seemed to tolerate it. Then the druid said in a cold and serious tone, "We have much fighting left to do today. Rest quickly and prepare yourselves to move back into the city. We have blood vengeance to repay in the name of Jael'Kutter."

* * *

The Dae'gon Alliance forces had pushed forward far enough to recover Landermihl before the commander of the enemy forces joined the fray. The noble paladin was gravely injured and would have been dead, if not for the power of his deity which preserved his life. The priests quickly called upon their own powers and laid their hands upon his body. The numerous wounds slowly closed, and the sparkle of life returned to the holy warrior's ice blue eyes. He was far too weak to return to the frontlines, but he would live to fight another day.

Grimtusk hit the dwarven line with all of his considerable might. The orc's ancestral ax met with a reinforced dwarven-steel shield, creating a shower of sparks and knocking the shield-bearer back into his companions. He was alive, but unconscious from the power of the blow.

Gaedron called from five ranks back, "Fill da durned gap! Press fo'ard! Archers, fire at will!"

The stocky legs of the dwarven Blade-Breakers knotted and bulged with each step, but the Bloodcrest Forces and Commander Grimtusk were pushed back. The archers let loose a shower of arrows that converged on the giant orc, but failed to penetrate his black armor. He laughed and swung his great obsidian weapon again, and just as before, dwarf-forged steel saved the infantryman's life, but left him stunned and incapacitated. The dwarves had to fill the gap and retrieve the limp warrior from the battle lines, which cost them the initiative.

Neggish Grimtusk was amazed at the hardiness of the dwarven infantry, but he had fought in hundreds of battles and knew the best way to deal with dwarves. He called to the rear in his native orc tongue, "Shock troops, break the lines!" No sooner had he called than his remaining platoon of tauren charged the Dae'gon Alliance frontlines. With the commander at the front of the battle, and the shock troops driving into the dwarves, the orcs renewed their attacks, and the dwarven lines lost ground, leaving an opening for their weapons to exploit. Five dwarves fell, and the battle line buckled like a thatch roof with far too much winter snow. Chaos erupted where the Bloodcrest Forces thrive.

Dwarves fought the orcs head to head, and the tauren pushed through to the elven archers who killed the first dozen before dropping their longbows and drawing razor-sharp steel. The wizards could no longer cast the fireball and lightning bolt spells, or any other spells with an area-effect, for fear of blasting friend and foe alike. Most drew wands and set to blasting the tauren with a myriad of mystical energy. The priests moved from soldier to soldier, trying in vain to stem the loss of life. When confronted directly by enemies, they called great pillars of fire down from the heavens in their defense. The Dae'gon Alliance was pushed back to the far side of the courtyard, and the enemy was quickly taking advantage of the chaos.

Just as Gaedron gave up barking commands to join in the grand melee, he saw a flood of dark shapes moving into the flank of the evil army. Da'Shar and the Forest Runners had arrived. The swift skirmishers dodged in and out of the formation like a wave of water released from a dam. They found the path of least resistance and left many orcs and most of the undead casters cut to ribbons. It all happened so fast that many had no idea the elves had penetrated the rear troops. The Forest Runners turned inward, trying to envelop Grimtusk's forces, making them fight from both the front and rear. It was the turning point in the battle.

Gaedron called to his cousins, "Blade-Breakers, reform da block o' stone! Archers fight back to da rear. We got 'em in da pinch!"

The battle began to regain some semblance of order. The orcs were back on the defensive, the tauren were scattered and fighting for their lives, and even the mighty Neggish Grimtusk was unable to swing his massive ax amid the two-sided attack. The Dae'gon Alliance had the advantage, but the Bloodcrest Forces still had enough warriors to fight to a stalemate. But a stalemate would never suffice for the ambitious orc leader. He needed a victory before he lost many more soldiers, or he would never hold the city, and his dreams would be at an end. With a mighty shove, he disengaged himself from the frontlines and called to his great worg. The gargantuan demon-wolf shoved past the surrounding orcs and tauren, enabling its master to quickly mount and ride to the rear of the fight where the lightly armored elven skirmishers were fighting. On the back of his war-mount, Grimtusk easily towered over the elves and cut though them with malice. He planned to single-handedly turn the tide of battle by cutting down the company of elves. So far, it was working.

Chapter 21
Final Combat

Rosabela, Wavren, Granmillo, Saresh, and Stonetalon had moved from the outskirts of the city through the southern entrance and were closing in on the field of battle. There were hundreds of bodies scattered across the courtyard, and most were already being ravaged by carrion-eating birds.

As the troop headed past the burned-out great hall, Rosabela again felt the pull of something beyond this world coming from the ruins. She paused for a moment and noticed someone moving about the ashes. She turned toward the great hall and felt compelled to investigate.

Wavren called to her, "Rosie, what are you doing? There is no time. We must hurry to aid our allies."

Granmillo, noticing that the she-elf was unresponsive, interjected, "I don't think she hears you over the roar of the battle."

Saresh spoke in his raspy wicked voice: "No, master, she has been beckoned by the dead. I can hear the voice of a spirit calling to her. It is the guardian of this place."

Wavren and his companions followed Rosabela to the ruined hall and saw a haggard looking woman who was bent with age sifting through the ashes with her mule a few paces away. They overheard her saying, "It is here, I just know it … I must find it."

Rosabela walked up to the old crone and said hollowly, "What are you seeking in the rubble, ancient one?"

The old hag looked up for the first time, showing her obviously orcish heritage. Two large tusks protruded from her mouth, and the upturned porcine snout was all the evidence the heroes needed to draw their weapons, but Rosabela did not seem afraid. She merely patted the old woman on her hunched and twisted back with reassurance, saying, "I will help you find it. You can trust me."

The onlookers were baffled, but became drawn into the magic of the old woman's helplessness. They simply stared until the she-elf pulled a soot-covered necklace from the ashes and said, "Is this charm what you were looking for?"

The crone nodded and began chanting. She moved over to her mule, where she uncovered a large metal object that looked a lot like the fearsome double-bladed polearm Captain Jael'Kutter had used in battle. The chanting continued. Rosabela stared wide-eyed and spellbound as the wind swirled into a tiny vortex. The hag danced around with amazing agility and threw several small stones and a bright red feather into the vortex. She spun the mighty polearm above her head and planted it into the ground in one swift move. Finally, she took the necklace from Rosabela and cast it into the spinning windstorm. She danced around some more, saying most curious words.

Your son was the key to unlock your demise
The charm has the power to make this one rise
A feather from the phoenix and stones from below
Wind from the North, where elf-kind will go
All cast together with elemental fire
Bring back the warrior from his funeral pyre.

The sky darkened and lightning flashed, hitting the polearm with a deafening clap of thunder. A flame appeared, and the swirling winds pressed the ash into the outline of a body. Elven boots rose from the soot and filled with ash. Blackened metal greaves moved into unformed shins, followed by thigh coverings and the codpiece. A broad elven breastplate slowly spun into place with the gauntlets, followed by forearm bracers and shoulder pauldrons. An elven helmet hovered just above the soot covered necklace and orcish charm. Blue and red flames swirled and brightened. The ash became solid. The wind surged mightily, and two blood-red dots blinked behind the elven visor. A blackened hand stretched forth and grasped the polearm. Lightning flashed again, the magical explosion of energy silencing the battle and drawing all eyes to the ruins of the great hall, where an elven warrior stood reborn in eldritch glowing armor.

In a voice that was both thunder and howling wind, the warrior said, "I am Jael'Kutter of Celes'tia, Protector of Forestedge, and Spirit Avenger. By the Laws of Honor and Vengeance, Neggish Grimtusk, you must die!"

The Bloodcrest Forces were stunned by the direct challenge to Commander Grimtusk, and the Dae'gon Alliance was amazed to see the elven warrior appear from beyond the grave and then walk right toward the battle as if nothing was more important than his vendetta. Equally astounding was how Jael'Kutter's armor glowed like moonlight and how his mighty polearm danced with eldritch flames. But his eyes were the most unsettling. The once dark and foreboding orbs now blazed with an inner fire of their own. Jael'Kutter had been reborn, but into what exactly, no one knew. The only certainty was that he was coming for the orc commander, and neither orc nor tauren would stand in his way. After all, it was part of the Warrior's Code to end disputes, or in this case, to end war in single combat.

The enemy soldiers immediately spread their lines into a great semi-circle that reached more than fifteen rows back. The Dae'gon Alliance followed suit with nearly the same number of troops packed in numerous rows as well. It became an arena of sorts, and the main attraction was about to begin.

Rosabela had followed the reborn elven warrior to the battleground, where she still did not fully comprehend what had happened. One moment she was feeling drawn to the great hall, and the next thing she remembered, Jael'Kutter was alive; and now she was standing by, preparing to watch him battle the deadliest orc she had ever seen. She suddenly remembered the old crone, who had somehow resurrected him from the ashes. When she turned to find her, the hag was nowhere to been seen. She had simply disappeared, leaving only her mule as any indication that it wasn't just a dream. She turned to her brother.

As if on cue, Wavren was there beside her, smiling knowingly. He said, "It consumed her."

Rosabela said, "What consumed her?"

"The spell," he replied. "It consumed her somehow. The stronger Jael'Kutter grew, the more she seemed to fade away, until there was nothing left. She simply became the wind that restored our good friend."

Granmillo added, "I have studied the tribal traditions of orcs, as well as how their shamanistic magic works. They are not so unlike druids in that they call to the elements and to Nature for their power. But unlike the druids, who protect their surroundings, shamans usually destroy them for personal gain. Interestingly enough, just as some druidic magic requires payment in the form of the casters life force, also called *mana* or chi, the shamanistic magic that the old crone used to restore Jael'Kutter required her entire essence. It was the most powerful display I have ever seen."

Rosabela began to understand how everything had happened, but she was certain she would never understand why. Never before had an orc sacrificed itself to help another. Their ways were too self-serving, too wicked. The end always had to justify the means, and usually that meant profit of some sort; but how could the old hag profit from resurrecting an elf at the cost of her own life?

The conversation died down as the two combatants entered

the Circle of Honor. Commander Grimtusk passed through his forces high atop his great worg mount. They parted with fear and respect, then returned as he passed through. When Neggish entered the circle, he leapt down from his mount, landing squarely on both feet with a deep *thump* that reverberated through the ground. At well over three-hundred-and-fifty pounds of dense muscle, he was more than imposing. He was terrifying. His coal black armor, which sprouted white spikes across his shoulders, elbows, knees, back, and chest, added to the promise of destruction, but nothing was more intimidating than the ancestral blade he carried.

The giant orc swung his great ax in a tight circle before him, showing great confidence and skill. When the spin stopped abruptly, he held his weapon high in the air and yelled, "FOR THE HONOR OF BLOODCREST!" The soldiers behind erupted in great cheers and howls.

Jael'Kutter made a simple entry by comparison. He merely walked through the crowd with his mystic glowing armor and flaming red pupils and planted his viciously curved, double-bladed polearm into the ground. He bowed nobly to his enemy, then turned to the crowd of Dae'gon Alliance soldiers and said, "FOR HONOR AND VENGEANCE!" The elves, humans, dwarves, and gnomes cheered mightily for their champion.

The two combatants turned to face each other. The elf was large among his people, more than six feet tall and easily two-hundred-fifty pounds, fully armed and armored, but he was dwarfed by his adversary. It didn't seem to matter to the warriors or to the crowd.

The combatants took up their weapons, nodded to signify they were ready, and began. Jael'Kutter crouched slightly, knees bent, weight evenly distributed, and weapon at the ready. Grimtusk took a few steps to the left, turned, and took twice as many to the right. He moved like a pacing tiger assessing its prey. The entire town seemed to grow quiet until only the whispering wind was present. The two stood still, locked in mental combat. Both took full measure of the other, not moving a muscle or even daring to breathe. Everything was considered, beginning with the arms and armor they wore and ending with their physical stature and confidence.

Grimtusk moved in first; his ax was poised high, held aloft by twisted cords of orcish muscle. In a flash, he crossed the ring and slammed his weapon down hard with enough power to crush any other warrior. Jael'Kutter accepted the downward stroke mid-shaft and turned his polearm to the right at the last moment to deflect its raw power. The obsidian ax slid off and buried itself in the ground just as the left polearm blade came around and smashed into the orc's helmet. The elf's attack didn't have near the power that the orc's attack had, but the strike was solid, and one of the white spikes came off with the blow. Neggish barely felt it. He summoned his inhuman strength and tore the ax from the ground, bringing with it a sizeable chunk of earth. He stepped back with renewed respect for his adversary's speed and precision.

"You fight well for a stripling. I will teach you the meaning of pain before I feed your corpse to the crows," the orc commander taunted.

Jael'Kutter came in quickly. He thrust with the left blade straight forward, and as the orc dodged to his left, the elf followed with an upward slash from his right blade. Neggish blocked downward with the shaft of his ax at the last moment and spun to his left with a double-handed horizontal chop. The smaller warrior ducked and countered with his own reverse spin that set up a rearward thrust into Grimtusk's side. The keen blade found a narrow opening in the plate armor and penetrated the chainmail beneath. Neggish howled more in anger than in pain. The Dae'gon Alliance cheered as their champion skipped back a few steps and took up the low guard position with his left blade forward.

It was Jael'Kutter's turn to taunt. He said, "You would be formidable if you weren't so slow. I will return every ounce of pain Forestedge has suffered by your army. This will not be quick nor will it be painless for you, beast."

Neggish knew he had to be cautious with this slippery elf, but the fight was far from over. The orc had countless tricks at his disposal, and he would use every one of them if need be.

The two circled again, studying each other's defenses for a weakness or even the mere chance of an opening. Neither saw anything that could be taken advantage of. The elf knew he was faster; the orc knew he was stronger; and both were well-experienced fighters. The elf knew he had the advantage of reach with his weapon, but the orc knew he had better armor. It was as close a match as had ever been fought. It all boiled down to strategy, tactics, and patience.

Jael'Kutter dashed in and pulled up short, hoping to lure the orc into a defensive swing, but Neggish shuffled back with excellent agility, despite his mass and size. The orc turned his body somewhat to the side to hide the movement of his right hand. In the blink of an eye, he drew and tossed a throwing ax with an underhanded grip. It was an unorthodox move, but one Jael'Kutter half-expected as he easily dodged the spinning weapon. He did not expect to find Neggish charging in right behind it. The orc's attack was a left-to-right diagonal cut that continued around in a circle over his head into an over-handed chop. The left blade of his polearm went in behind the first cut and guided the black blade past in a perfect parry. The right blade came around just in time to intercept the downward chop. The right blade came back quickly in a reverse thrust, but Grimtusk had moved in too close to be skewered and plenty close enough to counter attack with an elbow to the elf's face.

The spike on the end of Grimtusk's elbow left a long gash across the angular features of the elf. Jael'Kutter's initial reaction was to roll with the strike, which minimized the damage, but gave his enemy the distance and time he needed to regain the initiative. The orc came in hard, swinging his ax in an upward stroke and then another in a reverse figure-eight pattern. Responding in kind, the elven warrior skipped backward and spun his polearm in a reverse figure-eight pattern. The blades danced together for several seconds, and then Neggish noticed the cut on the elf's face heal itself right before his eyes. It was more than coincidence that his son, Hath'or, had similarly been healed. It was then that he noticed the same charm around the elf's neck that Hath'or had worn and that he had been sure to destroy.

Neggish muttered, "Blasted curse. When I get my hands on that witch's throat, I'll be sure to repay her for this treachery."

Jael'Kutter noticed the anger and frustration on his enemy's face. He smiled and said, "You should be more careful with whom you make enemies. I can sense the spirit of the one who wore this charm before me. He yearns for your death, as does … his mother. They await your arrival in the abyss. I will grant them their wish."

The infuriated orc came forward with his ax held in front of him as if he planned to ram the haft of the ax into the elf's face. Jael'Kutter slipped under the attack and angled left, while sweeping his right blade across the charging orc's ankles. The blade was unable to slice through the enchanted armor plate, but the goal was met when the brute stumbled forward headlong into the dirt. The spikes dug into the ground, making it difficult for the orc to recover. Jael'Kutter spun around to face his prostrate enemy and slashed downward at the only exposed flesh in reach. The polearm bit deeply into the orc's meaty calf, leaving him hamstrung.

Neggish rolled to his back just in time to block the following overhead chop that would have severed his spine. He kicked out with his good leg and sent the elf backward several steps. Injured but not defeated, Grimtusk scrambled to his feet. He didn't have to look down to know that he was bleeding severely or that his leg would never support his weight. He had to win quickly now or the fight would be lost. He whispered the arcane words of his ancestors and the ax hummed with power. Neggish swung his savage weapon in concentric circles above his head, gaining momentum with each circuit. He set his balance and weight on his good leg and gritted his teeth as he willed the other leg to withstand the remaining pressure.

In a howl, he called to Jael'Kutter: "You are nothing to me; I am Neggish Grimtusk, Commander of the Northern Bloodcrest Forces, and Regent of Forestedge. I cannot be beaten!"

Jael'Kutter's response was a look of profound hatred and

utter disdain for the beast that had sacked his town, slain his people, and dared to conquer the noble elves. He charged in with his polearm trailing in the low rear position. The orc timed his attack perfectly as the elf approached. The elf called upon the eldritch flames of his own weapon and swung upward with all of his might just as Neggish drove his blade down to cleave him in two. The weapons met in a titanic explosion of sparks, mystic energy, and raw strength. The great obsidian blade of Grimtusk's ancestral ax shattered, sending the orc backward in a colossal blast of black shards. The elf remained standing and glowed brighter than ever. His magnificent polearm danced with blue-gray flames, and his eyes were ablaze with red elemental fire.

The elven warrior moved toward the fallen orc and surveyed his handiwork. Neggish Grimtusk lay on his back, barely breathing. He had hundreds of black shards embedded in his armor, but in the exposed places where no enchanted chainmail or plate armor was present, the obsidian had penetrated deeply. Both eyes were gouged out. His face was ripped to the bone, his neck torn apart. Only his orcish constitution kept him alive now, as he slowly suffocated on the blood pouring into his lungs.

Jael'Kutter leaned down and whispered, "You fought well, evil one, but now I must send you to meet your son and mistress in hell. When you arrive, tell them I send your soul in return for their assistance in your destruction. Die well, foul beast."

Jael'Kutter waited until the last breath escaped the orc commander's mouth, and in one swift motion, he separated the orc's head from his body. He reached down, removed the massive helm, and grasped the severed head by its black, greasy hair. He held it aloft and said, "Your commander is dead by my hand, and by right of combat, I am now the Commander of the North. Unless one of you dare face me in battle, you are bound by the Warrior's Code to obey."

None dared step forward, but none lowered their weapons for fear of being cut down where they stood. Jael'Kutter spoke again: “As your commanding officer, I order you to return to your homes in the South and never return to elven soil.” The remaining soldiers were unsure how to respond. Jael’Kutter looked to Da’Shar, who was the senior commander of the Dae’gon Alliance forces.

The druid called to the Dae’gon Alliance troops, “By my orders, let no one bring harm to any soldier who leaves this battlefield in peace. Conversely, any enemy soldier who remains will be slain on sight. Give them five minutes to depart.”

The evil army had been beaten, and the battle-weary troops wisely took their leave and departed quickly. When all of the orcs, tauren, and undead had gone, the army of the Dae’gon Alliance cheered in great celebration. Forestedge was once again a city of elves.

The great rejoicing was not only a celebration for the victory over the Bloodcrest Forces; it was a reunion of separated and even lost friends. Wavren walked up to his mentor and nodded stoically, but the master hunter grabbed him in a powerful bear hug and said, “Ye did good, boy-o. I be one proud dwarf, an’ I couldna be proud’r if’n ye was me own son. Ye done learn’d ta fight like a real dwarven hunter.”

Wavren was not used to such praise, but he smiled with his boyish grin and replied in his best dwarven accent, “Aye, ol’ friend, I jes’ did what me ment’r tol’ me ta do!”

This brought a great roar of laughter from the dwarf, who called to his bear and started walking northward to Port Archer with the bulk of the dwarven Blade-Breakers in tow. They had fought well and would be heroes in Dragonforge when they returned.

Da’Shar was not nearly so boisterous, but he placed his hand on Rosabela’s shoulder and said, “You no longer require my guidance. You have earned the right to serve in your calling as a Governess of Nature and no longer require the title of apprentice.”

She smiled sheepishly, threw her arms around his neck, and said, “I saw you fall. My heart nearly broke when I thought I had lost you forever. Can you ever forgive me for attacking you?”

In barely a whisper and with a tear in his eye, Da'Shar replied, "I already have, dear child. I already have." He motioned to the few remaining Forest Runners, and they slipped into the woods like elven phantoms.

Vlaad, Granmillo, and Landermihl shook hands with the other heroes and shared smiles, respect, and great appreciation for the success and teamwork that had prevailed over the enemy.

In a strong Eastern accent, Vlaad said, "The Bloodcrest Forces will be back one day, and when that time comes, I will stand against them with you. Call on me. My sword and shield are waiting for your command." He bowed low and waited for the other humans before departing to Griffon's Peak.

Landermihl was next to speak. He said, "The dead must be properly tended, and the graveyard will be blessed and consecrated to prevent future reanimation. The dead deserve our deepest respect, and no one should have to fight those who have fallen in this battle. Let us conclude this business with Charon, the boatman of the river Styx." He remained to finish the work of his deity.

Granmillo smiled, showing his pointy teeth, but for once, he had nothing to say. He had accomplished much here and was anxious to get back to selling his wares at the market. The gnome and his imp dashed off to catch up with the dwarves who were also heading to Stou'lanz.

The heroes had tied up all the loose ends and were leaving when Wavren stopped at his sister's side. He saw the overwhelming sadness in her deep green eyes and did not understand. "What is it, Rosie?" he asked. "I have never seen you so lost in grief."

Rosabela pointed to Forestedge's great hall, where Jael'Kutter was standing. Tears streaked down her beautiful elven features, and her heart ached over the loss of the captain of the guard. No words could express her empathy for him.

"Rosie, just go tell him you love him. I am sure Jael'Kutter feels the same for you," Wavren urged her.

She smiled, lovingly embraced her brother, and said, "Of

course he loves me, but he is no longer of this world."

Just as Wavren was about to ask his sister what she meant, Jael'Kutter stepped into the ashes of the ruined hall. He turned to his friends and sadly waved goodbye. The elementally enchanted eldritch armor flashed brightly. The sky grew cloudy, and lightning struck Jael'Kutter's mighty double-bladed weapon. His body burst into flames, and the wind howled at his departure. When the heroes looked back, he was gone, but Rosabela could still feel him near. He would always be near. He was Forestedge's Spirit Avenger.

Chapter 22
A New Beginning

Wavren and Rosabela stayed behind in Forestedge to help with the rebuilding and to ensure there were no lingering villains around. Wavren took Stonetalon on several patrols around the city and scouted the area thoroughly, but found nothing significant. He was able to reconstruct the mass exodus of the orcish army. Less than one company of orcish infantry and barely two platoons of orcish elite warriors had survived. The troll cavalry had been crushed, and only a handful of tauren escaped. The undead were also eradicated, thanks to Da'Shar's final attack into the rear ranks. All in all, he was convinced that the area was secure.

Rosabela had taken up residence in the aid station where numerous soldiers had been receiving treatment for their wounds. Hundreds of Dae'gon Alliance troops had perished, and many of those who survived were severely injured. The priests had done amazing things for them, including restoring sight to various elven archers who had been severely burned by enemy fire spells. The she-elf had considerable healing powers as well as a pack full of medicinal herbs that she contributed to the cause.

Wavren walked into the treatment area. He found his sister casting restorative magic on a human mage who had been at death's door following direct hits from the undeads' black bolts of unholy magic. Rosabela finished her work and walked over to her brother.

"The area is secure for now," he said.

"But for how long?" she wondered.

Wavren smiled slightly and said, "At least for now. We will keep constant vigil until the scouting company can be reconstituted. Once they return, my work will be done here."

The she-elf asked, "What will you do next? Do you plan to go back to Port Archer for more messenger runs, like the one that got us into this mess?"

Wavren laughed and replied, "I am a Protector of the Vale. I will do whatever the realm needs of me. It is ironic that we were supposed to start with such a simple mission and by the time it was finished, we had been through a full-scale war."

Rosabela thought about all that had happened. She thought about Da'Shar and Jael'Kutter. She thought about her brother and even Gaedron. Her mind raced back to Sarim and the two brave warriors who had saved her life. She even thought about the enemies who had died at her hands. Da'Shar had been right when he said few Protectors could be druids and those who were druids were at risk of being consumed by the trials that came along with it. She was already feeling stretched beyond her emotional limits, and her career had only just begun.

Wavren broke through the silence and her recollections. "Rosie, I just want you to know that the realm is safer with you here fighting for it. You have saved my life and the lives of dozens of our allies. I just want you to know that even if no one ever thanks you for your contributions, I am grateful for your hard work and sacrifices."

Rosabela felt warm inside as she considered the fine words and loving sentiments her brother conveyed. Her brother had really grown up over the past few months. He was an honorable warrior and a fine Protector of the Vale. She didn't seem to have the words to express it, so she just hugged him and said, "Thanks, Wav. You're the greatest!"

The day passed into night, and as the number of injured soldiers remaining in the aid station grew smaller and smaller, Rosabela found herself slowly healing as well. It wasn't a physical healing as much as an emotional recovery from all the death, destruction, and despair. Two days later, she awoke to find a herald of Celes'tia at her door.

"Lady Rosabela of Celes'tia, Governess of Nature, Druid of the Grove, and Protector of the Vale," the herald began formally, "you are hereby summoned by the Speaker of the Stars of Celes'tia, High Councilman Joram Panni of Port Archer, High Councilman Xaeris of Forestedge, and Master Druid Da'Shar of Celes'tia to attend the awards banquet held in honor of the Dae'gon Alliance victory over the Bloodcrest Forces at Forestedge. You will be escorted by the elven honor guard and flown with all expenses paid to the Capitol City of elves and your homeland, Celes'tia."

Rosabela was at a loss for words. She was not sure if she really had a choice in the offer, but she knew it was her duty to attend. She smiled and said, "I will be ready soon. Where should I meet you to depart?"

The herald replied, "There is one other who will meet us at the northern end of town. We will wait for you there, in one hour."

She knew the other person had to be her brother. She smiled again and said, "That will be fine. Thank you."

The herald bowed deeply and turned sharply about. He walked away briskly.

Rosabela was still sad over the loss of so many soldiers. It almost seemed an insult to their memory to celebrate, but she knew the celebration was for the living, but in honor of the dead. She also knew that her duty as a Protector of the Vale was not always about fighting off the Bloodcrest Forces or other assailants. It was about setting the right example and showing strength for others. Sometimes that was far more difficult that simply blasting her enemies. She had to smile at that last thought. Da'Shar would never approve of it, but Wavren's mentor would likely smile and nod in agreement.

As the slender she-elf washed off in the stone basin, she looked up and saw her reflection in the bureau mirror. She noticed the thin scars, newly healed from battle. They would fade from view complete with time, but she wondered if they would ever be truly gone. She also noticed the slightly down-turned expression on her lips. It was a look of stoicism and determination. Maybe grim determination was a better description. It would simply never do for this occasion, no matter how well it served in combat. She took a moment to practice her smile. It felt uncomfortable at first, like stretching muscles that had been neglected too long. It was all part of being strong and looking the part. It was still her duty. After a few moments, she realized how silly she must look and actually giggled as she imagined the sight.

Clean and fully dressed in her leather worg armor and a forest-green cloak, Rosabela stepped out of her quarters and was escorted by half a dozen warriors from Celes'tia. Each wore ceremonial armor and carried a longbow on his back and a long sword at his side. They walked over to Wavren's quarters and escorted him as well.

Wavren was dressed in his traditional leather hunter apparel. He had his pitch-black hair tied up in a topknot, and his face was cleanly shaven. Rosabela thought that his face was so sharp and angular that it could have been chiseled out of fine marble. He was a handsome elf, and that boyish, almost devilish smile was utterly charming. She was so glad they were going to the banquet together. He was always able to make an occasion lighthearted and enjoyable.

"So, Wav, have you ever ridden a griffon before? They are amazing," Rosabela mentioned with a touch of excitement.

"Nope, but I am sure it is going to be exciting. Is there anything I need to know, or is it like riding any other mount?" he asked.

"It's even easier! All you do is strap in and enjoy the ride. I just know you are going to love it!"

The two siblings and the six escorts walked up the path to the griffon master who had eight of the regal mounts waiting. They strapped in and were airborne soon after. Rosabela was naturally excited, but when she saw her brother's smile stretching across his face, her mood turned from excitement to joy to pure elation.

The flight to Port Archer was short, and it wasn't much farther to Celes'tia. As they approached the island city, she was amazed by how beautiful her home was. It surpassed Port Archer and Forestedge by leaps and bounds. They landed and were escorted from SurCeles'tia Village on the outskirts of the elven capital to the city proper.

Wavren jumped off the griffon and began massaging his cheeks from having smiled the entire trip. He turned to his sister and said, "We have got to fly more often. That was incredible!"

Rosabela smiled. "I'll see if I can get you a griffon for your birthday. I think it will be worth it to see you smiling all the time."

Wavren winked and said, "We can have matching mounts, maybe even twins, like us!"

The twins entered the great causeway that led into the main grove of massive trees that made up the city. As they entered the entire city everyone erupted in applause and cheering. Hundreds of youngling elves ran up and touched the elves as if they were magical beings or royalty.

Three beautiful elf-maids each brought Wavren a lei of flowers sewn into a beautiful array of blue petals and green leaves. It was a sign of virility. Each kissed him on the cheek as she bequeathed her gift. Wavren blushed, and Rosabela giggled.

Three stout male elves brought Rosabela similar leis of flowers that were sewn into an equally lovely array of white, yellow, and pink petals that signified innocence and beauty. Each of the gifts was followed by a kiss on the cheek from the elven men. Now it was Rosabela's turn to blush, but it was not nearly as obvious as Wavren's change in complexion had been.

As the twins walked up the causeway toward the Great Temple, the elves on either side of the walkway bowed in sincere respect. Among the elves were scores of humans, gnomes, and dwarves from all over the realm who also bowed as they passed. It was quite a show for the two young Protectors of the Vale. Upon arriving at the base of the Great Temple's stairs, they noticed all of their friends and companions were waiting for them.

Gaedron was as clean as Wavren had ever seen him. His hair and beard were braided and bound with forest-colored beads and shining metal bands that were undoubtedly made from mithril and probably cost more than a handful of gold coins. He wore the shining mithril chainmail armor under a fine silken tunic with the crest of Clan Ursa emblazoned on it. He smiled proudly and nodded to his student as they approached.

Da'Shar stood opposite the dwarven hunter. He wore the formal headdress of the windwraith with intricately patterned leather armor that had raised etchings of the great redwoods that made up the druidic grove. His mustache and beard were perfectly trimmed to frame his features into a salt-and-pepper-colored goatee. He never even blinked as the two climbed the white marble stairs. He held the same serious look that he always had, but his eyes glistened with pride as they approached.

Landermihl, Vlaad, and Granmillo were also present. They were dressed in their finest formal garments and were sitting off to the side and behind the two senior mentors. They stood up and bowed as Wavren and Rosabela came into view.

The Speaker of the Stars, Daenek Torren, and the Grand Seer were gathered among the leadership beyond the stairs. As Wavren and Rosabela walked toward them, Da'Shar and Gaedron turned and walked alongside. As the twins passed Granmillo, Vlaad, and Landermihl, they fell in behind the growing party of honored guests. When all had come together before the elders of the city, the Speaker held up his hands for silence.

He spoke with magically amplified words so all would be able to hear: "Honored Guests, Elders from every nation, gallant humans from Griffon's Peak, noble dwarves and gnomes from Dragonforge, and valiant elves of the Western Kingdom … I bid you welcome on this fine day of celebration, as we gather to recognize the heroes of Forestedge—" the crowd cheered mightily—"and to honor those who fell in battle defending their homes, their city, and their brethren. They gave the ultimate sacrifice that we might live in peace and security. Our fallen comrades will be remembered this day and forever."

The crowd stood silently for a few moments in remembrance of those who died in combat. It was a solemn moment, and for many, a mournful moment, but death on the battlefield was a noble and honorable death and one that deserved celebration.

The Speaker of the Stars began again, "Let us never forget those who have died fighting for the freedom we hold dear and for the values we hold sacred. But this is not a time for sorrow. It is a time to rejoice, for once again, we have defeated the beastly invaders!"

The crowd cheered and applauded.

"We have retaken Forestedge, and now we will recognize those who have contributed most significantly to our victory," the Speaker declared.

The Speaker motioned to Gaedron to move forward.

The dwarf cleared his throat and said, "I ain't ne'er been mush fer speeches, but I felt it was our duty ta show great thanks fer da heroism and courage of one o' me kinsmen. I got 'ere a medal o' valor fer da one who was responsible fer startin' dis 'ere battle 'ginst da Bloodcrest Forces. Will Granmillo da Great step for'ard."

The tiny gnome had no idea the hunter was referring to him. After all, gnomes were distant relatives of dwarves at best, and he hadn't done anything special. Granmillo paused for a moment, while Saresh appeared and whispered through clenched teeth, "Get over there, ye crazy old conjurer. Yer making a fool of us both."

The gnome took the hint and walked up to Gaedron, who said, "Attention ta orders," which made all of the soldiers snap to the position of attention. "His Excellency King Magni o' Dragonforge and High Sheriff Thermadore o' Silvershire have awarded da Mithril Hammer o' Valor ta Granmillo da Great o' Silvershire fer heroism in battle 'gainst de Bloodcrest Forces during de Dae'gon Alliance counter attack at Forestedge. His willingness ta single-handedly attack de enemy as a d'version, enabled de main force ta breach da defenses. Dis action saved countless lives (e'en tho' I didn' git ta build no siege weapons)," he said, mumbling the last bit under his breath. "And he and his minion, Saresh, kil't 'bout four score o' dem rottin' corpses ta top it off."

Gaedron draped the medal around the gnome's neck and said, "Ye done us proud, ol' boy. Ye deserve dis, our thanks, an' more. May Moradin be wit' ye always. Oh an' by de way, dis ain't just a medal ta put on yer wall. It be an enchanted item o' protection an' will serve ye well in battle."

The crowd applauded the tiny hero, who blushed from his tiny neck up to the tips of his overly large ears. The gnome took his place with the others.

The dwarven hunter bowed and took a step back to his original place.

The Speaker of the Stars nodded to Daenek Torren, the ancient elven hunter.

The withered old hunter came forward, using his fine elven longbow for a walking stick. He looked as weathered as an ancient piece of parchment, but he still had the fire of life blazing in his eagle-like eyes. He turned to face the crowd and said, "Among all of the hunters I have ever met, there is one who stands out above them all. Ever since his first day of training, I have been watching Wavren of Celes'tia, and it is my sincere honor to present him with the Armor of Elvenkind to protect him as he has protected the lands of his kinsmen. Post the orders."

A much younger elf came forward and said, "Attention to orders. In recognition of conspicuous gallantry against overwhelming odds, during the Battle of Forestedge, the Armor of Elvenkind has been awarded to Wavren of Celes'tia, Hunter of Clan Ursa, and Protector of the Vale. May it protect him always as he serves the people of Dae'gon."

Wavren bowed humbly to the venerable hunter and accepted the amazingly light chainmail armor. He backed away respectfully and took his place by Granmillo.

The Speaker of the Stars came forward once more. He turned to Da'Shar and motioned for him to come forward. The druid came over to the Speaker and bowed deeply with great respect. The Speaker slid his hand into his robes and withdrew a shining green gem. Da'Shar looked amazed, his eyes wide open and his mouth slightly open.

He quickly recovered and asked quietly, "Sire, are you certain?"

The ancient elven leader merely nodded and said, "I have foreseen this. Daenek Torren will serve in my stead."

Da'Shar looked to the oldest of hunters who smiled knowingly and nodded his approval. Da'Shar turned abruptly and with a very serious look, called to Rosabela, "Dear child, come forward and receive your commendation."

Rosabela was very uncertain about the entire affair, but she found herself moving toward her mentor. She looked deeply into his eyes, deep pools of endless mystery and love for her. She was lost for a moment as she heard his spirit speaking to her.

Without a word being spoken, Da'shar sent his spirit into her being. Another elf was saying something very formal about being recognized for her duty, dedication, and courage, but it seemed very distant to her as Da'Shar entered her mind and touched her soul.

Da'Shar noticed that the landscape of her spirit was not the calm grove that he had seen last time their souls communed. The grove was gone and in its place was a desolate city in ruins. It was the destroyed elven town of Forestedge. Da'Shar found the avatar of his student's spirit kneeling beside the burned-out great hall. As he approached, he could feel the utter sadness that radiated from Rosabela. She had her hands over her face, but tears ran through her delicate fingers. He placed his hand on her shoulder and said, “You know he is not truly gone; you can feel his soul, can’t you?”

The she-elf looked up with tear-reddened eyes and said, “Da’Shar, I cannot get him out of my head. My heart aches for him, and I feel as though I will suffer his loss every day for all of my long life.”

He replied, “Now, I know that you are worthy of the Speaker’s gift. It is no trinket or simple bauble. It is a gem of rare power. Take it, and use it. You will understand in time.”

The connection ended and Rosabela found herself holding the brilliantly shining green gem. As the Speaker of the Stars withdrew his frail hand, he began fading into nothingness right before her eyes. Just before he had completely vanished, he smiled and said, “With my life, you will bring about an era of peace for all elves. This will come to pass.”

The crowd gasped, not knowing what had happened to their king. Da’Shar walked to the edge of the platform and spoke with a powerful voice: “The Speaker of the Stars has named his successor as Daenek Torren of Celes’tia, master hunter, and Protector of the Vale. All hail Daenek Torren, the Speaker of the Stars.”

The crowd was stunned, but the oldest people of the elven community, who seemed to understand what had just transpired, took a knee in deepest respect and reverence. The others soon followed suit. Even the humans, gnomes, and dwarves bowed before the new elven leader.

Daenek Torren spoke: “Goodly citizens from all Dae’gon rise and let us remember why we are here today. It is a day of celebration for our heroes. My formal coronation ceremony will come soon enough.”

Da’Shar spoke then, saying, “All hail the Speaker!”

The crowd called back, “Hail to the Speaker!”

Da’Shar called again, “All hail our heroes!”

The crowd called back, “Hail to the heroes!”

Among the renewed energy of the celebration, all of the heroes were congratulated and patted on the back. The youngest elves present begged the heroes to tell their tales, which had always been the main attraction at these celebrations. Landermihl and Vlaad moved to a gathering of children and began their stories. Granmillo and Gaedron moved to another spot and began their versions. Wavren noticed that it was a grand event for everybody but one. He watched Rosabela quietly slip away from the massive group and all of the festivities. He followed her to ensure she was going to be all right.

* * *

The hunter moved quietly through the great redwoods that towered over Celes'tia. He was careful not to get too close to his sister. He did not want to be intrusive, but he was concerned and observed her actions from afar.

Rosabela moved from the celebration to the edge of the city. She shape-shifted into her travel form and sped away toward SurCeles'tia Village. Before long, she saw the woods open up and the sea stretched out before her. She took a turn and headed up the hill toward the griffon master. She paid her fare and mounted the great mystical beast. The griffon master strapped her in and said, "What is your destination?"

Rosabela said one word, "Forestedge." And seconds later, she was flying southward through the air.

Wavren watched her depart and moved up to the griffon master. "Excuse me, sir, where did that she-elf ask to go?"

The griffon master said, "She flew to Forestedge. Do you mean to follow her?"

Wavren said, "I do."

The hunter mounted up and paid his silver to the man. He took off in pursuit of Rosabela. The sea passed by quickly, and Port Archer came into view. The flight path took him south over Port Archer and slightly west toward Forestedge. A few minutes before landing, he saw Rosabela's mount already returning to its aerie in Celes'tia. He landed and headed into town. He was certain where Rosabela was heading. He knew as if she had told him herself. He was her twin. He always knew.

Rosabela passed by dozens of craftsmen busy at work rebuilding the city walls and structures. Many acknowledged her, but she saw no one. She was too focused on her objective. She moved quickly toward the great hall where she had felt the spirit of the fallen captain. It was there that she hoped to find solace. It was there that she hoped to end her suffering.

Wavren picked up the faint trail his sister left behind. He really didn't need to follow it. He knew her final destination would be the great hall, and although he had no idea what he might do when he got there, he simply had to follow. He picked up his pace. In no time at all, he arrived in the courtyard of Forestedge. Not far ahead, he saw his sister standing among the ashes of the great hall. She held the magnificent gem in her hands. He stayed far enough back to observe, but not intrude. This was not his affair after all, but he had to ensure his sister was safe in more than a physical sense.

Rosabela held the gem that the Speaker of the Stars had given to her. It was glowing brightly and exuded powerful magic waves that were not unlike the beating of a drum. The steady *thump-thump* resembled something very familiar indeed. It beat in time with Rosabela's heart. The waves of magic radiated outward with ever increasing intensity. The druid felt her heart quicken, and the beating of her own heart seemed to directly affect the gem's magic.

A crowd began to gather around the great hall and the willowy she-elf. Wavren could see something was going on, but he was unsure exactly what. He did notice that the gem gave a brilliant glow and seemed to be sending out waves of magic. He moved forward a few steps and felt the pulsing of the magic like a gentle breeze on his face. As he drew closer, the pulsing grew stronger and stronger. Before he knew it, he was standing right behind his sister, who was oblivious to his presence. He stared wide-eyed at the gem as he peered over the she-elf's shoulder.

A voice manifested in Rosabela's head. It spoke in whispered tones of the recently deceased Speaker of the Stars. It comforted her as it said, “You who have served your people so valiantly are due a reward befitting your personal contributions and sacrifices. By your own efforts, many elves live, and the land is free from the grasp of the Bloodcrest Forces. The lives you saved and the land you have helped to preserve entitle you to more than the tales of bards and the immortality of fame. It entitles you to much more.”

Rosabela stood perfectly entranced as she stared into the depths of the gem. It was mesmerizing as it spoke to her. The gathering of elves grew as if drawn like moths to a flame.

The voice continued, “You could have claimed enchanted armor, powerful weapons, mystic tomes, or any of a dozen other items to help you serve as a Protector of the Vale, and they would have been readily given, but the emptiness in your heart called out for something far greater. It called for something more valuable and far nobler.”

The waves of energy grew more powerful as the druid began to add her own hope and strength to its power.

The voice continued, “Rosabela, I saw the pain in your eyes and felt the despair in your heart as Jael’Kutter fell in defense of Forestedge. I felt your elation as he rose under the summoning of the orc witch to destroy Neggish Grimtusk. Again, your heart was nearly torn from you as he returned to the netherworld upon completion of his mission for the old crone. There is no greater honor than to lay one’s life down in defense of one’s friends. Jael’Kutter died well, but perhaps before his work here was done. This gem holds the key to your heart’s desire. If you focus your own inner strength, then the last remaining essence of his being can be recalled to this plane of existence, but only for a short time. However, if you give more than your mental focus, something miraculous can happen.”

The voice faded and Rosabela felt the warm comfort of the Speaker dissipate, but it was replaced by another presence. She was overcome with the same feeling she’d had when the captain had been alive. Rosabela concentrated and felt her life force being drawn into the gem, weakening her. She concentrated harder and felt even weaker. The wind blew in hard from the north, and clouds appeared just as they had when the old crone had been taken by the powerful summoning magic. Lightning flashed, and the outline of Jael'Kutter formed.

Just as she was certain the gem would overwhelm her, a hand touched her shoulder gently. Somehow, she knew it was her brother, Wavren. He had always been there for her. He had always watched over her and been there to help her when no one else could, but this was something he could not help with. Lightning flashed, and the eldritch armor arose from the ashes.

She summoned all of her strength and poured it into the gem, but as her own heart grew weaker and weaker, so did the power of the gem. It pulsed less and less. The elven warrior was nearly returned, but she knew she would be unable to sustain the magic for long. As death approached, she felt Wavren holding her gently in his strong arms. He was saying something, but she couldn't hear the words over the wind and thunder. She looked up and saw tears flowing from his eyes. His lips were moving, but again his words were drowned out. She thought he might have been saying, "Don't die. Please, don't die."

Rosabela was so near death that her normally radiant appearance was ashen, her eyes darkened. The gem had taken all that she had, and nothing miraculous had happened. She had given all that she had, and it hadn't been enough. What else was there to give?

The hand of Jael'Kutter reached out. He was nearly resurrected as the elemental fire flashed in his eyes.

Rosabela closed her green eyes and said, "I am so sorry … I have failed … but I will love you for time and all eternity."

Wavren screamed a feral howl, sending the onlookers scrambling backward.

The gem flared to life and began a high-pitched humming. A deep, forest-green energy surrounded Rosabela's limp form and the raging tempest that was the elven captain. The two elves were lifted up as if by the hands of the gods themselves and brought together. The storm clouds dissipated, and the sun appeared suddenly. Wavren fell back and had to shield his eyes from the brightness of its rays.

A familiar voice came from the gem, saying, "There is no greater honor than to lay down one's life in defense of his friends or in the name love. Jael'Kutter and Rosabela, you deserve life for your ultimate sacrifices. My time has finally passed."

The gem exploded in a shower of brilliant rays, and the brightness of the sun ebbed. Wavren uncovered his eyes and saw his sister locked in the arms of the mighty captain. Both were very much alive. The hunter stood up, wiped the tears from his angular cheeks, smiled broadly, and whispered, "I knew you could do it, Rosie. You just don't know how to fail, even when it requires a miracle."

The crowd of onlookers cheered and came forward to welcome the great warrior back from the dead. It was a joyous reunion with endless clasping of hands and hugging for all, but none as joyous or heartfelt as Jael'Kutter and Rosabela. He looked deeply into her now brilliantly glowing emerald-green eyes and said the only words he could think of: "I love you, Rosabela." This was their moment and nothing else mattered.

Epilogue

Nightshade had returned to Dek'Thal to find that the regional commander, a half-orc named Gorka, had personally dismantled the remnants of Grimtusk's army after his defeat at Forestedge. Nightshade was now alone. At first, the cunning assassin thought he might seek employment as a mercenary or perhaps with an assassin's guild, but nothing seemed to work out. With no other options, he bought some supplies and headed for the coast to the neutral port city of Goblin Port. There was always employment to be found abroad for an orc with his skills.

Goblin Port was a busy little outpost with a wide variety of shops and traders who were brave enough to make deals with races of the opposing faction. It was a place of tolerance, if nothing else.

Nightshade walked into a dark tavern called the Swashbuckler. He moved up to the bar and sat on a sturdy stool. He motioned for the barkeep to come over.

"Gim-me a black ale, ex-tra stout," the orc said in broken common.

The bartender said, "We have Thunderbrew and Dwarvendark."

Nightshade was surprised to hear that this remote port had such a selection. He had never cared for Dwarvendark, but Thunderbrew was his favorite, so the choice was easy. "Thun-der-brew," he replied.

The bartender drew a pint of thick black ale from a massive wooden keg on a rack behind the bar. He served it to Night-shade and said, "That'll be a silver for the drink, sir."

The orc flipped a silver coin to the man and said, "I am look-ing for work. Is any-one in need of a quick blade?"

"There is a man from Shadowshire, across the Great Sea, and south of Blackmarsh, near Jaggedspine Valley, who passed through here. He was looking for bodyguards, but by the look of the man, I would guess he wanted to hire some thugs more than reputable warriors. He mentioned a gold coin per day as payment for any qualified employees," the barkeep said with a wink and a nod.

That was a sizeable fee for hired thugs. The orc assumed the work would entail high payoff assassinations. It would be perfect for the time being. Nightshade flipped the man a silver piece for the information, gulped down his ale and headed for the docks.

There were quite a number of passengers waiting to board a ship to the southern tip of Jaggedspine Valley, but the large schooner had plenty of room for more. Another silver piece was given as fare, and in no time, they were pulling into yet another neutral port. The sights and smells of this port were very different from the ones at Goblin Port. The merchants here were heavily perfumed, and the wares were more to the liking of the Dae'gon Alliance than the Bloodcrest Forces. Nightshade wasted no time there and headed northward through a small pass in the dense jungle and over a rope bridge leading into Shadowshire.

This land was cursed, according to legend, filled with un-natural creatures and undead, none of which would be much trouble for the veteran orc. Nightshade noticed that immedi-ately upon crossing the border into Shadowshire, the woods seemed to twist inward, cutting out most of the sunlight. The wind carried howls of wolves or worse … worgs. It was exactly the landscape an orc in his profession was trained for.

A short journey eastward brought the assassin to the town's center. The city guard was easily circumvented as he worked his way toward the tavern. It was dusk, and the unnatural darkness had become an oppressive gloom, but Nightshade felt comfortable here. He was in his element.

Upon entering the tavern, a few humans made note and eyed the orc suspiciously. Most never looked up, not wanting any trouble. That was good, since the orc was looking for work, not unwanted attention. He leaned forward on the bar and quietly slid a silver coin to the human behind the counter.

Nightshade said, "I heard there is work to be had for those with blade skill."

The bartender slid the coin back to the orc and said, "I can't help you, but a word of advice to you for free: silver is not common currency around here. It is better used in weapons."

The imposing orc replaced the silver coin with a gold one and said, "I think you can help me with this in-stead."

The bartender took the coin with a grim look and whispered, "Walk north a few miles, and then turn west as the road splits. Go another mile and look for the abandoned mineshaft. If you live long enough to see the mine, then you can ask for work, but you'll likely find death … or worse."

Nightshade nodded and left quickly. He had to dodge the city patrol again, but with his skills, it was not a problem. An hour later, the orc had passed the split in the road. He was nearly to the location where he hoped to find his next employer. The entrance to the mineshaft seemed unguarded. There was a torch illuminating the opening. As silently as the wind, the assassin entered. The smell was strong with decay and fresh blood. Unconsciously, Nightshade's hands went to his weapons. He continued to move among the shadows until he came to balcony overlooking the lower levels of the mine.

What he saw was gruesome, even for one of his upbringing and profession. There were shredded human bodies scattered all over the place. It looked as if half of the city had been torn apart by savage beasts and then left to rot. Nightshade was uncertain how to proceed when a presence raised the tiny hairs on the back of his neck. He spun and drew his enchanted blades as several humans filled the only way in or out of the mine.

Nightshade spoke confidently, as his orcish heritage demanded that he never show fear or weakness, but something felt very wrong with this situation. He said, “I have come all the way from Dek’Thal seek-ing em-ploy-ment.”

One of the humans with an unnaturally evil look about him stepped forward. He wore no armor and carried no weapons. His body language told the trained assassin that he was well trained and supremely confident in his ability to kill. He said, “I have heard of the capital city of orcs. I am surprised to see that you have come so far, and alone at that. You must be a fearsome warrior, trained since birth to survive, and no doubt, quite deadly with your blades.”

Nightshade spun his weapons with a quick demonstration of agility and skill and sheathed them in the blink of an eye. He remarked offhandedly, “I am.”

The leader smiled, showing slightly enlarged cuspids and feral canines. He bowed low and said, “I am Lord Carnage, lycan-druid of the Worg Pack, and soon-to-be-ruler of Shadeshire.”

Nightshade had never heard of a lycan-druid and the look of confusion and curiosity was apparent on his face, but he bowed in return as a matter of respect to his potentially new employer. He asked, “Do you have need of an experienced assassin? My services can be yours for the right price.”

Lord Carnage laughed loudly and was quickly joined in his laughter by his entire troop of twenty other humans.

Carnage slowly composed himself and signaled his men to do so as well. He responded, “We are indeed looking for new talent. I am offering a gold coin per day, but we don’t simply hire anyone off the street. We must keep the pack strong and pure. You appear very strong, but your kind would only pollute our bloodline and that, I cannot allow. I will repay your courage and audacity for making the journey, however."

Nightshade did not like this turn of events, but he was well armed, well trained, and an orc. He held his composure and asked, "What will my pay-ment be?"

The leader of the group said, "I will give you the first strike. If you slay me, you will be allowed to live and even return to your home in Dek'Thal. If you fail, then we will tear you apart."

The words were barely out of the man's mouth when Nightshade's weapons sprang into his hands. The massive orc rushed in with his wickedly curved saber and drove it cleanly through his enemy's chest. The orc had certainly struck a killing blow, but the human who remained impaled on his blade merely grabbed the orc's sword arm by the wrist and twisted it with such speed and force that the bones loudly snapped and the hand hung limply at an unnatural angle. The orc howled in agony and came in with his dagger, but the lycan-druid caught his much larger forearm in mid-swing and held it at bay easily. His hand seemed to grow in size, and vicious black claws sprouted from his fingertips which sank into the orc's flesh.

Staring wide-eyed and open-mouthed, the orc watched the human's face twist into a lupine visage with fiercely red glowing eyes and long, razor-sharp teeth. It was the last thing the orcish assassin ever saw as Lord Carnage tore out his throat and effortlessly snapped his neck with one quick yank. The rest of the pack shape-shifted and shredded the now headless body of the powerful orc.

Here's a preview of Curtiss Robinson's next book, *Defenders of Griffon's Peak*

Prologue

The Race for the Eastern Kingdom!

Having beaten back the Bloodcrest Forces at the Battle of Forestedge, the Protectors of the Vale and Heroes of the Dae'gon Alliance return home victorious—but the war is far from over.

Lusting for power, the half-orc commander Gorka Darkstorm looks beyond the borders of the orc and troll realm. He sees opportunity for future conquest as he stretches his influence into the human lands of Griffon's Peak and Darkshire to recruit elite assassins and fearsome werewolves to his destructive cause.

As news travels throughout the realm of this uncanny plot, Vlaad, Champion of Griffon's Peak, is called by the King himself to build a team who will embark on a quest to prevent the Bloodcrest Forces from joining with the worst villains humanity has to offer. It is a race for the Eastern Kingdom that pits feral beasts, demonic creatures, and bloodthirsty orcs against the shining arms and armor of the Defenders of Griffon's Peak.

About the Author

Curtiss Robinson is a full-time soldier, lifelong martial artist, science fiction/fantasy enthusiast, and RPG gamer. It is from this unique perspective that he constructs worlds of fantasy and adventure. Currently, Curtiss lives in Irmo, South Carolina, where he serves on active duty with the National Guard and enjoys spending time with his amazing wife and children.

Printed in the United States
142915LV00003B/67/P

9 781606 934708